"Were you told to seduce me?"

She swallowed. "No one told me anything."

He still had hold of her hair; he began to wind the lock around his knuckles, forcing her to step toward him. "Pity. You can still give it a go, if you like. All this hair . . ." He laughed softly. "I could tie you up with it."

She would bite his throat out first. But if he thought she was a blushing virgin, apt to be scandalized by such threats, then the advantage was still hers. She pitched her voice low. "Let go of me, and I'll do my best."

Now his hand nudged her chin up. His dark eyes narrowed on hers. "Oh, I don't think so," he murmured. "I don't leave knives unsheathed."

In the ensuing pause, she could see the calculations working through his expression. It came to her, very strongly, that it was better he not be allowed to finish them. Heart drumming, she leaned forward and pressed her lips to his.

He held still for a moment, and then spoke against her mouth, his voice obscene in its gentleness. "You're going to have to do better than that, Mina."

Written on Your Skin is also available as an eBook

ALSO BY MEREDITH DURAN

The Duke of Shadows
Bound by Your Touch

MEREDITH DURAN

Written on Your Skin

POCKET BOOKS

New York   London   Toronto   Sydney

Pocket Books
A Division of Simon & Schuster, Inc.
1230 Avenue of the Americas
New York, NY 10020

This book is a work of fiction. Names, characters, places, and incidents either are products of the author's imagination or are used fictitiously. Any resemblance to actual events or locales or persons, living or dead, is entirely coincidental.

First Pocket Books paperback edition August 2009

POCKET and colophon are registered trademarks of Simon & Schuster, Inc.

For information about special discounts for bulk purchases, please contact Simon & Schuster Special Sales at 1-866-506-1949 or business@simonandschuster.com.

The Simon & Schuster Speakers Bureau can bring authors to your live event. For more information or to book an event contact the Simon & Schuster Speakers Bureau at 1-866-248-3049 or visit our website at www.simonspeakers.com.

Designed by Jill Putorti
Hand lettering by Dave Gatti
Illustration by Jon Paul

Manufactured in the United States of America

10 9 8 7 6 5 4 3 2 1

ISBN 978-1-4767-8891-3

For groceries delivered, for help in brainstorming plots;
For Road Runner, chicken soup, and pep talks in parking lots;
For itineraries: moldarama; Phase III; the Andes and the zoo;
For offering a space heater when my hands were turning blue;
For kidnapping the modem, for yacht rock and joie de vivre,
This object from the near future is dedicated to Steve.

ACKNOWLEDGMENTS

When a deadline falls two days before a cross-country move you discover anew that friends are the greatest secret weapon in a writer's arsenal. Thanks to those who helped me across the various finish lines: Maddie and Elizabeth, for their astonishing generosity (and packing skills!) despite the many deadlines hanging over their own heads; Janine, for the email I reread at least a hundred times; Rob and Betsey, for bringing Christmas to me from across the ocean; Steph, Mom, Dad, and Shelley, for cheerleading. I am also grateful for my own New York heroines: the amazing Nancy Yost, the team at Pocket Books, and especially Lauren McKenna, Megan McKeever, and the eagle-eyed copyeditor who caught Mina running up a flight of stairs that did not, in fact, exist. Magical realism, or a segue into the paranormal? Thankfully, readers will not have to decide.

Chapter One

HONG KONG, 1880

Trouble walked in around midnight. She was swaying on her feet from too much champagne and had a man on each arm, though neither seemed to interest her much. Phin was leaning against the wall, nursing a glass of brandy and the beginning of a headache. He watched as her eyes skimmed the crowd. The line of red paper lanterns strung across the threshold shed a bloody light over her white-blond hair. When she spotted him, she smiled.

Loose ends, he thought blackly. A man could hang himself with them.

He handed off the brandy to a passing servant, a Chinese girl with a face as round as the moon. She balanced the tray high on her fingertips as she moved toward the exit, and he found his eyes following the glass, envying the way it coasted over the heads of the guests. A neat escape. Christ, he wanted out of Hong Kong. Every society luminary was in attendance tonight, save the governor and the American consul. As soon as he'd noted their absence, he'd known the arrest was imminent. His job here was done, no reason to linger. But Ridland had forbidden him to sail until tomorrow evening. The man was out to prove something to him. *What matters is the results, Granville. Take some pride in your work; you've a goddamned talent.*

Pride, Phin mused. He wondered if a dog took pride in heeling to its master. The chain at his throat was tight enough that he saw no need to learn to like it; it would tighten or loosen at Ridland's direction, whether or not he saw fit to lick the man's hand. And if results were all that mattered, he should be gone by now. There would be other agents hereabouts, as ignorant of his identity as he was of theirs, tasked to handle the aftermath. It was not his business to watch the consequences unfold.

He glanced across the room. Miss Masters was coming straight toward him, maneuvering boldly between couples who twirled like puppets to the musicians' bidding. His brief flirtation with her had turned into a grave mistake. In the end, he hadn't required her. Limit complications— that was his policy. Alas, he had started to realize that, in this case, his policy was the problem. Miss Masters was not accustomed to being abandoned by erstwhile suitors, and the novelty seemed to intrigue her.

As he watched, her advance overwhelmed her companions. First one, then the other, was knocked away by collisions with waltzing pairs. She seemed to take no notice. That obliviousness had probably served her well, till now. With Gerard Collins for a stepfather, she would not benefit from too much insight. The things she might learn would trouble her beauty sleep.

But the featherbrain was about to awaken into a strange new world. Once Collins was in custody, her admirers would scatter like rats from a stripped corpse. Her mother would probably try to leap out a window. Both women would learn, very quickly, what it felt like to have one's choices torn away. He saw no good outcome for them; the mother's family did not speak to her, and neither woman had a marketable skill. Their beauty would sell, of course, but it would not survive a few rough handlings.

The thoughts darkened Phin's mood beyond repair. A veal calf in yoke, worrying for two lambs led to slaughter: it made for little more than a very bad joke. The women were not his concern, and flogging himself for what he could not prevent would profit neither them nor him. He turned and walked out.

Laughter and squeals swarmed the front hall. He shouldered without caution through careless elbows and dark-suited shoulders, making for a darkened corridor where lamps flickered dimly in windows left open to the humid breeze. Hong Kong was glossy and green, fragrant with flowers after the evening storm; the whole damned city smelled like a debutante.

"Mr. Monroe!"

She had followed him? Phin turned. She paused a few feet away, beneath an archway of red and black tiles; how she'd moved so quickly in that gown, he had no idea. It was tight and narrow, deeply bustled at the back, a sky blue silk that was probably meant to match her eyes. A mistake, in his opinion. Her eyes were such an unlikely hue that they really needed no complement.

Paired with the silk, they took on a brilliance that seemed almost outré.

He could see why Hong Kong society disagreed on the question of her beauty. Her coloring did border on the freakish. "Good evening," he said to her.

"Mr. Monroe," she repeated, stepping forward. Her voice was breathless and distinctly triumphant, as if his name were the answer to a puzzle that had vexed her for some time. A drop of sweat curled down the delicate line of her collarbone; its progress riveted him. He had no idea why his body had the bad taste to be fascinated by hers. She looked breakable, and he was not a small man. "How does the evening treat you?" she asked. "Surely you don't mean to retire so soon?"

He mustered a smile. "It treats me very well," he said. "And, no, I was only going to fetch something from my rooms." He paused, giving her an opportunity to excuse herself. Of course, she did not take it. "And you, Miss Masters? You looked to be enjoying yourself."

"Oh, thank you very much! I *was* enjoying myself. Happy as a clam at high water. But as I was telling my English friends . . ." She glanced over her shoulder, as if only now realizing that she'd left them behind in the ballroom. Turning to face him again, she somehow managed to trip. The little hop she made in recovery brought her stumbling into his chest.

He caught her by the forearms. She smelled like a distillery, and as her eyes widened, they caught him like a fist in the gut. Such an odd shade. He would not argue with her beauty, but he preferred a woman to look like one. With her white-blond hair and huge eyes and petite figure, Miss Masters more closely resembled a porcelain doll. Alas, she could not behave like one. Dolls were mute; she chattered incessantly. He knew a way to silence that mouth.

Christ. The girl made his brain misfire. He set her away from him more forcefully than the instance required. "Have a care," he said.

She arched a silvery brow. "A care for what?"

For falling on men in darkened hallways. For placing your hopes in a stranger. "For your balance. Stumble in front of company, and people might decide you're intoxicated."

"Oh, dear." Her lashes batted. "Is that not allowed?"

He sighed. Even had circumstances not conspired against her, she would have managed to ruin herself eventually. Her little society world was perfumed and creamy, but it had its rules, and she grew increasingly rash in breaking them. "I don't think there's a law against it, no." His mouth had gone dry; he paused to clear his throat. Good God, this headache was ill timed. Her glance flickered up, and he realized he was rubbing his temple. Come to think of it, this headache had something in common with her: they both grew more irksome by the moment. What had he been saying? Ah, yes. "But you wouldn't want others to think you intemperate by nature."

The officiousness of his tone belatedly struck him. She had a knack for inciting such asinine behavior. She was artless in the way of children or puppies; watching her, one found oneself braced for an accident. Puppies got stepped on; children fell from windowsills; Miss Masters was dancing at the edge of a cliff, and no one, not her wan, withdrawn mother or even her tyrannical bastard of a stepfather, cared to leash her.

She was protesting. "But that is so unfair, Mr. Monroe! I drink nothing but champagne, which is very respectable indeed. And if I've had a bit too much—why, then it's only to anesthetize my boredom with the company!"

He laughed despite himself. Occasionally, he came near to being convinced that she was having everyone on with this empty-headed routine. Certainly, from another woman, the remark would have served a masterful set-down to his pomposity.

But no, she smiled along with him, sunny and vacant, ignorant of her success as a wit. "Unless you propose to entertain me?" As her eyes dropped to his mouth, his laughter died. She had better watch out. "Oh," she said softly, "Mr. Monroe—you have such lovely lips."

And then she launched herself at him.

At first, he was too surprised to resist. She was forward, yes, but he hadn't expected a seduction. Not that this *was* seduction, precisely—she grabbed his hair and pulled down his head with all the subtlety of a crank. Her lips banged into his so forcefully that he anticipated the taste of blood. He pulled back in simple self-preservation, and she followed him, her breasts pressing hot and soft into his chest. The small, breathless noise that burst from her lips bypassed his brain and went straight to his balls.

No. He was not going to kiss her back. She was a reckless, harebrained child, and if he dreamed of her, it was only from boredom.

She opened her mouth and he felt the wetness of her

tongue. He took her by the elbows, intending to push her away, but her skin, so astonishingly soft, scattered his intentions. He stroked his thumb down her arm, just to make sure that he wasn't mistaken, that it really was as smooth as his midnight thoughts had suggested. She moaned encouragement. God save him, but no doll had ever made such a noise. And she was twenty, not a girl.

To hell with it. His mouth opened on hers. She tasted of champagne and strawberries. Her small body, so sweetly curved, pressed against his. The top of his head seemed to lift off. Sweet, so much sweeter than he had expected; she was sinuous as a flame, writhing against him. Her hands pressed into his shoulders, persuading him to step back against the wall. She needed a lesson in subtlety; she needed to be taught some truths about the world, quickly, before the morrow came. He would be glad to teach them. It would be a favor to her—

What the hell am I doing?

He thrust her away, breathing hard. She stumbled backward, and his idiotic hands reached out to catch her; he balled them into fists and made himself wait.

She caught her balance against the opposite wall. Her breasts rose and fell rapidly; her eyes were wide. "Dance with me, Mr. Monroe?"

Good God. He ran a hand over his face, up into his hair. She had no sense whatsoever. That, or rejection was simply unfathomable to her. He sought for some remark that would recall her to propriety, assuming she even knew the meaning of the word. But his body mocked him and his brain felt like sludge. He settled for, "I beg your pardon?"

"My friends from England were complaining of how poorly Americans dance." She reached up to finger the diamond teardrop dangling from her ear. She had recovered herself now; her manner was perfectly casual, as if she hadn't just given him a taste of her tongue. "I simply cannot agree. *I* dance very well, and I feel sure you do, too. Shan't we prove it? For America, sir!"

Perhaps he *was* wrong to underestimate her. Certainly, to his continued astonishment, he was a damned fool to overestimate himself. "I don't think that would be wise."

She frowned. "Why not? Because I kissed you?"

He glanced down the hallway. "Precisely, Miss Masters." At this rate, someone was going to catch them together. That was the last thing he needed. Maybe a bit of plain speaking would serve where manners had not. "Unless you have a burning desire to be fucked against a wall."

The image those words conjured made his own voice hoarsen, but the language did not seem to register with her. "Well, I would never wish to do such a thing in a *ballroom*," she said, and took his arm.

He should have used a more genteel word; it was clear that she hadn't taken his meaning. Or maybe she'd taken it all too well, for her grip was strong, as though the last shred of maidenly decorum had abandoned her. Either way, she was a force of chaos, and her insanity was contagious; he was letting her tow him down the corridor toward the ballroom. He felt thoroughly light-headed.

A dance, then. Simple enough. He could keep his hands to himself for one dance, even if he had to bite off his tongue to distract himself. It wasn't as if he actually had anything to fetch from his rooms. And God knew, if he tried to act on the pretense, she'd probably follow him into his bed.

The music came spilling out to greet them, much louder than before. Aggressively loud, in fact. He found himself flinching from the clamor as she drew him inside. The current set was concluding. She said something, but he could not make it out. Why was he humoring her? His head ached. She was needless temptation, pretty flesh wrapped around a brain filled with air; there was nothing in her for him but a whole lot of trouble.

The dancers were parting ways. The next set was soon to begin. She turned to him expectantly. When he did not immediately extend his hand, she reached for it. He realized something was wrong when he couldn't feel her fingers.

He drew a breath, and the floor rocked beneath his feet.

He staggered backward, dimly registering a collision. A cry. The world disassembled, then swam back together. Miss Masters was mouthing something. It felt like twin screws were being forced into his temples. God in heaven. Was this some new variation on malaria?

The girl's face grew very large. Leaning toward him, that was all. He struggled to focus. Her visage faded in and out. God, he was cold. "Are you all right?" That was what she was asking.

As darkness washed over him again, he realized that malaria did not strike so suddenly. The image of the brandy flashed through his mind, the glass gliding away from him, its contents sloshing. Half full. Only half. "No," he managed. He was not all right.

He'd been poisoned.

He fell forward, straight into Mina's arms. His chin slammed into her nose, *pain*, good Lord, she actually saw stars, and then his chin was settling onto her shoulder. It took a moment, through the shock, to work out what was happening: she'd caught him beneath the arms, quite by accident. He was too tall and too heavy; his knees were buckling. He was going to pull them both to the ground.

She leapt away. He plummeted, face-first. His head bounced against the floor with an awful *crack* that promised blood. She stared down at him. A few feet away, someone screamed. Silken trains hissed across the floor, ladies whirling to gawk. For three weeks, she had been waiting for Phineas Monroe to fall at her feet. But he had proved to be unnaturally graceful, immune to gravity and flirtation both. Naturally, when he finally succumbed, he did it in the most vexing fashion imaginable. For all his charms, he was, after all, a man.

Dimly, she registered the faltering of the orchestra. That was fine with her. Their Beethoven had sounded a bit tart; only the cellist really deserved a hearing, his bow flowing down the strings like honey off a spoon. She sank to her knees as people began to crowd in around her. "Drunk," someone guessed, but Monroe had seemed sober enough to her, although he was out cold now; a pat to the face could not rouse him.

Her hand lingered on his jaw a bit longer than necessary. She was tempted to touch the cleft in his chin. His lashes lay against his cheeks, unusually long, all the more striking given that his face was so starkly masculine. Her attraction to him, at least, was not feigned. But she liked him better with his eyes open. They stayed on hers when she spoke, which was a novelty.

She rose and stepped back. That her concern felt genuine made her a little anxious. More and more, she was confusing her hopes for him. He did not snap at servants, and he had saved her once from a very unpleasant interlude with Bonham, but that might mean nothing; she hadn't been able to tell whether his well-timed entrance was by accident or design. And in the past week, he'd seemed increasingly aloof, distant and curt with her.

She should not allow herself to care. It was asking for trouble.

"My goodness!" A hand crept around her elbow. Jane's face was pale beneath her crown of chestnut ringlets. "Are you all right?"

"Yes, I'm fine."

"You don't look fine."

She sighed. Collins had hired Jane for Mina's sixteenth birthday. *A young lady needs a traveling companion*, he'd said. The friendship that had grown between them in these last four years was her most treasured possession, and also, occasionally, her greatest inconvenience. Jane never failed to see through her like a window, and she had cautioned Mina, more than once, against Monroe's charms. *You don't know the man. Don't be indiscreet.* "He fell onto my nose," Mina said. "It hurts."

Jane's hazel eyes narrowed. "Let me see." She took Mina by the chin, turning her face. People were crushing in around them now; elbows knocked into Mina's side, passing feet pulled at her skirts. It was rather novel, to be pushed past without a second glance. She let herself be rocked by the crowd; keeping her balance was like a game. "It looks intact," Jane decided. "A bit pink. What ails him? Is he dead?"

Mina shook her head. She had felt his breath, hot against her neck, as she clutched him. It had sent a lovely sensation down her spine—perhaps that was why she hadn't reacted immediately. He kissed splendidly, even better than she'd hoped. But his vocabulary was filthy. Why had he talked to her that way? What had she done to alter his attitude? It irritated her that he had the power to make her worry over it. He was only a friend of her stepfather's.

Dr. Sullivan's son shoved past them, jostling them into each other. They turned to follow his progress. He crouched beside Monroe, his fingers reaching for the man's pulse.

"I should go find Mr. Collins," Jane murmured.

"Try the card room." After he'd terrorized Mina's mother into retiring, he'd ensconced himself at the poker table, where admirers queued to greet him like peons before a king. Every time she passed the card room's open doors, he winked at her and blew a smoke ring, as if inviting her to congratulate him for his popularity. The effort to laugh for him was scraping her throat raw.

"All right. I'll just be a moment." Jane looped her skirts over one wrist and glided away. Mina now found herself the lone spot of color in a sea of broad, dark backs. The gentlemen had closed ranks around Monroe, and the hubbub was taking on a strident tone, each man deploying his loudest, most authoritative, most positively *manly* voice.

"Move back—"

"Loosen his tie—"

"Is he breathing?"

"Collins's guest, ain't he?"

"Hot to the touch—"

Mr. Bonham shouldered through the crowd. When he saw her, he gave her one of his peculiar smiles. She had never seen him smile at anyone else that way. Did he think it attractive? It looked as if he were trying to suck his lips down his throat. She could not smile back. If Mr. Monroe was seriously ill, everything would be ruined.

Dr. Sullivan's son rose, his bright red hair catching her attention. "Breathing," he announced, and the gathering sighed.

She went up on tiptoe for a better view. Ten years of her life for two more inches: this was the trade she'd offered God at thirteen, but he had ignored her completely.

Through the forest of shoulders, she saw Mr. Bonham kneel. He lifted Monroe's head by his dark brown hair and took a sniff. "Too much to drink," he drawled. "Or perhaps . . ." He looked up, finding her. His leering grew so tedious. "Perhaps he was simply overwhelmed by Miss Masters's beauty."

A laugh swept the crowd. Eyes turned toward her from all directions. Several gentlemen who'd been crowding her now found their discourtesy made conspicuous; they took quick steps away and a circle of space opened around her, the better for the crowd's examination. Inspected like a prize pig on fair day. She felt the urge to cross her eyes and screw up her face.

But at the center of so much attention, she had no choice but to smile. Mr. Bonham took this as a good sign for himself; his own smile widened, baring teeth. He was ambitious and moneyed, a self-made man; in the colonies, this was not a mark against him, and society beauties were expected to flutter in his presence. Had Mina known nothing more of him, she might have done so authentically. He was slim and elegant, with the long white fingers of an artist and hair of deepest black. *A banker's talents, and the face of a poet*; his sea-green eyes set the ladies to whispering such nonsense when he passed.

But she had cause to know other things about his nature. His hands ranged more freely than an octopus's arms. His lips tasted like gutter water. He had a soft heart for the street dogs that gathered outside his gates every evening, but he slapped his servants with the same smile he wore when he fed the strays. He had partnered with her stepfather in a coca plantation in Ceylon, and now he wanted to marry her to boot. She had no opinion on the former, but the latter made her light-headed with panic.

She did not allow herself to dwell on it. She was not Mama; she would not sit around weeping and wringing her hands. Action was the answer, and the man currently napping on the ground was meant to help. Mr. Monroe also wanted to do business with Collins. He was American by birth and wholly Irish by blood, an advantage that Bonham—born to an English father in Singapore—could not rival. Moreover, if he won Collins's favor, or was caught kissing Mina in dark hallways, she rather thought Bonham would lose interest in her. His pride would demand it.

She took advantage of all the eyes on her. "It might be typhoid. Or cholera? What do you think?"

At the mere suggestion of contagion, the gathering began to disperse. Bonham did not move, but his regard narrowed on her. Like Collins, he had a talent for recognizing the subtler forms of insubordination.

A hand closed over her arm. Collins pulled her around with the same carelessness he would use to turn a puppy by its scruff. "What happened?" he asked as his bloodshot eyes slid to the spot where Monroe's long body lay.

She thought it was rather evident what had happened, but Collins often asked questions merely for the pleasure of being answered. "He collapsed, sir," she said.

"Collapsed? Without warning?"

It was rare to hear the brogue in his voice; he must have been drinking quite heavily in the card room. Usually he sounded more American than she, whose diction had been addled by a childhood spent traveling the world and a parade of English governesses handpicked by her mother.

She spoke very carefully. "He did look a bit flushed." Out of the corner of her eye, she spotted Jane approaching, two burly servants in tow. "If you like, I'll see that he's settled into his room."

Bonham rose. "Perhaps it would be wiser to take him

to the infirmary in Aberdeen. Miss Masters is right, after all; he may be infectious."

Mina traded a glance with Jane, who shook her head the barest fraction. Not difficult to guess what would happen to Monroe in the hospital. Bonham did not like competition for her stepfather's favors; he would make sure one of the nurses confused her medicines.

With a light touch to Collins's arm, she said, "I would be glad to attend to him, Father."

He generally liked it when she called him that, but tonight, in the wake of his fight with her mother, he could not be pleased. He shook off her hand. "Can't understand what happened to him," he growled. "Seemed fine earlier, eh?"

"Take him to his quarters," Jane said to the servants.

"Hold," said Bonham, and gave Jane a sharp look. "With such a sudden attack, the hospital will be better for him. If he's contagious—"

Mina pitched her voice louder. "Why, Mr. Bonham, I am shocked! Mr. Monroe is our guest. *Surely* you'll agree that it's our Christian duty to care for him."

Her strategy worked brilliantly: Collins swelled up like an affronted rooster. He swept the gathering with a fierce glare, daring anyone to challenge his hospitality. "Mina is right," he said. "My household doesn't turn away a guest in need. Bonham, if you want to be of use, fetch Dr. Sullivan."

"Of course," Bonham murmured, and sketched a shallow bow.

"He's down in Little Hong Kong," Dr. Sullivan's son said. "Called to Mrs. Harlock's childbed."

"Well, send a boy, then. And someone strike up the music." Collins turned away, finished with the matter of Monroe. So long as there was liquor available, and cards to be played, he would postpone his sympathy.

As the servants gathered up Monroe's limp body, Jane took Mina's elbow. "Mr. Bonham will not like this," she murmured. "Are you certain you wish to risk offending him?"

Mina nodded, although the question was misjudged. It was not a risk, not when there was no other choice.

Chapter Two

Only the faintest light shone from beneath her mother's door, but Mina knew better than to knock. The handle moved soundlessly beneath her palm. Harriet Collins was curled up in the window seat, her legs tucked beneath her, her face turned toward the night sky. Her blond hair fell loose over one shoulder, exposing the slim line of her throat and the softness of her jaw. She looked very young, sitting there in her nightgown. She looked very nearly like the reflection Mina saw in the mirror every morning.

She crossed her fingers in reflex. *Never.* She would never look so crushed, and all for the sake of pleasing a man. Such love interested her not at all.

Some small noise must have betrayed her entrance, for Mama spoke. "Have the guests gone, then?"

The question made her frown. It was not even midnight. She glanced at the mantel, and found a bare space where the clock had been. A quick search discovered it facedown by the wardrobe, shattered glass all around.

She looked quickly back to Mama's face, but it appeared unmarked. "No, not yet." She pulled the door closed. The latch was well oiled and made no sound. Everything in this house was well tended, expensive, and ornate, the better to illustrate Collins's standing. In that regard, she and Mama were no different from the silk rug that cushioned her feet. "Not for a few hours yet."

"What?" Mama turned. Her eyes were reddened from crying. "Then what are you doing here? Go back into company. You play the hostess in my absence. And, my goodness, your hair! Have Jane fix that, if you please!"

Startled, she reached up to touch her coiffure. A bejeweled pin dropped loose into her hand. She cast it onto the carpet, a reward for whoever swept up the glass. "No, I've retired for the night. Mr. Monroe took ill, and Mr. Collins asked me to care for him."

Mama frowned. Clearly, she disapproved of the order, but she would not dare to contravene it. "All right, then." She reached up to fiddle with the locket at her throat. Her voice was thin from crying; she sounded resigned. "What's wrong with him? Have you sent for the doctor?"

"Yes, but it may take him some time to come. Apparently, Mrs. Harlock's baby doesn't want to be born." As her mother tightened her wrapper, preparing to stand, she added hastily, "Jane is with him right now—there's no need for you to attend." Mama tended to frailty; if Monroe really was contagious, there was no call to expose her.

Mama settled back, relief on her face. "Good. I should have hated to risk running into a stray guest." She hesitated, then held out an arm. "Come tell me about it, then. Quickly, before you go."

This show of interest was heartening. More and more of late, Mama seemed to move in a daze, as though her mind had detached from her flesh. Mina sat down on the chintz cushion and gave her a smile. "Well, I was speaking to Mr. Monroe—"

"No, start at the beginning. Were you the most beautiful girl at the ball?"

She rolled her eyes. "Must that always be the first question you ask?"

"I like to begin with good news, darling."

"Well . . ." Mina considered the question, for in Mama's view, it was never only a matter of looks. Her gown was costlier than any other she'd seen. The pearls at her throat would have paid for five copies of Miss Morgan's. And the gentlemen had flocked to her; she'd been hard-pressed to sit out a dance. "Yes, I believe so."

Mama nodded. "Miss Kinnersley is not in attendance, then?"

Mina pulled a shocked face. The Kinnersleys had recently transferred from Rangoon, where the daughter had been the reigning beauty. "Why do you ask? Surely you don't think her prettier than me?" She leaned forward, squinting into her mother's face with mock concern. The lines at the corners of Mama's eyes seemed to have deepened recently. All her creams and potions would be for naught, so long as Collins drove her to cry so regularly. "So young to require spectacles!"

Mama laughed. "Don't be silly."

"I can't help it. I'm a very silly girl."

"Is she here tonight?"

"Yes, she's here."

"And what is she wearing? With whom has she danced?"

Mina shrugged. "Why does it matter? Are we in competition?"

"It is *always* a competition." Mama's hand on Mina's chin drew her face around. "A woman has only three assets to trade on. Her beauty, her breeding, and, if she is lucky—"

"—her fortune, *yes*, I know." Mina pulled free. Her eyes fell on the abandoned clock. The glass glittered in the dim lamplight, pretty as diamonds. No wonder people were often fooled by paste. "You've only told me a thousand times."

"Well." Mama shrugged. "In the third department, you're outmatched, and you mustn't forget it. That's all I mean."

If she had a penny for every time Mama had reminded her, she'd be wealthy by now and free to do as she liked, rather than primping herself like a prize at auction. "A pity Mr. Bonham doesn't see it that way."

Mama sighed. "I know you've gotten off on the wrong foot, but he's a very likely gentleman, Mina. And he takes a very strong interest in you."

Not in *me*, she wanted to say. In her face and figure? Of course. But she knew better than to say it. Mama would not have acknowledged a difference. Mama thought American girls terribly forward. *A young lady is not meant to trade on her opinions.* She could not understand the license New York society permitted its daughters. *In England, a girl does not consort with gentlemen unchaperoned.* It seemed that mothers made all the decisions in England, and what decisions they made were designed to crush the fun from life. *If you had grown up in England, you would be drinking lemonade, not champagne.* England sounded terribly tedious, and the girls there must be as boring as Sunday sermons.

The brief silence had allowed Mama to recall her troubles. She pressed her lips together and fumbled in her lap for her handkerchief.

"Did he throw the clock at you?" Mina asked softly.

Mama pressed the hankie to her eyes, then drew a hitching breath. "Of course not."

"But he threw it, didn't he?"

No response. Well, what did the specifics matter? If he'd thrown things away from her tonight, there was no guarantee that he wouldn't adjust his aim tomorrow.

Mama's shoulders trembled. The handkerchief muffled her sob.

Take her in your arms. But Mina's muscles wouldn't permit it. They balked and contracted like hardening clay. "I fear for you," she said.

"Oh—" Mama cast down the handkerchief and came into her arms. She held still, feeling tears slip down her chest, under her bodice. Mama's body shook with a grief that seemed too powerful for her frame. The cotton batiste of her nightgown disguised nothing; every bump and knob in her spine translated clearly to Mina's fingertips. They were of a height and could wear each other's dresses, but Mina always felt so much larger, so much more solid in comparison. It worried her, how fragile Mama felt.

She tightened her hold. The angle was terribly awkward, the two of them sitting side by side on the bench with their knees knocking. The tears soaking her bodice made her feel clammy, claustrophobic in her clothes.

Mama could weep more copiously than the marble angels in the Rockefellers' garden, the ones with the fountains hidden inside.

Her own impatience shamed her. She shifted a little, trying to make herself comfortable. But as she drew a breath to start the routine—reassurances (*he did not mean it*), denials (*he will not leave you*), promises (*he will never leave you*), for God's sake all the manufactured optimism, the *lies*—she could not muster much feeling beyond exhaustion. *You are not meant to cry in my arms*, she thought. *You are my mother. I am meant to cry in yours.*

She tested herself. "It's all right," she murmured, and marveled at how kind her voice sounded. Yes, she could do it again, after all. "Shh. It's all right." She set her chin atop Mama's head and stared out the window. White petals floated down from the camellia trees, eddying like snow in the moonlight. Down the mountain, along the path taken by the warm wind, the harbor lights were dying as Hong Kong settled to sleep. The sails in the bay rocked gently, like clusters of strange white flowers caught in the breeze.

The sight pulled something strange from her, cold and fragile as a strand of ice. Loneliness, perhaps. The champagne had left her mouth dry. She always hoped these nights would go differently. "Stop crying," she whispered. "It will be fine."

"No. It was a . . . *horrible* fight. He is so angry with me! Sometimes I think . . . he *hates* me."

"Don't be silly. Of course he doesn't hate you." She could not quite bring herself to finish the equation. She could not say, *He loves you.* It seemed too close to speaking well of him. "He'll say he's sorry soon enough."

"Not this time. He means it, this time."

She closed her eyes. So many times Mama had scared her with this sort of talk. Mina would lie awake with worry, fearing for their safety, envisioning all sorts of horrors for the morning to come: Mama's eye blackened, her arm broken, Collins's guards waiting to throw them onto the street. *If only we had money, we would not need to worry.* How awful it was to be helpless. On such nights, Jane tried to calm her, but it did not help, because Jane had family in New York who would care for her, and letters of reference and a profession, whereas she and Mama were as useless as those stupid Ming cups Mama collected. Tossed from the china cabinet, they would roll about aimlessly. Soon enough, someone would step on them.

"He will apologize," Mina said. Certainly he would. It all looked very black right now, but experience had taught her better. Tomorrow she would go down to breakfast and find Mama and Collins smiling at each other. And later, in the hallway, Mama would draw her aside and whisper, *He apologized, darling. He realizes how badly he behaved. He's simply mortified by it. We'll forget it ever happened.* Apologies cost nothing, so Collins found them very easy to give.

Perhaps he shouldn't even be blamed for it. If a woman's broken trust could be healed with a few words, then maybe he was right to think it worth nothing at all.

She swallowed her anger. It felt as though it was directed at Mama, which made no sense, like wanting to kick a puppy.

Mama spoke in halting jerks. "I don't even know what I *did*."

"You did nothing." Collins criticized her for the strangest things. *Your long face is depressing me.* Or *God above, can you not make ten words of intelligent conversation?* Always it started with something trivial. But these inconsequential complaints seemed to trigger something in him; very quickly, his rage inflated. And her mother, who as a young widow had led a string of admirers by their noses through the grandest ballrooms in New York, could do nothing but cower before him and make herself sick with apologies. *I am sorry, I did not mean to, I did not think I was being so, I never intended to*—

"Unless . . ." Mama drew a broken breath. "Unless it has to do with Mr. Monroe? But that is not *my* fault. How can it be?"

"Mr. Monroe?" Mina pulled away, just far enough to wipe a wet strand of hair from her mother's eyes. "His illness, do you mean?" But no, that couldn't be. There'd been no sign of it until this evening.

Mama shook her head. "No, Gerard ran into someone this afternoon at the club, some American freshly arrived from Chicago, who claimed not to know Mr. Monroe. All I said was that perhaps he travels a great deal. I was only trying to smooth over the discomfort. But it was clumsily done, I suppose. It must have seemed that I was contradicting the gentleman." She retrieved the handkerchief, dabbing at her eyes. "I did not mean to embarrass him. I never used to be so clumsy."

"You aren't clumsy."

"I cannot please him."

"Then leave him."

Mama froze.

So did she. She had not meant to propose this right now. But the words felt right to her. Her lips felt powerful for speaking them. In fact, she wanted to speak them again. *Leave the brute.* "In Connecticut," she said very softly, "they will grant you a divorce for common cruelty."

"Don't . . ." Mama drew away to the end of the window seat. "Don't be foolish." She spoke so quietly that Mina could not make out her tone. "We would starve in the streets."

"We could ask Uncle Edward for help."

"My brother!" Mama laughed bitterly. "He would be glad to see me in the gutter. He says I'm already there, anyway."

"I could take a job—"

"You? A *job*?" Mama's laughter started bitterly, but ended on a sigh. "And anyway, Gerard would never allow it."

Mina felt her heart quicken. This, the heart of the matter, she could address. "You're right, maybe he wouldn't." She hesitated, then grasped Mama's cold hand where it clenched the little button sewn into the seat cushion. If Mama was trying to hold herself down, she did not need to. They could fly—tonight, even! She had been saving for it from her pin money. A meager amount, but enough to book passage to San Francisco. And there was the small trust from her late grandfather, which she came into on her next birthday. "California, then. He would never think to look there. I have researched it." She tightened her grip and spoke over Mama's gasp. "All you need do is publish an announcement in a local paper. You need never even tell him your intention! Some newspaper in a small California town, which he would never see—"

Mama ripped her hand away and stumbled to her feet. "Stop it! Do you hear what you're saying?"

She should never have mentioned the research. It bespoke too much forethought. She dug her knuckles into the cushion. Mama was staring at her in horror, as if she'd just proposed they light a candle for the devil. A weird embarrassment touched her. But there was no need to feel ashamed. This was the modern way to handle such difficulties. "Mama, he—"

"Divorce." Mama pulled the wrapper tight around her body. She looked peaked, as if the word itself were enough to nauseate her. "Do you hear yourself? That is what you mean. Well." She gave a short laugh. "You take after your father, no doubt. An American through and through. But Peppins honor their marriage vows. Do you know—have you any *idea* what people would think? And if Robbie were to hear of it, good Lord!"

Mina knew a sudden, powerful urge to rip the button straight from the cushion. It was incredible. Robbie, some twopenny Englishman whom Mama had jilted twenty years ago, was going to guide her actions? "What does he care? He forgot about you decades ago! Who cares what *anyone* in England thinks? You yourself said it—they would be glad to see you dead in a gutter!"

"Stop it." Mama stalked to the dresser to grab a comb. She smoothed her hair with an angry hand, twisted it up, then stabbed in the comb to hold it. "I am shocked by you." As she pivoted back, her chest rose and fell on a long breath. "That you *dare* to speak such things to me. . . . It's clear that I've failed you somehow. He is my husband, whom I vowed before God to love and obey. And as his daughter, it is your duty—"

"I am not his daughter," Mina said flatly. "And I made

no vow to him. But he made one to you, didn't he? Has he kept *his* vow?"

Mama gave a queer laugh. She wiped her eyes with the back of her hand. "Oh, Mina. You're so young. Far younger than I ever was. I expect it's your father's fault; he spoiled you so terribly. What do you know of marriage? Nothing at all."

She knew enough about it to feel uncertain that she ever wished to learn more. "Would Papa have made you cry like this?" When Mama pressed her lips together and did not answer, she felt resentment twist in her throat. She spat it out with her next words. "Would *Robbie*?"

Mama's frown faded. She stared into space for a long moment. "No," she said. "Robbie was everything good and kind. Though one can never say, I suppose. Love does fizzle, with time." Her gaze focused on Mina. "And your father was quite good to me as well; don't mistake me on that. But when he died and left us without the first red cent, *that* was not love. That was not caring." As Mina gaped at her, she made an impatient noise. "You think me mercenary? You'll learn in time that there are all manners of caring. Some are far more useful than others in this world."

Mina rose. It felt almost like relief, to be given a credible reason to be angry. "You are lecturing me on the value of money? *You?* The woman who bemoans that she tossed away her true love for a share in Papa's dirty American fortune?"

"You will address me with respect, or you will hold your tongue!"

"I know I should speak with respect, and I would try to do it, but when you slink behind Collins like a dog with its tail between its legs, I begin to think you don't deserve any!"

Mama stepped forward and slapped her.

The pain was not so great, really. She would not cry. Mama cried very easily, but Mina never wept; even when Monroe had cracked her nose, she'd shed no tears.

But as she lifted her hand to her face and felt how the impact had left her cheek hot, something inside her seemed to shift, to break away and dissipate. The sense of its loss touched her so sharply that she made a low noise. "And now you hit me. For what? For *his* sake? I see whose love you find more *useful*."

"Don't be foolish."

Her voice barely found the strength to serve the words. "Oh, Mama. I am not the fool here."

Her mother's mouth flattened. "I lost my temper, and I am sorry for it. It is a terrible example to set for you. But I will tell you that this episode makes me agree with Gerard. You are too headstrong for your own good. Mr. Bonham claims to admire your spirits. Very well, let *him* deal with them."

Mina laughed in disbelief. "You made your path, and you chose to walk it. But I'll certainly not walk it with you. I want nothing to do with Bonham."

Mama's brows lifted, and her shoulders squared. For a moment, she looked like the woman Mina remembered from earlier years—proud, composed, assured of her own worth. "That path keeps you in silks," she said. "But I see how much it pains you to endure such luxury. Poor Mina. How terrible, to be paired with the most eligible bachelor on the continent."

"As if that has anything to do with it." She gritted her teeth. "Listen to me, Mama: it will be a cold day in hell before I marry Collins's protégé."

"Then I suggest Jane pack your furs. We expect an offer any day now, and we are planning to accept it."

Mina drew a hard breath through her nose. This was important news. She should be glad to know it, regardless of the manner in which it emerged. *Leave*, her reason bade her. *Go figure out what to do.* Maybe it was time to risk speaking with the consul. She'd collected a bundle of documents, some in code, others suggestive enough to provoke his interest, provided that his honor proved stronger than his friendship with Collins.

But her emotions were clamoring for a hotter conclusion to the conversation than her reason desired. She struck a compromise, speaking quietly. "I could have run away, you know. So many times I was tempted to do it. Every time he screamed at me, every time he locked me in my room because I dared to disagree with him, I stayed for your sake. For *your* sake, I learned to grovel."

Mama's expression softened. "Darling. I know it hasn't been easy for you. You've always been so high-spirited. And as God is my witness, I've never wished to see you hurt." She lifted her hand, and Mina turned her head to avoid the touch. "Mina," she whispered, and her hand fell back to her side. "I love you more than my life. But the world has no use for a woman's spirits. Trust me: if you learn that now, it will save you a great deal of grief in the long run."

"There is only one thing I've learned tonight. I was wrong to stay with you."

"Brave words," Mama said gravely. "I expected no less from you. But my brother no longer acknowledges us. So tell me, child. Where else would you go?"

They had tied Monroe to the bed. "He started to thrash," explained Jane. She was holding a cold compress to her eye and looked unsteady on her feet. In the corner, a Chinese maid was mixing powder into a cup. "Blackened my eye and threw a manservant into the wall."

"Poor Jane." Mina spoke absently. Her cheek still seemed to burn. Was it wrong to feel envy? A black eye would heal, but the numbness in her bones felt unreachable by common medicine. *Where else would you go?* "Perhaps you should sit down."

Jane accepted her help into a chair. "I've never seen such behavior. First he was laughing hysterically, and then he began thrashing. Do you see how red he looks? His pupils were the size of saucers! And he's hot as a bedpan to boot. I'd think it some queer tropical fever, but he hasn't voided himself. We're giving him quinine anyway, and laudanum to dill him—just until the doctor arrives. It can't hurt, I think."

"Probably not." She couldn't marry Bonham. He was so much like her stepfather. He would expect her to sing on command and to fall silent at his bidding, and when she failed to do so, he would consider it his right to punish her, for he was, after all, a man of power and reputation, whom any woman should be grateful to have for a husband.

But if he took after Collins, she did not take after her mother. She would kill him before she let him cow her.

"Mina. Are you all right?"

She exhaled. "My mother has decided to marry me to Bonham. As if *she* has had any success in choosing a husband. As if her judgment hasn't been proven wrong in a million different ways!"

"Did you tell her of your objections?"

"Of course. She thinks me too *high-spirited*."

Jane sighed. "You must have a little compassion for her, I think. She regrets her own choices, and wants to make sure you don't do the same."

No. She was done with compassion. "I told her not to marry him." She remembered the exact moment she had seen Collins as he really was. He had just arrived to pay a call; it had still been early in his courtship. She had come in from the garden, laughing, and greeted him as he was handing over his hat. He had looked over her muddied gown in a cold silence, then instructed her to go and change; she was too old to be frolicking like an urchin, he said sternly.

It had not been his right to upbraid her. But he had taken it anyway. And at twelve years old, she'd already been wiser than Mama. She had known to suspect any man who claimed entitlements that did not belong to him. "I told her it would be better for us to starve," she whispered. "But she didn't trust me. She said my fears were girlish."

Jane spoke very gently. "And how could you expect her to trust you? Or anyone, for that matter? Dearest, she doesn't even trust herself."

Her thoughts now felt too raw and hot to share. Looking up, she mustered a smile. Sometimes the act of aping cheer made her feel more cheerful. Lies were like medicine, that way. "Dear heart, your eye must feel awful. Why don't you go and rest, and let me watch him for a while." She did not want insightful company at present. If she had to share a room with someone, better that he be unconscious.

"Are you sure?" But Jane had come to her feet. "I admit, I have a terrible headache. I only wish I knew what ailed the man."

"Malaria, maybe."

"A very odd case of it, then. He doesn't sweat at all. In fact, it reminds me of nothing so much as that poor Wilkins boy who used to live down the street from my parents. The doctor tried to cure his tetanus with belladonna, and ended up killing him with it. I would give Mr. Monroe a little morphine to see if that improved things, but—well, why would he have eaten nightshade? Unless he's an epileptic, and didn't tell us?" She shook her head. "Has Mr. Bonham sent any word as to when the doctor might come?"

"No, but I'm sure he'll come soon." Mina glanced at the bed. "I hope he will," she added more soberly. Mr. Monroe looked very poorly.

When Jane had departed, Mina perched on the little stool by the bed. It was no normal flush that stained Monroe's cheeks, but an angry rash that rose in welts. She reached out to touch his cheek, but at the last moment, her fingers curled away. He had not wanted her to touch him in the hallway earlier. She hadn't understood it. Only a week ago, he'd been so attentive . . . and she was Collins's stepdaughter, after all. Spurning her overtures was like refusing a shield in the midst of battle.

Her eyes strayed down his length. They had removed his jacket, and the white lawn of his shirt clung to his lean torso. If he really was contagious, she'd certainly caught it when she kissed him. She touched her lower lip. He had bitten her, very softly, there. And she had liked it. For three weeks, she had liked *him*—his wit, and his quiet way, and how closely he listened. She had liked him so much that once or twice she had been tempted to cast aside all caution and speak to him honestly. *Do not do business with Collins*, she'd wanted to say. *You're too good for him.*

The memory made her sigh. So naïve. He had shown his true colors now; how she would have regretted it if she'd revealed hers beforehand! She was usually smarter than that. Maybe his looks had blinded her.

She considered him critically. He was handsome, no doubt. But she should have seen the arrogance in his face. The sharp blade of his nose seemed designed for looking down on women whose behavior did not match his standards. *You wouldn't want others to think you intemperate.* Well, and people might think him an overbearing, painfully sober bore, but she had not remarked on it, had she? Those sharp cheekbones bespoke haughtiness, and the stark square of his jaw, inflexibility. *Have a care, Miss Masters. I don't think that would be wise.* She could not interpret the cleft in his squared-off chin, but it probably accounted for his vanity.

She sat back, irritated with herself. To think she'd chased him down a hall! He was a typical specimen . . . apart from those delicious lashes of his, which lent his eyes such arresting gravity. *No*, she told herself sharply. His looks would no longer impress her.

He whispered something.

"Are you awake?" She came to her feet on a wave of relief. But his eyes remained closed, and he did not respond.

The Chinese maid said something. Mina could not make it out. The maid shook her head and waved a dismissal; she was to ignore Mr. Monroe.

"Delirious?" she asked the girl, who shrugged helplessly, then pillowed her hands against her face to mime sleep. Mina nodded, resuming her seat.

"Aberdeen," Monroe muttered.

She smiled reluctantly. It figured that an associate of her stepfather's would mutter of the dockyards in his delirium.

"Midnight," he whispered. "Take the schedule."

How odd. He was a Chicagoan born and raised, but he pronounced the word *schedule* like an Englishman.

"Go quickly," he mumbled. "Tide . . . the tide is low."

She leaned toward him. When he repeated the phrase, her eyes followed his lips.

A chill brushed over her. She was not imagining it. He was speaking the Queen's English, his intonation as crisp as her mother's.

Chapter Three

"*Pilgrim's Paradise*," Monroe said, and sighed.

Mina came to her feet, her hands fisting at her waist. That was the name of one of her stepfather's ships, but not one that he publicly claimed to own. And why would he? He used it to transport guns bound for Irish revolutionaries; he had no wish to get himself hanged. Even Mama did not know of that ship. Mina had learned of it quite accidentally—and at great risk to herself, she suspected. Had Monroe somehow found the documents she'd squirreled away?

He pulled against the ropes, a sharp yank as his muttering grew louder. "At midnight," he said clearly. "Go then."

The maid was watching him as well, a frown on her brow. She did not seem to understand English, but one never knew for sure. Collins kept a network of spies, and the household would not be exempt from it. "You may go now," Mina said to her.

The girl tilted her head in puzzlement. Not for the first time, Mina bitterly wished she had some Cantonese. She had thought to learn it once, during one of their longer visits to Hong Kong, but Collins had forbidden it. Ostensibly, he did not want her to "go native, like those damned missionaries"; but later that season, he'd made a remark far more telling. *A monopoly on knowledge is tantamount to a monopoly on everything else of value*, he'd told one of his cohorts. And when he'd caught Mina staring at him, he had winked at her and smiled.

Mina pointed toward the door. "Out," she said, and added a smile for good measure. Her pulse might be racing, but her demeanor would not betray her. She had learned better than that. She could smile and blink more vacuously than a cow.

The girl's face cleared. She bowed and slipped from the room. Mina crossed to turn the key behind the maid, then leaned back against the door. "So," she said. Her voice hitched on the syllable, and she paused to compose herself. Nerves were useless, and in her experience, they bred on oxygen; give them voice and they flourished. She cleared her throat and spoke very coolly to the man on the bed. "Interested in breaking monopolies, are you?"

He did not reply, of course. The door latch dug into her back like a prodding finger. She drew a long breath. The air smelled bitter from the quinine Jane had administered.

Monroe might be in league with her stepfather. That would explain his knowledge. But why then would he pretend to be American?

The energy coursing through her demanded an outlet. She walked a tight circle between the washstand and the window, wrapping her arms around her waist to make sure she did not indulge the urge to tremble.

"To Bantry," Monroe mumbled. "Three ships."

He was correct. Her stepfather had three ships in the harbor, only two of them legitimate. The other was bound for Bantry.

She sat down on the edge of the mattress, watching him. It seemed he was not so typical after all; suddenly, he looked even more fascinating than he had in her dreams. Was Mr. Monroe even a businessman? The profession of collecting secrets through deception was generally called *spying*.

If he was a British spy, then he was here to stop her stepfather. He was here because of the guns Collins supplied to the Fenians.

She realized she was chewing on her knuckle. It was an old and very bad habit, which her governesses had tried to break with admonitions and whacks from a ruler. *The hands declare the lady.* She bit down harder. If he was here for the guns, Collins would kill him. Collins detested liars and brooked no interference in his plans. Once, in Manhattan, a new maid had gone into his study to clean. Only Collins's personal attendant was allowed into that room unsupervised. The maid had disappeared shortly afterward, and the gossip among the staff was that she'd been found dead in Five Points.

Holy God. Mina lowered her hand. What had her mother said tonight? *Gerard ran into someone from Chicago who claimed not to know Mr. Monroe.*

She sprang off the bed. She had to get out of here. If Collins thought she knew about Mr. Monroe and had failed to inform him, it would go very badly for her. Oh, he claimed to love her, but then, he claimed to love Mama, too. He liked the familial image that they helped to create; in public, he was a very Christian man indeed.

Two steps from the door, she realized she was running like a rabbit, and all for concern over Collins. She came to a stop, staring at the doorknob. Mr. Monroe was muttering on the bed, helpless as a child, his tongue spelling his own undoing.

She would not let that brute make her run.

She turned back to Mr. Monroe, rubbing a hand over her chest to soothe herself. Her heart was drumming so strongly that she feared it might break from her rib cage. The man was beautiful, even unconscious. Her instincts had not been wrong about him in the largest sense. He was not Collins's ilk at all. He was Collins's enemy. Not a financier, but a *spy.*

Actually, it was not so difficult to believe. Earlier, immaculate and sneering in his expensively tailored jacket, he had seemed the embodiment of a self-important businessman. She easily could have imagined him dispatching some thug to finish off his competitors. But now, in his rolled-up shirtsleeves, with the corded muscles of his forearms exposed, he looked like a man accustomed to heavier burdens than bank drafts. He looked fit to play the thug himself.

She took a deep breath and walked back to the bed. She had never met a man whom she considered a match for her stepfather, but this could be her opportunity to revisit the question. She would not even have to risk going to the consul.

His hair was sticking to his brow. She leaned forward to brush it back, then indulged herself by rubbing a strand between her fingers. As soft and thick as she'd suspected, a pure, true brown, like ebony wood. It matched his eyes and complemented his skin—which was too tanned, she saw now, to belong to a man who did business indoors. "You grow more interesting by the moment," she murmured. But that tanned skin was horribly mottled, and his breathing sounded weak. "Oh, Mr. Monroe . . . I think boring would serve you better."

He made a small noise. It put her in mind of a whimper from a puppy. But that was a ridiculous comparison. He was almost too tall for the bed, and in his delirium he had tossed one of the manservants across the room. By nature, a spy was dangerous. And she was a small woman.

She must remember that. *She* might be the one in danger when he recovered. She knew his secret, after all.

A bitter taste came into her mouth. It might have been nausea, but it felt curiously like anger. Couldn't he have trusted her? She put on a good act of loving her stepfather; Collins required no less. But if only Monroe could have seen the truth of it—if only she *had* spoken to him! She would have told him everything, given him all her information. She would put a gun in his hand this second and point the way to her stepfather's quarters, applauding—if only he could walk. Really, how *sloppy* of him to fall ill. And what poor timing. If Collins already suspected him of bad business, he would be dead by morning. It seemed a miracle that he hadn't died an hour after Collins returned from the club.

Her breath caught.

It reminds me of nothing so much as belladonna.
She lunged toward the medicine chest.

Someone was muttering secrets. Here they were, the facts that Phin guarded more closely than his life, being recited like a children's rhyme. He knew what it meant. Someone was going to die tonight.

Light rolled over him. It shot through his bones, boiling them to liquid. Bones, sweat, tears spilled from his eyes, rolling down his temples. He would not blink until he managed to focus, to see into this luminescence—

It flared out. Ashes and darkness. Someone was coughing. It was the cough of an old man, a dying man, his father had coughed up blood at the end. His skin had yellowed by the time Phin found him, the same shade as the peeling wallpaper, dried out, God, that hellhole, if he never had to return to Calais he would thank God for it. The smell of the deathbed all around him—blood and shit and the mold creeping up the baseboards. The old man grew angry. Phin emptied his pockets: *I am not lying. I have no coin to give you.* Coughing seized Pater again, great wrenching gasps, but he continued to shake his head; this fever had rotted his brain long before his illness, cards and liquor his only concerns. When he regained enough breath, he said, *Goddamn you, Phineas. You are lying.* His curses flew, flecked with blood, and when Phin turned away he found he had to wipe his face clean.

"Wake up!"

Eyes. Blue like cold things, deep seas and winter skies. He fastened onto them. They made his mind go still. He knew them from somewhere. "Hush," came a voice, and he saw the lips beneath those eyes, parted around tiny white teeth like threats unveiled. "*Quiet*. Swallow this. Now!"

The bitter taste of the liquid recalled him to the existence of his mouth. His tongue was so dry. God above. It was he who'd been speaking. He who'd been telling secrets.

He would die tonight.

"No," the voice whispered. Something wet and blissfully cold moved down his cheek. He thought of snow tigers with tongues of ice, blue and crackling, lapping his skin. Their tongues dripped in the heat. They began to crack, to splinter. Chunks of melting tongue rained across his face.

"Shh."

Hands pressed at his shoulders, holding him down. He had held Tanner down. He had used ropes to do it, *taking the easy way*, Tanner had sneered, but he was wrong, there was no scope for cleverness in killing a man, talent was not required; *I knew you were a natural*, but Ridland was wrong to say that, there was no art to murder, you simply pulled the trigger. You gave them forewarning, but not because you wished to be honorable. *Take some pride in your goddamned work, Granville*, but there was no honor in killing. You told them they were about to die because you wanted to scare them, once they pissed their trousers then they would talk, they babbled like children and then you killed them, you killed them once you could start to see the infant they'd once been, the little boy who was afraid to tell a lie. Tanner had taken a long time to break in that hot, airless room. He had laughed, at the beginning. *I'm to die, you say? Do you see the future, then?* But, no, it was an easy prediction. It was easy to predict death when one held a gun in one's hand. The blood sprayed. *I am a killer*, he thought, *the man was not even attacking me, I am a killer*, but it was difficult to grasp, when he felt no different in his bones. His hands still felt breakable, even with a gun in them.

"You must keep quiet." The voice caught his attention. It floated to him through layers of darkness, pulling him from—memories, they were memories, they were not happening to him now, he was—in a bed. The darkness was beginning to fracture, bits splitting away, revealing a ceiling, blond hair, a woman's eyes. Her lips, parted like petals, flowers, the smell of roses. *No. Focus.* She was speaking to him. "We are alone in this room," she said. "I have covered the spyholes. But I cannot say who listens at the door."

Her statement implied something. His instincts recognized a cause for alarm, but his wits could not work out the reason for it.

"You need more morphine." She turned away, and her figure, the room around her, receded.

His eyes opened. He was looking at a girl. He had done this before. She was speaking to him, but he could not hear her. His bones felt as if they were trying to break out of his skin. His tendons, his sinews, were stretching and vibrating with the effort to hold them in. Every cell in him sang with a sensation so extreme that he could not say whether it was agony or bliss.

She slapped him across the face. He was staring now at a wall, wallpaper, patterned with flowers. This pain in his jaw was clearer, simpler; he focused on it, and her voice emerged over the babble in his brain. "Breathe," she said, and something pressed against his nose, cold and metallic. A spoon. It felt vaguely familiar, as if she had done this before. He tried to avert his head. She covered his mouth with her palm, and when he moved to knock it away, he realized he was tied down. "Breathe," she said, and he breathed.

Fire raged up his nostril. Bitterness flowed down the back of his throat.

"It may kill you," she said. "I don't know how it interacts with morphine, much less the nightshade." Her laughter sounded ragged. "Well, at least you'll feel very cheerful as you die. Collins's way would not be so pleasant."

Collins.

The word acted like a catalyst. He felt his thoughts reordering, forming straight lines. Collins. Right. He was in Collins's house. Christ, this girl was Collins's stepdaughter. The intemperate little flirt who conspired with his body to turn his brain to mud.

He tried to speak, but his lips and tongue felt like cotton, too thick to shape the words. He throbbed. Everywhere. Looking at her, it was not an entirely unpleasant sensation. He watched through a dreamy haze as she leaned across him. The rope of ebony pearls at her neck fell over his chin, cool and smooth. They felt no smoother than her skin. Her shoulders were white and slim as a child's, her breasts like the snow-covered slopes of mountains, a dark, scented valley between them. *Think.* He remembered that dress she was wearing. It matched her eyes, but did her no favors.

She straightened, a cup in her hand. He could not feel it against his mouth, but liquid splashed onto his chin. The sharpness of alcohol stabbed his nostrils.

"Swallow," she said.

The flirt looked very pale. Her hair was escaping her chignon, white-gold locks framing her face like parentheses. She moved to cover his nose, to force him to swallow, but he twisted away. What the hell was she about? His wrist was bound to the bedpost. That knot looked goddamned professional.

"It's only Vin Mariani," she said. "They call it the French tonic sometimes."

He knew the wine. He'd told Collins he wanted to create a brand of it for American distribution. Its main ingredient was not alcohol, but syrup of—"coca." The word was his, the voice unrecognizable. Hoarse, as though he'd been screaming.

"Yes." Laughter escaped her, a low string of it, obscenely musical. She had tied him to the bloody bed, and she was laughing. "And the powder you inhaled—also from coca." Her lips quirked into a strange smile that made her appear much older. "Mr. Monroe, you will be so full of coca by the time you leave, you won't even feel a bullet."

He felt as if he'd woken into a play whose script no one had shared with him. At least he now recognized the feeling coursing through his body, the cause for his mounting strength and the numbness in his mouth. It was the drug she was feeding him. He knew something of it; they sometimes used it in the field. The effects wouldn't last for long. He cleared his throat, focused on schooling his vowels. "You have me trussed up like a roast pig." Passably American, there.

"You were thrashing," she said. "But now you must go."

She was making no sense. "Where is your stepfather?"

Her brows arched. "I recommend you avoid him. Unless, of course, you wish to explain why you are so interested in the *Pilgrim's Paradise*, and speak in your sleep like the Queen." She spoke so lightly that he wondered if he were still dreaming. "Oh, also—why nobody in Chicago has ever heard your name."

He blinked. He was not asleep. "Christ."

"Really, Mr. Monroe! And I thought you were a gentleman."

Why was he not dead already? He looked past her, expecting to see Collins holding a gun.

"He's not here," she said. "I didn't tell him about it. About—whatever you mean to do. What is that, if I may ask?"

He looked back to her. She gave him another pretty smile. Was this her technique of interrogation? If so, she needed to work on it. Her dancing eyes promised things far too sweet to frighten him.

The thought echoed in his brain, sounding more ludicrous and unfamiliar with every repetition. His brain was well wrecked, all right.

She sat back, her smile dimming. "Of course. You must have some sort of code that forbids you to tell me such things. Simply say yes or no, then. Yes, if you plan to do it soon, and no for—for *maybe* soon. I can't bear to have my hopes wholly dashed, you see."

"Soon." Good God. Had that just come out of his

mouth? He could not blame the poison; the girl was a toxin all her own.

"Oh, good." She rose, going to the washstand; when she turned, she had a long, wicked blade in her hand. "Don't move," she said, and went to work on the rope at his ankle. "I'm fine with fever, but blood doesn't agree with me." As she sawed at the rope, she rambled on. "Now, you must go quickly, because he *will* be coming to see if you're dead yet. And I say this because I believe you are not ill so much as poisoned. Otherwise, the morphine would not have worked so well."

He considered her as she moved to his other foot. He had no idea what she was about. She considered herself to be aiding a man she thought to be her stepfather's enemy. It was not the act of a brainless coquette, but he could not imagine another role for her. *She's a fast piece*, Bonham had said to him earlier tonight, with ribald good humor. *The man who catches her will have to cage her.*

As she freed his left wrist, he muttered, "You're even faster than he realizes."

"Stop that. There will be no more delirium for you, sir." She cut the final binding, then grasped his forearms and pulled. He sat up slowly, feeling his limbs warm to his command. But when he swung his legs off the bed, his head swam, and scarlet blotches swarmed his vision.

A hand threaded through his hair, pressing his head down to his knees. The girl's voice came from above, damnably cheerful. "Take this, please."

Something was pressed into his hand. A little vial; more of the coca, he assumed. He slowly straightened, wondering what new surprise she might offer him. She was waiting, face composed, although the foot tapping beneath her skirts and the quick glance she threw to the door suggested she was not so calm as she liked to appear. "The doctor will be coming," she said. "He sent a note a half hour ago. You will want to be gone before he arrives." Her mouth curved, wry. "He is Collins's particular friend."

He found himself staring at her. He should be on his feet. This lack of urgency did not bode well. Sicker than he'd realized, with the dizziness coming in waves; cocaine did not combine well with morphine, no. How many grains had she given him? How far apart? The white curtains were glowing with the blue light of dawn. His heart felt as though it were battling through quicksand. In another quarter hour, he would be flat on his back again. Dead or very near it. All her efforts in vain.

She was looking back at him steadily. She was startlingly beautiful. He had not allowed himself to acknowledge the full extent of her beauty until now; her effect on him had been his greater concern. But she was small. He did not like how small she was. Collins could break her with his fist.

She cleared her throat. "You're gawking, sir. It's unoriginal."

"Forgive me. I am . . . not at my best, half dead." He realized that he no longer knew how to speak to her, for he had no bloody idea what she was about. "You shouldn't be doing this."

"Why not?"

"Collins won't like it."

She retrieved the knife from the ground. "Probably not. Try to stand."

Yes, he should be on his feet. He felt curiously remote from his own concerns. "What say you? Will I be dead in an hour?"

She put a hand to her mouth, considering him clinically. "Do you know, Mr. Monroe—I have absolutely no idea."

"Well," he said, for want of any other reply; and this time, when she began to laugh, he surprised himself by laughing with her—a slow, rusty noise that hurt his chest and left him slightly breathless.

She cupped his elbow and helped him to his feet. Slowly they walked toward the window. He could not make his mind grasp it: he was nearly dead, and his savior was a half-wit with a vice for giggling. But clearly, she was something more than that. He had not been the only one pretending here. How well she had fooled him.

The answer came to him with sudden clarity. She would not risk herself so flagrantly for a stranger. She must be part of the game. That knife sat in her hand as though she were accustomed to wielding one.

As she unlocked the bottom shutters, using the blade to break off the latches, he touched her shoulder. "Whose are you?"

She looked up. "My own, of course." Straightening, she looked deeply into his eyes, and then startled the hell out of him by pressing a kiss to his mouth. When she drew back, her lips held an odd smile and his own had awakened; they felt full and sensitive from the lingering sensation of hers. "Remember that," she said. "Remember whom you owe."

He forced himself to look away, to the tree outside.

It was not an impossible escape route, although most of the branches looked unlikely to hold his weight. But the doctor was coming, Collins's special friend. If she was telling the truth, if she had no experience in this business, then he couldn't leave her here undefended.

"And what else would you do, Mr. Monroe? You're trembling on your feet."

Sloppy. To have spoken that aloud—he was very bad off. "You'll be alone."

"Is there any choice?" She sounded genuinely curious.

There was never a choice. But the repercussions of his helplessness had rarely tasted so bitter. Running with his tail tucked between his legs might count as a far milder offense than murder, but he had never been so slapdash that someone else was left to face the consequences of his mess. Much less a slip of a girl. "I'm indebted to you," he said roughly. Such empty words. God help her if she thought it would serve her to have the favor of a man who was not even allowed to make his own decisions.

"Yes, you are," she said. She gently urged him onto the windowsill. He paused there to locate his balance; his legs shook, and the dizziness was gaining on him again. She touched his arm as though to aid him—her skin was softer than silk, and he had shoved her away earlier, thinking her useless, a nuisance, an inconvenience he did not need—and then, as if recognizing the futility, she let her hand fall. It occurred to him to wonder what she had meant when she asked if there was a choice. Perhaps she had not been speaking of his choices. *You'll be alone.* That was the remark she'd been responding to.

"You cannot go with me," he said.

She laughed, as if he'd said something very foolish. Perhaps he had. He felt off balance, wanting—something, he was not sure what. He set his foot on the nearest tree limb and cleared his throat. "Today." He could give her this. "By sunset, I think."

She understood at once. Her whole face lit. "So soon? I should kiss you again."

The doorknob rattled. "Mina," came Collins's voice from the hallway, and her smile stiffened. "Are you in there? Why is the door locked? The doctor is here."

She did not look at the door. "Just a moment," she called. Her voice sounded strong and calm. "Go," she whispered to him.

The door shuddered beneath a blow. Collins was not waiting. He was going to break in.

The disgust climbing Phin's throat made him feel sicker. He released the tree and stepped back into the room. "Give me the knife." The floor was swaying beneath him; he had to put a hand to the window frame for support.

"Don't be a fool." Finally she remembered fear; it drew lines around her eyes and made her voice shake. "I'm safe. He won't hurt me."

Another voice sounded from the hallway—deeper, unfamiliar to him.

"They will have guns," she said more sharply. "Blast you, I want him arrested!"

To hell with this. He reached for the blade, intending to wrest it from her—he could manage that, at least—but she tossed it away and shoved him, two solid palms straight into his chest.

Ordinarily, it would not have budged him. But in the split second that followed, as she fell into him and continued to push, he counted on reflexes, strength, a sense of balance that the poison had burned away. His fingers scraped past the window frame—his head smashed into tree branches—branches crashing up around him, limbs thumping his back like mallets, leaves scraping his cheeks, lashing at his eyes as he fell—

His hand closed over a tree limb. He hung there for a moment, a few feet off the ground, dazed by his fortune.

An explosion came from above—the shattering of a lock, the splintering of wood. He looked up and saw her silhouetted in the light. She was watching him, her bright hair lit like a corona, the most unlikely angel of salvation he could imagine. If in her terror she abruptly regretted her decision, if she realized she was risking her life for a man who did not deserve it, then her wisdom came too late; he could do nothing to help her but return her regard, and search her face for some reason not to remember her.

An arm came around her and yanked her from sight. Another head popped out, male; he peered toward the ground and, as his eyes met Phin's, lifted a pistol.

Phin's fingers opened. The ground thudded into his feet. Time seemed to slow, the moment stretching interminably: the cool night breeze swept over him, scented with roses, and the lawn stretched before him, another gauntlet among too many to remember, and his thoughts piled one on top of another. He did not want to run. He was tired in his bones. Sinking into the earth would be so easy. He would die smiling, here, for it would spite Ridland beyond any imaginable thing.

But his body had never heeded his brain. Its dumb cunning knew no other choice than survival. The first shot rang out, but as his mind lingered on the room above, on the girl and her laughter and everything about her that made no sense, his feet were already moving.

Chapter Four

It was lovely, so far as prisons went. Mina's hotel suite at Claridge's had not been so resplendent. The three rooms were spacious, furnished in Chippendale and Axminster, with Boucher tapestries on the walls and gas jets fringed with crystal. They might have been junk-bottle glass, for all it mattered. So long as the windows would not open and the door locked from the outside, she could not breathe easily.

Mr. Ridland was apologetic. He did not like to inconvenience her. The first night, he reminded her that the British authorities were making every effort to find her mother. The second night, he assured her that the American ambassador had been made aware of her detainment, and considered it an unfortunate, temporary necessity. "And lest you have forgotten," he reminded her on the third, "I am not a stranger to you. We met in Hong Kong once, four or five years ago."

He spoke as though that should reassure her. But for the first time since Mama had disappeared, panic threatened to break her composure. If Ridland had been in Hong Kong, she couldn't trust him to shine her shoes, much less find her mother. The effort to charm him suddenly seemed futile.

After he left, she realized she'd been clutching the locket at her throat. Mama's locket. Mama had taken it off on the morning of her disappearance; it had clashed, she'd announced, with her new pewter gown.

Irritated to be so transparent, Mina stalked over to the window, snapping apart the curtains. On the eave opposite, a gray cat lay across the gutter. She tapped at the glass, but he showed no interest in her. After a minute, he bounded out of sight.

She stared out at the huddled rooftops. The clouds pressed so close atop the buildings that it seemed even the air lacked room to wander. Only a week ago, dancing through mirrored ballrooms and flirting with handsome men, she'd professed herself enamored of London, and Mama had laughed in happy astonishment. *Why, Mina! I never thought I would see the day when you had a kind word for anything English.*

In fact, it was her mother's joy that made Mina feel so generous toward the city. After Hong Kong, it had taken Mama two years to find the courage to reenter New York society. Months more to recover her old confidence. Thus to watch her move so boldly through her oldest Waterloo, as fearless and self-assured as though Collins had never existed, seemed like a miracle. *You are completely healed now*, Mina had thought. For the triumphant thrill that revelation had afforded her, she would have endured those last days in Hong Kong a hundred times—much less agreed to love London.

Now, though, the sight of the city seemed to smother

her. So many people in this dark sprawl, but only two who would care if she never emerged from these rooms. And if Mama was no longer in the city—well, then, that left only Tarbury. And Mina paid for his devotion; she would not delude herself.

She sighed. Really, from one perspective, it didn't matter where in the world she was—apart from Jane, Mama was all she had. Such were the consequences of her independence; they had never troubled her before.

But then, she had never viewed them from this particular window.

She shut the curtains and turned back to the writing desk. Ridland's admission left her no choice. Her hopes now came down to trickery, and a very slim chance that a stranger remembered his debt to her. Whether he would be better than Ridland, she could not know. But it seemed likelier than not, and so her pen began to move.

Dear Jane,

I did receive your letter. Forgive the tardiness of my reply, and the shock I must deliver to you. I pray you, sit before continuing to read.

I will not be returning to New York as planned. In short, Mama has gone missing, and it seems probable that the artist of her disappearance is Gerard Collins.

I can only give you a brief account, for much remains unclear to me. Suffice it to say that on the eve of our planned return to New York, I came back from a meeting with the gentlemen at Whyllson's to find our rooms in disarray, Mama gone without a trace. You can imagine my panic. The concierge summoned the police. Along with them arrived Mr. Joseph Ridland, a representative of one of Her Majesty's darker arms of government. Forthwith I was packed off to his house on Park Lane, where I currently reside as his most unwilling guest.

It was Mr. Ridland who revealed that my stepfather has escaped from English custody. He feels certain that Mama is with Collins, although he seems undecided on the question of whether or not she has gone willingly. He believes they are still in England, though, and hopes that my continued presence here may serve to lure them from hiding. What a charming role for me!

Of course, my main concern is for Mama. Today, a very peculiar note arrived at the hotel for me, which Mr. Ridland was generous enough to share. It is Mama's writing, but how oddly it reads! She says nothing of where she is or with whom she travels. She only sends her love, and reassures me that she leaves her welfare to Providence—and urges me, for her sake, to do the same, at the end.

I have puzzled in vain over this request. When I read it this morning, it seemed to me the sort of statement a captive might make to her loved one, when she finds herself in the custody of a man whom she knows to be capable of any manner of depravity. I read it and thought, "She is afraid that I will try to find her, and that he will hurt me for it." But when I read it again tonight, it seemed to me, against my will, to be the advice of a moralist, lecturing me for my great betrayal, and chiding me to look to my soul and reform myself.

Is it terribly wrong that I am desperate to believe the former interpretation? Yes, it is, isn't it? For that would mean that she is fearful in his presence, and that she suf-

fers at every moment from thoughts of what he may do to her, or to me. Perhaps, then, I wish that Mama has gone with him willingly. But if this is the case, then all the hope and life that we worked to return to her during the last four years—and the courage she unearthed during those dreadful days in Hong Kong, and the admiration I came to feel for her in their aftermath—all must be counted for naught.

I cannot accept that. In fact, I will be very honest with you: I cannot accept it, for I know it to be false.

I wish above anything that I could share with you the source of my conviction. But you have a husband to care for, and a child to mother, and it seems to me that some knowledge is too dangerous for a woman entrusted with so much love. I promise you, though, that if you knew what I know, you would share my conviction that Collins holds her by force. And you would understand why I must take the course of action that I have designed.

I am signing power of attorney over to you. The company is yours. Run it as you see fit, and it will flourish. Before Her Majesty's lapdogs began to yip at me, I managed to secure the contract for the lavender. It has been sent along to New York. Have Cavanaugh draw up some advertisements that extol the vaunted superiority of English perfumery. Do try not to laugh too much in the process.

I apologize if this letter leaves you shaken. I would prefer not to have to write it, and I eagerly anticipate our happy reunion. In the meantime, I remain

> *Your ever-loving sister in spirit,*
> *Mina*

The next morning, when the maid brought breakfast, she handed over the letter. It did not take long for Ridland to appear.

On his previous visits, he had made the most of his gray hair and wrinkled cheeks, hobbling and gesturing with the aid of a cane. Today he strode in boldly, her crumpled note clutched in his upraised fist. "What interesting letters you write."

He meant to scare her, of course. She jumped to her feet compliantly. "Sir, what a surprise! Did the maid misdeliver my note? And I see you've forgotten your cane! Please do sit; you mustn't overtax yourself."

A vein along his temple throbbed into prominence. "We do not detain you for our own amusement, girl. Toy with me, and you will regret it."

He had assured her, on the drive from Claridge's, that she put him in mind of his granddaughters, and that he would not wish harm to a single hair on her head. But his solicitude had not been nearly as convincing as this tyrannical turn. "I cannot imagine why you're so angry, sir." She sank into her chair as if faint. "Won't you take a seat? I promise I don't mean to distress you."

As he stared at her, she had the impression that he was rethinking his strategy. "I have explained to you," he said more calmly, "how very *critical* it is that Gerard Collins be recovered. The Fenians have bombed Scotland Yard; do you doubt that your stepfather had a hand in it? He attempted to fund a war against this country, and every moment he remains free, we must anticipate a new disaster. If you still doubt it—"

"Oh, no, certainly not." Men always claimed to have

very good reasons for caging a woman in a cell. Routinely, all across the world, they convinced themselves of the necessity. "I have a clear view of Mr. Collins, I assure you." He was a rabid mutt who wanted his bone back. Mama was nothing but a *thing* to him; her very independence challenged his manly authority, and therefore could not be tolerated. "But when I come to my own role in these events, my vision grows murkier." She paused to bat her lashes. "Dr. Morris tells me I could benefit from spectacles, but I feel certain they would detract from the general effect of my eyes. What think you?"

He came forward to toss the balled-up letter into the butter dish. "I think you are funning me."

He should not sound so smug. It had taken him four days to figure this out. "Do tell," Mina said, feigning astonishment.

He spoke through his teeth. "Yes, Miss Masters, I will do. Despite your best efforts to act the flibbertigibbet, I think you could not run a company with so much success if your head were as empty as you pretend it to be."

"How kind," she said softly. Of course, he had it wrong; her feebleminded act had won over businessmen who never would have lent money to a woman who dared address them as equals. "I must admit, I have a great deal of help with my company." Social climbers in particular had been glad to patronize a society beauty's little project. "And it is a very *small* business, you know. Only hair tonics. And the occasional cream. Oh, also a few lotions—we are expanding our offerings this season—"

His hand slammed onto the table. A fork clattered from the platter to the table; the eggs quivered in anticipation of calamity. "Enough. You have managed to rile me. Victory is yours. But now you will tell me whether that letter"—he pointed toward the butter dish—"was a stunt, or whether you do in fact have information that interests me."

She was still caught on his preposterous statement. "Victory is mine?" She ran a meditative finger around the rim of her cup. "No, Mr. Ridland, that does not ring true. So long as you keep me imprisoned here—"

"I like this no better than you," he said harshly. "Oh, I promise you, Miss Masters, I *very* much dislike the role I'm charged to play. If there were another way—"

"But there is." She tapped the rim of the cup twice, a decisive little conclusion to her featherheaded routine. "I will cooperate with the government gladly. I will take daily strolls through the park with a bull's-eye painted on my parasol. But it would be *so* much a comfort if I were allowed to choose my captor. Why, I think my attitude would quite transform."

Ridland rolled his eyes. "Mademoiselle, surely you do not expect us to simply leave you with one of your friends and trust that you will stay *put*."

"Of course not," she said in surprise. He really did think her an idiot, didn't he? "In fact, there's a man who I believe is in your employ who would suit the role very well." Her teeth itched. She wanted to bite her knuckle. Ridland did not seem the sort of man who would look kindly on small weaknesses, so she stuck her hand beneath her skirts. "I had occasion to meet him in the Orient, shortly before my stepfather's arrest. He went by the name of Phineas Monroe."

Ridland's face became so rigid that he looked like an effigy of himself. "No. That will not be possible."

His strong reaction puzzled her. A horrible explanation presented itself. "Is he dead?"

His expression did not change. No, she decided, Monroe was still kicking. Something else accounted for this iciness. "I am not able to divulge such information. I *am* sorry, Miss Masters."

She sighed. He wasn't sorry at all. "So am I." After all, Monroe was the only man in the service of the British government who she knew for certain had not worked for her stepfather four years ago.

Ridland was still staring at her. "Is that all you have to say for yourself?"

"Yes," she said. "I think it is."

His expression darkened. His hand on the back of the chair curled into a fist. Not promising, that. She rose to put distance between them, deciding on the fly to go to the bookshelf. She lifted her chin as she walked, the better to display the line of her neck, which a number of gentlemen had assured her put them in mind of a swan's. Surely it would prove harder on the conscience to hurt a swan than a hedgehog, although she could use a few sharp quills right now, and the helpful capacity to curl into a bristling ball.

"I hope you will not force me to harsher measures, Miss Masters."

She selected a volume at random. *Harsher measures.* Such terrible poetry in two words, such evocative power: a lightless, windowless room, thirst clawing at her throat, the air thickened with heat, her mother's distant screams. If he thought to scare her, he was going to have to work harder; she rather thought she'd already seen the worst. "Yes," she said, and took a seat at the window. "That would be unfortunate."

The book was an atlas. How lovely. She could look at all the places Ridland wouldn't allow her to go.

"I will return in an hour," he said. "Consider your nails, Miss Masters. Do you like them? If you cooperate, you'll be allowed to keep them."

When the door slammed, she tossed down the book. Her hands were shaking. She pressed them together against her mouth. It struck her as a prayerful gesture. Maybe what she needed to do was pray. But God helped those who helped themselves; the past four years had proved that, at least. Now was not the time to begin to doubt her own ingenuity.

The floral pattern on the wallpaper seemed to ripple before her eyes. How *stupid* it had been to gamble on writing that letter. Now he would want secrets, and she had none she felt able to give him. *I know of a traitor in your ranks*, she might say, but if he happened to be the turncoat, such tidings would hardly gratify him. She had taken his measure now, and it seemed likely that her nails would not be the last thing she lost to him.

Open the curtain, she thought. *Look again.*

The prospect of finding an empty rooftop made her tremble.

Just do it. Wondering is harder than knowing.

Her eyes fell on the discarded book. And then she blinked, and focused on the print. The hairs on the back of her neck lifted. *Providence.* Providence, Cornwall, located very near to a place called Land's End. Could that be a coincidence?

A sign. She wrenched the curtains open.

Nothing. A sob broke from her throat. And then, through the rising tears, she caught a brief stir of movement, and everything in her seized and lifted.

She pressed her nose flat to the glass, her fingers splayed against the cold pane. Mr. Tarbury crouched on the roof opposite, in the shadow of a chimney. The gray tomcat was preening beneath the stroke of his hand. Mr. Tarbury was a great admirer of cats; it took him a long, agonizing minute to look up and notice her. Then he tapped his chest and gestured in her direction.

Yes, she mouthed, nodding so energetically that she felt dizzy. It was very good to know that at least one gentleman existed who felt the need to consult with her before making decisions on her behalf. She stepped back as he came to his feet, hugging herself to keep the elation from bursting through her skin. *Freedom.*

Phin came awake, his eyes still closed. A stranger was in his room. His body wanted him to know it.

Air stirred by his cheek. "Good morning, dear."

He lunged up, his hand clamping around a throat. The man stumbled back. His head slammed into the wall. Gray eyes. Hands lifted in surrender, rings glittering. "Pax," the viscount croaked.

Christ. He'd done it again. His ears began to burn, but the irritation turned outward, staying his hand. Unexpected and disorderly entrances were Sanburne's stock-in-trade; at university, he had once arranged to enter a lecture, late, in the escort of a rented llama. But they were not at Oxford anymore, and these boyish games grew tiring. "Pax?" His fingers tightened. "Let me consider it."

Sanburne lifted a brow and glanced past him. Abruptly he became aware of other, more familiar sounds, only now resuming: the faint scrape of the fire iron, the rustle of paper. His valet and a chambermaid were bearing witness to this idiocy. More proof, if they needed it, that the new earl was a madman.

He dropped his hand and stepped back. The embarrassment felt reflexive, not even sharp enough to shorten his breath. Five months since his return, and he was growing near to resigned. Drugs did not dull this reflex. His logic could not rule it. He had no enemies in this city, save Ridland. But old habits did not die, and the slightest unfamiliar noise continued to wake him.

Sanburne was studying him with a frown. "Coffee? And some light." With a flourish of his gloved hand, he yanked open the drapes.

The weak light of a murky London morning pricked Phin's eyes as he sat down on the edge of the bed. Chimneys smoked in the early chill, and a stray bird wheeled against the gray clouds. He'd slept through the night. That was something, at least. "What time is it?"

Sanburne cocked his head. "Too late? Or too early, maybe." His tawny hair was bare, disheveled in a manner evoking scuffles in which hats got knocked away. From the smell of him, he'd breakfasted on alcohol, although the rumpled look of his jacket suggested he'd never gone to bed. "Eight o'clock," he decided. "Somewhere there-abouts. How long does that make for you?"

"Five hours." Almost.

Sanburne made a mocking *tsk*. He could not appre-ciate the magnitude of this achievement; he found the project itself misguided. *Sleep as little or long as you like*, he'd advised last week. *The world will bend to suit you now.* And to be fair, he was right; letter after letter proved as much. The solicitor would visit at whichever hour suited Phin best, dawn till midnight or shortly thereafter. The estate managers, the complaining tenants, the ambitious young men in search of a mentor, God help them—to a man, they assured him it would be a privilege to be an-swered at his leisure.

At first, after so many years of taking orders, Phin had found these reassurances startling. He had saved the letters simply to reread them, to wonder if this could be true. He'd never tested it, though. He replied immedi-ately, and held his meetings during the daylight; that was when normal men did business, and if there was some obscure point to delaying, or to demanding special ac-commodations, he'd missed it.

It seemed possible he was missing a great deal. San-burne seemed to think so; his regard, more and more of late, suggested that Phin was an object of deep concern. It grew irritating. "Why are you here?" he asked curtly.

"You need a holiday."

The rest of his life was a bloody holiday now. "You have an idea, I take it."

Sanburne laughed. "The whole city has an idea. What, don't you remember? Much ado at Epsom Downs, old fellow! Couldn't let you sleep through it. Carriage is waiting at the curb. Look lively," he added, with a jerk of his chin in the direction over Phin's shoulder.

Fretgoose, the absurdly named valet—*his* valet now ("If you wish it, sir"), a rotund, graying inheritance from his cousin, and his uncle before him—crept forward to proffer a robe. Phin stood and stuck out his arms, feeling, as always, faintly ridiculous to be dressed like a child's doll. "Who's aboard?"

Sanburne reached into his jacket, producing a flask. "The usuals. Dalton, Tilney, Muir. Elizabeth threatens to join, no doubt with Nello in tow, so we're working on a plan of concealment. I said your counsel would come in handy."

This was Sanburne's new tactic: to allude, regularly, to whatever he imagined Phin's expertise to be, no doubt by way of inviting a conversation on the matter. It would be a simple thing to put his curiosity to rest. *I stole things. I killed people. And I drew a few maps.* But it had occurred to Phin that the viscount was too bored to receive these tidings with the proper revulsion. He might see them as novel options for keeping himself occupied. "I thank you for your faith," Phin said.

Sanburne smiled back, all cheerful transparency. "You'll come, then."

He shrugged. "I had a meeting scheduled with someone at Stanfords. Great batch of maps coming up for sale in Rome."

"Good God, don't you own enough of them already? It's the Derby, Phin! If the whole city does not exit to Epsom Downs by noon, a calamity befalls the town. I believe Nostradamus wrote of it once."

Phin sighed and scrubbed a hand over his face. He'd finally gotten a handle on the business of holding a title— of managing estates and finances, and of occupying a chair in a thoroughly useless section of Parliament, where fat-cheeked men debated the occupation of countries they would never visit and proposed wars so readily it seemed the blood of strangers flowed more cheaply than water.

The social program still eluded him, though. He was expected to make appearances, he understood that much. To find a wife, to lend his name to a few charitable committees. It seemed easy enough. All the rules had been laid out plainly; he need only follow them. But he hesitated. Why, he could not say. He wasn't going to make a mess of it; he was nothing like his father. And if he were, why then, he would only be like Sanburne, whom London society seemed to adore.

The thought struck a nerve. He dropped his hand to consider the man. They had been very close as schoolboys, bound by that peculiar camaraderie only possible between opposites. Sanburne had enjoyed getting into scrapes; Phin found a strange satisfaction in fixing them. Sanburne spent money like water, and watching him waste it on empty pleasures made Phin feel better about not having any to spend. It had been Sanburne's family with whom he holidayed during university. *We are brothers in every way that matters*, Sanburne used to say. The rings beneath his eyes spoke of dissipation, but to liken him to Stephen Granville felt . . . disloyal. Dishonorable.

Sanburne, slouching loose-limbed against the wall, mistook his examination for hesitance. "It's all in good fun," he said.

"All right." He wanted an opportunity, perhaps, to disprove the aptness of the comparison before it could take root in his brain.

"Brilliant." The viscount pocketed his flask. "I predict a reprise of the Cremorne glory. You made a tidy sum that year."

On money Sanburne had lent him. He'd been three sheets to the wind, to decide to gamble. But back then he'd fancied himself in training for the army, where real men drank just as hard as his father, yet still managed to wake up at dawn to pursue noble ends. It seemed very distant now. If Sanburne expected a reprise, he was bound for disappointment. "Give me a quarter hour."

Sanburne sketched a mocking bow. "I'll wait without. The plebs are no doubt ripping apart my coach." He exited, the smell of liquor trailing after him.

As the door closed, Fretgoose spoke. "Sir." He was standing at the foot of the bed, his hands abnormally empty of sartorial suggestions. "Another letter has come from Mr. Ridland."

Phin was halfway to rising. He sat down again, exhaling through his nose.

"I would n-not have informed you of it, but his man emphasized the absolute urgency of the correspondence."

Ridland lived close by. Down the street, catty-corner across Hyde Park, ten minutes by foot at most. Those times when Phin entered a room and found him in it, Ridland left directly. Last month, the man had walked out of a tea held for the prime minister. He was a right bastard, but he knew how fragile his neck looked at close quarters.

If he was writing so insistently, there was a reason for it.

"I-I do hope I have not offended." Fretgoose's bulbous nose had begun to redden. "Shall I burn it also?"

Perhaps Ridland had heard tell of his meetings with the secretaries of the Colonial and India Offices. He might be writing to plead his case. What sweet irony that would be. The possibility should tantalize him, Phin thought. He could frame such a letter and raise a toast to it nightly.

He held out his hand. The note was carefully sealed. Expensive paper. He merited the best stuff now, soft as a baby's cheek, not that scrap Ridland used to send him in the field. Directives scrawled on brown wrapping paper, the sort one might use to carry fish home from the market. *So cheaply your life tallies:* that had been the other, implied meaning of those messages.

He'd had no choice but to read them. Initially, his own oath of service had bound him to obey. Gradually, with his unfortunate peers as examples, he'd learned the more urgent, unstated cause for compliance: Ridland had no scruples in disciplining defectors. Had Phin chosen to disappear, a price would have been extracted from others: casual acquaintances, old comrades, perhaps even an elderly man who fancied himself Ridland's friend and Phin's mentor.

It had occurred to Phin that a single well-aimed bullet would solve these worries. But the vast web that Ridland spun ultimately supported a great many lives, some more innocent than others. If the bastard died, a great many people would suffer for it.

For a decade, then, Phin had known no choice. Ridland's notes must be opened. They must be heeded.

No longer, though. The title nullified all of Ridland's advantages. A common foot soldier was easily ignored, but each time an earl murmured words of concern into governmental ears, another strand broke in Ridland's web. And Phin had been murmuring a great deal recently.

Yes, he thought, and felt his lips turn in a smile. If Ridland was writing, there must be a grave reason for it.

His wrist snapped. The letter spun away, smacking into the mantel and landing conveniently by the fire basket. "Burn it," he said calmly. He came to his feet and started for the newspaper.

The valet darted forward, reaching for the paper. "Allow me, my lord!"

"No."

Fretgoose ducked his head and crept away.

For God's sake. "But thank you," Phin added, then regretted that, too, for in the man's hurry to turn back and bow, he managed to slam his shoulder into the half-open door of the wardrobe.

Fretgoose pretended not to feel the pain. Phin pretended not to notice the collision, scanning the headlines as the valet picked out his clothes. Not much happening in the world. More arrests made in the bomb plot foiled at Birkenhead. There was certainly a more interesting story behind that, but as a member of the public, he would never know it, nor did he want to. Still, the official version made him snort; it was bland as toast.

He turned to the next page, dominated by a very splashy advertisement for hair tonic. *Special American*

Formula: New Technology. Five Shillings for Spectacular Shine.
Leave it to the Americans to demand a crown for a bit of
soap. He glanced to the next sheet.

Everything in him went still.

". . . Sir?"

It had only been a matter of time. There was nothing
to be surprised about. And in fact, he wasn't surprised.
He simply felt—suspended. Like a figure in a flipbook,
halted by a forceful thumb. He forced his attention upward. "Yes," he said.

Fretgoose held up a jacket. "Will this serve, sir?"

He nodded once, absently, and then, gathering his
thoughts, said, "Tell Gorman to cancel my appointments for tomorrow." He would need to pay his respects
to the bereaved.

Phin set out for Eton at nine the next morning. It was
a short journey by train, but he chose to travel by carriage. They had improved the roads since last he'd traveled them. It did not take as long as he'd calculated.
When the coach pulled up outside the modest cottage,
it wasn't yet noon.

He remained in the vehicle, studying the house.
It looked no different from what he remembered. The
wooden gate had a fresh coat of white paint, and the
rosebushes flanking the path seemed tamer. Otherwise,
he might have been seventeen. The red gingham curtains
in the front parlor stood open. Deliberately, he called to
mind the arguments these curtains had occasioned. Mr.
Sheldrake liked a great deal of light—any mapmaker

would. Mrs. Sheldrake had protested; the sunshine bleached the upholstery, she complained. The war over the curtains had become an ongoing joke, and he should smile at the memory.

He forced himself to smile.

A maid came trotting by with a basket on her arm. As she passed, she craned to peer into his window. Well. A large, glossy coach bearing a coat of arms did tend to draw attention. He should have taken a brougham. But he was going to pay his respects to Sheldrake. If he had to do it as the man he'd become, then he would present himself in every aspect. Would it have mattered to Sheldrake that he'd come into the title? He doubted it. But it would have been a far more cheering piece of news than all the others Phin might have shared.

He stepped out of the coach and waved off the footman who had been riding on the box seat and now wanted so very desperately to open the gate for him. God forbid a nob should break a fingernail working a latch. There was a trick to unfastening it so as not to make any noise; his fingers remembered it before his mind did, and the gate swung open soundlessly before him. He saw his feet moving along the path. The number of steps to the door, the door itself, the whole house seemed so small. A surreal feeling took hold of him. He'd been at his full height during his last visit, hadn't he? It made no sense that everything should look so much smaller.

The door opened almost instantly at his knock. Expecting to see the maid, Alys, Phin instead found himself staring into the face of Laura Sheldrake. Gone, the rounded cheeks of girlhood; in the scrappy tomboy's place stood a pretty woman in her mid-twenties, her auburn hair rosy in the light. He had dreamed, once upon a time, of marrying her.

For a moment she smiled at him blankly. Her eyes moved beyond him to the coach. And then she looked back to him, clapping a hand over her mouth. "*Phin!*"

"Miss Sheldrake." She wore no wedding ring, so he knew to say that much. From there, he was flying on nothing.

She did not wait for formalities. Taking his arm, she drew him inside. The hall smelled of freshly baked bread and rosemary. He had never determined Laura's stance on the curtains; in the spirit of diplomacy, she had maintained a neutral façade. Perhaps it was she who'd opened them today, in honor of her father. "Phin, I can't believe it's you! But—" The joy faded from her face. "Oh. Oh, dear. You *have* heard, haven't you?"

He removed his hat. He did not have to look for the peg. This was the one house in the world where he could reach out blindfolded to deposit his hat, and know that it would not fall. Curious thought. "Yes," he said. "I'm so sorry. I read of it only yesterday. Otherwise, I would have come sooner." And what good that reassurance was, he had no idea. *I would not have come if he were alive, but I would have come at the very moment of his death, had I known of it.* Yes, that must be very comforting to her.

But she did not seem troubled by the remark. "It was sudden," she said softly. "Apoplexy, they said. But in his sleep. I comfort myself by thinking it never woke him."

"Yes. Of course." In his experience, it always woke them.

The thought left a bitter taste in his mouth. He knew a moment of startling fury at his rebellious brain, at the habits it had acquired so easily that they now seemed ingrained. His body woke him to attack his friends, and his mind derided a girl's hopeful narrative by supplying the nasty truth. He would not think such things here. It would be profanation.

She was looking at him expectantly, her brown eyes alight with an interest that he had no idea how to satisfy. Had he stayed, had he chosen some other path, they might have had children together by now. He did not flatter himself with the thought; she'd nursed a terrible *tendresse* for him, and he would have liked, very much, to make her happy, only in part because it would have made her father into his own. He should feel something more than this numbness. He should have something meaningful to say.

But small talk was often beyond him these days. He had yet to accumulate acceptable anecdotes. Clearing his throat, he fell back on etiquette. "I'm so deeply sorry for your loss, Miss Sheldrake. I came to pay my condolences to you and your—" It struck him suddenly that he had no idea whether Mrs. Sheldrake was still alive.

The realization took something from him. He had no idea of *anything* about them. In light of that, did it matter a bloody bit that he knew where to hang his hat?

"And to Mama," Laura finished for him, and smiled, as if she saw his fear and was shyly pleased to relieve it. She'd always been a kindhearted girl. But naïve. She shouldn't open the door to strangers. Someone could so easily wrap his hand around her throat and push her inside, out of view of the street. Nothing in this hallway would lend itself to her defense. She would be killed right here, where she stood, in a matter of moments.

Good God. He was unfit for decent company.

She was still chattering. "She will be so pleased to see you, Phin. She has gone on a walk to the market . . ."

He ran a hand across his eyes, up through his hair; her glance followed the gesture, and he realized it was very unmannerly.

". . . but she'll be back very soon," she finished, as he dropped his hand and squeezed his fingers together at his back. "You will stay, of course—won't you?"

The front hall seemed to be closing in on him. He never broke things, he could walk a tightrope if he had to; but he felt too large, unbalanced, jumpy. His elbow was touching the banister, and the hem of his coat brushed a vase filled with umbrellas; these ordinary domestic touches penned him in. "I'd like that," he said. She smiled again; she had no idea he was lying.

But he knew. He saw now, very clearly, how deep all of this went in him. If one didn't know whether a woman was alive or dead, it was good to find out that she was well. It did not solve the basic problem, though. He should have known already. He simply hadn't cared to find out.

"Such a long time," Laura murmured, and shook herself, as if to wake. "Come along," she said, and reached for his hand.

She acted as though they were old friends, smiling so kindly, but she no longer knew him at all; out of nowhere, a paranoid conviction flooded him that if he took her fingers, some dark urge would compel him to crush them, simply to find out how much force it took to make her cry out. *Don't smile*, he would say. *See what I am.*

He stepped backward, away from her, into the umbrellas. They clattered in the pot, and her hand hesitated; she reached past him to adjust one of the handles, as if this had always been her intention. But it was not a clever recovery, and she knew it; she ducked her head, blushing, as she turned away. "This way, please." With an awkward laugh, she added, "But you know that, of course."

He followed her in silence past the stairs to the parlor. Every inch of his skin prickled with self-contempt. What the hell was wrong with him? Would a country cottage destroy his composure, where bullets never had? Six hours' uninterrupted sleep each night, correspondence answered promptly, tenants provided for, base temptations avoided, swearing curtailed, regular visits to church—this righteous routine kept him on track, but he began to think it could not transform him.

She paused at the parlor door. "Unless . . ." She turned back. "Would you like to see his study?"

His study. No, Phin thought. He would not like to see the study.

She colored and continued hesitantly, "Or we can sit down and wait for Mama, of course. I just thought, since you spent so much time there with him . . ."

He mustered a smile. She did not deserve to be addled by his sick head. He could walk through a goddamned study. "It's a fine idea, Miss Sheldrake. Thank you for suggesting it. I would like that very much indeed."

"Are you certain?" She looked anxious now. "If it will be too difficult for you, I understand. I certainly don't wish to—"

"No, not difficult," he interrupted. "It would be— lovely." Christ, this was awkward.

"All right, then." She turned toward the back of the house. And then she stopped. "No," she said. "You go on alone. I'll join you in a minute."

He could not tell whether her reluctance was born of concern for him or from a well-founded care for herself. It occurred to him that it was not appropriate for them to be alone together, period. Alys was nowhere in evidence. And Laura had said that her mother was fetching groceries. Had Sheldrake made no provision for them? He would have Gorman make inquiries into their situation. Helping the women was the least he could do.

He bowed and set off down the hall. Framed prints on the walls flickered past the corners of his vision. The watercolors of Brighton Beach and the cliffs at Dover were souvenirs of the family's rare holidays. Sheldrake had apologized to him for going away. *Missed you, lad. Sorry for leaving you in the lurch.* The cross-stitch of the Queen Victoria roses that Mrs. Sheldrake had finished on Easter fifteen years ago. Sheldrake had declared it a work of high art. Phin had hidden his puzzlement (roses? three months spent on a picture of flowers?) and gamely agreed. He would have agreed to anything, then, that Sheldrake said.

The door to the study swung open with a squeak. No avoiding that. He'd never managed to enter this room a minute late without being caught out.

Inside, it was all the same. The shelves were laden with Sheldrake's equipment—the sextants and compasses and telescopes and Marquois scales, the mercurial horizon with which he'd tasked Phin to determine the pitch of the house's warped floors. At the center of the room, the two desks sat face to face, one of them covered in stacks of neatly folded maps and books, Peirce's *Elementary Treatise on Plane and Spherical Trigonometry* prominently showcased. The old globe sat on its brass pedestal, Russia spotlighted by the sunbeam slanting through the window.

He walked forward. The surface of the globe felt thick with wax beneath his palm. His finger fell on the Indian Ocean. This antiquated shading spoke of an older time, when Britons had known nothing of the Transvaal or Baluchistan, the Suez or Upper Burma. When he'd last looked at this globe, he'd known nothing of them either. Hot, humid, the river yellow with mud, moving so slowly it seemed to creak; it still amazed him that he had not died on that last expedition. The bounty on British heads would have bought the locals a decade worth of meals.

He tapped the ocean once, and looked up. On the uncrowded desk, a pen lay discarded across a sheet of foolscap. He picked it up. Brandauer's Oriental. Naturally. *Steel-crow quills, Phineas; that's the real secret to a drawing. Got nothing to do with your hand.*

As he set it down again, an uncanny feeling prickled over him. It looked as though Sheldrake had just left off drawing. As if he would return in a few minutes.

He exhaled and stepped backward, his throat tightening. In his father's generation, they had counted nostalgia a disease. The mind was believed to rot on impossible longings; it fixated on a time that would never come again, and cannibalized itself by embroidering memory until it collapsed into fantasy. He could see the logic in it. This library felt like a sickness. The scents of paint and paper and polish and ink filled his chest and turned to stone. More wholesome than the odor of baking bread in the hall outside, they conjured safety, peace, knowledge, everything he had once taken for granted. Such sweet and easy lies.

"We haven't sold anything yet. Mama couldn't bear to."

Laura had come up very quietly. Perhaps she'd meant to startle him, but he'd felt the disturbance of the air as she widened the opening of the door.

No. Don't think that way. Not here.

"He would want you to have some of his things," she said. "The globe, perhaps? Pick whatever you like. He spoke of you so often, Phin. He was certain that you were doing great things for our country." Her footsteps on the carpet were soft. Pale, sturdy fingers reached out to give the globe a spin. It made him dizzy. "We knew that you couldn't write us about it, of course. Secrecy in these matters is standard, I expect. But every time Stanfords announced the release of a new map from the subcontinent, oh, how he would pore over it!" Her laughter was husky, as though her throat were clogged. "Comparing it to the previous versions, pointing out the changes he felt sure you'd been responsible for making. He was terribly proud of you."

Her words were poison. The interior of the room felt

thick, smothering; he wanted to crank open the window for a breath of cool air.

Sheldrake might have been right, once or twice. He had contributed a few maps. But he had not been allowed to stay with the Indian Survey for long. Two years he'd been given to wander the mountains in the service of the Royal Engineers. Then Ridland had found other uses for him.

The globe was still spinning; he reached out, his forefinger halting the world. Sheldrake had advised him to study it closely. Sheldrake had believed that there were correct answers waiting to be found by those who looked closely enough; that countries had proper shapes; that borders were more than lines drawn in ink, washed away so easily by blood. Sheldrake had taught him that mistakes were wrong because of some error intrinsic to them, not simply because someone had decided that it would be more convenient to have certain facts counted erroneous.

Laura was right. Her father had died in his sleep and never woken. Otherwise, he might have realized that earth was only dumb matter, incapable of flaws or excellence. Sheldrake's boyhood friend could have taught him better. Ridland had known that the real challenge lay in charting the topographies of the soul. With a glance, Ridland had charted Phin's character, and found the fault line fracturing his nature from his idealistic intentions. *You've a talent*, he'd said; with those three words the fault line had widened, so that now, a decade later, when Phin crossed paths with his own ghost in this room, he felt no recognition as he looked across the chasm separating them, only a chill that lifted the hairs at his nape.

His heart had started to drum. A drop of sweat fell onto the globe, and he realized it had slipped from his temple.

It was happening again.

What would Laura think? She must notice the color flooding his face, but she would not dare remark on it. *Focus on the globe. It will pass.*

"Shall we take tea?"

His sick ears mistranslated her tone so that it sounded taunting, aggressive. *Can't you even manage to take tea?*

He had to get out of here. He knew what he was in for; another minute, and he'd be in the grip of a full-fledged fit. The panics came unpredictably, without warning, ever since he'd returned to England. The globe now felt like rubber beneath his fingertips; his heart was breaking free from his chest; he was going to vomit or die. *No, you aren't. It always feels so.* He could not meet Mrs. Sheldrake in this state.

"I'm sorry," he managed, hearing his voice as if from a great distance. The doctor had been unable to find any medical cause for these episodes; he had looked at Phin as though he wanted to say something, but feared the consequences. *I'm not a lunatic, am I?* Phin had smiled as he asked it, but the doctor had taken a long moment to issue a denial. "I have a pressing engagement in town."

He would never forgive himself for the way Laura looked at him then. It would have been better, perhaps, to tell her that he *was* a lunatic. Better than placing new pain on the face of the woman he'd once hoped to love, who as a girl had turned her face into his sleeve so easily when she needed to cry. *I am not fit for your company*, he wanted to tell her. But she would wonder, then, whose company he was fit for, and he would not be responsible for leading her innocent thoughts anywhere so dark.

As they walked toward the front door, she startled him by turning back and smiling. "I understand," she said. "It's very difficult, isn't it? But I'm so glad you've come back, Phin."

He wanted to tell her he had not come back. But when she reached again for his hand, his addled reflexes failed him; she had his fingers in hers before he knew it. He breathed out through his nose and found he was willing, in this state at least, to be led; and at any rate, he was glad to realize that he wouldn't hurt her after all.

He sent the driver and footman home with the carriage and took the train. At first his thoughts were black and twisted, making as little sense to him as the malfunctioning of his body. Gradually, however, they settled. Laura was unwed still. Why? She was lovely and sincere, earnest in her ideals. She would not tolerate a disorderly home; she would make certain it ran properly, and that everyone in it behaved just as they should. If he so deeply regretted his decisions and the consequences they had produced, then here was a chance to remedy one of his mistakes.

The thought of touching her made him feel vaguely ill. He thought of the way she had led him down the hall, the dignified set of her shoulders and the graceful slope of her neck, how pure her skin was, the innocence of her blushes. Embalmed dreams, rotted from the inside; he could not recover them.

Or maybe this darkness in him was simply blinding him to their appeal.

He stared out the window and contemplated exorcisms, ancient rituals designed to purge the soul. Chain mail that scrubbed crusaders' flesh of their sins. The cloistered booths where Catholics went to confess. London came rushing toward him, sprawling like a slut across the land, loose and dark and dirty, unconcerned with opportunities for absolution.

He saw no hope for himself in mundane routines, but there had to be hope somewhere. The world, the way one was properly meant to live in it, seemed so inarguably clear to people like Laura. If a man behaved rudely, baffled kindness was the only reply they considered.

His butler greeted him in the lobby to hand over a letter. Phin stuffed it into his pocket as he strode up the stairs. He was calmer now, clearer in his head if not cleaner, so there was no excuse for what he was about to do. Fretgoose was fussing about the anteroom; Phin sent him scurrying and locked the door.

The opium smelled repulsive, like dimly lit hellholes where rats scurried over bodies too stupefied to take note. It smelled like weakness, like the hungers that had driven his father so far down in the world, to that wretched garret in Calais. But as he inhaled the smoke—coughing only a little at the burn, for he had mastered the art of it now—everything began to dull. He breathed in a deeper puff, loathing himself for the scalding of his lungs, but distantly, clinically, comfortably. He did not feed his weakness, as his father had done; rather, he blunted it.

He put down the pipe and stared into the twilight,

watching the sky turn to pasteboard and the chimneys' cold, sharp lines dissolve into brushstrokes from an impressionist's palette. Azure and charcoal. Violet and viridian. The clouds above them looked like gauze tacked on by a clumsy hand. His thoughts drifted, formless as gauze, harmless as gauze, enjoying a freedom he did not dare permit them when his muscles were sober and his reflexes functioning. He pulled the envelope out of his pocket. The seal split beneath his lax fingers, and Ridland's bold, slanting script punched into his eyes.

He did not crumple it fast enough. As his fist began to close, the angry black swarm resolved into words that his brain could not unlearn.

. . . Mina Masters . . .

The syllables themselves were so ordinary. Their combination, her name, the rhythm of it, he had erased from his brain four years ago. He had never let himself think on her again.

The crumpled edges of the letter formed points, directing his eyes to a single word: *. . . help . . .*

He would gladly consign himself to the fires of hell before he helped Ridland. Eight months since he'd fired a gun. Ten since he'd snapped a neck. These were privileges to be guarded more carefully than diamonds, more jealously than freedom itself. To rebuff the title's gifts and return to the game when he had, of all things, a *choice* in the matter, seemed nothing short of blasphemous.

His fingers opened.

. . . claims that she requires your help, and I beg you . . .

Every door in the world stood open to him. He could not decide which one he wanted to walk through, or whether he could manage to walk through it properly, but that made no difference. Tangling with Ridland would be like sticking his finger into a wolf trap. He could not expect to retrieve it unscathed, if he managed to retrieve it at all.

I am indebted to you.

Yes, she had said. *You are.*

He let the letter fall from his fingers. Chain mail, he thought. Its great weight must have chafed crusaders' skin, but habitual pain was of no worth to them; still they had knelt on the cold stone floors of churches, and used whips to flog what flesh remained from their bones. True penance was not meant to feel comfortable, and numbness had seemed no excuse to them. *Whip harder, and ride straight into the enemy's lands:* this was the solution they'd devised for themselves.

Chapter Five

Bells were tolling from nearby Stepney. Their high, eerie chimes wound in muted bursts through the fog. Mina counted them off as she pulled out the gun. No light escaped from the cellar doors in front of her, but the corroded nameplate left no doubt: this was her destination.

A breeze coasted across her cheek, icy and moist, like the breath from an open grave. It riffled through the detritus of the dusk-lit street, sending fish skeletons skittering, stirring potato peels that had blackened in the damp. Tarbury had come here to Whitechapel this afternoon to seek Mr. Cronin, an old army comrade who might be able to help her. He had left her in a cramped garret a quarter mile away, promising to return by three o'clock.

All day she'd waited, her nose pressed to the window. But Tarbury had never reappeared. And as the clock ticked onward, her frustration had mounted. She hated this city. How small it made her feel. In New York, she never felt so powerless.

She counted seven gongs before the bells fell silent. Tarbury never missed his appointments. It was not unwise to come looking for him. What other choice did she have?

Taking a deep breath, she rapped her knuckles on the rough-hewn doors. Her hand was shaking. The cold, she told herself.

Silence.

Her fingers twitched around the butt of the pistol. The gloves she was wearing fit tightly enough to delineate the edges of her nails—a favorite, foolish affectation of London girls, which Tarbury had thought it wise for her to emulate so as not to appear conspicuous. But the constriction suddenly seemed unbearable.

She knocked again, harder. Then, on an afterthought, she reached up to knock the cheap shawl away from her hair. She did not want her peripheral vision impeded.

"Who is it?"

She moved the pistol behind her back. "A friend of Thomas Tarbury."

After a second, the doors creaked outward. A squat, rawboned man with black muttonchops stood looking up at her. He held a lantern in his hand, which illuminated the grease spots on his trousers and the rude wooden step beneath his feet. The shallow stairs descended to a straw-covered floor. She could see no farther into the room; he looked to have only the one lamp. "You'll be Miss Masters? Come in, then. He's in the back room."

He knew her name. It should have soothed her. "Have him come out to me."

"Can't, miss. He's bad off. Some two-bit sharper stuck it to him in the lane." At her gasp, he retreated a pace down the stairs. "No call for worry, I've bandaged him up. But he ain't goin' nowhere tonight. I would've sent a message, but he'd not tell me where you stayed."

Still she hesitated. The darkness beyond him made her stomach jump. She did poorly in darkness. "He can call out to me, at least."

The man gave her a disbelieving look. "I've given him enough laudanum to drug a horse. He was bleedin' his life out in the street, and his only thought was to go to you. A man has his duty, and I can respect it—but I couldn't let a friend kill hisself, could I?"

"No," she said, but her instincts troubled her.

"Come in quickly, if you please. He said someone's after you. Best not to draw notice."

She glanced behind her and saw a curtain twitch in the house opposite. "All right," she said, and took a step inside. He retreated onto the packed floor. It reassured her that he willingly gave her a bit of space, but she didn't want him to know just yet of her gun.

At her next step, her foot knocked against a pile of chain. It lay coiled around a padlock, which she supposed Mr. Cronin must use to secure the doors, although . . . she hadn't heard the scrape of a chain before he'd opened them.

The doors hadn't been locked.

He would have locked them had Tarbury been attacked.

She whirled and lunged up the stair.

A sharp curse and a clatter. Darkness washed up the stair; the lantern had dropped. One more step—

A heavy weight slammed into her back. She fell across the threshold, the uneven floor stabbing her ribs. Hard hands closed over her arms, pressing down to her wrists. Fingers closed over her grip on the gun.

She twisted, pushing her weight down more firmly, the better to secure her grasp.

"Easy." The fingers squeezed a demand. "You'll shoot yourself in the stomach."

She panted, holding very still. That wasn't Cronin's voice. Nor Ridland's. Of course it wasn't. Ridland was not spry enough to tackle her.

"Let it go." The voice spoke quietly, its composure a jarring counterpoint to the vise on her wrist. "I don't want to hurt you, Miss Masters."

She stiffened in realization. It was *Monroe.* She did not recall his voice being so deep. But then, he had never spoken in his natural accent, save when the poison was in him. And then, he'd been muttering and hoarse.

The revelation rattled her. He owed her gratitude, not violence. She stared out at the free world, forced to new calculations. She had no desire to go back into custody. But Monroe owed her. She had liked him, in Hong Kong. And it seemed he had Tarbury. Without Tarbury's help, she was good for nothing in this blasted country. "Let me up," she said. The long body that pressed into hers felt immovable, hard as granite. "Please," she added softly.

He made some adjustment that brought his cheek against her hair. Stubble tickled her earlobe. His skin was hot. "Give me the gun first." With that voice, low and golden and slightly rough, some women would have counted the words poetry.

She resented them anyway. Why could she not keep the gun? She was not his enemy, but he tackled her like a wolf on a rabbit. Maybe she could not count on him at all. Her grip slackened reluctantly. "Take it, then."

His weight eased off her. His left hand smoothed around her waist while his other plucked away the pistol. He pulled her up so quickly her vision sparkled at the edges. Obviously, the poison had inflicted no lasting harm; in one unbroken movement, he hauled her off the steps and set her on the ground below.

She pushed at the arm around her waist. It banded more tightly, pinning her as easily as though she were some querulous child. "Are you otherwise armed?" His manner was pleasant; he might have been asking her to dance. Which he never had, she remembered suddenly. *She* had asked *him*.

How ridiculous that such a trivial fact should increase her irritation. "No."

"Are you certain?"

Already she knew she liked him *much* better as an American. "Yes!"

His arm slipped away. As she turned, a match hissed. The flame illuminated a broad, long-fingered hand with a single ring on the fourth digit, gold, bearing some sort of symbol. The flame cut a sweeping arc through the darkness. It caught on a lamp wick. Light spread across Monroe's face, sliding shadows beneath his cheekbones and his full lower lip; his lashes were still long as an angel's, his jaw squarer and more inflexible than stone. His eyes met hers as he settled the lamp on the floor, and the contact made her flush. How stupid. But she had admired his eyes, in Hong Kong. Their steadiness had tempted her to trust him, despite all her reservations.

"We meet again," he said.

She opened her mouth, but suddenly thought better of honesty. She had saved his life, and he'd never gotten to thank her properly for it. Surely he should sound happier to see her? Something was amiss here. If he wanted her trust, he was going to have to demonstrate that he deserved it. "Oh," she said. "Do we know each other?"

A strange smile quirked his lips. He straightened, the motion unusually fluid. His grace, too, had made her breath catch in Hong Kong. She decided not to admire him anew. "Perhaps not," he said. "But we did once. Don't you recognize me?"

In fact, had circumstances not suggested his identity, and had she not gotten a good look into his eyes, she might not have known him. He seemed taller than she remembered, leaner, whittled down. Far more raffish, as well. Gone the clean-shaven cheeks and slicked hair; now he had a lion's mane, waving past the stubble that darkened his square jaw. The cut suited his dark eyes and skin, if his aim was to look criminal. Certainly, he no longer appeared capable of masquerading as a financier.

His devilish presentation also had something to do with how he held her gun. He toyed with it absently, turning it over and over in his hand as he considered her, as if a firearm merited no more caution than a child's toy. Or . . . as if he sought to remind her who was armed, and who wasn't.

What on earth had Ridland told him of her? It seemed she would need to disarm him, in every way, if their time together was to be comfortable.

She reached up, realizing too late that she'd bound

her hair very tightly, and not a single strand was available for twirling. "Perhaps . . ." She licked her lips. "Is it . . . oh, could you be . . . Mr. *Monroe?*"

"I could be," he said, and the faint trace of sarcasm in his voice struck her like a slap. She should have known better than to expect gratitude from him. Businessman or spy, no matter; he'd fitted in very well with her stepfather's friends.

In lieu of a lock of hair, she wound her fingers together at her waist. It was not difficult to make her voice tremble; she did not enjoy being knocked onto dirty floors. "Mr. Monroe. Thank goodness. You will help me!" And then, on a manufactured sob, she threw herself into his arms.

He caught her by reflex, and thank God the gun had a trustworthy trigger, or there'd have been blood all over.

As her small, warm body burrowed into his, a curious feeling broke over him, more complex than déjà vu. For a moment he thought another attack was descending on him, and then he realized the sensation was purely interior, a sense of things opening that he'd tried to seal off. Some things the body could not forget—the fit of her breasts against his abdomen, the way a gun balanced so comfortably in his palm. Touching her felt like brushing up against a dark part of himself, a place where his regrets had gone to die from studious disregard. *I was done with this*, he thought. God above, he should be done.

He wanted to reach up and scrub away the sensation prickling at his nape, but her arms wound around him and his own tightened without consultation of his brain. She was still toxic to him, then. "I'm so glad you came," she whispered.

As her head fitted beneath his chin, the subtle scent of her hair, like the first strain of long-forgotten music, touched off a whole symphony in his brain: his grim irritation with her, that kiss, *Dance with me, Mr. Monroe.* He had seen her as an obstacle, a temptation that laid bare all his inherited weakness, a needless weight trying to thrust itself onto his conscience. There had seemed no other way to view her, not until that moment when he'd fallen from the window. Rude shock: running down the lawn, the turf exploding from the bullets' impact, he had wondered, only once and without understanding his own feeling of loss, exactly what he was leaving behind. And then he had never allowed himself to think of her again.

He detached himself from her arms, a breath shuddering from his throat. For the first time in months, he felt fleshly, grounded, steady on his feet. He knew better than to like the sensation.

A delicate flush was spreading across her face, bespeaking, perhaps, embarrassment. "Are you all right?" he asked. He hadn't wanted to tackle her, but the gun in her hand had limited his options; had he attempted gentler measures, she might have shot him from sheer surprise.

She knuckled her nose like a little girl after a tantrum. "Yes. Forgive me, I'm . . . you gave me a scare, that's all."

He studied her clinically, trying to diagnose the accuracy of his memory. He recalled her being quite freakishly beautiful, but the reality was less unsettling. Her each feature seemed, in fact, too perfect to combine with the others into a harmonious whole; the eye, not knowing where to fix, grew frustrated in its search for peaceful lodging. "I've spent six days looking for you." She'd been damned hard to find, and at one point it had occurred to him that he might be the butt of some obscure joke of Ridland's. But, no, here she was, in all her soft, flower-scented flesh, and he should be relieved to know he'd not made himself a fool. "I feared you might vanish again," he said, and paused, recalling the question that had seemed uppermost to him before her appearance. "Where were you hiding?"

Her blue eyes swam like the sea off Amalfi, crystalline and dizzying in her heart-shaped face. "Six days, you say? Poor Mr. Ridland! He must be frantic. I didn't mean to worry him."

Those eyes did not distract him from the fact that she hadn't answered his question. "Didn't you? You disappeared from your rooms without a trace." From the looks of it, she had smashed the window and clambered down a wall—not an achievement he could match with the petite body before him, those wrists as slim as flower stems. Even if she'd had the help of her manservant, that climb would have taken a nerve of steel, and a temperament unlikely to be trembling after being knocked to the floor. Either there was more to her escape than he knew, or less fear in her than she wanted him to realize. "Surely," he said more slowly, "you expected *someone* to worry."

Her little shrug could have meant anything. She glanced past him to where Cronin sat on a stool, his boot heel scuffing the floor. The man had sold his loyalty quite cheaply, and for the past hour, at a guess, he'd been entertaining regrets about his price. "Is my man all right?" she asked. That she did not address this question to Phin seemed telling. Her apparent relief at his appearance did not extend to trusting him.

"Reckon so," Cronin muttered. "This one tied him up and had him carted off, but he was well enough, last I saw him."

Her large eyes returned to Phin. "Where is he, then? Does Ridland have him?"

Not *Mr.* Ridland. Simply Ridland. It seemed a peculiarly masculine form of address for a sheltered girl to use. *I drink nothing but champagne.* Had her tastes changed in the intervening years? "I have him," Phin said. "And it seems I have you, as well. Perhaps it would serve you better to wonder what I mean to do with *you.*"

"Why, you will protect me, I hope. That's why Ridland sent you, isn't it?"

He smiled, and perhaps she saw the grimness in it, for her eyes dropped. Ridland did not send him anywhere these days. He'd made that clear enough. *I am not going to help you*, he'd told the man.

Then why are you here? Anxiety had etched sweet shadows beneath Ridland's reddened eyes. *To gloat? I heard of your meetings at Westminster.*

Good, Phin had thought. Let him stew. *I came to tell you that she is no longer your concern.*

Ridland's laughter had grated. *Good luck to you, then. She is a hard woman to hold.*

The words had struck a chord. Someone had told him something similar once. Someone wiser than he, perhaps.

He recalled her as buffleheaded, and her quivering manner supported the recollection. But for all that her hands fluttered from her nape to her waist, tangling there helplessly, her eyes held his too steadily to silence his mounting caution.

There was always the possibility, however peculiar, that Ridland had facilitated her escape. Phin could think of no reason for it; but then, he'd been trying very hard not to think of Ridland at all. And certainly, the man had shown uncharacteristic restraint in his treatment of her, for Miss Masters's pearly nails appeared wholly intact. Indeed, the whole of her appeared too damned pristine for an innocent American girl who'd spent a week wandering the London slums.

Like a compass being turned, he felt his expectations realigning themselves. If she was more than she seemed—if she was working with Ridland to entangle him in some bad business—then she was bound for disappointment. As of now, he had no intention of underestimating her.

His close study was making her frown. "I have no need to worry, do I?"

"Oh, there's always cause for worry," he said mildly. It was easier like this, anyway. He felt curiously relieved. This role fitted him far better and more familiarly than that of the savior. "But I assume you did not mean to be philosophical. Do you realize where you are, Miss Masters?"

She looked around. "In a cellar?"

"In an area of London to which even I don't travel unarmed."

She blinked. "But I *was* armed, sir."

Yes, this pretty pearl-encrusted pistol might have terrorized a dollhouse or two. He flipped it again, wondering if it was loaded. The heft suggested so. "Let's go, then." When she looked nervously to the door but did not move, he said more sharply, "You told Ridland to fetch me, didn't you?" *Fetch* was a telling verb. Ridland had an interest in her, but she supposedly had no interest in Ridland. In one possible view of this situation, Phin himself was no more than a bone caught in the tug-of-war between a mastiff and a tiny, perfumed poodle. Which meant he'd stumbled right back into hell, of his own accord.

"But where do we go?" she asked.

Why did the answer concern her so much? "Do you have somewhere else to be?"

She blinked. "No. Only—somewhere safe. But I should like to see Mr. Tarbury, at least." She was twisting her hands so hard that he half expected to be picking up fingers in a moment. "To assure myself that he's well."

He remembered this, too—the way she put her sapphire eyes to use in making these girlish, pouting appeals. Even now, when she was attired more plainly than a scullery maid, she managed to come off the coquette. He gave a frown to her outfit, really noticing it for the first time. Apart from the locket at her throat, she wore no jewelry, and her threadbare dress seemed unlikely for a woman who was, Ridland claimed, doing well for herself. Some nonsense about a company in America that catered to female vanities by way of expensive hair tonics—Phin had not listened very closely; it was not relevant to the task of finding her. "Tarbury is fine," he told her. Tarbury was stubborn as a mule—three hours of grilling, and he'd yielded not so much as a hint to his mistress's whereabouts.

"You're taking me to him, then?"

"No."

"But Mr. Tarbury will worry about me!"

He had forgotten her arrogance also. Had it not occurred to her that she involved her manservant in dangerous matters? Or did she expect men to imperil themselves for the sheer pleasure of being allowed to serve her?

His own temper startled him. He drew a breath of the musty air, schooling himself. Whatever her motives, she hadn't forced his hand. He'd come of his own volition, God help him. He was going to get to the bottom of this and get her the hell out of his house as soon as possible.

A noise came from behind him. His body replied before his brain, pivoting, lifting the gun. Cronin's right eye lay in his aim. "Back," he said.

Cronin froze. His arms shook beneath the weight of the stool he held aloft.

"Don't shoot him," cried Miss Masters. "He is only protecting me!"

Even Cronin looked astonished by this idiocy. He retreated, dropping his weapon; as the stool crashed against the baseboards, it raised a cloud of dust that made Phin's nose tickle. He reached backward and caught hold of the girl's arm, hauling her toward the steps as he kept the pistol level on Cronin.

She called down to the man, "If you see Mr. Tarbury, tell him what has happened!"

Her tone struck Phin as inappropriately desperate for a woman who had deliberately enlisted his aid. But Cronin, uncovering a rusty streak of chivalry, straightened like he had a plan in mind.

Phin adjusted his aim to a spot directly between Cronin's legs and pulled the trigger.

Ah, yes: loaded. The report was deafening. Cronin dove into the shadows. Miss Masters made not a sound. When Phin glanced over, he found her face pale but composed, as though gunfire were a regular event for her. His mood turned grimmer yet. He knocked the doors apart with an elbow and pulled her up the last step, into the night air.

Chapter Six

Ridland must have shared her letter with Monroe, for he did not protest when she gave him to understand that she must stop by the boardinghouse. What he thought she was collecting, she had no idea. Secret documents, maybe. A bag of gunpowder, some terrible secret related to Collins. At any rate, he seemed unduly concerned. He followed her up to her room and watched from the doorway as she knelt to grope beneath the bed. Her gun still rested in his hand. Since there was no one here to shoot but her, she could not find it comforting.

At least she would have the small satisfaction of disappointing him, for all she wanted to collect was the gown she'd worn while escaping Ridland's. That, and the cat. Tarbury had taken a liking to the beast, and the scrawny thing seemed to reciprocate, although he did not show similar favor to Mina. It took her ten long minutes to lure him from under the bed.

When she finally straightened, the beast hissing in her arms, Monroe gave a cool nod, as if a cat were exactly what he'd expected her to fetch. He was in the middle of his own routine, she realized, playacting very convincingly. She wished she knew the point of it. With her free hand, she plucked her Liberty tunic off a hook and tossed it toward him.

Impassively, he looped it over his forearm. "Come," he said, and stepped back to allow her passage down the stairs.

As she passed him, it came to her again that he was much, much taller than she'd remembered. Descending the stairs, her feet made the rickety steps groan, but behind her he moved like a thief. Had his shadow not fallen down the steps before her, surpassing her own by a foot at least, she would never have known he was there. She tightened her hold on the cat and wished, for the hundredth time, that she and Mama had never come to England.

The landlady stood holding open the front door. She appeared in a fine humor, Monroe having settled with her at some extortionate rate for the use of the rooms and her silence. As Mina passed, she tossed off an arch "Well done, dearie."

The remark jolted Mina's intuition. As she stepped onto the pavement and Monroe went to speak to the coachman, she gave his figure a concentrated survey. He did, in fact, look like a rich man. His suit was first-rate, tailored closely to his broad shoulders, the stitching exquisite and nearly invisible. Those cuff links he wore made an excellent imitation of gold. Where did he get the tin for such clothes? Wealthy men didn't gamble their lives in pursuit of criminals. Perhaps spycraft paid better than she'd imagined.

The thought deepened her unease. If Ridland provided for him so generously, then his loyalties might well be uncertain. His sour attitude could bode real harm for her.

Her hesitation drew his notice as the coachman opened the carriage door. The dim illumination from a dirty streetlamp lent the curve of his full lips a brooding cast; his dark eyes looked her over as though he were sizing her up for sale. "Is there a problem, Miss Masters?"

No, she thought, only that she was about to board a coach to heaven knew where, in the company of a man who might as well be a stranger and who seemed to have forgotten completely the great favor she'd done him. And now not even Tarbury would know where she'd been taken, or be able to help her escape.

"Of course not," she said brightly. Monroe held out his hand and she adjusted her grip around the squirming cat, trying to free a hand so she could accept his help into the coach. The beast took advantage, trying to leap to the ground. She clamped down with one arm, and he clawed her wrist. "Bad cat!" As she tried to free her arm, his tail swatted into her open mouth. She turned away from Monroe to spit out cat hair. Tarbury was going to thank her for this charity, *more* than once.

"A fine beast," Monroe said blandly. "Is he rabid?"

The hint of sly humor in his voice startled her. It was one of the reasons she had liked him in Hong Kong, in the beginning, at least. He had made jokes for himself, expecting no one else to catch them, and indeed no one else had; she'd felt hard-pressed to disguise her amusement. That he could joke now at her expense seemed very encouraging, suggesting that he counted her no threat. A much more useful attitude, on the whole, than the one that inspired him to play with her gun.

"Indeed, no," she said with a smile. "The cat is an

original." Although, come to think of it, rabies was a distinct possibility. "Would you like to hold him?"

His answer was to cock a speaking brow, then reach again for her hand.

She had left her too-tight gloves upstairs, for the benefit of the landlady or whichever unfortunate girl took the garret next. But when Monroe's bare fingers closed on hers, she abruptly regretted the decision. The press of their naked flesh refreshed her awareness of his size, of the strength in his hand and the roughness of his palm. Time had worked in his favor; had she seen him across a room and known nothing of him, she would gladly have looked twice at his dark, lean face. As she stepped up into the vehicle, his eyes connected with hers, sharp and steady, and her stomach contracted.

The corner of his mouth lifted. The attraction she had felt between them in Hong Kong was alive and well, and he looked quite comfortable with it.

She settled onto the bench, her pulse tripping. She had not counted on such complexities surviving, but the goose bumps rising along her arms suggested that her body didn't catch on as quickly as her brain. She drew a calming breath. When he had all the power, it seemed unwise to accord him unnecessary advantages.

He tossed her gown inside, then put his hand to the opening of the carriage to pull himself in. His ring caught her attention. The suit, the cuff links, the unbreakable composure—they assumed stronger significance as he took the bench opposite. He was a man without worries. This carriage, too, was conspicuously well appointed. Cream velour cushions trimmed in silk did not come cheap, and they would require constant replacement from all the mud. The wood paneling was etched in a delicate scrolling design. "Did Ridland lend you this vehicle?"

He banged the roof with his knuckles. That casual gesture and the languid way he sat back, draping an arm across the back of the bench as he crossed his legs, answered her before his lips did. "No," he said. He owned this space, in every way. "It's mine."

"Oh." Oh, dear. This called for a recalculation of strategy. She'd supposed he would hail from a family of middling status at best. Indeed, during her quick calculations while corralling the cat, she had counted on it: if guilt failed to motivate him, cash would prompt his conscience. But men with money often proved immune to the more common brands of manipulation. "It's lovely." She drew a breath and nodded toward his hand. Might as well ascertain the extent of it. "And what a fine ring. Does it have particular significance?"

His eyes were steady, but again she had the unmistakable impression of amusement, as if he'd guessed exactly what she was about. How? She felt certain her memory did not fail her; he'd thought her quite the brainless flirt in Hong Kong. "Not really," he said.

She feigned dumb interest. "Really? I noticed a symbol. . . ."

He glanced toward the hand draped over the back of the bench, then spread his fingers as though to admire the jewelry. There was nothing effeminate about his face or build, which was lucky for him; his movements were imbued with an elegance that she might otherwise have accounted feminine. "The family crest," he said.

In her arms, the cat gave an angry yowl. She hastily loosened her grip. "Doesn't that usually signify aristocracy?"

He spoke dryly. "Difficult to say, these days. More often it signals a very imaginative genealogist."

"And are you . . . imaginative?"

"Not to any notable degree."

The cat sank his claws into her lap. She could hardly blame him. Her idiocy astonished her. An aristocrat! And she'd thought Ridland high-handed! "Well," she began, but words failed her. A blue blood running around the Orient, playing spy! What an idiotic notion. How was *she* to have guessed?

His brow lifted. "Ah. You're one of *those* Yanks."

"What Yanks?"

"Blinded by democratic prejudice."

She flashed him her teeth. "Oh, no, I can see very well. It's a lovely ring." The cat's tail was straying into her face again; she was forced to expel air in a most unbecoming fashion to avoid a mouthful of hair.

"Are you sure that's your cat?" Monroe asked.

She was out of patience with him. An *aristocrat*. "I'm carrying him. It seems very likely. Why?"

"He doesn't seem to like you."

That wasn't a very gentlemanly observation. "He is high strung, and does not like strong handling." *Such as being tackled.* She gave him a pointed look, but he missed it; he was too busy frowning at the feline.

"Is he domesticated?"

She thought with satisfaction of the various stinking spots that now dotted the landlady's garret. Wherever

Monroe was taking her, she would not be without one weapon. "Sufficiently. Are you some sort of lord, then?"

"Some sort, yes."

The coach jolted as it began to move. Thrown against the wall, she freed a hand from the cat's warm belly to take hold of the strap. Monroe remained balanced. It could grow irritating, this easy self-possession of his. "Is your name really Monroe?"

"No."

She smiled at him and waited.

He smiled back, but there was a taunt in it. For some obscure reason, he seemed to be enjoying himself. Had she been a woman given to faint spirits, it might have overset her.

Happily, she possessed a few useful pieces of knowledge about him. He was handsome, skilled at lying, and disposed to suspicion. The threat of bullets would not faze him, which no doubt had something to do with the arrogance she'd read in his bones. In Hong Kong, it had surprised her; now she knew the source. It was bred into his blood. He hadn't even needed to labor at acquiring it. How very *English* of him.

Well, she had dealt with arrogant men before. The haughty young heirs among Mrs. Astor's four hundred occasionally gave her trouble. They imagined that her reputation, her independence, and her commercial enterprise entitled them to misbehave. But they learned better at once. She slapped very hard when forced to it. Of course, Mr. Tarbury was always waiting nearby to make sure that they didn't slap back, and Mr. Tarbury wasn't here right now.

She forced her smile to remain steady as she scratched the cat's ruff. Smiling made one feel braver. Washington was what Tarbury had dubbed the cat. It seemed an auspicious name for an ally in a battle against Englishmen. Maybe he could be trained to piddle on command. "What's your real name, then?"

"Phineas Granville."

It had a ring to it that put her in mind of prune lips and castor oil. She racked her brain for Mama's lectures about English etiquette. She had never paid much attention; they painted such a tedious picture of her mother's homeland. Musty homes filled with animal heads. Stiff-lipped hypocrites who fainted away at the suggestion of honest work. Reams of rules and a long list of consequences for those who dared disobey. *If you should find yourself in one of the great houses, Mina, you must never speak to the footmen directly; rather, you will ring for the butler and he will relay your order.* It figured that such tightly buttoned snobs would saddle a boy with such a name. "Lord Granville, then?"

"Lord Ashmore, actually."

"Baron Ashmore?" These barons were apparently a dime a dozen.

"Earl of, I'm afraid."

Well. At least he wasn't a duke.

"Don't bother yourself over it," he said gravely, but the gleam in his eye put her on alert. "You may simply call me 'my lord.' I tell you this as a kindness, you understand. I know you Yanks are not so familiar with the way of things here, and I would not want you to feel embarrassed."

"Oh, I *do* appreciate that," she said sweetly. If he thought to intimidate her through snobbery, he would have to revise his strategy. "In fact, I'm rather old-fashioned. Traditionally, we New Yorkers don't acknowledge foreign titles."

"I see," he murmured. "How awkward for you."

"Not at all," she said cheerfully. As she sat back, Washington attempted to jump from her lap. She tightened her fingers over his belly, and he bit her finger.

"How charming," Ashmore said, equally cheerful.

She tugged on her hand, growing annoyed when Washington's teeth proved obstinate. "Heel!"

"That is for dogs, Miss Masters."

"And what is it for cats, then?"

"I don't believe there's a word for cats."

She sighed, not at all surprised. She much preferred dogs, so dependent and grateful for kindness. Cats had no manners whatsoever. Jane's tabbies hid when she visited, or crouched in the doorway to hiss. She'd hoped Washington was possessed of better judgment; during daylight, he made a show of indifference, but the last three mornings she'd woken to find him curled up on her chest, warm as a brick, purring. What good taste! She'd been charmed.

More fool she.

Ashmore cleared his throat, then sniffed. She glanced up in time to see him lean over to the window. The sound of the pane being slammed down startled the cat; he loosed a yowl and sprang away to the floor.

A muffled noise came from Ashmore's side of the coach. It sounded like a laugh, but when she darted a glance at him, he appeared perfectly straight-faced.

Lovely. What else might make him unbend? Poison had done it. And kisses had worked well, too. She supposed that was another approach to consider.

She eyed him up and down, growing doubtful. That moment when he had handed her into the coach—well, she did not want to invite trouble. The dizzy damsel in distress seemed a safer route, so long as it continued to serve. She offered him a wide smile. "I'm not a cat person either."

His brow rose again. Just one of them. That was a clever trick. Very aristocratic. Probably bred into them, along with big noses.

"No need to deny it," she said casually. "It's very clear to me: you can't abide cats."

"Actually, I don't mind them."

"It's all right to admit it. I can't stand them either."

"Oh?" He relaxed into the bench, assuming the posture of a man prepared to be entertained by a featherbrain. She didn't plan to disappoint him.

"Yes," she said. "I prefer dogs. I had a Scottish terrier when I was young." She sighed. "Quite tragic. He was murdered, actually; the priest from St. Patrick's got drunk one night and ran him over with a wheelbarrow. I always wanted another. Why don't you like cats?"

"As I said, I don't—" He hesitated. "Did you just say a sodden priest killed your dog?"

Got you. Mina settled herself more comfortably, mimicking his position. On the floor, Washington paused an industrious cleaning of his paw to deliver a baleful glare. Was he only interested in sharing a bed with her, then? Such a typical male. "Well, the priest felt very bad about it, though I can't say I was forgiving. He had to buy me monstrous amounts of chocolate to keep me from telling anyone. A box every week from Dominique's, actually." She smiled and tapped her lower lip with one finger. When Ashmore's eyes remained on hers, she let her hand fall. "You can't imagine the power chocolate has over me. I'm sure it's quite indecent." That part was true enough.

"So you blackmailed a man of the cloth," he said.

"Blackmail? We called it a friendly agreement. By the end of the year, I wished I had another terrier for him to kill. But not really," she added quickly. "Wouldn't that be too bad of me! I much preferred Mongol to chocolate. Dogs are always better than chocolate, of course, because they're *alive.*" She paused to frown. "Then again, if one counts mold, I suppose some of the chocolate was also alive by the end . . . the cherry-filled ones, you understand; I never liked cherries. Well, it's all rather confusing." She looked to Washington for support. The cat lashed her with its tail.

Lord, she hated cats.

Ashmore was sitting up now, smiling in disbelief. "Are you having me on, Miss Masters?"

"Oh, dear. Do you take exception to my dismissal of mold? But it's not a very entertaining form of life, is it? I'm sure you understand why I preferred Mongol."

He spoke very soberly. "Mongol was the dog's name?"

"Yes. But in retrospect, I should have named him Attila." She paused to radiate astonishment. "My goodness. Isn't it amazing how after years and years of remembering something, it's still possible to have new thoughts about the memory?"

"I wouldn't know," he said. "Memories hold little purchase on me."

Was he warning her not to count on his debt to her? "I'm so sorry to hear that. You've suffered some injury to the brain, then? I suppose it could have been the poison. I thought I'd treated you in time, but, yes, that would account for a weakness of the memory. Although if I had as many names as you do, I should have a hard time keeping track of things as well. Granville, Ashmore, Monroe— Monroe was fictional, I take it?"

"Fictional," he said slowly, "yes. You understand, I did not want to advertise my identity to Collins."

"Or to anyone," she said sweetly.

He paused, studying her. "Or to anyone. And I did not mean that I *lack* memories, Miss Masters. It was a figure of speech only."

"Oh!" She giggled. "A *figure*. Really, sir. You must not think me a loose woman simply because of these unusual circumstances."

He made a choking sound. She gasped. Leaning forward, she cried, "If you cannot breathe, flap your hands!"

The advice seemed only to exacerbate his respiratory ailment. She moved onto his bench and began to pound his back, more enthusiastically, perhaps, than a doctor would recommend. It felt good to hit him.

And lo, her ministrations wrought a miraculous recovery. "Miss Masters!" He twisted to catch her hands. Two impressions struck her as his fingers tightened around hers: he could subdue her as easily as lint, and he moved with shocking quickness. "I was not *choking*," he said. "Rather I was *laughing* at you!"

"Oh." She bit her lip and retreated to her side of the compartment, stuffing her hands into the depths of her skirts. His agility unnerved her. He was trained to move quickly, she supposed. Even if she'd been armed, she wondered whether she would have managed to squeeze off a shot before he struck the gun from her hand. *Remember that*, she told herself. "I'm sorry. Laughing at me? You've grown unaccustomed to American girls, then. We speak very plainly. Don't you remember? Still . . . I can't think of anything I said that was *remotely* amusing."

He shoved a hand through his dark hair. "I think it amusing that you are of this planet, Miss Masters."

"Is there another option?" She opened her eyes very wide. "You can't mean you credit that rumor about the man on the moon!"

His chin cut down. He considered her narrowly. "What are you about here?"

"What do you mean?"

"You cannot be serious."

It seemed she'd been cutting it rather too fat. "Can't I? Why not?"

"Not even you can be this . . . obtuse. "

Not even she? Apparently she'd made a *very* good impression on him, four years ago. She wondered how he'd managed to explain her cleverness to himself, as he fled the scene of what otherwise would have been his execution. He deserved a bit of twitting. "No, indeed, I'm hardly obtuse!" She lifted her voice. "Why, I can recite history and paint watercolors and play the piano—"

He clapped both hands to his ears. "*Pax*, Miss Masters! I will concede anything to keep that shrill note from your voice."

"I do get a bit loud," she conceded. "But I am death on the pedals; you should just hear my sonatas!" When she said no more, he slowly removed his hands. "Shall I tell you," she began, but stopped when he promptly covered his ears again. "I am not being shrill," she said loudly. "I am speaking in a perfectly pleasant manner!"

"But *why* are you still speaking at all?"

"Because I have yet to finish my thought!"

"And why, pray tell, is that necessary?"

"Well, really, sir! As the saying goes, a thought or meal left half complete ends the battle in defeat."

He caught his breath. "By God," he said, and clapped a hand to his mouth. A laugh slipped out through his fingers. He really did have remarkable eyes, dark and thickly lashed, and when he was amused, they looked deceptively kind. "Did you make that one up on the spot? *Did* you?"

"Of course not. It's a famous proverb. My father—my real father, my goodness, *not* Collins—used to say it all the time."

"Oh, he did?"

"He did."

He lowered his hand, unveiling a grin. "How . . . remarkable."

"Yes, but the credit must not go to him, for he did not coin it. Although who knows who made up those sayings? No one even tries to find out. I tell you, I have often suspected a vast conspiracy revolving around this gentleman, Anonymous. Who was he really? Why all the secrecy?" With a sniff, she tightened her shawl about her shoulders. "I sometimes think that he didn't exist at all. Just think of what would happen if we learned we'd been cozened into crediting the advice of some no-name charlatan! Someone should really undertake an inquiry into Anonymous's origins. I say, wouldn't that be a fit calling for you? I seem to remember that you had a gift for uncovering information."

His expression sobered. "And now we get around to it."

"It? Where?" She looked out the window. "All I see is fog."

"Ridland believes you to be in possession of information that could assist the search for Collins." When she turned back, he was studying her very closely. "He says something I find very curious. He says you vowed not to divulge the information to anyone but me. Is that so?"

Ridland had misrepresented her. She had not promised to divulge any information to anyone. Only if Ashmore proved himself newly trustworthy would she reconsider her stance. "Well, I supposed you would help me."

"Why is that?"

"My memory occasionally falters as well," she said. "But I seem to recall—oh, forgive me if I'm wrong— that I did you a favor in Hong Kong."

"Oh, your memory seems fine to me." He paused. "You did me a great favor, in fact. But I believe it was of your own accord. If I might be so bold as to advise you, I suggest you never depend on a man to repay what he did not willingly borrow."

She nearly snorted. "Oh, I do not depend on anything, sir. Believe me." When his eyes narrowed, she cursed herself. Clumsy to speak sharply unless there was an aim to it. "You know my mother," she went on more softly. "You've met her. I'd hoped you might have it in your heart to help me find her."

His stony expression did not suggest the soul of a humanitarian. How a man with such beautiful eyes could use them so coldly, she did not understand. "Then I advise you to adjust your expectations. I agreed to protect you; that is all."

"But—"

"And you should consider it a very special favor to you. Once I came into the title, I stepped out of the game."

How nice for him. He had decided to wash his hands of the matter, but he *deigned* to keep her prisoner while other men mucked it up. "Silly me. I supposed you would grant me a favor that matched the magnitude of the one I did for *you*."

"And so I am," he said. "I'm keeping you alive and safe."

"From whom?"

He made an incredulous noise. "From Collins."

"Collins doesn't give two figs about me. He already has my mother. Why should he care about me?"

He looked her over very skeptically before he nodded. Somehow, that small hesitation managed to invest his agreement with an insult, as if he, too, doubted that any reason existed to care for her at all. "Then you shall have to learn patience," he said. "The government's best men are searching for him."

Certainly they were. But some of them did not answer to Her Majesty. At least one of them answered to

Collins. "If you cannot help me, I've no interest in stay-ing with you. You may drop me at Claridge's."

He had the gall to laugh. His teeth were very white; had she any interest in impressing him, she might have covered her own mouth and regretted her weakness for a good Bordeaux. "Claridge's." He snorted. "Miss Mas-ters, you seem to be laboring under a grievous misap-prehension. You are no longer on a pleasure tour. The Crown has taken you into custody. I gave my word that I would supervise you, and I mean to keep it."

Her breath was coming shorter. She dug her finger-nails into the seat cushion. "Yet you have no care for your debt to *me*. But really, why should I be surprised? I already knew that you have no honor."

He went very still. "Oh? And what cause have you to know that?"

The old anger leapt up in her, roughening her voice. "You break your promises."

His face darkened. He braced his hands on either wall of the coach and leaned toward her. The banquette was not yielding enough to accommodate the withdrawal her instincts demanded. "Speak plainly," he said, and the softness of his tone, paired with the natural roughness of his voice, made the words sound like a purr. "What promises have I broken?"

Her fingers were knotting. She forced them to relax, and tilted her head to affect puzzlement. "Do you not remember, then?"

His mouth quirked into a half-smile. He tilted his own head, mocking her posturing. It was mean of him, really, because he thought her too much of an idiot to realize it, which meant the joke was private, made at her expense. "Remind me, if you please."

She had not seen this rotten streak in him before. It chafed her temper to realize she'd misjudged him so badly. Even had she been as dim-witted as she pretended, she would not have deserved such treatment. Setting aside his impoverished logic about unsolicited favors, she had saved his life; of all people, he owed her a bit of respect.

Ah, but she'd forgotten to factor in her new knowledge of his status. Men in his position were not taught how to give respect. They knew only how to demand it.

"Very well." Forget featherheaded; it would only give him further excuses to belittle her. She leaned forward, too, coming so close to him that their mouths almost touched. He smelled . . . clean. She inhaled. Yes, he used bayberry soap. Heat radiated from him. The scent diluted her annoyance; one could almost luxuriate in his warmth, as one did before a fire.

His eyes fell to her lips. "Oh, I remember that," he murmured. "No need for a reminder."

She laughed in surprise. He was referring to the kiss, of course, and her humor was all for herself: how absurd that her vanity should be pricked by his disinterest. Something about the man, some inherent quality that she would like to excise with a scalpel, simply destroyed her better sense. "Yes," she said, "it was terrible, wasn't it? I would do a far better job of it now—had I any interest in doing so."

His lips curved. "Good to see you do not want for pride, Miss Masters."

"Oh, it is not pride that speaks there," she said. "It is truth."

His brow arched. He caught on very quickly. "By all means, then, give it a go. I am game to be taught better."

How smug he was. She should have realized he was titled from the moment she'd first met him. He fit every description her mother had ever given of an overbred Englishman. Alas for him, she was no milkwater London girl.

She lifted her hand to her mouth and bit down on the tip of her middle finger. He was not expecting this; it won his immediate attention. She sucked her finger into her mouth, and color crept over his cheeks. Not so immovable now, was he?

She released her finger with a wet, sucking noise. "I do not kiss men who might as well be strangers." She set her wet finger to his mouth, feeling the cool pull of his startled indrawn breath. He had a long, lovely mouth, with a sharply grooved philtrum that lent his upper lip definition. His lower lip seemed to pout a little; she gave it a soft, slow stroke, fighting the temptation to move down farther, to stroke that dimple in his square chin. *One step at a time, Mina.* "But perhaps we will get to know each other better," she murmured.

His breath exited in an audible rush. He sat back, staring. She found him far more beautiful like this, rumpled and off guard, not smirking anymore, not smug.

He drew another breath, slower, as he held her eyes. He licked his lips and said quietly, "You don't taste foolish, Miss Masters."

Her heart tripped. A prickle moved down the backs of her knees. "I don't take that as a compliment."

"I didn't mean to praise you. Perhaps what you taste like is cunning. I should warn you," he said meditatively, and cupped his jaw with one broad hand, his thumb rubbing across his lip as hers had done. Watching him touch himself caused a stirring low in her belly. Oh, yes, that was a useful warning, all right.

Letting his hand drop, he smiled a little, as if he saw the response she fought to hide. "I react very badly to manipulation," he murmured. "I have no idea what you're about here. But you should know that I have decided, very recently, to brook no interference in any corner of my life."

"What a marvelous luxury for you." It took no effort at all to sound sober. "Myself, I would like the opportunity to make such decisions."

He frowned and looked out the window. "Yes," he said. "It is a privilege."

The reaction encouraged her. Did he feel a twinge of pity for her? She pressed on. "And I react very badly to being held against my will. But I will endure it, if the end result is my mother's safe return."

"Well." Still refusing to look at her, he drummed his fingers on his knee. "You may tell Ridland I made an attempt to win the secret from you. As for the rest, you and he will have to reach some sort of compromise."

"What?" The carriage was slowing. As she followed his gaze, her stomach pitched. She recognized that dark, glowering house. He had brought her back to Ridland's. "Wait!" He was gathering himself to open the door and descend. She reached out to grab his wrist. "You can't leave me here."

He looked from her hand to her face. "Why not? You've given me to understand how loathsome you find the thought of remaining with me."

"Because—" Did she really wish to give away the secret of the traitor *now*? What would stop him from tossing her back to Ridland once he had the information he'd been tasked to retrieve? What would ensure her safety after she divulged it?

There was another tack she might try. The last one, the one that would lead to discussions she very much dreaded to have. "Sunset," she said. "That was the promise you broke. For they didn't come then." She released him and sat back. "They didn't come for two days." How calm she sounded. But then, words meant nothing, so long as one didn't allow oneself to feel their connection to the meaning they expressed. Hearing her own calmness made her feel calm.

In Hong Kong, the intensity of his dark-eyed regard had seduced her into idiocy; she had mistaken it for genuine interest in her. Now she knew better, and braced herself. "No," he said, studying her. "I told you that I *thought* they would come for Collins at sunset. I didn't guarantee it."

This lawyerly hairsplitting nauseated her. "Fine. I confess that the details are vague to me now. Lost in what followed, I expect."

He looked away again. His profile seemed grim and ungenerous, and as the silence drew on, his unwillingness to ask the natural question began to unnerve her. She had felt sick at the prospect of answering it, but this silence made her sicker: it underscored his determination to remain uninvolved, to return her to Ridland and be done with her. Did he not even wonder what had happened? She had saved his life! Was he not the *slightest* bit curious about what had happened to hers as a result?

"What is between you and Ridland?"

The question confused her. "What do you mean? There's nothing between us."

"Then you should have no objection to staying with him, should you?"

The door swung open and a servant raised a lamp to light the footman's arrangement of the coach step. She thought of the plush rooms waiting for her above, and the roof that would remain empty now whenever she parted the curtains. Her thumb moved nervously across the edges of her nails. "Please," she whispered. Trapped like a lamb awaiting slaughter, not even a chance of escape—her throat was closing. "Don't send me back to him. I . . ." God above, it sounded as if she were begging. She could loathe him for this alone—for reducing her to groveling like a spineless child.

But it had an effect. Of course it did. Arrogant men liked it when one flattered their authority. With a terse motion, Ashmore waved off the footman and pulled shut the door. For a long, silent moment, they stared at each other.

And then he smiled. "You are a great deal cleverer than you let on, aren't you?" When she rolled her eyes, he laughed. "No, really. What a fantastic little act you've worked out for yourself. How many men walk away thinking you can't add two and two?"

Her temper snapped. This episode had not been at all

amusing to her. "It's no fault of mine if men don't bother to look past a pretty face."

"And you are very pretty," he said solemnly. "But I see you need no reminder of that."

He was mocking her, even now. "Do you know, I find myself wondering why I bothered to save you."

"Yes," he said thoughtfully. "I've wondered the same. Certainly your decision has borne some damned inconvenient fruit for me now."

Exhaling in a rush, she glanced pointedly toward the door. "Open it, then." At least she would not give him the pleasure of forcing her out of the vehicle. "I grow tired of your company." But he made no move. Perhaps it had sounded too much like an *order* to him. She shifted impatiently; if he did not let her out immediately, she would crumple and do something utterly beneath her dignity. "I said, open it!"

"Perhaps . . ." He rubbed his mouth. "Perhaps, if you are willing to abide by my rules, you may stay with me until your mother is recovered."

Relief swept through her. "Yes." This gave her an opportunity. Anything but Ridland's death trap. "What rules?"

Again his eyes flicked over her. "Any rules." The smile he gave her blotted out her relief; it started out dark, and only grew blacker. "Any, Miss Masters, that I choose."

Chapter Seven

Mina's eyes opened on darkness. It took her a moment to realize where she was. Ashmore's.

Slowly she sat up. The thick rose-patterned carpet swallowed noise; the double-paned windows shut out the sounds of the world. In such silence, she might well be the last person alive, some catastrophe having taken place outside without her knowledge. Locked up here, she would languish until her flesh rotted.

She drew a hitching breath. It was only the dark making her think these things. Some nights she could not sleep for it. She would lie awake remembering the time when Jane had slept on a cot at her bedside, and the memories would stir something in her that felt strangely like grief. Those nights had been so peaceful, so deeply restful, despite all her worries and frustrations. In comparison, the days and years since seemed like one long stretch of exhaustion. She had managed to do so much, but she'd never reacquired the art of sleeping alone. It was always a battle now.

She fumbled for the candle and matchbox at her bed-side. There was a button around here to call the electricity; the shy blond maid had showed her this evening. But it would be difficult to find in the blackness.

As the wick caught, the shadows contracted. She sat studying them for a frozen minute. That one was from the little table. That one came from the pitcher atop the washstand.

An oblong patch of darkness spilled from behind the curtains. She squinted. There seemed to be no source for it. And it looked to be the shape of a man, standing very quietly, watching her.

Her heart thudded painfully in her throat. *Waiting and wondering is always harder than knowing.*

She lunged off the bed. Her fist swung into the curtain, and her knuckles cracked against the wall.

She shook her hand, trying to laugh at herself. But the sound emerged in a whisper, not reassuring at all. As she turned full circle, the candle summoned strange shapes to dance across the peach silk walls; the rosy blossoms on the brocade upholstery seemed to shiver. The room felt like the interior of a jewelry box, thick and smothering, designed to coddle her into immobility.

She went out into the sitting room, but pacing it afforded no pleasure; the thick nap of the carpet felt like quicksand, trying to suck her down. Ashmore said she was safe here. But how could he know to defend her against his own government? She would warn him, but she had no idea if he was trustworthy himself. Damn her instincts; he himself had cautioned her against trusting him. Although, in her experience, true villains did not advertise themselves.

In the corridor, the clock began to chime. The sound drew her to a stop. Somewhere, her mother also might be listening to a clock strike the hour. She closed her eyes and felt for the locket at her throat. It seemed as though her concentrated thoughts should be able to fly, out through the glass panes, across the darkened streets of Mayfair, over the emptied parkland, past all the dying lamps and the sluggish rivers, to her mother's location. It seemed as if she should be able to sense Mama, and that Mama should be able to feel her concern as well. *Hold on. I am coming for you.* But what she sensed instead was the vastness of the world, and how distant was the sun, shining down on the other side of the globe.

Her eyes opened. In New York, it was also time to sleep, for children at any rate. Jane would be putting her daughter to bed, the lamplight filling that small bedroom with a cozy glow. Henry would be at the Tuxedo Club or Delmonico's, dining on lobster and crab cakes. Mina was done with him; he had grown too demanding, constantly disappointed by her. But tonight, had she been in New York, she might have invited him to her bed anyway. Sleeping next to him, she did not feel afraid of the dark, only of herself.

The thought opened a weird sadness that made her feet itch. But there was nowhere to walk in these rooms. She held up her candle near the outer door. The keyhole looked to be a familiar type. In New York, she had hired a man to teach her to pick locks. It had been necessary to her peace of mind, after Hong Kong.

She carried the candle back to the dresser in her bedchamber, fumbling through the drawers until she found the hairpins she'd removed before bed. Taking up two, she returned to the anteroom, kneeling on the soft carpet. The lock's interior mechanism was stiff and hardened with age, but Mr. Goodger had taught her well. She fancied the last chime was still echoing through the hallway when the latch clicked.

Slowly, her fingers crept up to the knob. The door swung open.

She laughed softly, pleased with herself. Of course, until she knew where Ashmore had stashed Tarbury, it would not profit her to escape. But what if Tarbury was somewhere down the hall? Unlike her, he would not have been wearing hairpins when caught.

If she found him, they could be gone from here within the hour. No need to deliberate about Ashmore's character at all. They could amass their own force of men and rescue Mama themselves.

The thought electrified her. She blew out the candle.

Outside, the corridor was dark and cold, the hall rug chill beneath her bare feet. She found herself holding her breath as she sidled along the wall, testing knobs, discounting any rooms that were not secured.

The hall opened onto a broad balcony that followed the curve of the staircase down to the lobby. The space was flooded with moonlight from a glass dome two floors above, casting the statuary and walls in a cool, pale glow. She put her back to the wall and slid into the next wing, where the first doorknob rewarded her with a promising refusal to budge.

The tumbrels on this latch were better oiled. It took less than a minute to coax the lock open.

As she slipped inside, a strange scent overwhelmed her, sweet and cloying. The room looked to be an ordinary study, lined with books and framed maps, furnished with a few easy chairs, a couch, and a desk. That it had been locked made her curious enough to investigate the desk. A wedge of light fell through a slit in the curtains, illuminating the pens neatly arranged atop a blotter.

Slowly, she sank into the leather chair. The pens were ordered by size and thickness, longest to shortest, thickest to thinnest. A man who valued such trivial disciplines would certainly embrace the larger ones. *Any rules that I choose.* Such a man, she thought, would also take great care with his correspondence.

The uppermost drawer held nothing of interest: some strange metal instruments she did not recognize; a few scraps of paper, covered with mathematical equations; a heavy seal resembling the marking on Ashmore's ring; and a newspaper clipping of an obituary for Mr. David Sheldrake, geographer.

In the deeper drawers, she found letters. She flipped through the first bundle quickly. Most were fawning solicitations of Ashmore's time, with notations inked in the corners regarding the dates and substance of his replies. The second bunch held drafts of his own letters, and she paused when Ridland's name popped out from one.

After twelve years of service under his direct supervision, I feel well qualified to caution you regarding his fitness for any position that necessitates adjudications of an ethical nature.

"Find anything interesting?" He spoke quietly from the opposite side of the room.

She dropped the letter. The moonlight coming in behind her blinded her to the subtleties of the darkness ahead; all she could see, when she squinted, were the outlines of the furniture.

"I asked you a question."

She rubbed her chest, trying to soothe her pulse. *Brazen it out.* "Yes, I suppose so. I found out that you work directly for Joseph Ridland."

A beat. "And that's a concern for you, is it?"

She wished she could see him. Some peculiarity of his pronunciation—the laziness of his vowels, perhaps—suggested he was less than sober. "No."

"Are you certain? Think carefully before you reply."

She frowned into the darkness. He would not hurt her; he couldn't afford to. There were people who knew she was with him, and they had charged him to care for her. But his voice unnerved her. Floating disembodied from the darkness, it had a presence of its own, dark and soft, like black velvet wrapped around a rough stone that could easily bash her skull in.

It comforted her to realize that the lighting would also render him blind to her expression. She only need worry about the composure of her voice. It sounded strong as she asked, "Should it concern me?"

A faint rustle came to her ears. His eyes appeared first, catching the moonlight, and then his square jaw, rendered in dramatic shades of charcoal and ivory. He had discarded his jacket and rolled his white shirtsleeves to the elbows; his waistcoat hung open, revealing his suspenders and the muscular breadth of his chest. He had changed his clothes since capturing her in Whitechapel.

He had gone out after he locked her up, perhaps to a party, for his waistcoat and tie were white, in the formal style. He had caged her and abandoned her as though she were of no larger consequence than a bird.

"Then why," he asked softly, "do I find you in my desk?"

Because I was stupid enough to get caught, she was tempted to say. But the rapid beat of her heart warned her that she should not answer flippantly. "I want to know where Tarbury is. You wouldn't tell me."

He prowled around the desk toward her. One hand landed on the desktop, positioned in precise alignment with hers, ring glittering in the moonlight. Her fingers curled into her palms as his other arm came around behind her shoulders, his right hand bracing beside hers on the opposite side of the blotter. He had caged her in truth now. How charming for him. "This is not necessary," she said.

"I didn't think it was. But apparently I was wrong." He leaned over her head, inspecting what lay on the desktop.

"I was worried for Tarbury," she said stubbornly.

His breath touched her neck, causing goose bumps to rise along the backs of her arms. "I don't believe you."

Out of nowhere, she remembered the caution that had touched her in Hong Kong. Spies were dangerous, and she was small; in his shirtsleeves, the breadth of his shoulders had not escaped her. Maybe her confidence in her own safety was misplaced. While his body touched her nowhere, she could sense the mass and energy of him all along her back, like a storm cloud threatening to unleash lightning. One did not linger in a storm that threatened violence. "I was worried," she whispered. "He's my responsibility."

"And you are a responsible girl." He spoke slowly, as though he enjoyed the feel of the words rolling over his tongue. "You take great care with the tasks you're given."

The phrasing confused her. It seemed to hint at something beyond her knowledge. She trained her eyes on the pens, and their ordered arrangement took on a bleaker significance. Collins had relied on others to maintain an orderly household. Even his anger had been sloppy. Until the end, she had always been able to find loopholes in it. But this man would not provide her with such easy escapes. "Surely . . ." She cleared her throat. "Surely, with such a great household at your disposal, you can understand an employer's concern for her staff."

His soft laughter ghosted over her ear, heating her temple. "Flattery?" It took a trick for him to press so closely, yet not touch her at all. Forget the pens; his own body was subject to a discipline of exacting precision. "I think you overestimate me," he murmured. "It's becoming more obvious by the hour that there are a great many things I don't understand. You, for instance. How did you get out?"

His tone was casual, almost playful. But her survival instincts were well honed; she knew better than to doubt them when they told her he was furious. "Someone left the door unlocked."

Hot, dry fingers threaded under her unbound hair, taking her neck in a gentle grip. They tightened slightly, giving her brief insight into what it would be like to be strangled. And then they slid around to her chin, yanking it up to an awkward angle that directed her face toward the ceiling. "Look at me," he said curtly.

She drew a hard breath through her nose to channel her sudden anger. He manipulated her with the same rude economy that a farmer used when trussing an animal for slaughter. Was this her repayment for saving him?

"Look at me."

She slid her eyes to his. The angle at which he stood required her to glare from the very corner of her vision, and the muscles in her temples stabbed protest. His pillowy lips looked hard in the moonlight, chiseled from marble. "How," they said. "Did you. Get out."

"Very easily." Her voice emerged hoarsely, by virtue of the awkward bent of her neck. "I picked the lock."

His face revealed no opinion of these tidings, but his thumb skated down her cheek, pulling a shiver from her. Loathing, fear, she could not name it. "I see." The pad of his finger was rough and warm; it stroked her skin like the touch of a lover, as though to suggest that he saw a great many possibilities and was considering each of them. "Is this a skill particular to American girls? Or are you . . . unique?"

She thought it a rhetorical question, but as the silence lengthened, his fingers firmed: he would require an answer. Collins, too, had liked to demand answers to questions that did not puzzle him at all. "No. It's not a common skill."

Now his thumb fitted into the corner of her mouth. She tasted the salt of his skin. He was wrong to tempt her. If she bit it off, he'd have a harder time holding her gun. "And where did you learn it?"

She inched her head away, freeing herself of his taste. "My neck is starting to cramp."

"Then you had better reply," he said coolly.

"I hired someone to teach me." She ripped out of his grip and slammed back her elbow, aiming for his gut.

He caught it and snapped her around. Her face smashed into his chest; she jerked back, and his hands caught hold of her wrists, pinning them at the small of her back. "Disappointing," he remarked, as she gave a furious pull. "All the lessons went to locks, hmm?"

"Let go of me!"

"What were you looking for?"

Kick him. But he must have felt her muscles tense; his lower body twisted away and his hands yanked her into a backward arch, forcing her to bend at the waist. Her shoulder blades banged into the desktop. His grip on her wrists changed, transferring them to a single hand; his forearm, freed, settled lightly over her throat.

She froze, her breath scraping loudly against her ears. He loomed over her, a dark silhouette, his wild hair haloed by the light coming in through the window behind him. "Answer me," he said very softly, and all at once, she felt herself blush. There was a terrible intimacy in the way his lower body pressed against hers, and his whisper seemed better suited to hot, hushed secrets, the sort she had once wanted to extract from him. "What did he set you to find?"

She realized suddenly that there was far more to this interrogation than she understood. "Who? Who do you mean?"

His forearm slipped away; for a miraculous second she thought he had come to his senses. Then he set a finger to the underside of her chin, rubbing teasingly. "Last chance," he said. "Then I find some other more entertaining way to amuse myself."

"I don't know what you're talking about!"

"No?" He sighed. "What a pity they know I have you."

"And to think I actually liked you," she muttered.

"Seeing me clearly now, are you?"

"Maybe I am."

His hand lifted, resettling on her arm; with impersonal thoroughness, it skated over her breasts and waist, then down to her hips, sliding briefly between her thighs, moving away too quickly for her to get out a protest. He was looking, she realized, for a weapon. "You already took my gun," she said breathlessly.

He grabbed her arm and pulled her upright. Not letting go of her, he leaned away toward the wall. Light rose. His square jaw was clean-shaven now, the white shirt a startling contrast against his golden skin. His cold regard seemed no more reassuring for the new clarity with which she viewed it. "I should have known when I saw your nails." An unpleasant smile tipped up the corners of his mouth. "He always did have an eye for beauty." He flicked a finger at the trailing ends of her hair where it fell past her breast.

Such a small touch. But the hairs lifted on her skin, and a shiver broke over her. Even in this terrible moment, her body was attuned to him. She loathed it.

He noticed. His brow lifted, and he made a low, interested noise. With two fingers he caught up the lock of hair, winding it around his knuckles, until the pull at her scalp forced her to step toward him, her lips coming within a hand's width of his chest. "Miss Masters," he mused. He spoke her name as though testing a new interpretation of the syllables. "Mina Masters, damsel in distress. How sweetly you do play that role."

Hearing her own phrase from his lips made her feel horribly obvious. She was glad for the return of her anger. "You're wrong," she said. "You think you're being clever here, but you're mistaken."

"That makes two of us, then. What did he tell you? That I'm clawless now?" The idea seemed to amuse him; his gaze unfocused, looking through her, and he laughed beneath his breath. His eyes were such a dark brown that they bordered on black. Shadows for eyes, made deeper and more mesmerizing by those long, almost girlish lashes, which lured one into trusting them against one's better judgment; she should have known better than to try to enlist his aid, or to mention him to Ridland. "No," he said, and his attention dropped down her body. "He chose badly for this job. Unless the task was to seduce me? What did he tell you, that I'd inherited my father's taste for trollops?"

"No one told me anything," she said stonily.

He did not seem to hear this. His eyes lifted now to her face, roaming across her cheeks and lips. "Well, and perhaps you could have managed it. I've always thought you a sweet little package." His hand lowered, pulling down her hair and her head along with it, so she had no choice but to watch as his knuckles skated across the upper slope of her breast. "You can still give it a go, if you like. All this hair . . ." He laughed again, a low, distinctly sexual sound. "I could tie you up with it."

The vision formed with startling clarity in her brain. The day she let a man tie her down was the day she died. She would bite his throat out if he tried it.

It seemed unwise to share that intention. Besides, if he thought she was a blushing virgin, then the advantage was all hers. She pitched her voice very low. "Let go of me, and I'll do my best."

Now his hand rose, to nudge up her chin and force her eyes to his. His regard narrowed on her. In the silence, she heard the distant chimes of the clock again. Only a quarter hour. It felt like a century. "Oh, I don't think so," he said. "I don't leave knives unsheathed."

Silence fell. She did not know how to break it, but she could see the calculations working through his expression, and it came to her, strongly, that it was better he not be allowed to finish them. Heart drumming, she leaned forward and pressed her lips to his.

He held perfectly still. It disconcerted her. She ran her tongue along his upper lip, and he exhaled, his breath coasting across her mouth. His lips were much softer than they appeared. She set her teeth onto the bottom one, very lightly. If he did something dislikable, she could bite it clean off him.

His fingers brushed against her neck. The gentle touch startled her; she let go of his lip and he spoke against her mouth. "You're going to have to do better than that, Mina."

Her face prickled. She could not believe she was flushing, that some base part of her was suddenly warming to this charade. Bodies were so stupid. "Let go of my hair and I will."

He leaned forward and kissed her. His tongue opened her lips and forced itself inside, touching and tangling with hers as his hand loosed her hair and came around her waist. He bent over her and knocked her off balance so she fell backward, relying on his arm alone for support.

He tasted hot and dark, and his kiss was like the onset of a fever; the angle, the stroke of his tongue, and the dig of his fist into her back left no role for her but submission. He held her in such a way that her instincts kept telling her she was about to fall. She found herself grabbing his shoulders to offset her dizziness, and his mouth pressed harder into hers, forcing her to a new awareness of his knuckles digging into her spine, the solid density and thickness of his shoulders, how easily he was overwhelming her.

Nothing in her should have responded to it, save that his strength was somehow not hurting her. His grip on her was brutal in its absoluteness, but it caused her no discomfort, and his kiss pulled her into pleasure despite herself. He kissed as gracefully as he moved; she could not predict it. His mouth sucked at hers, his teeth caught her lip. He spoke into her mouth. "What were you meant to find?"

"Nothing," she gasped.

Abruptly, she was standing on her feet again; he had set her away and stepped back. His chest was moving more rapidly than normal, but as he wiped his mouth with the back of his hand, she realized it was not arousal that made his eyes so heavy-lidded. A muscle ticked at his temple as he stared at her. Why, he was not enjoying himself at all.

All at once, she felt a weird urge to laugh. His action said everything: he had no intention of hurting her, or of ravishing her, either. How badly he'd scared her—and for what? "You've cooked up this drama yourself." Her voice sounded only a little unsteady. He kissed as well as she'd remembered. "Yes, I was an idiot to come in here. But you took me from that cellar in the rudest manner possible. You can't blame me for trying to figure out if I'm safe with you. Locked up here, at your mercy—what would *you* do in my situation?"

His brow lifted. "The same thing, perhaps. But not so clumsily."

Stupid to feel stung by his criticism. "Yes, well, I have little experience in spying, and *not* much interest in acquiring it, I must confess."

His mouth thinned. "One thing you will remember," he said. "I am not, and have never been, a spy."

"Oh, yes," she said, "you are a *tycoon*, I forgot. You trade in coca, when you're not jumping out windows."

"I am a mapmaker," he said sharply. "Raised ludicrously high, which is cause enough for interest, believe me. Once you leave this place, your imagination will be counted as running wild if you claim anything more extraordinary."

That he mentioned her departure as an inevitability moved her to smile. Maybe they could get along, after all. "Oh, I'm no more imaginative than you," she said. "Perfectly boring, really."

He sighed as if she had disappointed him. But then he rubbed his eyes, and she wondered if he wasn't simply tired. "Would that were the case, Miss Masters." He ran his hand through his hair, setting it into furrows; if he'd had a gold ring in his ear, he might have played the pirate right now, with his wild mane and billowing shirtsleeves and suntanned skin. He had not looked nearly so handsome in Hong Kong. "I will ask you one more time," he said as he dropped his hand. "How long have you worked for Ridland?"

She was stubborn and refused to admit anything. But why the hell else would a pampered American girl know how—or care—to pick a lock and go rifling through his private documents? Phin set a footman outside her door that night, a brawny, weathered fellow he'd found at one of the pubs Sanburne liked to frequent for boxing. Gompers, his name was, and he showed no sign of curiosity or concern when Phin informed him that Miss Masters was not to be let out of her rooms, making him just the man for the job.

The next morning, Phin had the locks replaced on her apartments. Unless she had the hands of a virtuoso, she'd be going nowhere now unless he willed it. And the hell of it was, he *could* permit her to go nowhere, not even back to Ridland's, until he knew her aim, and his own role in it. Ridland's rot had invaded his own home; he was helpless to expunge it. *And thus*, he thought, *I add jailkeeper to my long list of accomplishments.*

He should not be so angry. He told himself this over

breakfast, and again during a very unrewarding meeting with the Oxford trustees. At first, they balked at the proposal to name the chair in cartography for Sheldrake, and to his own surprise, he lifted his voice. It worked to alter their attitude, though; they left amidst a shower of gratitude and apologies, no doubt fearing that otherwise he might revoke his endowment. His father had often gotten his way by yelling, but Phin had never needed to stoop to it. Thus did one day of Miss Masters's company erode his control.

He could not say for whom his frustration was larger, himself or her. He had been an idiot, all right, believing that the repayment of his debt would be simple. An unexpected epilogue to an already-closed book, he'd told himself, as if anything were simple where Ridland was involved. But there was the rub: Some part of him had known this. Some part of him had craved it. He felt more clearheaded than he had in weeks. Scaling the cliffs at Dover, stroking an eight across the Channel, rubbing shoulders with the royal family—realizing these boyhood dreams, nursed for so long in a heart made ambitious by disappointment, had left him strangely numb. But a letter from Ridland set his heart drumming. A trollop sent to raid his study, who spoke lies more easily than a false oracle—*she* could made his skin flush.

He put it down to the fact that he hadn't touched a woman in months. He had no taste for the sorts of arrangements, or the diseases, that his father had contracted with whores, and mastering his new responsibilities had left him little time to find and woo some agreeable widow. With Mina Masters laid out like a feast on his desk, her eyes flashing defiance, he had simply discovered the cost of his abstinence.

But the explanation did not quell his disquiet. Her lips against his had conjured dark possibilities, all the various fleshly punishments a beautiful woman could expect for poking her nose into other people's business. His imagination proved fecund and disturbingly depraved. She roused in him capacities that he had tried to forget he possessed; she reminded him that, for a decade, he'd done very well as a villain.

Worse, she had kissed him back as though she had a taste for depravity. The flavor of her mouth still lingered on his tongue.

He did not want her in his house.

After the trustees' departure, a note arrived from the Sheldrakes, stiffly worded and ingratiating. They asked permission to call tomorrow to deliver their thanks in person. He almost wrote them to stay away. *My house is unfit for you; keep clear of this tangle.* But of course he could not refuse them; they would take it as an insult, and reinterpret his generosity as condescension.

A note came from Sanburne in the early afternoon, inviting him to the club for what he assumed would be lunch. But when he arrived, the majordomo escorted him past the dining room, down the hall into the shooting gallery. Sanburne was lounging on a bench, a bottle and a pair of protective earpieces by his boots. He was watching a slim blond man take aim at the painted figure on the wall. A shot rang out. The resulting hole, a good foot from the figure, suggested that the man was nearsighted or nervous.

"Deuced bad luck," the gunman said as he turned around. Neither nervous nor nearsighted, then, but a waste of breath all the same. Phin had known Tilney since Eton, and time had not improved him; he was still prettier than a girl, and as bad with wagers and wine as he was with a gun. Sanburne was keeping bad company these days.

The man broke into a grin as he spotted Phin. "What ho, Granville! You've cost me five quid."

"Ah," said Sanburne, turning and lifting his chin in welcome. "That's right, he told me you'd never be pried from your maps."

"Glad to enrich you," Phin said.

Tilney lifted the pistol. "Newest model from Webley. Have a go?"

Phin glanced to Sanburne, who shrugged. "Just had my turn."

That accounted for the hole in the figure's arm. Not the place to shoot a man if you meant to stop him from coming at you; Phin had seen rage that numbed a man's pain more effectively than morphine. But such skill would prove sufficient for a society darling whose main concern was making a good show at the summer hunting balls. *I've grown into a mean bastard*, he thought as he walked forward.

"Oh, cheers," said Tilney as he held out the pistol. His grip was three-fingered, a damned foolish way to hold a loaded gun. "Say, you didn't stop by after the Derby. We had a nice little rout."

The revolver nestled in his palm. Nice balance, good proportion, enough weight to focus the mind. "I was busy."

Tilney's smile now looked strained. "Yes, well, it got me thinking. I do hope you're not still grudged about the piss on the pillowcases. Told the lads you weren't Irish, but you know how boys can be."

"Oh, third form," said Sanburne easily. "Decades ago."

Phin shifted his grip. "Old hat," he agreed with a smile. "So long as you're not still sulking over being dumped into the latrine. And thrashed," he added thoughtfully. With a glance toward the painted figure, he arched one brow. "I hope your vision recovered? I never did remember to ask."

Tilney looked a little more uneasily now at the gun. "Brilliantly, thanks." He cleared his throat. "Quite a growth spurt you had there, Granville."

"It's Ashmore now." Phin lifted the gun and took aim. The sound of the shot exploded through the room. They were doing themselves no favors by forgoing the earpieces. "And, yes," he said as he lowered his arm. "I quite enjoyed it."

Sanburne was applauding. "Straight through the eyes. This calls for celebration."

He felt an increasing sense of unreality. "Celebration, yes. Good to know I could kill you both quite easily."

"I've got to beg off," Tilney said. "Prior engagement, what?"

In the dining room, Sanburne was full of light, amusing news. An artifact he'd bought had been denounced as a fake last week at some public event, and he seemed delighted by the sympathy flowing to him from all corners of society. "I've dined out on it for five nights," he said. "I may arrange to buy another forgery tomorrow."

The Cornish hen was tough, the wine sour. Phin attended to the conversation with half a mind; the other half wondered what the hell was wrong with him. This was his life now. Sanburne was genuinely witty. Phin should not be laughing mechanically at these jokes.

He realized silence had fallen when Sanburne broke it with a poke at his arm. "Are you in love, then?"

"Good God, no." He was in something, all right, but it was the furthest thing from love. In fact, he rather suspected it to be a great pile of shit. "Why do you ask?"

"You've got that dreamy, idiotic look about you."

He considered this for a moment. "Perhaps I've formed an interest," he said. "Sheldrake's daughter is coming to town tomorrow. She's turned out quite well."

Sanburne's brows lifted to his hairline. "Sheldrake's daughter! Bit long in the tooth by now, surely." He paused, a smile creeping over his mouth. "Not that there's a thing wrong with a spinster. They accrue a bit of flavor on the shelf. Well, well. Phin and old Sheldrake's daughter. I think this calls for a real drink." He lifted three fingers to the bearer, who showed no sign of surprise at this stiff order. "For you?" he asked.

Phin shook his head. "Coffee." He'd halt the deterioration where he could; liquor had smoothed his parents' road to hell, but he would feel every bump, if he had to.

"Ah? Gone the glory years, then? I remember when no resident of Oxford could count on a night's sleep without being regaled by your fine, drunken baritone."

He laughed. "Oh, I'll sing for you. Like a canary in a

goddamned mine shaft. But best you keep drinking; you won't like it so much if you're sober."

"Hmm." Sanburne gave him an irritatingly thoughtful inspection. "I expect your sleepier toxins don't inspire much song," he said. "Thanks to you, I spent a good deal of my own party last week talking to the bloody flagstones."

Phin sat back as his coffee was delivered. "Yes, the ether was a bad choice." He'd heard it lauded for its sedative properties, but it had been the furthest thing from soothing. Perhaps he would try chloral next. He needed something to alternate with the opium, lest he end up enslaved to the substance.

"No harm done." Sanburne took up his drink, tossing back nearly half at one go. "It called my attention to a pressing philosophical riddle. A man comes to a crossroads. Down one road lies everything loathsome and dutiful—"

"Are they one and the same?"

"—obligations he never asked for, a life of comfort and empty honors. Yes, I think they are one and the same. They both lead to the same end, anyway: a slow suffocation by way of doing the done thing."

Suffocation was an apt word. Phin thought of his fit in Sheldrake's study. A touch of that feeling had come upon him in the shooting gallery, which worried him. Generally, these fits came farther apart. Well, it had ebbed fast enough when Tilney departed. "Better a slow suffocation than a quick beheading," he said. He was not sure he privately agreed, but for Sanburne, at least, the wisdom was sound.

"Indeed, no. A quick and glorious end is always preferable to a slow and painful one. And it makes a hell of a show for those left behind." Sanburne's smile looked calculated. "Even those who don't wish to watch."

Phin repressed a stir of impatience. This crusade Sanburne had launched against his father kept London entertained, but it seemed the height of childishness to him. Sanburne's sister Stella was no victim; she'd put a knife through her husband's throat. If their father thought her better kept in an asylum, the men of London certainly breathed more easily for it. "And what lies down the other road?"

Sanburne took another swig from his glass. "The man has no idea. He can't see that far. But it promises to be more interesting by half."

"You should have been a mapmaker."

"Christ, no. The point isn't to chart one's course. Simply to stumble along, enjoying the pratfalls as one goes."

The coffee was dark and bitter, done in the Turkish style. Phin crunched down on the thick dregs; they suited his mood. "How does the man know he'll enjoy these pratfalls, if he can't see down the road?"

"He can guess."

"But blind guesses often miss their mark."

Sanburne swished the contents of his glass, contemplative. "Marks are overrated. Guidelines only serve the uncreative. Hew closely enough to duty, and one day you'll look into the mirror and see a stranger."

In fact, Phin thought, that sounded like a damned good goal. "But duty isn't meant to provide pleasure."

Stella's tragedy, it seemed to him, had only given Sanburne the excuse he'd always looked for. He had never been reconciled to his own privilege, not when it required him to fall in step with his father's wishes. There were worse fates than conventional luxury, of course, but Sanburne was fortunate enough never to have learned of them. "Duty is meant to keep one from going astray," Phin concluded.

The sharpness of Sanburne's glance put him on alert. This conversation was not as idle as he'd imagined. "And what if one already has gone astray?"

"Walk very carefully, then. Some roads keep you safer than others." It took an effort to restrain himself from looking pointedly at the glass in Sanburne's hand. The man had no cause to swallow his sorrows; his problems were borrowed from his sister, even if he'd managed to blame himself for them. "Some keep you safe from yourself."

Briefly, some dark emotion worked its way across Sanburne's face, and Phin thought, for a puzzled second, that he was going to have to catch a fist.

But then Sanburne laughed. "Rubbish. I see no reason not to go astray. In fact, I go astray quite regularly, and I always manage to have a jolly good time at it. Besides, that's the whole point, no? By the time lunch is over, I won't be able to walk a straight line if my life depended on it."

The tight feeling was back in Phin's throat. "Then I can tell your life never has depended on it." Fed up with this nonsense, he stood. "I'll be going."

The viscount leaned back in his chair, to all appearances amused by this abrupt announcement of departure. "Perhaps my life *does* depend on it. The crooked way, I mean."

"Oh, you'll get wherever you're going," Phin said, "no matter how you choose to proceed. Your luck always has been with the angels." It was true: Sanburne was a social Midas. Even his gaffes turned to gold, and when he stumbled, the road rose to meet him. "Good day, Viscount."

As he walked away, Sanburne began to laugh. This time his mirth sounded unhinged; at other tables, diners craned their heads to stare.

Phin turned against his will. "Are you going mad, then?" Trust Sanburne to do it loudly, rather than in slow, throat-closing, heart-pounding silence.

Sanburne waved a hand to dismiss this idea. "Phin," he wheezed, "you are in for a surprise, old fellow." He drew a long, choking breath. "At least I know there are two paths, and can take a clear view of them. You? You tell yourself you've got choices, but you have to keep blinders on to make sure you're heading straight."

All right, then, they would have this out. It had been coming for weeks now, with every silent smile Sanburne cast him as Phin turned down a drink or left a party before someone puked. He walked back to the table. "Speak clearly," he said. "You disapprove of the fact that I've not followed your lead? That I actually take my responsibilities seriously?"

Sanburne lifted his arms in an ostentatious stretch. "If you enjoyed your own righteous rigmarole, it would be one thing. But, good God, man, whom are you fooling?" He dropped his arms and exhaled. "Whether or not you sleep through the night won't make a damned bit of difference to the world. Drink or don't drink; it won't change a whit. You'll never be your father."

Phin drew a hard breath. This was friendship, he reminded himself: plain speaking and hard truths. But they were meant to cost something; one did not toss them out like dynamite simply because one anticipated the entertainment of an explosion. "You think you know me still," he said. But Sanburne had no idea where such roads could really lead. "There is your mistake."

Sanburne shrugged. "I've always known you. Better than yourself, maybe. You fancied yourself the grubby one, yes? The diseased offspring of a rotten line. Meanwhile, you tossed future earls into pig troughs and barely took note of the splash. Oh, I know you thought the lads sneered when your back was turned, and perhaps at first they did. But they learned better very quickly. Even as children, they saw you more clearly than you do."

Phin stared at him. "Your point?"

The viscount made an impatient noise. "That you've always been more than a mapmaker. Now you've got the title to prove it. But the only one who still needs convincing is you."

"Ah, yes, the title," Phin said flatly. It was a license to life, all right, but in a far more literal sense than Sanburne imagined. Drink and debauchery did not cover it. "That does change everything, don't it, old fellow."

Sanburne sighed. "Of course it doesn't. That's precisely my point. You are who you are. And unlike you, I've never minded it."

With great difficulty, Phin made himself smile. "Forgive me if I do not trust the judgment of a man whose standards are notoriously low." And as Sanburne pulled a mocking, shocked face, he pivoted and walked out.

That afternoon, as he passed Miss Masters's rooms on the way to his own, the doorknob rattled. Just slightly.

He wheeled back, looking at the footman, who'd been standing at attention. "Has she been trying to get out?"

Gompers shrugged. "On and off about every hour, sir."

The rattling ceased. She'd heard his voice, maybe.

He exhaled. Something about that small sound scraped his conscience, which irritated him. He did not care if she'd saved his life, or a thousand lives, for that matter. No cause on earth would compel him to feel sympathy for Ridland's minion.

Of course, he, too, had once been a minion. Ridland had subtle ways of enlisting the unsuspecting. *We require a cartographer for this task, a man of unusual skills. The river, you see, has never been mapped; it is not in friendly territory.* Ridland preyed on naiveté and idealism, and trapped his victims in cages strung from their own ambitions. Mina Masters was clever, but Phin had been clever, too. He'd still fallen victim.

Cursing himself, he fitted the key into the door. Here was the real danger with boredom, he thought. One was too vulnerable to being intrigued.

Miss Masters was sitting in an armchair that she'd drawn up to the window. Her eyes were closed, and the mellow afternoon light lent a warm glow to her ice-blond hair. Had he not heard the evidence of her foray to the door, he would have thought her well settled; she had a rug over her lap, and a book lay open on the floor. She was a brilliant fraud; even on the off chance she worked only for herself, he'd do well to keep her locked up anyway.

Except, of course, that her genius had saved his life once. In light of that, her innocence would make him a scoundrel.

He waited a moment, but she did not turn to acknowledge him. "Where is your cat?"

"Washington? Hiding from me." She spoke absently, as though her thoughts were elsewhere.

Silence fell, and she showed no inclination to break it. He leaned back against the wall, crossing his arms. What had he hoped to achieve by coming in here? She hardly required his compassion, even if he was foolish enough to feel it.

He supposed he only wanted another chance to examine her. He was not accustomed to misjudging a person, and it unsettled him. He did not want to make the same mistake again.

Oh, hell, he would not lie to himself. Laura Sheldrake smiled, and he wanted to smash her fingers; Mina Masters pried into his desk, and he wanted to lift her skirts and lick the frown from her brow. He was bloody perverse, a hypocrite beyond measure. He frowned on Sanburne's waywardness when within himself there lurked far darker inclinations, irreconcilable with any form of reason. Overnight, the dirty, bloody, murky maze he'd known as the world had collapsed into a single orbit, with him at the center; life should be so easy, but this woman made him want to plunge right back into the muck.

A beheading or suffocation: to Sanburne's options, he might add Miss Masters. She threatened to lay waste his remaining shreds of self-respect. She would be his own special form of suicide, if he permitted it.

He was not going to kiss her again. He was not going to touch her. And yet, he stood there. He stood there, and he cleared his throat to speak. "Are you comfortable?"

"Comfortable?" Her shoulders rolled, an impatient little gesture, but still her eyes did not open. "Answer a question of mine, and I'll answer yours."

His temper stirred. In Hong Kong, too, she'd exhibited a peculiar talent for irritating him. At least now he had a way to account for it. How did one reconcile such wicked resourcefulness with a pampered beauty who made her fortune selling shampoo? Answer: one factored in the hand of Joseph Ridland. It should relieve him to know that her skills were professional. It recast his irritation as the product of expert manipulation, rather than proof of his personal weakness.

Unfortunately, the fact that it would relieve him made him wonder if he was not biased in his evaluation of the matter.

"Are you in a position to make demands?" he asked gently.

She lifted her face so the sunlight caught it in full. Her profile was as pure and lovely as a cameo, and she knew it, no doubt. "Demand? I'd thought it a request."

His curiosity was no sin. Even the most wholesome sorts suffered from it. "Ask away, then. Maybe I'll answer."

"I'd assumed that you still worked for Ridland. But now, I think you don't. Which is it?"

An interesting question, if disingenuous. Its motive seemed obscure to him. "Why do you want to know?"

"I don't trust him, and I wouldn't trust any man in his employ."

He paused. "Are you really looking for someone to trust?" Perhaps she wanted out of Ridland's service.

Her eyes opened. "Everyone needs to trust someone. Particularly in a strange country where one has no friends." She began to smile. "Look as hard as you like, Ashmore. I'm being perfectly frank with you."

There was no harm in telling her, he supposed. He ceded no advantage by giving her the truth, and if she'd guessed the answer already, his honesty might compel her to relax her guard. "When I came into the title, I ceased to answer to him."

She nodded and looked back to the window. He wished she wouldn't; her expression might have told him something. "As for your question—no, I'm not comfortable at all. My mother used to sit like this, you see. And I'd vowed never to do it myself."

"Sit by the window, do you mean?"

"Yes, exactly. No matter where we were in the world, I would enter her boudoir and find her sitting like this, staring out. It made me quite impatient. I used to wonder what she was looking at, but when I asked, she would never tell me. Today, though, I realized the answer. Would you like to know it?"

It seemed she'd finally run out of fresh tactics, for she'd already tried to incite his guilt. "Let me guess. Freedom?"

She glanced back to him. There were shadows beneath her eyes, as though she hadn't slept well. This apartment was as rich as his own; he would not allow her appearance of delicacy to stir a whit of remorse in him. "No, I don't expect she saw freedom anywhere she looked. She doesn't have the imagination for it."

He hesitated. He was like Pandora; he did not like a puzzle, and even if he knew that uncertainty was healthier, he still wanted to open the goddamned box and put a period to his curiosity. All right, he wanted to put far more than a period to it; the light across her face highlighted the grainless purity of her skin, and he remembered, with tactile intensity, how she had felt pressed beneath him.

Besides, she was in his house, which made her his problem. He could not leave her unquelled. "Then tell me, Miss Masters, what was it she saw? And don't disappoint me," he added dryly. "I depend on you to make the answer as affecting as possible."

She laughed, which took him off guard. The uneasiness that had been stirring for the past few minutes raked its claws through his gut. He did not understand her at all, but he saw why Ridland had tapped her. Impassivity would be impressive, in her circumstances, but this smile was nothing short of miraculous. "I've never disappointed you," she said.

He smiled back at her, although he could tell that his smile failed to match hers for sheer, brash effrontery.

That was fine; she was the one with something to lose. "And here I thought you'd disappointed me in my study last night."

She shook her head. "No. To be disappointed, you must have expectations. And you've never thought enough of me to form any. What did you think of me in Hong Kong? That I was some daft, silly girl?" She paused. "You asked me whose I was, that night. Do you remember?"

It gave him a start. Yes, that was right. Even back then, as she broke apart the shutters to expedite his escape, he'd assumed she was part of the game. But she had denied it. *I am my own,* she'd said. It occurred to him now that the phrasing had been odd and perhaps revealing, though he could not work out the significance. "Yes," he said. "I remember that."

She tilted her head as though his admission had surprised her; that was something, at least. "I wonder, then. Assuming you believed me, how did you explain what I'd done for you? Did you tell yourself that I'd saved you on a whim? For my own amusement, without a thought to the possible consequences?" Her mouth pulled in sarcasm. "Did you tell yourself that I'd regret it when you were gone?"

Her words cut uncomfortably close to the truth. For four years, he had worked very hard not to remember her. If he had ever thought himself cowardly for the insistence with which he shut out her memory, he need only look at her now to recognize the wisdom of his decision. Sitting there in sunlit splendor, she could not be ignored. She drank up the light, absorbing every measure of his senses; had Cronin been creeping up behind him now, he would never have noticed. She was not safe to look upon, much less think of. "I never gave it much thought," he said curtly.

"How odd. I believe I would have given it thought, had someone saved me. No matter," she said more briskly, and rose. The throw fell from her shoulders, and his breath caught. She was wearing the gown she'd collected from the boardinghouse. Done in the aesthetic style, it fell in a sheer white column from her bust to her feet, and against the backlighting of the window, it revealed every line of her body: her slender waist, the full curve of her hips, the sweet pout of her inner thighs.

His temper sparked. It was one thing to gawk, and another to be manipulated like a puppet on strings. She had planned this goddamned scene.

He forced his eyes up to hers. She was still smiling, and he had the unnerving feeling she had divined the exact order of his thoughts from his expression alone. "What I did last night was surprise you," she said gently. "If you think on it, you'll realize I'm right. I've surprised you a great deal, I think, and not just in London, but in Hong Kong, too. And you cannot account for it, so you resent me. You tell yourself there must be some explanation other than the real one. You think I'm *working* for someone who's clever. You can't even consider that *I* might be clever, because that would mean—well, that between the two of us, *you're* the one who's the idiot."

"Sharp words," he said. "Cleverly spoken. But if I'm the idiot, Miss Masters, then why am I the one holding the key?"

"Ah." Her appearance of good humor faded. "For

the same reason my mother stared out the window, I expect. She has a great love of nature, Mama does. It's been decades since she left England, and she still talks constantly of the green fields, the streams, and the forests. But when she looked out the window in Hong Kong, or New York, or Singapore, what did she see? Everything *you* have done to it. The asphalt men have laid over the grass, the waterways they've redirected, the trees they've turned into hovels, every manipulation and modification and *improvement* that suits their short-sighted desires. Of course you have the key, Ashmore. Even when it comes to the arrangement of pens, you like to be in control." She smiled. "Don't forget to lock the door when you leave."

And then she walked into her bedchamber, and shut the door.

He stood there, wrestling down an anger that seemed as damning as her little speech—which grated him, no doubt beyond her wildest hopes. He took no pleasure in imprisoning or managing anyone. This imprisonment was not by his *desire*, but by necessity.

But the thought echoed unpleasantly in his brain, magnifying his hypocrisy until he could not avoid facing it. Of all men, he knew how bitterly it burned a soul to be deprived of choices. And yet, even as he gloated over his own new freedom and loathed Ridland for attempting to infringe on it, he told himself he had no *choice* but to keep her like this. Sanburne was not the only one who had a right to mock him.

He locked the door behind him, all right. Objectively, his guilt was irrational; it seemed clear that his thoughts were not functioning properly. By her own actions, she had proved herself untrustworthy.

But when he had walked far enough down the hallway to get free of the witchcraft she'd worked in that scented little room, the uppermost feeling that replaced it was not anger, but amazement. She was the prisoner, but she had managed to dismiss him as effectively as a queen.

At best, he should be amused by her. This admiration was entirely unwelcome.

Chapter Eight

The next morning, Mina was wakened by a sound in her sitting room. She rushed to the doorway quickly enough to see the maid slip a key into her pocket as she stepped inside. Sally, her name was. She was Mina's new friend, even if she didn't realize it yet. "Good morning," Mina said brightly.

The maid gasped and nearly dropped the tray she held. She was a skinny thing, bred on thin gruel and a weak English climate, and her mobcap wanted to escape. She set the food on a sideboard and clutched at her cap, white-faced, as she sank into a curtsey. Trust the English to demand groveling where a simple *Good morning* would serve.

"None of that," Mina reminded her. "As I said yesterday, a nod will do."

After a moment, the girl nodded, slowly and deliberately. "I've brought your breakfast." The door behind her began to open, and she slapped a palm against it. "Hold!" she called, surprisingly authoritative. "Mum—I mean, miss—that's the footmen. They'll be fetching in the rest of your luggage."

"Oh, excellent." She was worried about her oils. She'd packed them very carefully, but she did not put it beyond Ridland to smash them for spite. She waited expectantly, but Sally remained frozen in her guardian posture. As the moment lengthened, the maid's expression took on an anguished cast. "Won't you let them in?" Mina asked, puzzled.

"Um—" The maid cleared her throat. "I expect you wouldn't want them to see your . . . your nightclothes, miss."

"Oh." Mina glanced down at herself. The robe Sally had provided more than covered her. But for the sake of the maid's nerves, she retreated into the bedchamber and closed the door.

The room seemed to shrink around her. Waiting was her particular strength, but she had felt it faltering last night in this pretty, perfumed prison. She had to get out of here. Today, somehow, she would.

She crossed to the window. She had not lied to Ashmore; the view fascinated and depressed her. The little garden below was walled in by oak trees. A gridded path segmented it into perfect squares. Severely trimmed shrubbery emphasized the linear dominion, marching in rows around boxed-in plots of flowers that hunkered obediently beneath the strengthening sun. It was no garden for dreaming or romance; rather, it offered a study in the taming of wayward whims.

She almost preferred the view from Ridland's. Almost, but not quite. For a full day now, she had puzzled over Ashmore's behavior in his study. It seemed to her more and more likely that he was no friend to Ridland. That letter she'd found had not been written in support of the man. And when she had asked him whether he still worked for Ridland, his phrasing had suggested hostility.

She was going to trust him, she decided. If the decision did not feel wholly right, then the sight of the rising sun reminded her that she had no choice. Another day begun, and soon to pass. When there was no choice, one could not properly think of risks, only necessities. Some stupid part of her had wanted to trust him from the moment she'd first laid eyes on him. Necessity would compel her to indulge her stupidity.

A knock came at the bedroom door, and Sally's voice announced the departure of the footmen. Mina emerged to discover that her trunks were bound in cord differently colored from that which Tarbury had used. Ridland had gone through her things, and he wanted her to know it.

He'd found nothing of interest. All the same, the sight made her queasy. One step forward, two steps back. She'd felt very clever, getting away from him. But with a simple switch of cord, he had sent her a message: she was still under his watchful eye.

"I'll get to the luggage next, miss." Sally was uncovering dishes; the smell of fried eggs and butter wafted over, rich and stomach-turning. Mina had no appetite. If Ashmore did not require money and would not listen to reason, then there was only one thing she could trade him. Was she willing? Her body's answer was immaterial. Her brain recognized that only a most rigid and tyrannical person would trim his hedges into the shape of cubes.

On the ottoman beside her trunks sat a small enamel

case, familiar and heartening. She sank to the carpet to open it. A muffled noise came from above; when she looked up, she had the impression that Sally had just turned away from gawking.

Ah. She was still in her nightclothes.

Or perhaps it was because she was sitting on the floor.

She returned her eyes to the latch. It was tricky, requiring a patient hand. "I had a very unusual childhood, you know. My father was a banker, but when I was six, he decided that he should start his own trading company."

"Yes, miss."

"We traveled a great many places when I was growing up, looking for things he might buy and then sell at a profit back in the United States." She opened the lid carefully. The padded compartments held the vials of essential oils that she'd carted from New York to tempt investors. "India, Ceylon, even Africa—we went everywhere." She liked to think that she'd inherited Papa's daring. Better yet, she'd made good on ambitions that had disappointed him. She was no fragile piece of porcelain any longer; if someone tossed her out of the china cabinet, she had more than a meager inheritance to bank on. *In New York*, she thought blackly. Here, she might as well be flotsam, for how easily these men were tossing her around. She drew a breath and schooled her thoughts. "I suppose I picked up all manner of strange habits," she finished casually. A glance showed Sally was watching her. She clambered back to her feet and carried the case to the center table. The sight of her oils made her feel much better. She could easily tolerate the smell of breakfast now.

The maid stepped back as she arranged the vials on the table. "This is jasmine," Mina said, lifting a bottle of violet glass. "Do you like that scent?"

"Yes, miss."

"You don't sound certain. Here—smell it." She popped out the stopper and held it toward the maid.

Sally's gaze switched suspiciously between Mina and the vial. Finally, her shoulders slumping, she leaned forward. Perhaps she had decided that mad American whims must be tolerated as part of her duty. "It's very nice, miss," she said obediently.

Mina reached for another. "And this one." She unstoppered the vial and held it out. "What do you think?"

Sally pushed up her mobcap with a rough and reddened hand. "That one's just lovely," she said with real enthusiasm. "What'll that be? Something with roses?"

"No, it's gardenia." Mina held up the glass, admiring the clarity of the oil in the electric light. Something brushed past her ankles; Washington had come out from his lair beneath the bed. She bent to pet him but he sidestepped, darting forward to snake around Sally's feet. The perverse creature! He deliberately ignored her. "I hate you," she said.

Sally jumped. "Pardon, miss?"

"The cat." Mina felt her own cheeks warm. "I do not like my cat."

"Oh!" Sally looked down, as if only now taking note of her new admirer. She reached down to scratch the cat, and he stretched and preened beneath her hand. *Traitor*,

Mina thought. She would change his name to Benedict immediately.

She cleared her throat. "I've agreed to supply some of my oils to Whyllson's in exchange for their English lavender. Lavender is all the rage in America at present, but we don't have any reliable production yet. I did try some from California, but the quality was shoddy. That's what distinguishes Masters hair tonic, you know—the quality of our ingredients." She caught herself; this was perilously close to a lecture. Sally, bless her heart, was nodding along as though it interested her.

"What terrible trouble for you, miss. Traveling all the way to England for lavender! Why, I can get that for a few pence at the apothecary down the lane!" She looked over the bottles on the table, then glanced anxiously toward the door. "Shall I leave you in peace, miss?"

"No," Mina said quickly. The last thing she wanted was to be alone and locked in. The passage of time would scrape on her nerves. She cast about for some reason to detain the girl. "Would you like to keep this one?" She pressed the vial into the maid's hand. When Sally looked hesitant, she added, "Lord Ashmore need not know, of course."

The girl was torn; her teeth worried her lip, but her fingers closed over the bottle. "His lordship is very kind," she said softly.

"Oh, yes," Mina agreed. "And so imaginative." Sally looked uncertain whether she should agree to this; how fortunate for her that she'd had no cause to experience that aspect of Ashmore's personality. "Perhaps you should smell all the bottles," Mina suggested. "Pick the one you like best. It would be very useful to know what appeals to English ladies."

The maid blushed, then ducked her head and nodded.

"Excellent. And I shall continue unpacking my things." She dismissed the maid's protests with a shrug. "Foreign ways, as I said. I'd like to do it myself. Some of the contents are breakable."

Foreign ways made Sally shake her head in astonishment. But as Mina knelt by a trunk, she heard the telltale sound of a stopper clicking in the neck of a bottle. She glanced over her shoulder and smiled. Sally was brushing wistful fingertips across the bottles arranged on the table, her lips moving soundlessly as she read each label. Every few seconds, though, she interrupted her inspection to dart a nervous glance at the closed door. Perhaps she'd heard tell of Ashmore's irritation the night before last, when he'd escorted her back from his study.

From now on, Miss Masters, locked doors stay locked.

But Sally had the key.

On a deep breath, she lifted the lid of one trunk. What on earth? She lifted out a globe, frowning at it for a moment before she replaced it and searched for the luggage tag.

Miss L. Sheldrake, it read. "This is not my trunk."

"What?" Sally hastily replaced a vial. "What's that?"

She tilted the tag for the maid's inspection. "It belongs to a Miss Sheldrake."

"Oh, Lord! That'll be his lordship's guest. What a mix-up!"

"Guest?" Here was news. "An unmarried guest?"

"Oh, no, miss, nothing like that," Sally assured her.

"It's very respectable. She's paying a call with her mother. They . . ." Turning a dull red, she shut her mouth—perhaps recalling too late that she spoke to *Miss* Masters, who had not arrived accompanied by a chaperone.

Mina almost reassured her. But perhaps the maid would be more shocked if she learned her temporary mistress had no interest in respectability. A pristine reputation was an asset only for women who desired husbands. For those who cherished their freedom, it could prove a liability beyond measure. "Foreign ways," she said gently.

"Foreign ways, miss." Sally sounded mournful.

Respectability did have its vicarious uses, though. In this case, upstanding houseguests would serve her well. Such women tended to frown on living down the hall from a prisoner. She would have to meet these new arrivals and make them very aware of her presence. If the encounter occurred in Lord Ashmore's company, he could not even accuse her of breaking his edict.

To sum it up, Miss Masters, the guiding philosophy is this: I will know your location at all times.

"What a masterful example of chiaroscuro," Miss Sheldrake said, gesturing toward the painting over the mantel. "His face emerges from the shadows like truth itself. And note how his hand rests on the scales of justice."

"Yes, quite," Mrs. Sheldrake said. "See how his horse's girth is loosened? It denotes compassion, I expect."

The smiles they directed toward Phin looked as thin as the script in a book of etiquette. He wanted to tell them to sit down. They had called to thank him for his great gift, and seemed intent on repaying it by complimenting his drawing room; this painting was the last in a long list of items to elicit their admiration. It was only common courtesy, but it was making him damned uncomfortable. They would be welcome here even if the rug beneath their feet was not, in fact, the most beautiful piece of art they'd ever had the pleasure to step on. "It *is* a fine painting," he said, and called up a smile of his own. He felt resolved today, firm in his determination to behave appropriately; Miss Sheldrake would not be subjected to more nonsense.

"Was your cousin a great horseman, sir?" This from Mrs. Sheldrake, who spoke stiffly. At first, he'd assumed that Laura's recounting of his odd behavior had put her on guard. But now he wondered if it wasn't this damned Versailles of a drawing room. Each time she attempted to meet his eyes, her gaze broke away to wander in a skeptical fashion over his shoulder. No doubt the cream and gold paneling, the gilded cornices and pilasters must seem very garish to her, compared to the cottage in Eton. She couldn't match him with it, probably. The Phin she'd known was all gangling limbs and empty pockets and bottomless stomach. Apart from his friendship with a young viscount, that boy would never have been welcome amid such gilt, much less have had the blunt to purchase the Sheldrakes' house for them.

Or, hell, perhaps what constrained her was the very fact that he'd purchased their house for them. But what else had he been meant to do? When he'd found out that they could no longer make payments on the lease, he'd acted without considering the more subtle repercussions. That house had been open to him when he'd had no other home to go to. He would not let them be expelled from it.

They were waiting for his response. He cleared his throat and set down his teacup. "I suppose he was a great horseman. But that isn't my cousin."

Pin-drop silence. A flush mounted Miss Sheldrake's cheeks. "Who is it, then?"

"I am abashed to admit I have no idea. I had the place furnished before I assumed occupancy."

"But why?" Her face disguised nothing of her thoughts; she found his actions bewildering. "Did the late earl leave you no furnishings?"

He hesitated. They clearly did not subscribe to any of the society dailies, or they would have known of his decision to let out his cousin's house to a family of foreigners. He'd borne William no ill will; it was Will's father who had ruined that house for him. The seventh Earl of Ashmore had provided him with an education, for which he was grateful, but the man had exacted a price for it. Phin had never been welcome there, and on the few occasions he'd visited, he'd been made to listen to lengthy sermons on his father's faults, when in fact he could have written a book on them with no help at all.

The Sheldrakes knew something of this strained relationship. When he'd been sent down from Eton for brawling with Tilney, it was to them he'd gone, for his uncle had refused to take him. Thus, to explain his decision regarding the family house would mean introducing a host of uncomfortable memories. His drawing-room manners were rusty, but he did not think that the echoes of that pungent antagonism would complement their biscuits and tea. "I wanted a fresh start," he said.

The absurdity of that statement dawned on him as soon as he'd spoken it. But the ladies nodded, as if a fresh start were not a very ironic policy with which to assume an earldom stretching back some three hundred years.

"A fresh start is always lovely," Miss Sheldrake said.

"Oh, yes," agreed her mother, "perfectly smart."

With the way things were going, if he told them that he'd used the earl's furniture for kindling, they would promptly express admiration for his thrift with firewood.

He sighed and rubbed his eyes. He'd slept poorly again, and his thoughts were straying with irksome frequency to the small, scented catastrophe sealed in a room upstairs. She was locked in; he'd checked the door thrice before receiving the Sheldrakes. But her very presence in the house scraped his nerves like a blade. He felt not at all prepared for this visit, and certainly ill equipped to play the suitor.

He schooled himself to the task as the ladies returned to their chairs, focusing on the simple economy of Laura's movements as she took her seat. *Here* was what he should dwell on. What a difference her manner posed to Miss Masters's artful flourishes. Laura had no need for artifice; she presented herself frankly, in a quiet green gown that neither accentuated her curves nor sought to disguise them. And the man who married her would not be purchasing entertainment, but comfort and stability. She would never throw him out of line. Rather, she would keep him within it.

They were making appreciative note of the fine brocade upholstery. He fought to keep his mounting frustration from coloring his tone. "I'm so glad of your visit," he said, because he was damned if he would thank them for admiring his brocade.

"Of course we had to thank you in person," Mrs. Sheldrake said. *You left us no choice*, her tone suggested, *with that outlandish thing you did*. "And I do hope you will enjoy the globe. Mr. Sheldrake would have wanted you to have it, although I fear it is small thanks for the great service you've done us."

"Thanks are unnecessary," he said. "But I greatly appreciate the gift." He was going to lock that globe away in the darkest, most distant corner he could find. He would have smashed it, had his conscience not forbidden him.

Miss Sheldrake's green eyes rounded earnestly. There was a soothing simplicity to her wide face; he felt he could chart entire countries in the blank expanses of her cheeks. "Oh, but we had to give it to you!"

"Of course we did." Mrs. Sheldrake did not sound happy about it.

An awkward silence fell. "Well," he said. "I very much hope that you'll be able to stay for a few days." Pray God they did not. Not until Miss Masters was gone.

"Oh, no," said Mrs. Sheldrake, sounding startled by the very idea. Laura was blushing. Had he committed some breach of etiquette, then? Perhaps it was only in the colonies that people paid house visits without warning.

Yes, of course, that was right. Damn it. He shifted uneasily in his chair. These small, crucial tidbits were coming back to him more slowly than he'd counted on. "Some other time, then," he said.

The women exchanged an opaque look. "We don't wish to impose upon your hospitality," said Mrs. Sheldrake.

"You could not impose," he said. "That is, I've imposed on your hospitality so many times throughout the years that the very idea is nonsense." Very carefully, he chose his next words. "Indeed, I want you to know that I would consider you more than guests. You should consider this to be your very own home in town." Mrs. Sheldrake pressed her lips together, shocked or disapproving, but Laura bent her head to disguise a smile. This encouraged him. "I hope," he said lightly, "that the lack of my uncle's antiques will not discomfit you too much, Miss Sheldrake."

"Oh, no," she said softly. "Not at all."

All right, he was remembering the way of it now. And so was she, apparently. She'd formed an ardent attachment to him when he was at Eton, doing everything possible to win his attention. Once she'd told him that she would name her first son Anaximander. The first mapmaker in recorded history; what a fine legacy to bequeath! And—he smiled a little, remembering his sober, officious tone—he'd cautioned her against it. *It will be your job as a wife to trammel rash whims, not to encourage them. Anaximander! Good grief, he'd be thrashed every night at school.* "Tell me," he said. "Are you still determined to curse your sons with terrible names?"

She remembered instantly; there was no need to explain it. She blushed and gazed at her feet. "Philip or Stephen would do, I expect."

Mrs. Sheldrake made a sharp noise and came to her feet. "Well, we must be off, I fear. We plan to see the Crace collection at the museum before our train departs."

Laura, looking startled, rose as well. He came to his feet, understanding from the narrow look Mrs. Sheldrake gave him that she saw him a bit more clearly than her daughter did. *You have bought us a house*, that look said, *but you have not bought us.* "I understand," he told her, and then, after a pause, added, "It's a very fine exhibit."

"Hullo!"

Good God. How the hell had she gotten out?

Her cheery announcement won the ladies' instant and wide-eyed attention. He turned. She was draped along one side of the doorframe, a small, curvaceous package done up in scarlet silk. "Miss Masters," he said. There was no help for it; he had to introduce her, as she well knew and had certainly counted upon. "Do come in."

As she let go of the door and slinked toward them, he caught sight of his pathetic, incompetent, bloody fool of a footman skidding to a stop outside the door. He gave Gompers a small shake of his head, which turned into an astonished double take as the full effect of Miss Masters's gown became clear. All at once, he understood that his earlier unease had been a premonition of disaster. The gown had no structure or tailoring, save for the high, square neckline and the capped sleeves. The gold sash tied at her waist drew the thin fabric tight around her hips, announcing, very bluntly, that she did not wear a corset.

At her next step, petticoats also began to seem doubtful.

He cut a glance to Laura, who was gawking. Eton had yet to embrace the aesthetic style, and this was a very rude introduction. "Mrs. Sheldrake," he said. "Miss Sheldrake. Allow me to present to you my cousin."

"How do you do," Laura said faintly. Mrs. Sheldrake managed a nod, and cast him a glance in which he read a story of deep disappointment, of sad suspicions confirmed.

"Smashingly," Miss Masters replied. "I got your globe, I think? Very pretty, very . . . round?"

Laura cast him a horrified look. God above, did she think he'd given the thing away so quickly? "Miss Masters's luggage was delivered today," he said. "The servants must have mixed your very kind gift with her things."

"Yes," Miss Masters said cheerily, "that's what I assumed." She reached up to tuck a strand of hair behind her ear. To complete the artistic effect, she'd left it unbound, and it fell in a shimmering sheet to the tops of her thighs, the shade of sunlight on a cold winter day. The ladies gawked at it. He could not blame them. It seemed she was a better businesswoman than he'd guessed; that hair was the best damned advertisement for hair tonic imaginable.

He wrenched his eyes away. Laura was looking rapidly between him and his new family member as though her opinion, too, was rapidly being revised. "But I thought . . ." She put a hand to her cheek. "How lovely to hear you've reconciled with your family."

"Laura," Mrs. Sheldrake chided, but without much force. Her eyes rested on the doorway, probably awaiting the appearance of the chaperone that etiquette demanded. *Damn it.*

Miss Masters seemed oblivious to the complexities of the moment, including the progressive stiffening of her new acquaintances as the doorway remained empty. No surprise there—she had, after all, been raised among wolves, or in America; he was not sure there was a difference. "Yes," he said. "The reconciliation was a surprise to me as well."

"But a happy one," said Miss Masters. She slipped her arm through his; she was *definitely* not wearing a corset. He could feel the soft weight of her breast pressing against his elbow, and for a second, his awareness contracted to that single sensation. He forced himself to attend to her words, to ignore the warmth of her body and how it brought back to mind, with sudden and searing immediacy, the taste of her skin. "We decided, why bother with all that silliness our parents started? Blood is thicker than water, after all." She paused as if struck; her expression gave him an inkling of what was coming. "Why, what a clever turn of phrase," she marveled, "how *striking*, don't you think?" He blackly congratulated himself: at least he had a handle on one of her routines. "Yes, I should find a way to use it in my advertisements."

Laura made a mild noise that might have signified interest, but also worked perfectly well to communicate disbelief. "Indeed, Miss Masters, very original." She looked to Phin, her brow arching.

He sighed. If Miss Masters had decided to masquerade

as the family idiot, then his own role had also been cast. He gave a small shrug, the noble, martyred relative.

It did not serve. Laura frowned. "I had no idea that you had *American* family."

"Laura," Mrs. Sheldrake said more sharply. Her daughter's stress on the nationality had unwittingly made it sound like a slur.

He cleared his throat. "In fact—"

"And I had no idea you had *country* friends," said Miss Masters. She was eyeing Laura head to toe; the gown did not appear to impress her. "How delightful. Wherever did you acquire them?"

He slipped his hand down to her wrist and squeezed a warning. In response, she snuggled closer into his side. He gritted his teeth and disengaged; he needed his hands free, in case he decided to throttle her.

Offense had tugged Laura's shoulders rigid. Brilliant. "We are from *Eton*."

"Precisely." His voice emerged curtly. "I am surprised, cousin, that you do not recall the many, many times I've regaled you with tales of the Sheldrakes' kindness."

Miss Masters gave a shrug that made her breasts bounce in spectacular fashion. He looked quickly away, and found he was not the only one astonished; Mrs. Sheldrake was adjusting her spectacles, her mouth agape.

"You cannot expect me to remember *everything* you tell me," Miss Masters said. "So"—this directed, laughingly, at Laura—"Eton, you say? Well, if I haven't heard of it, you mustn't blame me. I know very little of England."

"I thought everyone knew Eton," Mrs. Sheldrake said in bewilderment. "The school, at least."

Laura slanted a wry smile at her mother. "Perhaps they do not pay attention to schooling in America." Taking her mother's arm, she addressed her next words to a point somewhere over his head. "You will excuse us, sir? We have a very tight schedule, if we wish to see the exhibit before our train departs."

"Of course." So much for nurturing old affections. Miss Masters had dropped into the scene like a cannonball, and if the detritus could survive an awkward exchange of letters at the holidays, he would count himself lucky.

He waited until the door had closed behind them, then turned on her.

Her expression was sober now. "Do not lose your temper," she said. "I wished to speak with you, and your knockabout footman clearly did not deliver my message last night."

He stared at her, at her swelling breasts and loose hair and big eyes and small, grasping hands, and his irritation twisted into something more athletic. It was as if she were trying to make him misbehave. "Yes, he did," he said through his teeth. "And I chose to ignore it." She should be very grateful that he'd chosen to ignore it. The thought of paying her a midnight visit had appealed to him for darker reasons than conversation. "I will tell the footman and the maid to thank you for their sacking."

She looked unimpressed. "It was not their fault, Ashmore. But"—she shrugged, and by dint of sheer vexation he managed to keep himself from glancing downward like a dog in heat—"if you're really so unreasonable, *I* shall hire them. In the meantime, don't you even wish to know what I have to tell you?"

"*No,*" he said. "All I wish is that you will stay in your rooms. Is that so difficult?" Christ. He sounded as though he were imploring her. He hardened his voice. "Perhaps I'll have a hole cut in the door, so your meals can be slipped to you. What say you?"

She fell silent. And then a sarcastic smile bloomed across her lips. "I say, come and give a kiss to your long-lost cousin."

Chapter Nine

Phin's gaze narrowed on the quirk of her lips. It was not his lust framing this view; she did, indeed, goad him deliberately. "Are you having fun?"

Her smile did not waver. "At this point, I think I'll take an opportunity wherever I find it."

He shook his head in disbelief. After the incident in the study, after she had seen what he was capable of, the fact that she saw an opportunity with him made her foolish beyond measure. But then, the contretemps in the study was only one experience among many, and perhaps the others had misled her. Hurtling across dance floors at him, attacking him in dark hallways, tying him to beds, pushing him out windows—yes, she might have gotten the wrong idea. But all her triumphs over him had owed to favorable circumstances. And circumstances did not favor her now.

He took a step toward her. She cocked her head as if curious. He advanced another step, and her chin rose. At the third, it became clear that she was too rash to be cowed. He took her wrists and pulled them up between them. "Listen to me," he growled, ignoring the fluttering of her lashes, the pretty, sarcastic O her lips formed. "This is *my* house. So long as you are under my roof, you will live by my rules. You will behave yourself, or I will not bother to spare you the consequences."

The pulse beneath his fingertips was hammering, but the brat did a bang-up job of smirking at him. She was so short she had to crane her head back to meet his eyes. Her face was perfectly heart-shaped, and a small mole marked the corner of her right eye, as if the devil had pressed a dark kiss to the tender skin there, giving her his mark before unleashing her on humanity. She depended on this girlish appeal to excuse all manner of nonsense, but the world did not work that way. Her actions bore fruit, and she would eat the results.

"I haven't broken your rule," she said.

He applied pressure, forcing her a step backward. Her brief resistance gratified him; the full-bodied flush of pleasure was so intense that it awoke a stray wit, cautioning him to pause, to reconsider his strategy.

But then she smiled and retreated a step on her own, the slant of her lips framing it as a challenge, and by God, he was going to take it. His hands clamped down; they felt capable of doing things to her that his brain could not rationalize. *I will lead an honorable life*, he told himself every morning. But his body knew that honor was a luxury like any other; it required the right circumstances to flourish, and she seemed determined to deny him the opportunity. So be it. Let her *enjoy* herself.

He advanced, and she made a sarcastic little game of her retreat, hopping the first step, twisting her hips to sidle the next. She had no more sense than a child; alas, he could not turn her over his knee and spank her like one. The thought distracted him; he was barely aware when her back touched the flowered wallpaper. "Oh, how boring," she said, and made a face. "I had hoped we might have a go around the room. It's been so long since I've danced."

Her temerity amazed him. "You are beyond stupid."

"You said you should know where I am at all times." She went up on her tiptoes to make a dramatic survey of the room over his shoulder. "I believe," she said solemnly, going flat-footed again, "that this is the drawing room."

She had no instinct for self-preservation. Her wrists felt fragile beneath his hands, as easily snapped as twigs.

Christ. What sort of thought was that?

He threw her hands away.

They thunked into the wall on either side of her head, but did not fall. She held them there in a posture of mocking submission, like the bloody devil's handmaiden.

"Have a goddamned care," he breathed.

Her lips played with the idea of a smile. "So fearsome," she murmured. "Don't hurt me."

He recoiled physically. Those were words he'd vowed no one would ever say to him again, and she tossed them out like a *dare.* Did she think he'd been playacting in Hong Kong? Had it somehow escaped her what his role might have necessitated? Had she missed his rough handling the other night? "You bank on a great deal," he said, and had to clear his throat to speak without hoarseness. "A good many men would wallop you. They would do worse." He paused. "They would want to do worse," he said quietly.

Her sea-blue eyes were guileless. "That's very true, isn't it? But I have no need to fear that *you* will."

"Really?" He did not bother to restrain the mockery that entered his voice. "If you could hear my thoughts, you wouldn't feel so certain."

Her brow arched. "What? Do you want to strike me? To ravish me? You may speak them aloud; I won't faint."

The words seemed to brush directly against his groin. He dragged a hand over his face. There should be nothing erotic about this; God save him from his perversity. If setting her on him was Ridland's idea of revenge, the man was even cleverer than he'd imagined. But her aim in this instance baffled Phin utterly. Slapped, killed, or fucked—these were the only ends she seemed to be inviting. She *was* inviting them. She wanted to *hear* about it.

The warmth rising from her pale skin briefly invaded his awareness. Flowers, yes, she smelled of lavender. What a ridiculously commonplace perfume for her. She required patchouli, sandalwood, ambergris—something complex and grossly unsuitable, to serve as a warning to hapless men.

But he was not hapless. The very idea that Ridland might have told her to bank on his lust utterly infuriated him. He leaned very close to her, letting her feel how much larger he was, how completely he might dominate her. "I warned you," he said into her ear. Her hair was soft against his lips; he blew into it lightly to force her scent away from him. "I do not like being manipulated."

Her cheek turned into his. He pulled away to avoid the contact, just enough to see her glance downward. "Part of you is beginning to like it very well."

He realized with a shock that his lower body was pressed against hers, his cock as stiff as a poker. Good God. He withdrew a pace, his ears burning. "Are you shameless?"

"Not at present," she said. "It requires significantly less clothing."

He raked her with a look. "Judging by your costume, that could be accomplished very swiftly."

She looked down at herself. "You underestimate the trickery of Liberty gowns. There are quite a lot of strings and things in this getup."

He blew out a breath. He could handle this far better. Send her to her rooms, for a start. He did not need to tangle with her at all. That he was doing so bespoke a weakness on his part, and he knew well where the weakness resided. As she had pointed out, it was currently thriving.

Adopting a thoroughly, admirably, goddamned heroically reasonable tone, he said, "Miss Masters, I am going to take you upstairs. And you are going to stay there, if I have to tie you to a chair."

She blinked. "I think Ridland might be working for Collins."

It took him a beat to work out the meaning of this absurd string of words. And then he burst into a laugh. She created her own entertainment, all right. "Ridland." He snorted. That power-hungry bastard could barely bring himself to answer to the government, much less to a two-bit piece of American scum. "If I'd known you had a talent for fiction, I would have supplied you with a pen and paper. Or was that what you were looking for in my study? You should have told me. I would have taken dictation for you."

She lowered her hands to her sides. "Mock me if you like," she said, her manner jarringly sober. "There was another agent from your government in Hong Kong."

"Of course," he said. "More than one, probably. It was a large operation."

"Well, *one* of them was conspiring with Collins." She spoke as though this news were momentous.

"Yes, Ridland mentioned that. What of it?"

For the first time in perhaps the entirety of their cursed acquaintance, she seemed thrown off guard. She wiggled her torso as if trying to cuddle into the wall, then put a knuckle into her mouth. What an abominable habit; he actually had to grit his teeth to prevent himself from telling her to stop sucking on it. The sound would drive him mad. He needed to adjust his trousers, but he would not do it in front of her; she would enjoy it too much. "But I don't understand this," she said, and her hand, thank God for small mercies, fell to her side. "Ridland knew about it? I didn't mention a thing to him."

He almost dismissed her remark. Of course Ridland knew there was a traitor; any thinking man would have assumed the existence of a turncoat the moment Collins slipped from prison without the aid of dynamite.

But as he started to speak, her denial abruptly reminded him of something: his own surprise at Ridland's carelessness. *I believe Miss Masters has some cause to fear a traitor among us*, Ridland had told him. *She will not be frank with me. I wonder if she hopes to trade her knowledge for her mother's safe return.* And Phin had thought, *You're growing sloppy to tell me that; it isn't information I need to have.* "You told him you had proof," he said slowly.

"No, I didn't." Her blue eyes were watching him steadily. "Of course I didn't. I thought *he* might be the traitor. It seemed wise not to mention it at all."

Her words plucked at his intuition, sounding a low, ominous note. If she was truthful, there was only one reason for Ridland to advertise her supposed knowledge: to draw the traitor to her.

Phin ran a hand over his face. Brilliant. Trust the bastard to have a card hidden up his sleeve. He was using her as bait, but in a very different fashion from what he'd given everyone to believe.

And me, he realized belatedly. This was a brutally efficient way of gauging *his* loyalty: If she remained alive, it proved his innocence. If she died, it damned him as Collins's man.

Phin eyed her. Rather crucial that she stay alive, then. "Have you a reason to suspect Ridland?"

If she noted the shift in tone, she showed no sign of it. "Only that he was also in Hong Kong. I met him at the club once."

He hadn't known this. It did not bode well. "When?"

"Just before you arrived."

He nodded. There was a deeper game in play here than he'd realized. "And how do you know of a traitor?"

She pressed her lips together as though to hold in the answer. But he had practice in waiting. It was a truth of human nature that nothing could prove as cruel as one's own fears; in an interrogation, a stony silence and the wild imaginings it allowed to proliferate often achieved more than a knife under the nails.

Wherever her imagination led her, it was not sunlit. Her expression darkened; she blew out a breath as though to push away her thoughts. "After you escaped, I had occasion to learn a good deal. Collins was . . . indiscreet in his anger." Her mouth twisted, and in the second she hesitated, he felt a dark curiosity bloom, taking root too rapidly for him to crush. Now it was in him; now it would only grow; now he wanted to know what had happened to her.

He felt a flicker of sourceless rage, with himself more than with her; this would only lead him further into it.

"Collins wasn't the one who poisoned you," she said. "Your two-faced confederate did. I suppose he thought you'd found him out. Collins didn't elaborate to me. Only that it was clear he had no idea you weren't American until afterward. And he was angry that his stooge hadn't told him about you, not to mention that he'd botched your murder."

He took a long breath. "Names?"

"I didn't get any. I was not in a position to ask such things." Her eyes briefly broke from his. Something in him tightened. A memory of her face flashed before him, the way she had looked leaning out the window, the thick scent of roses. Whatever position she had been in afterward, it had not been pleasant; the recollection was causing her to pale.

He spoke quickly, to pull her back to the present.

"Have you ever told anyone else of this? Your honesty is crucial, Miss Masters."

"No. Who would care but your government?"

The implications clarified fully now. He turned away from her, his hand on his mouth. The signet ring pressed, cold and smooth, against his lips.

He lowered his hand to study the ring. For the greater part of his adult life, he'd worn no jewelry, no bright colors, nothing notable enough to linger in the mind of anyone who glimpsed him. It still troubled him when Fretgoose produced any article distinctive enough to stand out in a crowd. But he'd grown unexpectedly accustomed to wearing this piece. It had not left his finger since the day he'd first been given it.

The recollection of his triumph that day, the giddy sense of unbounded possibility as he'd slipped it on, seemed suddenly as thin as the gold leaf gilding these walls. If Ridland was guilty and managed to find Collins first, the man would never make it back to London alive. After all, Ridland would not be able to rely on his discretion during the interrogation that would certainly greet Collins's return. But if Collins was captured by honest sorts—and there were more men on the case than Ridland could hope to control—he might reveal the name of his ally. If guilty, Ridland would therefore need to act preemptively. And by turning Miss Masters over to Phin, he had arranged his own alibi. If she died now, Ridland would say, *Do not believe what Collins says; believe the facts. I told Ashmore she had proof of a traitor. He killed her to protect himself.*

In fact, her death would be convenient to Ridland in

more ways than one. It would give him an opportunity to destroy the man who'd had the bad taste to balk at becoming his protégé and now made a hobby of undermining his power.

He turned back, and caught Miss Masters chafing her thumbs across her palms. Another honest gesture: that made for two, in less than a minute.

Too late, she noticed his attention. Her hands relaxed, and she produced a smile. Her mask was well constructed, her weapons more than sufficient for drawing-room games. But not for this. In this game, she was the most vulnerable pawn on the board. And he rather thought now, when he turned his whole mind to it, that she was telling the truth. She was innocent of deliberate involvement, which meant he had mistreated her terribly. In fact, as he reconsidered all their interludes with this new view of her in mind, he realized that it meant far more than that. It meant that she was sharp, and frighteningly clever, and foolishly brave, and rash to a bone-chilling degree.

"I owe you an apology," he said.

She arched her brow, clearly unimpressed by his tardy grasp of this fact. "Several, I believe."

He nodded. "Several, then." And then, because that dark flower had taken root in him and all its tendrils were unfurling toward her, he found himself asking, "Why did you save me in Hong Kong?"

She shrugged. "Because I knew you were after Collins. It had nothing to do with you, really."

No, of course it hadn't. He found himself wishing it had. She was, without doubt, against all odds, quite obviously and all of a sudden, the most unlikely and extraordinary woman he'd ever met.

He smiled at her. She looked startled, and he felt his smile widen. How goddamned relieving to know he was not so perverse as he'd feared. His instincts had not sabotaged him. On the contrary, they had been drawn to her wisely, and so strongly that they had even managed, once or twice, to override his brain.

A wisp of hair had fallen across her cheek. He reached out to brush it away. The gesture had no conscious intent; he told himself, belatedly, that sympathy motivated it. Her composure would have fooled most people, but he had some experience with subtle and habitual pretenses.

But as his fingers traced across the softness of her cheek, he decided he wouldn't lie to himself. He simply wanted to touch her. Now that he knew he was right to want it, there seemed no reason not to do so, as often as possible. He lowered his hand to brush a knuckle over the locket between her breasts.

The corner of her mouth twitched.

From another woman, it would mean nothing. From her, it was a flinch as marked as a full-bodied jump. And that small, telling movement startled his own thoughts into a new direction. She was not so immune to him as she seemed. His touch put a crack in her mask.

As the revelation unfolded through his brain, it twisted, taking on a predatory intensity that made his muscles tense. His senses seemed to be stretching and sharpening; the scent of lavender was thick around her, and he could hear the whisper of her hair against the wall. He told himself that the motive for what he intended to do was nothing more complicated than convenience: in the days to come, he would need her cooperation. If he explained to her that he needed to protect her in order to keep his own throat from being sliced in some back-alley execution of justice, she would hear it as an invitation to create havoc, knowing that for his own sake, he could neither send her away nor mistreat her. But if reason would not sway her to behave, there were other methods at his disposal. Such as what he was about to do.

He told himself this, but he didn't bother to believe it. She stirred something acquisitive in him, as antique maps used to do when he couldn't dream of affording them. She was healthier than opium or bullets, more pleasurable, marginally safer. He searched himself but could find no scruples, only a gratified surprise that something should finally, after months, appeal to him so strongly.

In some ways, it wasn't so bad to be his father's son.

He put a hand on the warm, soft curve of her hip. No petticoats. "You really have no idea," he murmured. "You have no notion of how thin your defenses are."

It took her less than a second to recover the thread of their earlier conversation. "It'll serve. Liberty uses only the very best fabrics."

Saucy beyond compare. He smoothed his hand up to her unbound breast. As his thumb found the slight peak of her nipple, her throat jerked. "Will it serve? For what purpose, do you think?"

Her nipple began to bead under his thumb. God above, she was sweet to the touch. Her sea-blue eyes met his with maddening composure. "For that too, I reckon."

He laughed. Even in Hong Kong, dazed by drugs and poison and addled by the need to escape, he had paused to goggle at her self-possession. It was not a quality often praised in a woman, but then, most men were idiots—himself included, until now.

The smile lingered on his lips as he stroked her nipple. He'd had no use for her four years ago, but he had a use for her now. And she knew what he was; his own mask had slipped in his study and she had seen him very clearly. She had no expectations for him to fulfill or to fail. The thought was an aphrodisiac in itself. Her nipple grew harder. "You seem to be enjoying this," he said.

She tilted her head back, exposing the long line of her pale throat. "So it seems."

"I take it that means you don't want me to stop."

"I haven't decided," she said breathily. "Let me consider it."

How quickly she made him feel disadvantaged, like some servant boy tasked to pleasure his mistress. "Decide quickly. My patience is running out." The words did not even sound like a lie to him. The softness beneath his hand, paired with the stubborn, taunting tilt of her chin, made him feel sympathetic to villains. He could become one, if that was what she wanted from him. He'd been one before. Maybe she liked a challenge.

She turned her head, pressing her cheek to the wall, and a sheaf of blond hair spilled across her shoulder, falling cool and soft over his wrist. "Yes," she said, and her body arched into his hand. "Perhaps," she revised in a murmur. "Only vary it a bit, and you might be as good as Hans."

Hans? He grabbed her chin and pulled her head around. "Look at me."

Her eyes opened, deceptively innocent, wide as a babe's.

"I am not one of your damned lovers."

"No-o-o," she said thoughtfully. "Not by my preference, at any rate. Generally, I demand a bit more skill in the approach."

Five minutes ago, her taunt might have infuriated him. Now it only seemed like a very good opening. "Here's skill," he said, and laid his mouth to hers.

Her lips were a revelation of another kind. They parted beneath his, and her tongue flicked out like a challenge, daring his to chase it back into the sweet, wet space behind her teeth. She still thought this was a fight, but she was hardly chastened; if anything, he was the one who was humbled. Her mouth tasted cool and fresh, like summer ices in a hot climate. It was beyond all expectation, now that he could permit himself to like it; he licked her for more of the taste. She kissed as cleverly as she retorted.

It came to him, suddenly, that she knew this. She counted on running the board. It was what enabled her to look on him so composedly.

Not this time. He was going to seize the lead.

He pressed forward, pushing her into the wall, angling his head to go deeper. Her breast beneath his palm was a hot, heavy weight, the hammering of her heart proof of the vulnerability she tried to deny. A slippered foot pressed onto his boot; her breasts pushed out of his hand, up into his chest, mocking his attempt at jurisdiction. Holding her was like grappling with a current of electricity, and the hot sensation that streaked through him left him unbalanced. He was harder than a goddamned fire iron, his balls tight and heavy, all her softness begging to be fucked. Nails sank sharply into his arse. *You are being outmatched*, his wits whispered, and he hardly minded at all. She awed him.

The kiss had not started out with much promise. It was too full of design to speak to any part of her body other than her brain. She had seen it coming and had braced for it; he was trying to convince her of something, and no matter how pretty his eyes or clever his lips, kissing a woman into compliance ranked barely above beating her into agreement. Mina told herself she favored originality. She was not impressed.

But when he drew away for breath, his eyelashes fluttering against her forehead, she realized that his body was trembling beneath her hands. His broad shoulders, his muscled back, even the tight cheeks of his bum were shaking. She had turned the kiss around on him. Now he stood in *her* grip.

The thought was like the soft stroke of a finger between her legs. Her breath went from her. *I have you.* She pulled his head back and kissed him softly, licking the salt from his mouth. If a debt would not compel him to cooperate, seduction would do; she had already resolved on it, and this could be a good test of his mettle. His lips clung to hers and his hand palmed her body, from breast to waist to hip and back again, as though to convince himself she was real.

She pushed at one of his shoulders, nudging him around. It was possible that he didn't realize her intention; he did not resist her, and after another push, *his* back was against the wall. The mighty lord of the manor submitted to her as eagerly as a puppy, his hands reaching after her when she pulled back to look him up and down. Muscular, rangy, broad-shouldered, utterly defeated; she wanted to laugh, oh the poor man, she wanted to kiss his brow and pat his cheek. She grabbed his face and kissed his mouth again; all the penny dreadfuls were suddenly making sense to her. She could see why there might be a piquant pleasure in a trembling, unwilling response. Of course he would help her—he'd have no choice, caught up in his need. His hands slid to her bum, tightening against his good sense. In a minute he would regret this very much, and she would adore soothing him for it, *Don't fret*, *it's all right*, but she had him under her thumb right now, and he would never forget the experience.

"Wait," he said into her mouth.

"No," she whispered. And he listened to her. His hand tightened in her hair, and his tongue returned to hers. She said into his mouth, "Touch me," and felt a triumphant thrill as his hand slid between her legs, pressing lightly through the silk. She had been touched there before, but never compliantly, and it made all the difference; it made her feel powerful, an Aphrodite. She abandoned his mouth for his neck, biting him over the Adam's apple. Beneath her fingers, his biceps flexed, and his throat worked on a guttural noise. *Yes.* She bit again, sucking lightly. This time he remained silent, so she lightly blew on the dampened patch of skin. *There.* He did it again. And his fingers, below, pushed harder, setting up a rhythm that made her knees go weak, that made hunger uproot itself and migrate downward, from her breasts and her belly to the spot between her legs.

It was time to laugh at him again, but when she reached for her humor, all she found was the urge to rock against his palm. He was so splendidly muscled, his thighs like granite; how far could she challenge him, what would it take to make him toss her away and call her names? Henry had been easy that way; he'd never managed to surprise her. He had served his purpose, but he'd never given her a moment's surprise. This man might.

The thought slapped her sober. Yes, indeed, this man might give her a *whole* lot of trouble. Was she doing this from necessity, or because his hand on her mound made her go soft in the head? Pleasure was one thing, but she mustn't lose herself in it.

She yanked away. Their eyes locked, the sounds of their labored breathing twining in the air too intimately, now, for her liking. She forced herself to stare, to wait with a bold show of composure until she saw what he would do.

He pushed the back of his hand across his mouth. "Have you remembered morals, then? How disappointing."

The mild reaction so surprised her that it took a moment to register the absurdity of the question. *Morals?* He had been the one to kiss *her.* And anyway, when she was asked to submit idly to imprisonment while the search for her mother might rest in the hands of a traitor, how did morals factor in? She was between a rock and a hard place, so when he handed her dynamite, she struck a match. "Do I need to remember them?"

His eyes traveled down her, and the corner of his mouth quirked. "Good God, no."

But when he reached for her, she skipped backward. It was one thing to explore her options; it was quite another to let him dictate options to her. "Is this what it takes for you to let me out of my rooms?"

He grimaced and shoved off the wall. "No," he said curtly. As he walked past her, she turned to follow his progress. Most of his countrymen favored a stiff-legged, chest-pouting stride, but Phineas Granville was all slink and prowl, as if his muscles had reached some special accord that other men's had not, excusing him from the limitations of gravity and tight tailoring. Like a giant cat, she thought—and about as disagreeable as one, too. Still, her hands itched to reach out and touch his thighs, simply to learn how the muscles there moved as he walked. It was not her lurid imagination; his bum really did flex with every step he took. Thank God for his tailor! The man had an art for showcasing beauty.

I really am *shameless*, she thought, marveling at how hot she felt. This was how it was meant to be, perhaps. Not mechanical, but fluid with yearning, almost boneless.

The thought gave her pause. Boneless, yes. That was where all the trouble began: when one started wanting to bend and flex to accommodate a man. No doubt Ashmore would demand a great deal of accommodation; she already knew he was that sort. Most men were. *Any rules I please.* This would be a risky undertaking, if she went through with it.

He picked up a discarded teacup. The sip he took did not please him; he grimaced and set the cup down. The glance he threw over his shoulder was opaque. He no longer seemed angry, but a muscle still ticked in his square jaw. "We must reach an accord," he said.

This was encouraging. Before, the only accord he'd considered had been distinctly one-sided. "So we should," she said. She reached behind her head to gather her hair, which was tangled from their tussle; as she smoothed it over her shoulder, his attention followed the motion of her hands. He liked her hair; he had turned his face into it earlier, and the sensation of his breath on her scalp had been her first reminder that something lived between them that she couldn't fully control. "Of course, there would be no need to speak of accords if you would only agree to look for my mother. Then I should be as prim and agreeable as a schoolgirl."

He snorted. "I'd like to see that."

She tossed the twisted coil back over her shoulder. "I can behave very well when I have reason for it."

He sat—no, draped himself in a chair, his long legs sprawling out before him, one ankle hooking atop the other. Another promising sign—he would not have sat so comfortably in her presence an hour ago. "I'm flattered that you think so highly of my capabilities, but half the government is looking for your mother at present. And no," he continued, forestalling her protest, "not all of them answer to Ridland. In fact, you may rest assured that one or two of them are probably more honest than your mangy cat's namesake."

She sighed. Comparisons to that beast could not

comfort her. Besides, no matter their honesty, all of the men looking for Collins lacked the most important piece of information. And it was time to share that information, she supposed. She had tested Ashmore in every way possible today: she had insulted his guests, mocked his discipline, and kissed him with all the hot ingenuity she possessed. In reply, he had neither struck her nor forced himself on her. He hadn't even tried to strangle her again. What a glowing résumé, she thought dryly. Clearly, he was a knight in shining armor.

But caution checked her impulse. If seduction was to be part of it, there were still things she needed to know. "Tell me something. Do you think I'm to blame for that kiss?"

Most men stiffened when wary. Ashmore, it seemed, relaxed. He reached inside his coat to produce a pocket watch. Oh, very casual, that glance he gave the time. As he replaced the timepiece, he said, "Why does that matter?"

"I didn't mean to be philosophical." She saw in his little smile that he recognized his own line. "It only requires a simple answer: yes or no."

"And I didn't mean to avoid replying," he said. "I was simply curious about why you care."

"You won't answer, then?"

"No," he said.

His cool tone confused her. "No, you will not answer it?"

His eyes met hers. "No, the kiss was my doing. Amazingly, not every move on the board is yours. Are you asking for another one?"

She hesitated. It went against expectation that he

would claim responsibility, but his mention of games seemed unpromising. Henry had tried to control her with lovemaking. He'd seemed perfectly reasonable in all their private dealings until she had invited him into her bed. And then, overnight almost, he had developed expectations that baffled her, as though by giving him her virginity, she had contracted to shoulder all his faults and honor all his whims as well. "You called me shameless," she reminded him.

"And you promised you could be more so." He smiled. "Do let me know if you decide on a demonstration."

You decide—that was a phrase she liked very much. More hopefully, she said, "But the kiss is your fault. We agree on that."

"Oh, you incited me, no doubt." His lifted brow lent the words an ironic edge. "But it was my doing, and I will apologize for it, if that's what you're after." He shrugged. "If you bring out the worst in a man, that doesn't mean you're to blame for his sin."

She frowned. He counted a mere kiss as sinful? He was a man either of peculiar honor or of perversely monkish persuasions. The latter might explain his disinterest in Hong Kong, but she was not sure what to feel at the prospect—annoyance made no sense, and embarrassment seemed entirely too clumsy and unsophisticated. She had no cause for shame, nor for this creeping temptation to feel inadequate. "You certainly enjoyed it," she said sharply. "I know that much."

His dark eyes pinned her. "Yes. So I did. How delightful that you noticed. Are there any more questions you'd like to ask? Perhaps we can discuss how hard my cock was, or whether your nipples are pink or brown. Pink, I'm thinking, but you should feel free to educate me if I'm wrong."

She opened her mouth, but nothing came out. Her skin prickled hot and cold. Oh, bother! She would not let him shock her. He sat there so arrogantly, twitting her with practically the same breath he'd used to offer his apology—but only if she *wanted* one. "You have a filthy mouth," she said. "I remember *that* from Hong Kong."

He laughed. "Do I? Tell me, Miss Masters, how did my filthy mouth taste? If I recall, I was not the only one who enjoyed the kiss."

"I enjoyed it very much when I had you shaking like a baby," she retorted—and immediately, instinctively recognized it for a mistake. Playing with trouble was one thing, but she had just purchased it wholesale.

He did not reply. He did not need to. The frankness of the look he gave her, and the smile that toyed with the corners of his mouth, made her go red. "I think you will regret that remark," he said softly. "Your thoughts?"

She feared she agreed. Still, no use giving him further satisfaction. She mustered a snort that sounded passably brash. "Behold me all a-tremble. And you're right, they are pink. But I don't think I'll prove it to you."

His eyes dropped consideringly to her chest, then rose back to hers. "I fear I may insist," he said lazily.

She opened her mouth, but to her own astonishment, her wit failed her. Her own hot thoughts left no space in her brain for a reply.

She ripped her attention away to the wall. This tactic of seduction seemed the furthest thing from safe; if she could not rely on her own composure, she was giving away her most potent weapon. "All right," she said. He had routed her; she could not fathom it. But she had news that would distract them both. "I'll tell you the real secret, then." It was time. He had proved himself, albeit not in any way that she could feel comfortable with. "Here's why you're the best chance for finding my mother." She licked her lips and her stomach pitched, as though she were on a ship plunging over a great wave. When she looked back to him, he was sitting up a little, and his expression had sobered. Yes, this would amply distract them both.

On a breath, she said, "I know where Collins is."

Chapter Ten

The next day, just before noon, Mina found herself on the fast train out of Paddington Station, bound for Providence by way of Plymouth and Penzance. She had not even had to battle for the right to accompany Ashmore. "I can hardly ask you to stay behind when it concerns your mother," he'd told her with a shrug. He had even given her back her pistol, the comforting weight of which now rested in the reticule on her lap. Rarely in her life had a man delivered so fully on her hopes, and with so little apparent gain to himself. Never, in fact. It made her feel at once triumphant and gratified and also very . . . uneasy.

She sneaked a sideways glance at his profile. He lounged in the seat beside her, his long fingers holding a newspaper open. He looked far too unexcitable for a man who only yesterday had bluntly guessed the color of her nipples. She found herself flushing at the memory, and her eyes strayed to his lips.

His mouth curved. He knew she was looking.

She turned back to the window, her heart tripping.

Why encourage her? It suggested some new motive on his part that seemed necessary to know before she could chart her course. Did he not take this journey seriously? He had listened with all appearance of attention to her explanation. It was a single phrase in her mother's letter that had tipped her off: *I leave my welfare to Providence, and for my sake, I urge you to do the same, at the end.* The line was not remarkable per se, but coming from Mama, it was curious. Papa's mother had favored the saying greatly, and after he died, leaving them flat broke, it became her answer to almost any worry Mama put forward. Soon, Mama began to use it as a spiteful joke. "Providence never put money into anyone's pocket," she'd said. Still, Mina had not realized the significance of the line until her unlikely glance at Ridland's atlas. Quite near to Land's End in the south of England was a coastal village called Providence. *Providence, at the end.* Surely it could not be a coincidence?

Ashmore had made no strong objections, apart from asking her if she thought her mother was really that clever. She had not appreciated the question, and he'd immediately apologized. *Apologized!* The lecturing, bullying autocrat had apologized to her. And he had invited her down to dinner. And made very pleasant conversation, which put her in mind of his charm during those first weeks in Hong Kong.

His new manner seemed highly suspect.

She stole another glance at him. He really could benefit from one of her hair tonics. Perhaps the disorder of his dark hair accounted for the looks he was receiving from the matron across the way. Or maybe the lady was drawn to stare out of curiosity. He had a cravat tied about his neck, and it made a pleasing contrast against his browned skin, calling attention to that cleft in his chin, which any lady (even a tightly buttoned matron with a sneer on her lips) might want to touch, just to see if it could be as deep as it looked. But the stock cloth was also dreadfully old-fashioned. Mina might have shared the reason for his sartorial regression to the 1870s, but she doubted the matron would approve. He had chosen the necktie to hide the bite marks on his throat; she had no doubt of it. By the time he'd walked her back to her room yesterday afternoon, they had been purpling.

She rather liked the idea that he wore the marks of her teeth. He was tall and well built; for all his leanness, he filled the upholstered seat completely. His long, broad-shouldered presence made the compartment feel smaller, despite how gracefully he inhabited it. Probably everyone who encountered him felt a little less substantial by comparison. This would have irked her, normally. But she had bruised him, this man who topped her by a head and had held her down so easily that she doubted his muscles had remarked the effort. Yes, she liked that. If she had the chance, she would bite him again, harder this time, somewhere he wouldn't be able to hide it.

Her thoughts gave her pause. They put her in mind of her wayward temptations in Hong Kong. Biting him was not a very utilitarian plan of action, was it? Frustrated, she opened her fashion magazine. But it could not hold her interest; for all their proximity to Paris, English couturiers seemed wholly uninspired.

Bored, she looked around the compartment. The

other passengers—the matron and her newly bearded son, and the sober red-haired gentleman with the great mole on his chin, who shrank to the wall every time the matron cleared her throat—studiously avoided her eyes. As they had settled into their seats, Ashmore had leaned over to speak into her ear. "I tried to give a coin to the guard for our privacy," he'd told her, "but it seems there's no help for it; first class is fully booked today." She had gathered from his tone that he was apologizing, as if a train journey were not made livelier by company. The silence of the other passengers confirmed his philosophy: none of them even bothered to introduce themselves. The point, it seemed, was to ignore one another entirely.

Out the window, the dirty houses had given way to sunlit fields, a patchwork blanket sewn by a drunken hand, irregular plots of green and brown and yellow stitched together by zigzagging hedges. Mama's voice murmured through her mind: *When the horns sounded, nothing could stop us; I jumped every hedgerow without fear.*

It was easier to think of Mama now that the distance between them was closing; her throat no longer ached at every recollection. She felt certain they would not arrive too late. Mama's courage was subtle, but Hong Kong had proved her powers of endurance. And Ashmore had said that they would reach Plymouth before seven o'clock this evening, and by noon tomorrow they would be in Providence. She'd felt such gratitude to him when he told her that. He might not trust her, but he was taking her seriously. Why, he'd compared her to a knife. Even in the carriage coming from Whitechapel, he had been wary of her. His insight had seemed an inconvenience then, but now it made her feel almost warm toward him. He was right—she was not inconsequential, and he was smart to be cautious with her.

She was going to bite him again, very hard.

An instinct made her look away from the window. The young man on the opposite bench quickly dropped his eyes. His dull blond hair was greased so thickly that it was a wonder it hadn't slid off his scalp, and the creases in his trousers were sharp enough to cut glass. Did boys of sixteen not roughhouse here? Were all youthful spirits trammeled by this stultifying society? When he peeked up again, she gave him an encouraging smile. It misfired. He flushed and swallowed and directed a mortified glower at his knees.

Oh, this was silly; she would not sit three feet away from these people and pretend they were not there. She held up the magazine. "I never thought I would say it, but I much prefer *Godey's Lady's Book*."

Phin sighed into the newspaper. He'd been braced for some mischief for the last half hour, and he could not blame the boy for inciting it with sultry stares. Miss Masters had promised to dress inconspicuously for the journey, but she had failed. Her dress was high-necked, long-sleeved, and, thank God, corseted, but its red and white pinstripes also charted with dizzying precision the pronounced peak of her bust. It still might have served, had she managed to occupy her seat unnoticeably. But in spite of her petite size, Miss Masters overflowed. First her skirts encroached over his shoe. Then her elbow came up against his along the armrest separating their seats. Her every fidget gave him a sweet little nuzzle, and God almighty, did she fidget.

At least she was wearing petticoats today. He knew this because they rustled constantly, the noise evoking scarlet taffeta, black ribbons, garters and silk stockings, smooth white thighs, and everything between them. Also nipples. Pink nipples. What demon had bid him request that information, he would never know, but in the many long hours since he'd acquired it, his brain had been reminding him of it regularly. Pink, fragrant, busty, rustling—the wriggling Miss Masters was the stuff of adolescent fantasy, and the more she squirmed, the younger and more scatterbrained Phin felt. Later, he felt sure, all this would amuse him, but he had no desire to embarrass himself in a train. Meanwhile, with every brush of her elbow against his, his mind insisted more strongly that the contact was deliberate. She kissed like the devil's minion; torture would naturally find a place in her repertoire. And if she was driving a grown man mad, what chance had a boy?

The boy had his mother, that was what. The matron gave a loud sniff, and redirected Miss Masters's remark to herself. "I do not know the magazine."

With the easy cheer of the tone-deaf, Miss Masters mistook this rebuff for interest. "Oh, it's American," she said. "I am American, you see."

The boy bounced in his seat. "I knew it from the get-go!"

Silence, and a dark look from his mother, put a stark

period to his triumph. Slowly he subsided into the up-holstery.

But Miss Masters could not let the mute remon-strance stand. She had a very bad habit of speaking to people who didn't concern her; for instance, chamber-maids. This morning, when Phin had passed the scrawny blond maid in the hall, he had asked her, with some puzzlement, if she smelled gardenias. The girl's blanch had told him everything. Miss Masters was not content with threatening to hire away his staff, oh, no. First, she would *perfume* it. He had surprised himself by wanting to laugh.

Miss Masters's voice broke into his thoughts. "I must say, it's quite instructive to compare our respective rail-road systems." It was unclear for whom, among her in-voluntary audience, she intended this observation. "For example, why can't you check your baggage before you travel here? In America, after you book your ticket, a baggage wagon comes to your home, and they take all your luggage in exchange for a little brass tag—"

Phin cut in. "Yes. You mentioned this at the station." In great detail. He'd suspected that she was trying to test his patience, although her motive seemed obscure.

She gave him a wounded look. Whether it was genuine, or whether she defaulted to featherbrain when in public, was something else he hadn't figured out yet. "Well, I am telling *these* people. Perhaps they don't know of Ameri-can improvements. And if you don't know that a better system exists, how on earth can you agitate for it?"

Her endorsement of agitation appeared to alarm two-thirds of the opposite bench. The ginger-haired man craned fully from the waist toward the window, taking great interest in a passing cornfield. The matron glowered. The lad, meanwhile, gazed at her in a steamy, open-mouthed trance.

Phin refolded his newspaper and rose to replace it in the satchel on the rack above his seat. "Miss Masters. Will you step outside for a moment? I wish to show you a most interesting feature, thoroughly unique to the English railway."

They emerged into the narrow aisle that ran alongside the compartments; she clutched at the wall for balance and said something about superior American railway tracks. "This line is a twelve-gauge," Phin said with a frown. "Matches anything in the States." And then, catching himself, waved away her reply. "What I meant to say is that this journey will go better if you refrain from drawing attention to us."

The train was passing through a wooded area, and the dappled light danced over her throat, the shadows of leaves slipping suggestively downward toward her décolletage. "Ah, let me guess," she said, as his eyes followed the shadows, whose indecorous progress he fully envied. "The unique feature of your railroad is *boredom*. I see no harm in conversation with our fellow passengers. Do you *really* not converse on trains here? I expect it's because you sit in these stuffy little compartments. In America, the carriages are open, and everyone—"

"In America, gold rains from the sky, no doubt." She seemed damned determined to convince herself of English failures; he wondered what that was about. "But you're in England now, and not for a pleasure tour."

She hesitated. "You worry that Collins's men are after us."

In fact, it wasn't Collins's men he worried about so much as Ridland's. But it made no difference. "A talkative American will be remembered." He paused. "Don't you think?"

His solicitation of her opinion appeared to gratify her. "Perhaps," she allowed, making a regal nod. A brief pause opened, and he became aware suddenly that the steady thump of the wheels over the ties in the line registered in her flesh. *Thump* went the wheels, and her body gave a perceptible jolt. Her flesh quaked at regular intervals. It had never occurred to him that the smaller and lighter a body, the more tiring life must be.

She was studying him, a little frown on her face. She'd been frowning at him a great deal in the last day; clearly, she was more comfortable with antagonism. Or maybe nature endowed small creatures with special instincts for self-preservation, alerting them to suspect intentions even when their larger counterparts had yet to show their hand. His weight lent him a balance that made the train's passage unremarkable, but she clutched the wall for a reason, to hold herself on her feet. He planned on knocking her off them at the next opportunity. It had been a long time coming, four years and five months, to be exact. His cheerful anticipation was difficult to hide. "You have an objection?" he asked.

"No," she said. "Only, if there are men after us, we wouldn't be able to spot them at sight, would we? Drawing a man out is a good way to take his measure."

"Dear God." He swallowed a laugh. "Never say you're

claiming that *Godey's Lady's Book* is part of your strategy to safeguard us?"

As she smiled, it struck him that there was no need to hide his humor from her; even when wary, she seemed willing to encourage good fun. "You won't believe me if I do," she said. "And that is precisely why it's such an effective tactic. No one ever suspects it!"

His hypothesis intrigued him. One more crack in her mask, perhaps. He decided to test it. "Oh, certainly," he said. "Because conversations about fashion magazines so often segue into confessions of villainous intent."

Sure enough, she overlooked his sarcasm and laughed back. "You must admit, it's a much subtler method than pulling out a gun."

What a bizarre and charming tic. She encouraged his amusement, even if it came at her own expense. "Perhaps you should just skip right to the heart of the matter, then. Leave the magazines and bring along a dress. Whip it out and canvass for opinions."

Her face lit like a chandelier; the effect was so pronounced that he actually felt his heart skip. "Yes," she said. "The uglier the better. Something puce, or . . . magenta and orange."

Over her head, he noticed the guard lurking a few meters away. Wonderful; he told her not to draw attention, and then he lingered in the corridor with her to trade jests. He could not feel optimistic about how effortlessly she addled his wits; it had tripped him up in Hong Kong, and it could well do so now. The stakes were no lower for either of them. "All right, enough fun. My request is very simple. Go back inside, sit down, and keep silent.

I, and the rest of the compartment, I daresay, will thank you."

He felt a stir of regret as her face went blank. "Of course you will," she muttered.

He pulled open the door to the compartment. The ginger-haired man who'd been sitting opposite Miss Masters now stood at the entrance, rooting through a bag placed on the luggage rack overhead. Coincidentally, this position put his ear very near the door. The matron, who did not strike Phin as amenable by nature, had taken the man's former seat by the window. Phin eyed the fellow as he stepped aside to permit Miss Masters's passage. The man's jacket pulled beneath the arms; the bearer of a first-class ticket should be able to afford better tailoring. The shoes were a fine make, but they were worn thin at the soles.

Sloppy not to have noticed these things before. Phin would have blamed his distraction on the lure of flirtatious elbows, but the prospect was so absurd that he felt his self-regard slip several notches merely in the contemplation of it.

Miss Masters had also remarked the possible significance of the man's actions. As she resumed her seat, she gave Phin a charged look, then glanced onward to the man. *No*, Phin urged her silently. *Don't look, don't remark—*

"Oh," she said brightly to the matron, "did you decide to sit across from me? What fun. Did you want to see my magazine?"

"No," the woman said curtly. "It was not *my* idea to switch seats."

All right, that was cleverly done. Alas, Miss Masters felt the urge to advertise her triumph, humming a pointed bar of "Yankee Doodle Dandy" as she settled back with her fashion magazine.

Phin took his satchel and newspaper from the rack and sat down, snapping the paper back open with a pointedness that he hoped Miss Masters noticed. Their valises were in the luggage compartment and would have to be sacrificed, but that was all right; his gun was in the satchel.

"Such a fine day out," Miss Masters said. "Isn't it a shame we're cooped up inside?"

She simply couldn't let him take the lead. No doubt her successes in New York gave her cause to trust her own initiative. He remembered her mother, who had seemed to limp so obediently in Collins's shadow, and wondered whether she was even aware that between these two extremes, other options existed, such as, perhaps, *cooperation*. "Travel can be tedious," he said mildly, and scanned the columns for likely words. When he had found what he needed, he said, "Are you bored? Allow me to amuse you; have a look at this."

She craned over as he pointed slowly to various words: . . . *depart* . . . *without* . . . *announcement* . . .

"Oh, that is very interesting," she agreed. "When do you think it will happen?"

"Very soon, if the prime minister has his way." The train began to shudder; they were braking in preparation for the next station. "At any moment, really."

She smiled. "Well, I can't claim to acknowledge a foreign power. But in this case, I wouldn't argue with him. His judgment seems sound."

She was bloody clever. He wanted to pinch her cheek, an urge that startled him. "Glad to hear it," he said, and started to fold up the paper. But she caught his wrist.

"This story looks very interesting." Her gloved finger landed on *how*. "Have you heard anything about it?"

"It's one of those classic criminal scams," he improvised. "Very basic, really. The one man created the diversion, while the others ran off with the jewels. I expect the police will never find them."

The matron gave a loud sniff to communicate her distaste at such discussion.

"But how did the man who created the diversion escape? Or is he in custody?"

"No," he said. "I expect he's rather good at what he does."

"I see." As he folded the newspaper, she set her magazine on the floor, her hands folding very primly in her lap. But her lips fought a smile. "I had no idea, sir, that you had such intimate knowledge of criminal schemes. I find myself quite concerned by you."

He grinned openly now. There was something peculiarly delightful in this private conspiracy. "I am not the one who desires a dress striped in magenta and orange."

The train shrieked as the brakes fully met the wheels. Steam billowed up past the windows, casting the compartment in a dim light. She looked out the window, then back to him; as the smile fighting for her lips spread like sunrise, he felt something leap inside him. He should not be enjoying himself. Her, he could enjoy. But he had never enjoyed this sort of business. He would worry about that later.

"Shrivenham," called the porter. "All out for Shrivenham."

"A moment," he said to her, and came to his feet, as if to step into the corridor.

The man visibly started. He made to rise, then glanced at Miss Masters's still-seated form and subsided. It was all Phin needed to see. Turning back, he faked a stumble into the man's lap—his elbow angled to deliver a nicely aimed punch.

The man wheezed and curled over. Skirts brushed past Phin's trousers, trailing the scent of lavender; a quick sidelong glance confirmed that Miss Masters was disappearing down the corridor.

"Heavens above," the matron murmured.

"I'm so, so sorry," Phin said. "My goodness, are you all right?"

The man was wheezing. "I'm—to hell with you."

The matron gasped. But she was in for a worse shock—if the fellow could talk, the job wasn't done. Phin clapped a hand to the man's shoulder as though to apologize, squeezing hard. He had not rehearsed in some months; he felt a muscle pull in his arm as he clamped down, and for a brief second, to his own shock, he feared he wouldn't manage it.

The man flushed an angry purple and flopped forward from the waist.

"Dear God," Phin said, and sprang backward. "He's out cold. Let me call for the guard."

In a bad piece of luck, the guard had already heard the ruckus. He came rushing into the compartment; Phin sidestepped him, picked up his satchel, and walked quickly down the corridor, stepping off the train to Miss Masters's applause.

"Oh, lovely!" she cried. "I saw it all through the window."

He took her arm and led her at a quick pace off the platform and past the stationmaster's narrow strip of garden, alive in the breeze with bobbing blossoms of red and white. The sunny scene looked impossibly vivid, as though painted in primary colors by an artist who hadn't yet learned how to shade; it should trouble him, it really should, that he felt so goddamned alive. Was he never going to learn subtler pleasures?

Miss Masters seemed to feel it, too. She wrested free of his hold, skipping ahead a little, then spinning back to face him. Her eyes were as blue as the sky behind her, her hair as bright as the sun; she was not a subtle pleasure herself. "You must teach me that trick," she said. "Pinching him until he passed out!"

Her enthusiasm acted like an antidote; he felt his elation contracting. She would admire a circus freak show, too, if the contortions were strange enough. "Do it wrong and you will kill someone." He had learned that firsthand. He still remembered the small noise the man had made as he died. Not a victim to be mourned righteously; the man had traded primarily in flesh. But someone had wept for him, no doubt. Almost always, someone did.

I wept for him. His tears had baffled him at the time. For his own sake, knowing such mistakes were likely to happen again, he'd not been able to admit that he'd also been weeping for himself.

Beyond the booking office, the country lane lay deserted, dappled with light beneath the limbs of overhanging oaks. The air smelled of wild roses, honeysuckle, and hay, and a nightingale sang sweetly from some branch nearby. Miss Masters, undeterred by the possibility of murder, said, "Perhaps I would like to know how to kill someone."

Had she not spoken so calmly, he might have said something cutting. But her manner made him look before he spoke, and he saw in her expression some shadow that made him study her more closely. "Whom would you want to kill?"

The scream of the train whistle startled a cloud of birds from the trees. "No one in particular," she said. "A category generally. And perhaps I wouldn't actually do it, but to advertise my capability would be useful. Are we going somewhere? Why not wait for the next train?"

He consulted the map in his head. They could hire a vehicle in the village and cut to the Bristol-bound line. He took her wrist and started down the road. "That pinch can be unpredictable. If he hops off at the next station and backtracks, we don't want to be waiting. No, we'll go by road for a bit and bypass Swindon entirely. What do you mean, a category?"

She sighed. "I knew I shouldn't have worn a corset. And a category, yes—men, mostly. Not all of them, of course. But men like Collins." She made a sound of amusement. "Men who lock me in rooms."

He cut her a sidelong glance. If she was slotting him into the same category as Collins, he had his work cut out for him. "How fortunate that I let you out, then."

"You didn't let me out," she said. "I slipped out, and then I gave you information that made you decide to let me stay out. It's the *letting* that I object to, you see."

"And I apologize for it," he said. "Again."

She gave him a smile. "Apologies come cheap, Ashmore. And we both have a great deal of money."

Yes, he thought with a sigh. The next opportunity to knock her off her feet might not be as close as he'd hoped.

Chapter Eleven

In Shrivenham, the only postchaise available for hire had windows that would not shut and springs that had long since come unsprung. Mina did not think highly of its prospects, but it managed to rattle along for five miles before the axle broke, leaving them stranded "jest around the corner from the Twin Elms," the glum driver assured them, "and if there bean't a cab there, I'll eat my hat."

The Twin Elms turned out to be aptly named, a white stucco structure flanked by two massive elms whose knotty roots bunched up from the earth like scrabbling fingers. In the whitewashed parlor off the entry hall, a half dozen gentlemen and a young lady were gathered around a three-legged table at the fireplace, eating beefsteak and tapping tankards.

The talk paused at their entrance, the gentlemen gawking at Mina. Then the young woman rose, wiping her hands on her apron as she came over. She turned out to be the innkeeper's daughter, a pretty, wide-faced girl whose rosy complexion made a pleasing contrast to her night-black hair. Mina liked her at once, simply for the fact that she sat among men, drinking and conversing so casually. It seemed Mama had something to learn about modern English girls.

Alas, the girl could not meet her eyes. After one wide-eyed survey of Mina's face and gown, she swallowed and addressed herself solely to Ashmore.

"Lawks," she said, after listening to Ashmore's cursory summary of their troubles. "Well, tomorrow's a different matter. But today, there's only one coach, and it be out at the Holladay wedding. I expect they're be making a parade of the pair through the neighboring parts at present. But"—she glanced briefly at Mina, and began to stammer—"b-b-bean't need to vex yourself. They'll be coming for their supper; we're cooking a terrible grand feast for them. And John Marsh, what's the driver, goes back by Swindon way afterward." As her eyes darted briefly back to Mina, she shifted uncomfortably and tucked a stray curl back behind her ear.

Your hair looks lovely, Mina wanted to tell her. *We are not in competition.* But experience suggested that such reassurances more often embarrassed their recipients than comforted them.

"Ain't much, to be sure," the girl muttered. "But it will see you where you're going."

"It sounds perfect," Mina said.

"Well." She looked now at the floor. "If you bide an hour, I'll have a nice plate for you."

Mina might have liked to relax by the bow window with a glass of wine; she felt she deserved it, after walking so far in the sun. But a washstand and a cold cloth across her brow also sounded appealing. Why not combine them? At her request, the girl blushed and scrambled off into the kitchen to fetch the wine, then showed them upstairs to the only chamber remaining. The wedding, she informed them, had drawn people all the way from Wiltshire.

"How far is that?" Mina asked, when they had stepped into the room and shut the door.

"All of five miles," Ashmore said with a small smile.

The room was spacious, scented by sprigs of rosemary tacked along the wall and kept fresh by the mild breeze flowing through the open casement windows. Grateful for the respite of a soft carpet beneath her road-wearied feet, Mina fell into a wide-elbowed chair while Ashmore prowled the perimeter. He looked into the garden with an expression generally reserved for the sight of invading armies. Perhaps he was disturbed by how wildly the apple and damson trees grew, not a straight line to be seen in the lot. "This is unfortunate," he said.

He put her in mind of Benedict né Washington, tail lashing and hair bristling. She wondered idly how Sally was getting on with the beast, God save her.

Her eyes drifted shut. The rosemary was an honest scent, conjuring comfort and health rather than luxury. How unjust that such lovely herbs would favor this dreary climate. Beside the inn door, she'd spied a hedge of lavender growing as bushy and wild as a weed; her contract with Whyllson's was no longer looking as advantageous as she'd fancied. If she were only willing to spend a few months here a year, she could set up a lavender plantation and save the company a great deal of money. "Three hours," she said. "It's not so long to wait."

Springs creaked; opening one eye, she saw that he'd sat on the bed. It was too low for him; he had to straighten his legs entirely, lest his knees fall agape. "You misunderstand," he said. "Swindon is where he'll expect us to go. Until we find a vehicle that can take us farther, we stay put."

"Here?"

"Yes. For the night, at least."

"The night?" She sat up. The room seemed smaller, of a sudden. A bracing sip of wine did not change her view. That bed was far too small for the both of them, unless they planned to share more than the pillows. Her body stirred at the thought, and she found herself staring at his cravat. *Take it off*, she almost said. She wanted to see the damage she'd wrought.

He bounced a little, making the bed creak again. There was a boyish quality to his smile that made her brows lift. He should really consult his intentions. He had accused her of goading him, but he seemed no less guilty of the charge.

She closed her eyes, because to remark on his unspoken taunt might force a decision she was not yet ready to make. It was still new and interesting to her, this idea that her virtue no longer constrained her. Jane had not approved of her decision to sleep with Henry, and the mass of literature Mina had compiled during her considerations—essays by suffragists, pamphlets by a group espousing "free love" and the "New Woman" ideal, some medical tracts on contraceptives (Henry had balked at the use of rubbers, but she had insisted, knowing very well that his hopes were devious, his goal matrimonial)—

had not persuaded Jane. "It's a sacred gift," she'd said, "and a terrible sin to give it out of wedlock. What if you decide to marry later?"

Sin and sacredness were not concepts that spoke very strongly to Mina. Divorce was a sin, too, and as a result, her mother currently languished in the grip of a criminal who, in the eyes of the law, had no right to freedom, but every right in the world to share her bed and abuse her until he was caught. (*Damn sin*, she thought, and smiled at the conundrum.) Ultimately, Jane's advice had tipped her decision, highlighting as it did the burden her virginity had become. So long as it existed, one could still say to her, with confidence and perhaps even a trace of smugness, *But what if you decide to marry, Mina?*

No, becoming a fallen woman suited her well. She'd designed to be seen exiting Henry's home at a very suspicious hour, and overnight everyone had ceased urging their bright young boys in her direction. The men who continued to approach her did so frankly, with no aim of permanent ownership. She felt free now.

But certainly, freedom was meant to be exercised. *The pleasures of the body are the greatest gift with which nature endowed us;* so the free-lovists wrote. Henry had not done much to substantiate their claims, but she did not believe him when he said it was *her* fault. She owed him nothing, and it infuriated him that she did not feel obligated.

At any rate, there was much to learn, and Ashmore seemed a convenient tutor; he was a man of the world, and surprisingly obedient in such matters. Their bodies reasoned together in a very comfortable way. A little experimentation, maybe, followed by the successful rescue of her mother, and then she would put an entire ocean between them. It would be a choice, for she was starting to believe he would not compel a seduction. But as far as risks went, it seemed mild.

"Well, I suppose we are here for the night, then," she said, and the confidence in her voice impressed her.

"You look almost happy about it."

He expected maidenly flutters, did he? "I am trying."

"I thought you were concerned for your mother."

She opened her eyes, stung. "You think I'm not worried?"

"I don't mean to accuse you." His surprise appeared genuine; she relaxed again. "But you don't seem impatient in the slightest. It makes a rather dramatic change from your attitude in London."

Impatience was a terrible temptation; she did not like that he even spoke the word, as it seemed to bring the feeling into the room. Impatience sank claws into a person's lungs, making it hard to breathe. "What good would it do to be impatient?" One did not dwell on what one could not change. She had learned how to wait in more terrible situations than this one. Action was all that mattered; when it proved impossible, needless contemplation became its own form of torture, as effective as screams, as darkness and heat and hunger. Oh, she did not want to think of these things. "It's useless," she said sharply.

"It keeps you sharp," he countered. But his manner suggested he was willing to reconsider. "We know we were followed from London. He will report back to his master on the vicinity of our last appearance. This doesn't seem the time to nap."

"But this is precisely the time to nap." She looked at him in bewilderment, for his words mismatched his manner; he did not seem particularly tense, lounging on the bed. "Better to be well rested if and when they find us, don't you think?" And why must she explain this to *him*, of all people? "A man of intrigue should know such things."

A peculiar expression worked its way over his face. It was not the first time she'd caught this look from him today, and it made her feel warm and unaccountably awkward in a way his lust did not. She was accustomed to leers, but not to being examined so thoughtfully and with such careful interest, as though she were a specimen in a scientist's lab. "What is it?" she asked. She sounded a little defensive, and breathed deeply to quell a blush.

The breeze through the open window stirred his long hair, framing his slight smile. "I think you might be better cut out for this line of work than I am."

The idea surprised a smile from her. She liked that he could picture her as an artist of escapes, flitting across the world to bring justice to thugs. Such things took skill, and a good deal of cunning. The compliment—for that was what it felt like, all the more because she doubted he'd intended it as such—moved her to generosity. "You seemed good enough at it in Hong Kong. You fooled us all completely. It was terribly clever." Until the night he'd been poisoned, she would have wagered every future cent of her profits that he was American.

He shrugged. "I didn't say I wasn't good at it. But I did not choose it, and I never enjoyed it."

Now, that was claptrap. When he'd leapt out of the

train at the station, his expression had been animated, and he'd laughed when she applauded him. She set her glass on the floor, trying to decipher this altered attitude. "Not even today? You didn't feel the tiniest thrill, jumping from the train?"

His hand was lying flat against the sheets; he turned it over to consider his empty palm. Even his fingers managed a graceful curve. When he had leapt from the train, it had looked like a step in a dance. Had *she* been a scientist, she might have studied him simply to educate herself on the human body's optimal operation.

"Today . . ." He drew a long breath. "Well, yes, I will admit to a degree of enjoyment."

And he did not feel comfortable with that; it was clear in the way his fingers curled suddenly, as though to call back the admission. Again, she thought of his peculiar gloss on their kiss, how he had framed it as a sin. Maybe it was some quirk of the English character that caused him to interrogate his pleasure. Her mother, too, suspected all forms of entertainment. If a gown was beautiful, she would balance her admiration by finding fault with the way it fit her. If Mina laughed too loudly, she would take her to task for rowdiness. Small things, but they added up, day in and day out, to a regime designed to crush the fun from life.

To what end, though? The world exacted harsh tolls with terrible frequency: fortunes collapsed; children suffered at their parents' hands; illness struck good men in their prime, taking them from the world as their wives and daughters prayed fruitlessly at their bedsides. And men inflicted cruelties for no reason at all, save the sheer gratification of exercising their power. With such perils abounding, why bother to punish oneself? Prepare for the worst, and pursue the fun: this was her philosophy, which she tried to demonstrate. But Mama could never agree, and sometimes Mina wondered if what had drawn her to Collins was the promise he offered of predictable pain. Perhaps his terrible discipline had granted her a perverse sort of freedom; assured of his punishments, she'd felt able to neglect punishing herself.

Against her will, Mina felt a pull of sympathy for Ashmore. He had locked her in a room, but at least her prison had possessed walls, and windows that could be broken. People like Mama—if he was indeed one of them—carried their prisons with them. They never managed to escape, no matter how hard others might try to set them free.

Well, there was no call for him to feel glum about his successes today. "You got us off the train," she said. "You kept him from following us. And that bit with the newspaper was monstrous clever! I think you should be proud of yourself."

He laughed, but it was a kind sound; he seemed pleased by the encouragement. "Do you?"

"Well, *I'm* proud of myself," she said with a smile. "Come, now, didn't you think my question to the matron dreadfully well done?"

"Oh, yes, you're a natural."

"And so are you," she said.

His mouth pulled, as if the praise tasted bitter. "I expect there are better things to be proud of."

The urge came to her to go sit on the bed and stroke his hair back from his face. The prospect obscurely pleased her; more and more she liked the idea that this contained, arrogant man, who'd treated her like so much flotsam in Hong Kong, might recognize that he had something to learn from her.

She retrieved her wine. "Pride and enjoyment are different matters entirely." Indeed, she thought, so often enjoyment came at the cost of one's pride. For instance, if she did sit next to him on the bed, if she stroked his cheek and offered her counsel, would he snap out of this reasonableness and mock her? She would feel foolish then, embarrassed and exposed, irritated with herself for speaking so honestly. What was it about his eyes that made her want to trust him, even after he had proved himself unpredictable?

Risks, she thought. This was one she did not need to take. She tipped the glass and drank to the dregs.

"Perhaps," he said slowly, almost to himself, "I enjoyed it because it had nothing to do with before. Because . . . it was for myself, after all. My own actions, my own decision."

A curious thought struck her, that he was doing something deliberate here—peeling himself back like an onion, to show her his layers. "Yes," she said hesitantly. "That sounds right." When she had played dumb for Collins, it had made her teeth ache with anger. But in New York, she had batted her lashes and twirled her hair for a dozen social-climbing investors, all of them willing to waste a bit of money on a society beauty's harebrained scheme because they hoped a connection to her would serve them. Each time, she had walked away feeling perfectly at peace with herself. "It makes all the difference, larger than night and day, really."

He nodded. "Of course, to act on one's own decisions requires a good deal of faith in oneself. For instance, I will admit that you were right the other day. I often wondered if you'd regretted saving me in Hong Kong." His eyes lifted, catching hers. "And what price did you pay for it? I also wondered that."

Her good humor evaporated. Suddenly the air seemed scant, and his regard too close, as if no space separated them at all. His questions had not been so idle or self-oriented, after all; he had ambushed her somehow, and as his steady regard held hers, it began to feel horribly intimate, as if she were skin to skin with him, utterly exposed. "If you'd really wanted to know, you could have found out long ago."

"Perhaps I didn't feel able to learn it," he said quietly. "Not then. Not when I could do nothing to help you."

Her fingers tightened around the empty cup. He spoke as if he were making a confession. But she would not absolve him. He knew nothing of his sins. He had taken care not to learn of them, and the cause for his willing ignorance did not interest her; it could make no difference to her opinion. "And now it's in the past." It lived in her dreams, and in the darkness she faced every night, but in all other regards, it was done. "So there's no use speaking of it."

"I think there is."

"Why?" She felt angry now, and did not bother to disguise it. "So you can assuage your guilt by showing some concern? Very tardily, I might add. So you can express your *sympathy*?"

He was watching her very carefully, as if she were some rabid dog. "Or my regrets."

"I have no use for your regrets." The sediment from the wine still lingered on her tongue, gritty as the feelings clogging her throat. She ran her tongue over her teeth and swallowed. "I did very well for myself, and for my mother, too. That's all you need to know."

"At least tell me this." He waited for her to look at him again. "Did it even out, in the end?"

She tossed away the tankard. It banged against the chest of drawers, and she held his eyes, not speaking, until the clatter died away. "Yes, until he escaped. Ask me in Providence tomorrow, and I hope my answer will not be different."

He rose, one long fluid movement, shucking his jacket onto the bed as he went. She astonished herself by shrinking back, afraid—*afraid!*—that he was coming for her, as if he could do anything to her to make her speak of that time; she would not say a word if he throttled her—but when he only continued past, she felt foolish and unsettled, all at once. The air stirred in his wake; she caught a faint note of bayberry, and perhaps the barest trace of his sweat. When she'd kissed him again, her body had relearned his scent; it had acquired, overnight, a taste for him. It clamored now for her to stand and put her nose to his throat so she might breathe him in more deeply. She bit down on her knuckle and twisted at the waist to track his progress.

He stood at the washstand, rolling up his shirtsleeves.

His forearms were thick and well muscled, dusted with dark hair; she remembered admiring the way they flexed when he was bound to a bed. She'd had him at her mercy then. He hadn't liked it at all.

He felt too comfortable with his hold over her, maybe. Telling her his secrets did not give him a right to hers. *I am going to seduce him*, she thought. The conviction surfaced on an inexplicable surge of anger. If he exercised some sort of thrall over her senses, then she would break it by indulging them. He had trembled beneath her hands as she laughed at him; he did not have all the advantages.

He took up a pitcher, splashing water into the washbasin. When he reached over to retrieve the cloth draped on a hook in the wall, his shirt pulled taut, the fine lawn delineating the tight line of his waist. He dipped the cloth into the water, then began to fold it in precise increments, squeezing as he went. What a fussbudget he was. She didn't doubt he had a system for putting on his socks.

"I didn't mean to upset you," he said quietly.

She stared at his back, so maddeningly broad and expressionless. *Coward*, she thought. *Turn around and face me.* "Don't pretend to care," she blurted. The words horrified her; she put a hand to her mouth, too late to stop them. Flushing hot, she added, "A week, and you will never see me again."

He did not deny this. "We'll have to work together until then."

She watched as he lifted his arm, neatly wiping down his broad wrists and long fingers. Steady, methodical strokes. She wondered whether he had plotted this conversation in advance, if what she had perceived as twists and turns were only another series of carefully manipulated folds. Did he think her as pliant as the rag? He would not find her so, if she put herself into his hands. "We're working together already," she said. "I helped you on the train."

The cloth dropped with a splatter. He turned, one hand resting on the edge of the marble countertop, his handsome face sober. "And that was when I realized that the coming days will require trust on both our parts." He ran a hand through his hair, and it crossed her mind to wonder why a man set on order would be content to let his hair grow so wildly. "Let me take the first step, then. I trust you might be right: Ridland may be the traitor." He gave her a strange smile, far too cheerful for the tidings it announced. "In which case, we are not only trying to save your mother's life, Miss Masters. We're also saving our own."

They took afternoon tea in the parlor downstairs, at a little table lodged beneath the bow window, oak leaves fluttering against the glass. As the barmaid was clearing away their dishes, a great ruckus sounded in the yard. A herd of children came running down the lane, their passage lent outsize presence by the cymbals they were ringing. Now came the stately progress of a young man in a morning suit and top hat and a girl in a monstrously over garnished white dress, with a garland of orange blossoms crowning her unbound brown hair.

"And there's the coach," Ashmore said dryly. It pulled into sight at a snail's pace. Four young rowdies sat atop it, and an unlikely number of arms and hands sprouted from the windows, all of them tossing rice in the newly-weds' direction.

The innkeeper's daughter rushed up to the next window, laughing at the sight. To Mina and Ashmore, she said, "We're shutting up to join the merriment on the green. Come along, and I'll find John Marsh for you."

"We've changed our minds about that," said Ashmore. "We'll be staying for the night after all."

"But we'll come," Mina added, rising. Ashmore's brow lifted, and she made a face. "I'm curious. My mother grew up in the countryside. She talked about it sometimes—the village green, the maypole in the spring. Besides, re-call what I said about impatience."

He shrugged and came to his feet, surprisingly ame-nable. She decided to reward him by taking his arm. His other brow rose to join the first, but he made no remark, letting her lead him out the door.

The parade wound down a lane that became a stately avenue flanked by lime trees. Neatly thatched cottages cropped up to left and right, the walls between them topped with bright hollyhocks and wallflowers. The vil-lage green lay next to a stone bridge that arched over a small river; a crowd was gathering on it, chattering and drinking.

They took a seat on one of the bales of hay scattered about the perimeter. Refreshments were being dished out from a table at the edge of the green. Mina saw the inn-keeper's daughter looking over at them; the girl caught a man by the elbow and nodded in their direction. He brought over two tankards, raking Mina with an appreciative look. "Help us celebrate," he said.

The ale was dark and thick. Mina made a face at its bitterness, and Ashmore laughed. "Prefer champagne, do you?"

"Normally, I—"

"—only drink champagne," he finished for her. They smiled at each other, and he added, "I do hope you're not anesthetizing your boredom."

A blush heated her face. "That was mean of me."

His smile widened. "I'd suspected it was meant to be. But you did a bang-up job of keeping me guessing."

She laughed. "Yes, I did, didn't I? And you lectured me for it." She dropped her voice, imitating his gruffness. " 'People will think you intemperate.' "

His lips slipped into a more thoughtful curve. "Oh, yes, I was a terrible bastard. But you'd started to become a distraction. I felt I had no choice."

"No, nor did I. Bonham," she added, when he looked a question. "He was very determined to marry me. I was desperate to dissuade him, or to find an equally promising suitor whom Collins wouldn't object to."

A comfortable silence fell between them. Most of the attendees were on their feet, and a great many children were running through the forest of legs, screaming and laughing and ripping off great handfuls of straw to throw at each other. The bride and groom occupied a rude bench at one edge of the lawn; well-wishers were forming a queue to greet them.

"Is your curiosity satisfied?"

She sighed. "Actually, I doubt Mama ever visited such an event as this. She's a great stickler for propriety." Her mother had all but resigned herself to Mina's wayward tendencies, but she would never be reconciled to them.

"Is America so different then? Can people behave without a care for their stations?"

She glanced at him. Apart from the wildness of his hair, one would never guess that he'd had such an interesting morning; his starched collar still stood at attention and his cuffs were properly pinned. It took some sort of talent to survive trains so immaculately; her own skirts were wrinkled beyond repair. But for all his apparent propriety, he sprawled casually across the bale, one hand propped behind him, his boot slung over his knee—not, she suspected, a pose he would ever employ in polite company. "Is it a question of how people behave?" she asked. "Or of how women behave? You seem perfectly comfortable here—but I suspect your countess would not."

He smiled a little, as if the idea of his marriage were inherently amusing. "She might, Miss Masters. But the trick would be to enter the scene in a very different style. Sweep in as Lady Bountiful, condescend to greet the happy couple, hand them some coin, then depart as quickly as possible."

"And you? What would you be doing during all this?"

The clouds were flirting with the sun, the light shifting rapidly across his face from a bright glare to a cool glow and back again. She could not tell if the shadow that fell across his expression was wrought by the light or by some dark thought of his own. "I suppose I will have to work on that. For so many years, the trick was to slip in without anyone taking notice. And now notice is precisely what I'm meant to demand."

"Because of an accident of birth," she said. "Yes, that's why I can't approve of this country."

"And is it really so different in New York? Money or breeding . . . or beauty," he added, with a brief nod to her. "What difference does it make?"

"Compliments," she said suspiciously. "Ashmore, did that man on the train give you a knock to the head?"

He laughed. "I'm not blind. Only reticent to tell you what you already know."

His frankness pleased her; he had managed to flatter her in a way that demanded no false modesty of her. If only others might learn this trick, her beauty might not be so tiring. Otherwise, she could not think of what pleasure it had ever afforded her. It drew attention from men whom she would rather have ignore her, and it put her at a disadvantage with anyone who complimented her, since in return they expected a show of humility or a simpering display of gratitude, both of which were hard to perform without feeling slightly diminished. "I thought about cutting it all off," she said.

He frowned. "Your hair?"

"Yes. But it wouldn't have served. New York isn't an encouraging place for the female entrepreneur. It isn't enough to have money; one must have allies. And a gentleman who would hesitate to associate himself with a mad bluestocking is more than willing to take on the role of mentor to some misguided, fluttering girl with more money than wits. Hair flutters quite effectively, you know."

"I think even if you were bald, you could still manage to flutter," he said dryly. "And wrap men around your finger as well. But it's fortunate that you think otherwise." He reached up and ran a finger over her hairline, from the crown of her head to her temple, lightly skimming down her jaw before dropping away. "I would miss it," he said softly.

Her pulse tripped and her mouth went dry. "Well." She cleared her throat. "At any rate, long hair. For the company."

"Ridland mentioned your company. A considerable accomplishment for a woman."

That made her sigh. "For *anyone*."

"Yes," he said. "But particularly for a woman."

"But this goes back to my point about England versus America. Money is more egalitarian by far. If it doesn't recognize breeding, it doesn't recognize sex, either. Cleverness is what matters."

"Cleverness," he mused. "Oh, I think you're more than clever, Mina. To accomplish what you have—it takes a real degree of genius."

They were only words. She tried to focus on their workaday nature, to fight down the monstrous flush they occasioned. "What is this? Admiration?"

"And if it is? I think you do deserve a good measure of it."

"Careful," she said. "You don't know me at all. Perhaps you're admiring the devil." She made a little grimacing smile as she said it.

But he did not take the invitation to lighten the mood. "I know enough, I think."

"I'm sure you think you do." They always thought they did. *Marry me*, Henry had told her, *and your worries will be over.* But what he mistook for worries were the reasons she rose in the morning. She did not blame him for it, not really. The world bred men to see a woman's work, female pride and ambition, as threats to their own.

"I know that you want your mother safe so badly that you risked your life in Whitechapel to find her." He paused. "I know that you sit here so calmly, waiting for a country wedding to finish, despite your fear."

She hesitated. These were not the reasons she had expected—indeed, she could think of no reason for such generosity. "Why are you speaking to me like this?"

He smiled a little. "Because I am selfish. I'm wondering what your secret is. I could find a use for it myself."

"You?" The exclamation sounded rude, and when he laughed, she could not even blame him.

"Yes, me." He picked up a piece of straw, sticking it into his mouth as he surveyed the green. "Simple pleasures," he mused. "The art of patience." He glanced at her. "The gift, perhaps, for happiness."

She pursed her mouth dismissively. But the silence that settled in lieu of her answer seemed fragile and charged all the same. It made her shift uneasily on the bale. She was not sure she wanted to share anything with him so complex as this silence. They were traveling to find her mother, and perhaps she would pleasure herself with him. That was all. And no doubt a good show of wantonness would put an end to his admiration. Sex and admiration did not walk hand in hand for very long, in her experience.

She turned her attention back to the bride and groom, who were circulating now through the crowd. "I will tell you the secret to happiness for a woman," she said. "Never risk yourself where you don't need to."

He followed her gaze. "You mean marriage?"

"Among other things."

"Never, then?"

She shrugged. It seemed to her that if she were ever going to take that risk, she would have done so in those early days in New York. She had received more than a few offers, and it would have solved all their financial problems. But the prospect had made her feel claustrophobic, as helpless as if she were still locked up in that room, listening to Mama's suffering. She had told herself she would not make the same mistake her mother had; she would not count on a man to play her savior. To do so would be tantamount to locking herself into another room, gambling her future on her hopes that the jailer would prove generous with his key.

"I don't think so," she said.

"Collins is a bastard," he said gently. "He isn't typical."

She smiled. "No, not typical." But there were lesser shades of him everywhere. "And you? I suppose you will have to marry, pass on the title." He gave a curt little laugh, and she rolled her eyes, saying hastily, "Of course you will. Silly question."

"No," he said, "I was simply thinking that, by your philosophy, I shouldn't." His hand had been lying flat on his knee; he turned it over now, unfastening his cuff link. For the first time, she noticed a raised, reddened patch of skin that ran from the base of his thumb down his wrist, disappearing under his sleeve. "From a hot stove and a short round of 'cry uncle,' " he said. "My father had a peculiar taste in humor, when drunk."

She caught her breath. His smile bespoke no need for sympathy; he looked rueful, and a little apologetic. "That is different," she managed.

"Is it?" He shrugged. "He was not so unlike Collins. Less deliberately malicious, no doubt. But he disappointed my mother no less than Collins did yours. The alcohol freed some demon within him. I will confess, I have felt it stir in me at times."

"No," she said. "You would do nothing like that. And of *course* it's different. You were a child!"

"And so were you, when she wed Collins," he said. "She had poor taste. You don't." He bent his head, refastening his cuff. She watched his brown fingers moving with such easy economy, and she wanted to touch his hand.

When he glanced up, he smiled again, as though startled to find her watching. "It's all right," he said, and lifted a brow. "I never did cry uncle, by the way."

Nor did I, she thought. But she would not say it. She put her hand beneath her skirts, her heart suddenly pounding for no good reason, only that it seemed clear— thoroughly, irrationally clear—that if she touched him right now, their flesh would recognize each other. The wildest thought: these scars, his and hers, would speak to each other, communicating intimacies that could not be unshared.

Her fingers clawed into the scratchy surface of the hay. She wanted to touch him, simply for this: how casually he'd spoken of his suffering, and also how casually he dismissed it, returning to his ale as though he'd never mentioned it. He did not let the scar bother him. Why should he? It had healed into proof of his triumph. She had tried to feel the same, but Henry had never understood it. *Your beautiful skin*, he had whispered, his fingertips jerking away as if he could not even bear to touch them, those few little marks. She had told herself she should be reassured by his squeamishness; a man who balked at scars would not give her new ones.

Now she suddenly wondered if she'd had it wrong. A man without scars would always underestimate their value. He would not see them as marks of courage. What reassurance, then, that he would not also mistake them for fit forms of punishment?

"You're very quiet," Ashmore said. He gave her a smile, deliberately transparent in its attempt to lighten her mood, to encourage her to ignore what he'd revealed, if she preferred to do so.

She did not smile in return. All at once, it felt wrong to smile at him unless she meant it. He was helping her, and she felt that maybe she was finished now with her anger toward him.

He frowned a little. He was going to apologize for his honesty, she saw, which would be unbearable. She spoke quickly to forestall it. "So, yes, Ashmore, I highly recommend you marry." She gave him a bright smile. "But do be kind to us poor spinsters."

He tilted his head. For a second she thought he would push the other matter, but he said, "And what of love, then?"

She exhaled, glad for the return to simpler topics. "As a marriage does not require love, neither should love require marriage. In fact, it seems to me that marriage is the very antidote to love."

"I change my mind," he murmured. "Perhaps *happiness* was not the right word for you. You sound more like a cynic."

She shrugged, although the little sting she felt suggested that, despite herself, she had rather liked his earlier view of her. "I learn from observation. And do you mean to say you're not a cynic?" She glanced, against her will, at his wrist. Oh, she would not stop herself. She reached for it, her thumb finding his scar. "Can you be an idealist? When you found me in your study, was your first impulse born of optimism?"

"We've both walked a hard road," he said slowly. "But I like to think I still believe in more wholesome possibilities than those I've been shown."

"Wholesome?" She laughed. "I've heard it used to describe bread. But do note how fond everyone is of butter and jam; otherwise, the taste is too plain."

His hand turned beneath her touch, his fingers threading through hers. "There's no need to be flippant with me. You do realize, don't you, that we're both after the same goal now."

She was sitting down, but her knees were beginning to tremble all the same. "You are determined to be frank today." Her voice did not sound steady, either.

His dark eyes studied her face. "Perhaps I've decided not to be cynical about you."

She mustered a weak laugh. "I would give it a few more days before you decide. You don't know me at all."

"You keep reminding me of that." He smiled slowly. "But I have very good instincts."

A nervous thrill chased through her. It was as if he had read her mind, and knew what she intended for him. She broke from his gaze. On the lawn, the crowd was arranging itself into couples. A small group of musicians stepped up onto the hay bales; the fiddler flourished his bow and began a reel.

A memory came to her, making her smile. She rose to her feet, still holding his hand. "Dance with me, Mr. Monroe?"

He set down his tankard. "By all means, Miss Masters."

Chapter Twelve

As Ashmore's warm hands spun and guided her, Mina was glad they'd never danced in Hong Kong. It would have ruined her for all the other dances that had come afterward, with men who did not move so lightly on their feet. He steered her with ease through the other couples, and after the first song, she stopped bothering to watch out for anyone; she shut her eyes to give herself over fully to him and to her ambitions.

If he looked for wholesomeness, he must look elsewhere—that, she meant to make clear. She lifted her arms over her head as she spun away from him, and he pleased her by whistling appreciation as he caught her up again. She liked him more than a little, not least because he'd compared her to a knife; he spoke of instincts, and hers had always approved of him. It would have been enough to make her wary, for she did not seek entanglements. But there was no danger of that. This wasn't her country, and soon enough she would be gone.

Indeed, as they danced, she marveled at her lack of worries. Her spirits felt lighter than they had in so long. She was going to find her mother, and the joy that bubbled up within her was not only at the prospect of a reunion, of safety, but also at her own triumph: She was more capable than Ridland had realized. She had outwitted him and persuaded this man to help her, and very soon she would exorcise all her curiosity about him. Tomorrow, free, she would find her mother. Everything would be fine then, a tragedy turned into grand adventure. She felt empowered by the prospect; she felt aglow with her own capability. Put a mountain in front of her, and she would rip it apart with her bare hands. Ashmore's admiring eyes announced it: she was a force.

When the dance was over, another villager pressed fresh tankards into their hands, and they drank the ale down thirstily before agreeing, by a wordless accord of glances, to return to the dance.

This time, something felt different between them. She had planned to work up to a seduction tonight, but suddenly patience seemed superfluous. Her strange exaltation transferred its focus from herself to him. How could she resent a man who moved so beautifully, who did not fear being as graceful as a woman? A lion, a hunting cat, he had a talent for movement; his fingers were long and strong as they caught her and turned her by the waist, his teeth white and fine as they flashed at her. He looked boyish in his laughter, as though country dances and village scenes were his natural element; she could not square his face now with her old impressions of arrogance, although, when she thought on it, she liked his versatility, too. His body emitted a heat that called to hers when she came close to him in a figure. Her laughter was settling now into something deeper. She wanted to come right up against him. He had a great deal of potential, and her body wanted to realize it all for herself.

He seemed to feel it as well, for his hand began to linger and his expression grew sober, despite the merriment all around. When the fiddle slowed, his hands did not release her. In the small space between their bodies, a current was building that brought her closer to him; she could not move away even if the world rushed in between them. A warm breeze scudded through the crowd, perfumed with celebration: burnt sugar, the sourness of beer, the warm, golden scent of hay. Here was life in all its sweetness, surprising her when she least expected it, twisting forethought into revelation, reminding her that plans sometimes proved unnecessary, that occasionally everything came together spontaneously, as though the universe were an ever-resolving pattern that wanted to please her in the end.

They stared at each other, and as the music started up again, neither of them moved. He reached up to dislodge a strand of hair from her eyes, and for a moment, her stomach falling, she thought that his intentions ended there. But then the slow stroke of his fingertip traveled onward, past her cheekbone, down her jawline, along her neck to the edge of her bodice. Fire trailed in its wake, and a shiver broke across her skin. "You are a puzzle," he murmured.

"I am," she agreed.

"I give you fair warning, Miss Masters. I mean to unravel you."

Later, she would think back to this moment and wonder at how easily she dismissed his caution, discarding so many years of hard lessons, so much wisdom so painfully accrued. But now the words made her breath catch, and she could think of nothing better than finding out how he meant to do it, knowing it would involve his lips and his tongue and other parts of him, wondering if he would speak to her as he touched her, the way he had in his drawing room, as though nothing were too shameful to be put into language.

"Try it," she said, and then, going up on her tiptoes, she kissed him.

He did not hesitate. He cupped her elbows and kissed her back, deeply, his mouth bitter from the ale. Around them, cheers broke out and also, belatedly, a few good-natured admonitions. The alcohol had been flowing freely enough to erode the basis for moral outrage, perhaps. *There is no society so upright as an English country town.* Ha! Poor Mama would be so shocked.

Her calves began to tremble, and she pulled away. His hand followed, cupping her neck. "The room at the inn is ours," he said.

"Yes," she whispered. All that lavender growing against the windows, and the rosemary inside, promising comfort, and the pleasures of a warm, clean bed.

She was not sure what she had expected of Ashmore. Her liaison with Henry had been carried on in darkness, in the silent hush of silk-draped bedrooms with curtains drawn, lights doused, voices hushed at his request, lest his servants, his sister, his nephew, a host of ears overhear. Sex with Henry, in her memory, tasted of his shame, and darkness, and his mounting frustration with her refusal to let him make her "honorable," to wear his ring so he might lie down with her and turn the lamps up beforehand.

But their room at the inn, when Ashmore unlocked the door, gave her a foretaste of how different this would be. The chamber was flooded with the lambent light of late afternoon, picking molten highlights from the floorboards exposed by the edge of the rug. When she turned back, she found him still at the door, in no hurry to shut out the light. He made no move at all, in fact. He stood and stared at her, not at her breasts or her hips, but at *her*, his eyes dark and deep. He seemed to be deliberating on something, and her body appreciated the implications, although her mind was not so sure of them; pulses began to quicken in every secret part of her as he looked.

"Are you awaiting an invitation?" A marvel that her voice could sound so confident, in defiance of the weakness in her knees.

"No," he said. "The light on your face is quite beautiful. You look dipped in gold."

She took a breath. Compliments to her beauty were routine. There was no cause to find his words miraculous. But this time, at least, her reply was very easy to give. "Come and kiss me, then."

He smiled a little. With one hand, he flipped open the buttons on his jacket. It dropped to the ground and he stepped away from it, now working on his waistcoat. Even the finest jacket worked against him by disguising this silhouette now bared by his shirtsleeves, the breadth of his shoulders, the narrowness of his hips. Her gaze wandered lower, to the distinct bulge in his trousers. She felt a little foolish for flushing, as though the sight came as a surprise. He had been ready for her for some time; she had felt his hardness when she kissed him on the village green.

"Your turn," he said softly.

This startled her; he was not fully undressed yet. But her hesitation was brief; she had ingenuity at her disposal, if no experience in this sort of game. She started with her gloves, loosening them finger by finger as he settled back against the door to watch. He looked too comfortable lounging there, too indolent, as though this were all a game for his amusement, and so she drew out the process, taking each finger in her teeth to draw the gloves off bit by bit. But he seemed amenable to waiting; only when she reached up to her hair to pluck out the pins did a low noise come from his throat. "Let me," he said, and she turned, seeing the bright blue sky glowing through the tree limbs outside the window as his footsteps approached.

His fingers settled at the crook of her neck, warm and firm. Lips pressed against her nape, opening, a hot, moist pressure that lingered there as his hand slowly moved down to cup her breast. His teeth closed lightly on her neck, and for a long moment he made no other move. He simply held her there, as if to warn her that her decision was made now, and the view out the window should not concern her; all she needed to know was how wholly she stood in his grasp.

And then his other hand delved into her chignon. The

heavy weight of her hair fell coiled over her shoulder; a light touch threaded through it, pulling it behind her back, smoothing through the length of it. She closed her eyes, lulled by these strokes, surprised by his gentleness. This was not what she'd expected of him; she wasn't sure if it was what she wanted. It felt too much like tenderness, while what had sprung up between them outside was more elemental and fierce, nothing to do with caring.

Nothing between them had to do with caring. Her eyes opened; she was frowning. "Let my hair alone," she said.

His laughter was soft and hot against her neck. It sounded wicked, raising goose bumps along her flesh. "No," he said, and the mean edge to his voice lent his slow, deliberate strokes through her hair some new and mysterious significance.

"Yes." She tried to turn and face him. Her hair pulled by the roots; he had wound it around his hand to hold her in place.

His lips touched her ear. "No," he repeated very softly. His hand cupped her breast again, then slid down slowly over her abdomen, pressing into her skirts, finding the space between her thighs. He cupped her mound and pulled her back against his body, his cock pressed now against her lower back, while outside the oak branches waved against the sky. His fingers rippled, once, and she felt herself grow moist and heard a whimper die in her throat.

She forced herself to swallow. "All right then," she said coolly. "Do as you like. Maybe I'll be impressed."

"I do hope so," he said. A steady pressure exerted itself on her hair, gently pulling her head toward her left shoulder. She shut her eyes and submitted, feeling the delicate flick of his tongue along her neck. His hand released her mound, and she felt the loss as a pang, only slightly alleviated when she realized his hands had moved to the hooks of her gown. She should not have worn a corset, she thought distantly. It made things so much more complicated. In one of her artistic gowns, she might already be naked and this curiosity might be sated; already she would know what his lips felt like on her breast.

But she'd underestimated his cleverness. The gown parted around her, sagging with an audible puff as though protesting its mistress's lack of manners, letting a man handle it so rudely. Now came the hiss and slap of laces being loosened; his hands at her waist lifted her out of the tangle, and redirected her to face him.

His face was intent, almost fierce in the sunlight. His eyes and hair were no lighter for the sun on them, a deep rich brown immune to auburn. But the fine contours of his lips seemed newly beautiful to her, hewn with greater precision than those of Bernini's anguished saints. She reached up to touch them, and he sucked her finger into his mouth, watching her all the while, as though he wished to know what she thought of this, as though it mattered to him very much. Her own lips parted; she would have told him how her bones seemed to be liquid and a tremor was starting within her, but when he released her finger, his little smile told her not to bother. He took her wet finger in his hand and directed it down his chin, over his throat, trailing it to the hollow beneath his Adam's apple, never looking away from her. It came to her then that she had, perhaps, overestimated herself: she knew nothing of the games his smile hinted at.

"We are going to enjoy each other," he murmured.

"Yes," she whispered back. She did not back down from a challenge.

She broke from his hold to pull away his suspenders and yank his shirttails from his trousers, pushing his shirt from his shoulders. His upper body, bared, was an expanse of golden skin, chiseled with muscle. She touched his abdomen lightly, astonished by its sculpted flatness; she had thought these segmented bands of muscle a figment of artists' imaginations. When his belly contracted, she could see the working of his physique; she laid her palm flat against it, to feel how it moved. "You are beautiful," she said. She had never said such a thing to a man, had never understood the word could be so applied. The idea pleased her fiercely; it seemed powerful to her. "Very beautiful," she amended. And then, on a sudden weird burst of humor, remembering all the times she had been so praised, she added, "Why, you're a pocket Venus writ large, Ashmore."

He laughed, which surprised her; she looked up at him, and surprise turned to amazed gratification—he understood exactly what she meant. "I will not return the compliment," he said. "Venus was a hell of a lot less trouble than you are. But Helen . . ." He reached for her shift, and she raised her arms to help him. A silent breath came from him, passing over her forehead as he looked at her. "Helen," he confirmed softly, and then went to his knees in one fluid, soundless movement, to kiss her waist and then her breast.

Her arms came around his head, touching the softness of his wild hair. She wanted to close her eyes, but when she did she felt dizzy; she opened them and watched his tongue touch lightly to her nipple, and then his lips close over it. It drew an intense, almost violent feeling from her; her arms tightened around him, and then she wondered at herself, clutching him close as if he provided her balance, when she was standing on her own two feet. She did not want to be standing, suddenly; she wanted to be lying next to him, or no, she wanted to watch him, naked, walk to the bed. "Take your clothes off," she said hoarsely.

His teeth pulled at her nipple one more time before he stood. His hands moved to the fly of his trousers, but she pushed them away, unclasping the hook and sliding the fabric over his hips. She told herself there was no need to disguise her curiosity; he did not expect shyness from her. But she had never seen a man in the light, and it unsettled her to see him so openly bared. She put a hand around his cock, and realized the differences between men; she would have more trouble with him than with Henry, although her body seemed to like his better.

She tightened her grip, and he gasped. She exhaled, too, because the feel of him leaping in her palm made something within her pulse deeply. She felt open and clutching, ready for him. She wanted to tell him that. She wondered if she dared. The words were ordinary, but their order and meaning would be unprecedented for her; perhaps they required rehearsal, although she could not envision failing right now. Her fingers tightened again. "I want this," she said. It was the best she could do.

It served. He scooped her up from the floor—and she did not like that; she did not like the reminder of how light she was, or how easily he could carry her. But when he dropped her onto the bed, she saw the full length of him, his calves corded with muscle, his thighs flexing as he sank onto his knees on the mattress, and she forgot her irritation. *I am a woman of the world*, she thought, *bedding this man, the unwilling man of intrigue*, and she felt her lips curve; there was no harm in being pleased with herself, and anyway, it brought him up to her, his tongue into her mouth. Maybe he wanted to taste her smile; he himself tasted like ale, and dark hallways in times before she had learned to fear the darkness; she had gone running into it, in fact, full of plans and hopes that night, wanting him even when he had not wanted her back.

It all seemed to twine together now, their limbs, his low moans, her own murmurs, this hunger inside her writhing and swelling as his hand stroked between her legs, past and present, Hong Kong, a country village. She touched his cock and squirmed until the head of it brushed against her wetness, a solidity her body craved. Lust, she thought, this was not simply desire but *lust*, almost too large for her body to contain. What matter if the lights were on or off when one felt this way? She thrust her hips, and caught him off guard; he said something low and too garbled to understand, and she felt the pressure of him, caught at her opening. She took him by his hard, muscled buttocks and pulled him in, thinking strange thoughts that made no sense. *Anchor me. I have waited for this.*

His full width penetrated her slowly, little muscles in his face registering his effort to restrain himself. She knew a moment of burning discomfort, almost as sharp as the first time, when all she had felt the whole way through was pain. She had thought then that it was no wonder they called it a *deflowering*——flowers felt no pleasure when their heads were chopped off——but this time, a little revelation worked its way up from the place of their joining, and her body jerked once in the discovery of pleasure. Her thighs fell apart, then closed hard on his hips; he shut his eyes, lashes thick and finely arranged, orderly of course, falling somehow sweetly over his cheeks. Wrong to think, in this moment, that he looked as innocent as a boy. The body over hers was nothing boyish; her arms came around him and he was more solid, harder than anything she'd ever grasped, vibrating from the tension of his own private drama. She pressed a kiss to his shoulder, and tried to move with him. The rocking rhythm struck some nerve; a bead of sweat fell from his face, and it felt like a caress as it rolled down her shoulder. She was moving toward something, him pressing inside her so deep and with such intensity, again and again.

But the mounting sweetness was too liquid and formless to be trusted. She found herself clenching against it—taken, suddenly, by some strange fear that if she submitted to it, she would shatter against him, a million little pieces she would never manage to retrieve. *I don't know you*, she thought. *This* was the time for darkness, so they could be strangers. She realized with an unpleasant shock, almost of fear, that his eyes were open, resting on her face. Even now he was waiting for something from her. She did not like that. She would not give it to him. He whispered to her, "Come," and she did not understand the request; what more could she give him than this? "Mina," he said, but he had no right to demand anything of her; this act was done of her own accord.

And perhaps he saw the answer in her face, for the deep kiss he gave her then seemed more complex and sober than the wild assault of a few seconds ago. His thrusts strengthened, as though he had grown tired of it and wanted to be done. She dug her nails into his back and waited, beginning now to notice how his hip bones ground into hers, more painful than she had realized, and how her own joints ached a little, and how she could feel the soreness already coming on and anticipate the way, afterward, she would feel loose and drained, as though she had given away something that she missed and wanted back and had gotten nothing in return for.

He tore himself away from her and fell onto his stomach at her side, his breath coming in silent, fierce pants against her shoulder. Stupid, as she stared at the whitewashed ceiling, the giant crack running through it, the faint discolorations from a recent rain, to feel disappointment. She had set out to be wanton and seize the moment, and so she had. She had felt new things she'd never experienced with Henry; when Ashmore had taken her by the hair and reached between her legs, she had understood Cleopatra, and Jezebel and Eve.

She started to sit up. His hand caught her arm. "We are not done," he said softly.

She yanked out of his grip and pushed at his lean hip until he rolled onto his side, coming up on his elbow. Taking pointed note of the damp patch on the sheets beneath him, she lifted her brow and said, "I think we are."

He showed his amusement openly. "Very knowledgeable, aren't you?"

Was he mocking her? "Maybe I am." She reached for the sheet that had spilled to the floor, pulling it up over her breasts. He was still watching her. "What of it? Do you *disapprove*?"

"Not at all," he said easily. "But it seems to me that your education is incomplete. You didn't climax, did you?"

She looked away, up to the crack in the ceiling. Now that her body had cooled, it was becoming increasingly difficult not to feel foolish, and a little disoriented. It seemed as if she were waking from some performance she thought she had mastered, only to find the audience staring at her, bewildered, no applause. Ashmore looked slightly incredulous that she had thought she was doing well. Damn him for it.

"My *apologies* if you weren't pleased," she said.

"One could argue it has nothing to do with me, apart from the blow to my vanity." He paused. "Or is that it? You think this has to do with what *I* want?"

"I don't know what you mean." And maybe she didn't; as he continued to study her, she felt weirdly stubborn, and a little angry. She wanted to blame him for something. He seemed so determined to draw her out. But he'd already done so; she was naked, and he'd had his fun from her. He could look elsewhere if he needed additional entertainment.

"Sit up," he said.

"You already had your view."

"Such a worldly woman, afraid to flash her tits at me?"

She glared at him. "There's your filthy mouth again."

He gave a shrug of one well-muscled shoulder. "I can get filthier."

"Don't sound proud of it."

He began to smile. "Don't pretend you don't like it." He reached out and yanked the sheet away, exposing her entirely. "Spread your legs, Mina."

A quiver stirred in her stomach. She couldn't say whether it was the sound of her name, all done up in gold by his low, husky voice, or the command that made her hot. "Why? You're done."

"You're not."

Ah. He was going to try to impress her now. She held still as he touched her knee, nudging her legs apart. His survey was frank. "To be dirtier," he said meditatively, "I could use several names to describe this sweet little slit of yours. Have you any particular preference?"

She could feel a flush creeping down her throat. "No," she managed. She knew no names for herself; Henry had only addressed his own bits. "I don't care," she added. "Whichever you like, if you must speak of it."

One brow lifted. "*If* I must speak of it." He met her eyes. "Why not speak of it? You're a sophisticate, not wholesome at all. Less jam than foie gras or caviar, no doubt, and much"—his lips curved—"to my delight.

We've no need to dance around sensitive matters, then, do we. Touch yourself."

His meaning registered, and her throat closed. Oh, this was far more than she'd imagined when she'd realized he was not going to draw the curtain. This was . . . beyond imagination. "I don't take orders from you," she said thickly.

"I noticed," he said. "You're afraid to give an inch, which is why I'm sitting here, keeping my hands nicely to myself, despite this banquet laid out before me. Do it for yourself, Mina." He paused. "Unless . . . unless, of course, you didn't know that you've no need to depend on a man for your pleasure."

She felt pinned by his steady, hot regard. He purred the words, as though he was inordinately pleased with her, but although his voice seemed to cast some sort of sticky spell that kept her eyes glued to his, her hand would not move. To touch herself in front of him seemed beyond shameless.

But shame was not meant to concern her, was it? She had no truck with that emotion. She cupped her hand over herself, feeling her own heat, the moisture that lingered from their encounter. She did it defiantly, lifting her chin, and he watched her do it. It was appalling; her cheeks stung; she could not have felt more exposed had he peeled her skin away, bit by bit, the way Italians did with their grapes over breakfast, neatly with a knife and fork.

"Pretty picture," he said softly. "But not quite purposive, is it?" He reached out, and his fingers settled over hers, closing in a warm, hard grip that sent a shock through her, although it was such an everyday sort of touch that it should have felt like nothing after the more intimate contact they'd made. He moved her hand, pushed it up her body, so her middle finger brushed against an exquisitely sensitive part of herself. Her strangled sound won his immediate attention. "Yes," he said, "and now stroke."

He had shocked her. There was a piquant pleasure in startling a woman so determined to remain unmoved, and later he would savor the memory of her expression, the mounting flush on her cheeks and the sweet glimpse of her tongue between those parting lips. But at present, his awareness had contracted too tightly to allow for the contemplation of irrelevant victories. All that mattered was this: the unrealized promise of her flesh, her own stubborn refusal to pursue her pleasure, and his mounting conviction that another piece of her mask trembled by a string, ready to drop away if only he gave her a push.

He took her hand by the wrist and directed her fingers.

The feel of her heat and dampness stirred a growl in his chest. He bit down on the sound, focusing instead on her muffled breath. She was trying to hide her own noises. He guided her finger over her clitoris, feeling a moment of fierce satisfaction as her hips jerked slightly.

But then she grew abruptly paler, and her teeth closed around her lower lip. She was fighting, by habit, a battle that he was not going to let her win. Her eyes fixed on his, their glassiness sharpening into resolve. He gritted his teeth and exhaled and very gently removed her hand, pressing it to the mattress by her thigh.

Her shoulders slumped. Maybe it was relief that loosened her muscles, but her posture also spoke of disappointment. He did not flatter himself with the thought. She was a woman of passion, and her body, aroused, still trembled with need. She might tell herself that the need was purely physical, bearing no innate connection to him. Maybe that was even true. But not for long. How her need would be answered—he intended to have everything to do with that.

"We're done then," she whispered.

"Just about," he said gently, and took her by the shoulder, his thumb pressing lightly over her collarbone, his fingers firm on her back. He lowered her—for now she did not resist at all—onto the pillows, where her hair tumbled outward in streamers of gold. She watched him a moment longer, but when he made no other move, she closed her eyes and sighed.

He was briefly appreciative of the privacy. For to survey her in her fullness—to behold the blushing cream of her skin complemented only by the rose of her nipples and the light scattering of platinum between her legs—felt like being slammed against a wall: again and again his breath was knocked away. Such grand vistas, great waterfalls and scarlet sunrises and the perfection of a woman softer and sweeter than any ideal, demanded humbleness from the viewer, a sense of one's smallness when compared to the vast range of wonders the world offered.

But he did not feel humble. And there was the difference. She was some sort of miracle, yes, but it was not the world's place to look upon her. She was *his* miracle, and his intentions felt avaricious, as carefully calculated as trigonometric equations. He bent down and in one swift move—he would not allow her to think now—pushed open her legs and laid his tongue to her slit.

She gasped. He heard it dimly, but with the taste of her on his lips, it did not concern him overmuch. He took a long lick, and then another; her hips jerked and she tried to move away, but he caught her and forced her still, settling with intention on the one spot that would erode her resolve most quickly. *Pussy, quim, cunt, box*— earlier, he might have given her a great many synonyms, but now his mind was working with more euphemistic litanies. *Honeypot, nectar, banquet, heaven, heart, paradise, mine.* Had he offered these options before, she would have laughed and girded herself, but now if he chose to speak, which he would not because that would require removing his mouth, she would not have the breath left to mock him, for she was moaning, submitting to him very sweetly.

Her flesh trembled; she bucked against him. But there was nothing of resistance in her movements. Her hands settled in his hair, grasping hard, twisting. He didn't mind a little pain; he encouraged her by turning his head to bite, very gently, her inner thigh. His thumb claimed her clitoris and her voice broke on a long, low cry as he licked down to her opening, filling her with his tongue as he'd done earlier with his cock. She spoke his name, a breathy plea, and he moved upward to abrade her with short, steady laves, placing his fingers inside her, spreading them to fill her as her soft thighs closed over his cheeks.

With a low keen, she broke for him. Her sheath contracted in hard spasms as he continued to kiss her, more softly now, working from her slit to the edge of her inner thigh, up the sloping plane of her stomach to the hot well of her navel, which contracted and shivered beneath the flick of his tongue.

When the last quivers of her pleasure had subsided, he withdrew his fingers and pushed himself up by the elbow.

Her blush had grown violent. Scarlet-faced, she stared at him. The tic at the corner of her mouth, the clenching of her fingers on the sheet, suggested an embarrassment of continental proportions. He smiled and lifted the fingers that had coaxed her pleasure, and licked the taste of her away.

Her eyes dropped from his. She swallowed.

Whatever she wanted to keep from him, he was not going to have it. He leaned forward and took it from her mouth with a kiss, his tongue luring open her lips. By the time he pulled back, her hands were clutching his shoulders.

She did not want to let him break from the kiss. She was trying, she thought, to take back what he'd retrieved from her. But some shiver within her gave that the lie: she was not as strong as she thought, or maybe, just maybe, he was not the man she had assumed him to be.

Her body still trembled with the aftermath of what he had done to her, so easily, without any cooperation from her but sheer, quivering curiosity. God above, Henry had never done anything like that!

He pulled back, watching her, slightly breathless, his chest rising and falling in a rapid, shallow rhythm. She met his eyes and waited for him to do something. He was hard again, his cock straining toward his navel, but he did not move.

Either he was generous beyond expectation, or he was devilishly calculating. She could not make up her mind.

"I'm no boy," he said. "I can master myself. No call for worry."

"I'm not worried," she said quickly.

"Yes, you are." He paused. "You know, Mina, my interest in you is not idle. Does it help to know that?"

She shifted uneasily, not daring to ask what he meant. "I don't need help."

"All right," he said slowly. "Fair enough. And perhaps to the point. All this"—he gave a slight wave, to indicate the rumpled sheets, *God above*, she had felt so wanton— "only means what you make of it."

They would make nothing of it, of course. Why should he even raise the possibility? She cleared her throat, then managed a laugh. "Of course I know that. You think me more naïve than I am. And after this, even?"

He shook his head. A lock of brown hair flopped over his eyes, and her fingers curled into her palms; they itched to brush it away for him. His skin tasted of salt and musk; she had forgotten to bite him, and she regretted it. "What I mean to say . . ." He hesitated again. "It's not a matter of control, unless you want it to be. Unless *we* decide to make it so," he added softly.

Unless we decide. Her breath caught. He spoke as though this—the mussed sheets, the quilt clinging to the edge of the bed, his casual nakedness, the light pouring in, the tangle of hair scratching her nape, knotted from his hands—was not the aftermath of something finished and done, but a field of negotiation, a space for some new creation in which dignity and manly pride had no role. *We can decide how it will be.* Together, shaping something.

She sat up, wondering why the idea should move her so, increasingly uncertain whether he'd even meant it that way. One could read a million meanings into a phrase; that was, after all, the reason the world loved poetry. Her liking for him had addled her.

She smoothed her hands over the sheet, then plucked it back over her, making the movement as casual as she could. "I don't know what you mean," she decided.

But perhaps she did. Certainly he seemed to think so. His slight smile told her as much. "Won't you let yourself like me a little bit?"

"I like you," she said, then arched an ironic brow. "Obviously, I like you, Ashmore. What more proof do you require?"

He studied her face for a long moment. "Drop the mask, then. Of your own volition."

She inhaled sharply. It was not so much the words that shocked her; of course he knew now that she had been playing roles with him. No, the electric surprise that flowed through her was all for the idea that he would think to ask such a thing from her. That he might think she would consider doing it for him.

That she might want to.

She pushed out the breath. "I am who I am."

"Yes," he said. "Exactly."

No, she wanted to say. *You don't understand. I am whoever I wish to be, with you. You don't get to decide.* But her lips would not move. She thought of his scar, and could not bring herself to say it. He had been so honest with her. And the wonder he had wrought for her, at no gain to himself—

All she could do was wait silently for his eyes to release her, and wonder at her own disappointment when he turned away to retrieve his clothes.

By the time they went downstairs to sup, the episode in the bed might as well have been a dream. Phin watched, with amusement and then a touch of frustration, as she slipped back into her comfortable routine. She did it with deliberate thoroughness, rattling cheerfully to him over a hock of lamb about her make-believe dog, the perils of cats, how lovely his hair would look if he only used her tonics. And when they returned upstairs, she did not invite him to share the bed.

He didn't make the suggestion. He slept on the floor, or tried to; the soft sounds she made kept him awake. She had managed a composure today that impressed him; she had even tried to deny herself pleasure to preserve it. But asleep, with her lips parted as laxly as a child's, her body retaliated for her discipline. Whimpers, wordless whispers, limbs tossing across the sheets—these small rebellions, he told himself, bespoke pleasant dreams. But the longer he listened, the more skeptical he became.

He might have woken her, had his own intentions been less clear. But he knew better than to touch her. If he touched her once, he would touch her again. And he was starting to understand Mina Masters; like a book in a half-learned language, she yielded to him with increasing speed, although each new page suggested that the story would be longer and more complex than he'd expected. She had plans and strategies, and this afternoon had challenged her vision of how he might fit into them. He was glad of it. He had no intention of letting her incorporate him into her current narrative. To do so would give her the ending she'd already scripted. *A week, and you will never see me again.*

Only a week ago, he might have hoped the same. But she had caught his interest now. She had caught more than his interest.

And so he lay there listening with full attention to the symphony of her sleep: sighs, a murmur, and then the slide of her hand down the pillow, the starched sheets crackling as those pale, perfect limbs turned. She was a puzzle indeed, like a mountain range that resisted climbing, or a lake that seemed too deep at first to plumb. But he had spent years mastering difficult topographies. The process was arduous, requiring the painstaking collection of countless minutiae, their tentative assemblage into a larger picture, the willingness to disassemble them at the first sign of a flaw, to rearrange the pieces and begin again. But he was well fitted for the task; he was, after all, Stephen Granville's son, and a good portion of his life to date had been spent trying to school an obsessive disposition into more useful pastimes than alcohol and cards. Sheldrake had been the first to show him a better use for his talents, and Ridland had shown him another, but now he found his own use. He turned his skills on her. And a picture began to emerge, in the long hours of darkness, that he gradually realized would not assemble properly unless he incorporated himself within it.

It seemed to him, as he lay there, that Mina Masters's map had overlapped with his more intimately and for longer than he'd realized. There was no other way to account for what he'd felt today when he touched her, the eerie sense of accordance, as though, pressed against her body, his own skin had finally begun to fit him. It put him in mind of a phenomenon he'd first read of as a boy, of how once in a very great age the magnetic poles reversed, the earth reorienting itself. The thought of such disorder had alarmed Phin when he was young; he had dreamed of compasses going wild, their arms flying askew. He wondered now, with fascination, if his own compass had not been disordered for much longer than he'd suspected.

Certainly, the reversal had not begun when he'd opened that letter from Ridland. He thought back to the first moment in Hong Kong when he had wanted her and recoiled. That, perhaps, was when his poles had shifted. Missing the small signs, focused on other aims, he had reviled himself for wayward urges, mistaking them as signs of his own weakness. Had he realized then that she was well worth wanting, he might have found the courage to do what came to her so naturally: to look around a locked room, and see opportunities worth breaking windows for.

He sat up, taking advantage of the moonlight slipping in through the thin curtains, refracting from the mirror to bathe her face in cool illumination. Could desire refract like light, becoming stronger for its bounce between past and present? For the longer he looked at her, all his missteps with her in Hong Kong, all the moments in which she had frustrated and confused him and riled his temper and incited his contempt and his wanting, seemed more and more momentous, until more recent events seemed inseparable from the earlier ones, coalescing in one seamless confluence of steadily mounting revelation. In his new view of her, he saw how far he had traveled, and how much he had changed, since he had dreamed of sweet, pretty girls like Miss Sheldrake.

Why are you speaking to me like this? she had asked, and what he had realized in that moment, and known better than to say to her, was very simple indeed: *I am speaking to you like this because I know you understand, and I do not know how you bear it so lightly.*

Mina Masters understood compulsion. But she did not recognize helplessness. She would like to know how to kill a man, but she did not feel ashamed by her desire because she trusted her judgment. Blood-thirst was a strange thing to admire in a woman, and maybe it spoke ill of him, according to conventional philosophies. But not according to the philosophy by which she operated. *I am my own,* she'd said, and it was not a braggart's claim;

she meant it, and made no apologies for the measures she would take to defend her stake.

No, his admiration of her was not mistaken. If anything, it was understated, or *admiration* was too pale a word for it. A less elegant gloss, then: when he looked at her, he felt covetous. She camouflaged herself so no one would look closely enough to see her. He sat in the darkness, and looked his fill.

Chapter Thirteen

In Providence, it all went wrong. Maybe she had known it would. That morning, when she woke in the little lavender-scented room and found herself alone, she should have been glad of the chance to breathe free of Ashmore's regard. But all night she had dreamed, and when she sat up, rubbing her eyes, the perfect silence of the room and the radiance of the morning light sloping across the heavy oak furniture had stirred some echo of that foreign panic that had chased her through her sleep. She felt as if she had missed something in the night. She had let some crucial chance slip away but the world had taken no notice; the sun had gone ahead and risen anyway, into a cloudless sky.

The panic made little sense, but she found herself performing her ablutions with unaccustomed speed, then running down the hall to the stairs in search of him. There were reasons to desire Ashmore's company—good reasons, which had nothing to do with the way he had touched her. On her own, she could not handle Collins. He had better weapons, and practiced skills, and knowledge of this country. And he needed her as much as she required him. He had explained to her the tangle he found himself in; if she were to die, he would be counted the traitor. What had happened in the bed upstairs was only an extension of the trade between them; it should not unsettle her, or disrupt the balance between them.

And indeed, he made it easy for her to relax again. He smiled at her as she stumbled into the parlor, and called for her breakfast, and afterward bundled her into a waiting coach with the casual congeniality of a man with no vested interests. He behaved as a friend of a friend, perhaps, someone charged by circumstance to be cordial, but not ambitious for more than a pleasant hour of company.

They set off for Chippenham, some twenty miles distant, and arrived shortly before noon, in time to catch the line that ran to Penzance via Bristol. During the long train ride that followed, as the broad fields gave way to vast, gorse-covered moors where scrubby trees bent horizontal beneath the harsh hand of the wind, he entertained her very thoroughly. She answered his good cheer warily at first, and then permitted it to infect her, understanding that it was as manufactured as her willingness to be entertained. Anyway, this casual conversation kept her from having to decide how to feel about the more complex looks that she occasionally caught from him. He asked about New York; he had never been, which amazed her. Her amazement, in turn, amused him. "Perhaps I will go one day," he said. "You understand I was otherwise occupied, this last decade."

"Making maps," she said. "You were originally trained as a cartographer, weren't you?"

"Yes," he said. "Sometime I'll tell you about that."

"Sometime in the next week," she said.

His smile made her nervous. She abruptly asked him about London. He claimed still to be discovering it, thanks to the guidance of old friends. Some of the stories he told her about these friends, in particular Viscount Sanburne, surprised her; she would not have imagined him willing to court such wild company. But he seemed tolerant of his friend's antics, albeit slightly skeptical of a city that would support such shenanigans so easily. "On the contrary," she said, "I think it speaks very well of London. One should have room to cause trouble in a city so large."

"Then you would thrive there," he said.

"I considered it. Then Mr. Ridland soured my view."

"He has a talent for that," Ashmore agreed. "I've been trying to convince the powers that be to put him into retirement. Perhaps, when all of this is over, we can redeem your opinion of town."

Again, he implied a connection that would last considerably longer than a week. She flushed, and made herself think of his pens.

Just into Cornwall, a vendor came aboard to sell pies, and to congratulate them for their arrival in the safest county in England. "The devil won't enter Cornwall, miss, for fear of being put into a pie," he assured her. Mina could have disproved that; the devil had entered with Collins. But she was too hungry for argument. She ate the squab voraciously, bits of crust falling across her lap, ignoring the example of Ashmore's elegant system, the genteel flick of his fingers after each bite he ripped off. A small, tidy pile of crumbs began to form in a corner on his side of the compartment. Yes, she liked him, but he found a way to discipline even crumbs. She put out a foot and deliberately dragged them across the carpet. He arched a brow. "What?" she asked, and then, when he shrugged, "Must everything always be neat and tidy for you?"

"An insistence on the opposite is no less orderly," he said.

He had a point. Again she felt a flicker of this morning's strange panic. She changed the subject to cats and their general ingratitude.

By the time they arrived in Penzance, it was late afternoon. The look of the people was different; they seemed larger and darker, their Celtic origins undiluted by time. It was not difficult to find a coach in Penzance. The place breathed the spirit of commerce, its Market House a grand, domed marble palace that loomed over the railway station like an invitation to profit. Through the rattling windows of the post chaise, she watched the passage of carts clogged with white broccoli and potatoes, trucks stuffed with stinking piles of pilchard, and finally, at the edge of town, invalids partaking of the mellow, salt-sharpened air on an esplanade of granite overlooking the sea. The road wound up over Mounts Bay, along granite promontories polished by roaring wind and surf to a high, gleaming polish. The ocean beyond them was startlingly vivid, a rippling sheet of pewter and lilac and palest green.

She was about to find Mama. The certainty held her thoughts in a warm grip as they pulled into the small village and entered the little pub, until the very moment they asked after an Irish-American and his blond companion, and the innkeeper paled and told them of a fire.

The walk then from the inn to the magistrate's residence felt like walking into a nightmare. The measure of her senses grew disproportionate, touch and sound swamping vision. She was acutely aware of the murmurs from curious residents who came to join their progress, making a straggling parade. The innkeeper whispered explanations; the villagers issued muffled and eager replies. A mystery was being laid to rest. This mystery was not entertainment to her.

Ashmore had taken her elbow; she did not remember when she had first become aware of it, only that his grip had been tightening. He was not worrying about her comfort, she understood, only keeping her on her feet. She wanted to tell him, as they passed down the lane flanked by a low stone wall, that she was fine, but she could feel the wet drops from the ocean crashing on the other side of the wall, and the dry breath of the road where the wind stirred dust into her face, and it came to her that the beauty of the countryside might become meaningful; she might have to remember this as the place where Mama had died.

The idea brought with it a premonition of her own grief, how completely it would flatten her. Mama, only Mama, was hers. Mama was the reason for everything she had done. When the magistrate, startled from his afternoon tea, solemnly produced the items recovered from the fire—a mirror, a spoon, and a ring—she could not speak. She recognized the diamond. *Diamonds are the hard-*

est stone, Mama had told her once, and she had thought how fitting it was that men gave women diamonds to mark their love. *My heart is hard as diamond, it will not bend or flex for you*—yes, it made perfect sense. But this made no sense at all, although the man explained very clearly that bones had been found, in a house high on the cliffs that had burned only two nights ago. A man and a woman had been renting it. No cause for the fire that anyone could determine.

She found her voice when the man would not hand over the diamond. He needed more proof of identity, he claimed, before surrendering such a valuable item. "You are lying," she said. "You want to keep it."

He flushed, fat and ruffled like an overfed rooster in his red coat. She turned on her heel and walked out into the waiting crowd, bodies scattering away from her like ripples on the water. Bodies: she would not bury Collins's, but Mama's—Mama would want to be buried in England.

"Mina." A hand on her arm: Ashmore again, not attempting to stop her, simply walking with her. "Here," he said, and lifted her hand, placed something in it. The diamond ring, warm from the press of his flesh. The sight startled her back into the moment. A ruckus was rising behind them in the lane, a hubbub of speculation. It occurred to her that Ashmore had done something dramatic, that maybe the anger she should be feeling had found its home in him instead, in his fist against the magistrate's nose. But when she glanced over her shoulder, she saw the rooster conferring very thoughtfully with someone; he raised his head to look after them, and the other man, too, turned in their direction. She could not make out their expressions from this distance, but the tilt of their heads suggested that they were reevaluating something.

"What did you give him?" she asked.

"A good deal of collateral."

"It was not a good trade, then." Her voice sounded alarmingly dreamy. She tried to speak more forcefully. "Collins gave her this ring." Now she sounded as though she were proud of the fact. Her fingers squeezed the sharp facets of the stone. "She never stopped wearing it."

"Then it was hers," he said. "And it should be with you."

He was kind. She registered that factually as she turned her attention to the lane ahead. The houses flanking the main street were a dirty white, their roofs perfectly flat, as though a great thumb had descended to press them against the earth. A flock of crows swarmed onto one of the roofs, cawing, oily wings flapping. It was terribly depressing, the best example imaginable of how a landscape might be ruined. She did not see any burned buildings in the lot. "I'd like to see the house before we go."

"Mina—"

"I insist on it." She wanted to know if Mama had been able to see the sea.

Ashmore helped her into the coach before going to ask for the direction. She opened her palm and stared at the ring. Like the locket, it had been a gift from Collins. Mama had worn them for very plain reasons. Not to remind herself, as Mina had first supposed. *You are too sentimental, Mina. They're very fine pieces, and they draw admiration. Why should I surrender them?*

Mina had wondered at such cold pragmatism, in the beginning. Only later had she realized it was her mother's own form of strength.

She tilted her hand, letting the ring slip to the base of her finger. Mama had died wearing this. Such a weird temptation, to want to try it on. She and Mama had been of a size.

Nausea flooded her throat. She reached for her reticule, stuffing the ring inside it as the door to the coach swung open. Her fingers brushed over the butt of her pistol as she looked up, into a face that was not Ashmore's. The features took a moment to evoke a name, but she knew them; a full-bodied shock rocked her. She had not forgotten this smile, how his mouth looked as though it were trying to eat his lips; her fingers recognized it before her brain did. Her old suitor, so unwanted: *Bonham.*

As his booted foot thudded into the interior, her hand was clamping around the pistol butt. She lifted the silk purse and aimed the muzzle at Bonham's head and primed the gun, one sweet, practiced move. He had a gun in his own hand.

"Wrong," she told him. Wrong to think she would be so easy, that grief would transform her into a sitting duck.

He froze in an awkward crouch, half in, half out of the vehicle. "Wait."

Her finger itched on the trigger. Bonham, Collins's

particular protégé. *Mr. Bonham admires your spirits; let him deal with them.* "Throw away the gun," she said. Her arm did not shake; her hand held steady.

"You misunderstand," he said. "I want to make a trade."

"I said *throw it*."

He tossed the pistol out of sight. He had gone white.

He would go whiter. He would learn what it meant to deal with her spirits. "You are the traitor." Of course he was. "Did you kill her?"

He shook his head quickly. "She's not dead."

"Liar," she said flatly. "I have her ring."

"He wants you to think she is, maybe." Spittle flew from the corners of his mouth. "I'll make you a better trade. *You* stole the information, didn't you? Granville never knew a thing; it was you all along. I'll give you her whereabouts in return for the cipher."

His glance flicked to her pistol, and her muscles braced. *These men are trained to move quickly.* "Step backward. Put your hands over your head."

He put a foot down behind him onto the step. She could not risk killing him. What if he was telling the truth about Mama? "What cipher?" she asked, and his hand drew back and she realized he was going to strike and she aimed at his leg and pulled the trigger.

Nothing. The chamber clicked, an empty sound. His body flinched. A crow called, and the light shifted, sun breaking over his face.

He lunged at her.

The impact of his body knocked her back onto the bench. Her head cracked into the wall. His arm came around her waist and he dragged her toward the door. She braced her feet against the wall as his fingers dug into her flesh; the reticule thunked against the floor, and with a grunt she swung it up into his head.

Now the gun fired, blasted thing. Bits of wood rained onto her face. He jerked away.

Free. She shoved herself upright. Gravel crunched as he leapt to the ground. "Wait," she gasped. He sprang away, out of sight; he thought she was going to shoot him. She scrambled to her feet, stumbling out of the vehicle, then throwing herself back as he dove for his gun. "What do you mean? What cipher?"

A shot rang out, startling him back. She wheeled and spied Ashmore racing down the lane, his pistol lowering from its skyward aim. He had not wanted to risk shooting her, but now Bonham was fleeing; now he would have a clear shot. "No!" she screamed, but it was too late; Bonham was ducking down a side street, and Ashmore sprinted past her in pursuit. "Don't shoot him!" she screamed, but he was gone.

She sagged against the side of the coach, panting, dizzy, numb, the stupid gun still in her hand, how useless it was—if she had shot him in the leg, he couldn't have gotten away. A little crowd flocked in around her, all the vultures who had tagged along earlier hoping for a glimpse of tragedy. Bonham, of course. *Take Monroe to the hospital*, he'd said, *he may be infectious;* she'd been right to think he was looking for a bad opportunity.

You stole the information. Did he mean the bundle of shipping receipts she had taken from Collins's study in Hong Kong? They had chronicled his traffic in guns, but Bonham's name had not been mentioned in them; she would have taken note of that. What else could he mean, though?

Someone touched her arm, making her jump: a woman with kind brown eyes, nervously glancing now at the gun. They wanted to take her somewhere. They thought tea and a blanket would help her. She laughed, and they stepped away from her. Her eyes fixed on the street into which Ashmore had disappeared. *Do not kill him*, she thought.

After some amount of time—a day, a half hour, immeasurable—Ashmore reappeared. She saw no blood on his shirt as he jogged toward her. "Caves down by the cove," he said, sounding winded.

"Did you shoot him?"

He set his hands on his knees and breathed deeply. "No." He made a low, sharp, frustrated sound. "There was a goddamned pack of children on their way home from school. I couldn't get a clear shot."

"Thank God."

One of the villagers started to speak to him—more tea maybe, how ridiculous—but his dark, cutting glance silenced the offer. When he straightened, he pinned her with a sharp regard. "Thank *God*?"

"He says Mama isn't dead. He says he knows where she is."

"And you believe him."

Anger rose out of nowhere. "I'm sure it's very easy for you to doubt!"

He shoved a hand through his hair, considering her, obviously making calculations. "He knows the area," he said finally. "We need to get you away from here."

A couple of the onlookers muttered agreement. "We need to find him," Mina said. "We know he's here." More desperately she added, "Whether or not you believe him—he's the traitor!"

"So it seems." A grim smile curved his mouth. "Pretty little Bonham, working for Ridland. Of course." He looked down the empty road. "He pressed that brandy on me, didn't he? He must have thought that I'd uncovered his double-dealing."

They had no time for nostalgia. "So *find* him, then! All your worries will be over!"

As his attention returned to her, his expression flattened. "There's no need to try to find him. You're the one he wants, Mina. *He* will follow *us*." He looked back toward their audience, now muttering speculations, and sighed. "Better that he finds us in a place where we have the advantage."

The ruined cottage sat on a cliff overlooking the ocean. Little remained: blackened bits of timber, chunks of melted glass that glittered in the light. But the little white fence that bound the perimeter had survived unscathed, and the fuchsia and myrtle at its borders blew in the breeze, grotesquely picturesque. The ocean wind carried the smell of soot, a dark, sour weight that still sat in her lungs three hours later, as they waited in a private compartment for the train to depart for Plymouth. She could not rid herself of the smell, although she felt more certain now that Bonham hadn't been lying. "The ring would not have survived that," she said again.

Ashmore had purchased their privacy with a few coins to the guard; now he took the seat next to her. "It does seem unlikely."

He had said it before, but his delivery still failed to satisfy her. "He has no cause to lie."

"He has plenty of cause. Thanks to Ridland, he believes you have proof that he betrayed the service."

"And maybe I do," she said sharply. "We can still make a trade. I can wire New York for the documents. Jane can send a transcription."

He did not speak.

"It's the only thing he could have meant," she said.

His hand touched her cheek, and she blinked at how hot his fingers felt as he turned her face toward his. "We'll send a telegram," he said softly. "And we'll assume he is telling the truth. But don't fool yourself, Mina. He has cause to lie."

She jerked away. "But she *was* here. That much is true. The magistrate said as much."

"So it seems."

"And you didn't believe she would be, did you?"

A moment of silence. "No," he said finally. "Otherwise . . ."

Otherwise. She drew a shaky breath as she turned to look out the window. It was not a word she ever allowed herself to use. For those who depended on themselves, doubt was the most intimate enemy. She would not doubt herself. Bonham had been telling the truth.

She slipped a glance toward Ashmore. His face was dark with old possibilities, useless to everyone now. But he was not the only one to blame here. *Two nights ago.* Two nights ago, that cottage had still been standing. "I should have told you earlier." Words that burned. "I should have told you in Whitechapel. We could have been here and gone already."

He shook his head. "No. I gave you no cause to trust me. Taking you to Ridland's . . . you had no cause."

It was generous of him. He always seemed generous where his pride was concerned. It made him utterly singular, in her experience of men.

She wanted to repay him with truth, to confess that it would not have mattered. Had he fallen to his knees that night in Whitechapel and told her he'd been roaming the world in search of her, that every night for the last four years he'd lain awake worrying about what had become of her, she still would have suspected him. *The world is not your enemy*, Mama always told her, though she never listened.

But there was no room in her for charity at present, only this flat black expanding anger. Her eyes felt hot and swollen from the pressure of it. She drew a breath. *Not your fault*, she thought. *I should have trusted you.* This close, she could smell the scent of him, so much better than ash and soot. No bayberry soap to disguise him now; nothing but musk and sweat, a man who had sweated in pursuit of a villain. He had tried. So had she.

She put her forehead to his shoulder. The train shuddered around them as his hand settled against her hair. His palm was large; she felt cradled by it, oddly protected.

The train whistle screamed. Why did they make the

whistle sound so much like a shriek? It was as if the train were crying out in anticipation of agony, dreading the moment it would be forced to scrape its belly down the rails. Perhaps she, too, should be anticipating pain. All it had taken was a liar's quick words to make her cast off her grief.

A noise broke from her. She pressed her lips shut around it. There were so many horrors in the world, and now this journey might become another one.

He said nothing. His fingers stroked down her hair. He had liked to lecture her in Hong Kong. But he had never lectured her when she was being honest.

She drew a hard breath through her nose. "You're right," she muttered. "I have no cause to believe Bonham."

"But you are right about the ring," he said. "In such a blaze, it should have melted."

Tears welled in her eyes. Her hand crept up his torso, slipping under his jacket to fist in his shirtfront. He was warm and alive and his arm came around her, holding her tightly to him. The train lurched forward, groaning, creaking. She had thought this nightmare would be over by now, that she would be waltzing away from Providence with Mama. She *was* naïve. She opened her mouth to admit it, and her lungs seized so powerfully she choked with the effort to hold in the sob. Footsteps sounded in the corridor outside.

"Cry," he murmured. "It's all right."

"They—" Her voice broke; she swallowed and tried again. "They'll hear. And y-you said not to—draw notice."

"It's all right."

"Why?" She choked it out. "There's—no need to cry. If the ring didn't melt, he was telling the truth. There's a chance."

"Even if he was. There are still reasons."

She opened her mouth again and the retching sound dimly startled her. She tried to inhale deeply, to calm herself, but she could not breathe without this ugly sound reaching into her lungs and retrieving the breaths she drew. She was capable of ugliness, and he knew it now.

The thought relaxed her. He had heard her; she was not so adept at containing herself at all.

His hands moved to her waist. He pulled her out of her seat and onto his lap, cradling her against his chest. *Cry*, she told herself, and tears welled from her eyes, hot and as salty as seawater. To see so much water below, as one burned above . . . it could not be true; Bonham *must* be right. She wondered if she would faint. She could not draw a breath and the whole world seemed to be shaking around her; only the darkness behind her eyes seemed stable.

His voice came to her dimly as his fingers threaded through her hair, his low, golden murmur like the sun on her temple: In London, all would be well. In London, they would sort this out. Incantations for a child—she knew these words. So many times she had tried to soothe her mother's tears this way. She had soothed Mama in every way she knew how, but she had not possessed such a voice, or a lap large enough for Mama to curl up on. She had never been enough for Mama, and maybe now she understood what her mother longed for. It was not so bad to be held, to be small enough to be held. His arms closed around her, and something in her, something she had thought unreachable and incurable, began to calm.

I can comfort myself, she'd told Mama. And so she could, if she had to. But why should she have to? He had never made any promises that he did not keep. He had told the truth, that night he'd retrieved her from Whitechapel: he had never promised they would come for Collins by sunset. Perhaps she had resented his hairsplitting because she had so little practice with what the truth sounded like. The truth was not always pleasant; sometimes it made you hate a person, until you learned better and knew to be grateful for it. *I wish Mama had someone like you.*

Words wanted out, but when she spoke, they were not what she'd anticipated, because the thought that powered them was foreign and startling. *I want someone like you.* "You didn't want to touch me," she said.

"Yes," he said, "I did."

She swallowed hard. "No. In Hong Kong."

His lips touched her temple. "Yes," he murmured. "Mina, I did."

He was lying. Or he had wanted to entertain himself, but his profession had not allowed it. "You thought I was an idiot." Her voice jerked with the force of her hitching breath. "You thought I was a trollop. A forward, empty-headed flirt."

She could feel the hard beat of his heart beneath her hand. When one always felt the need for wariness, it became easy to forget that other people were made of flesh and not stone. Even cruelties were fueled by warm blood—Collins had wept for his brother's passing, and Bonham had made her laugh, once or twice. Even the greatest villain still sighed in the night, and ached now and then with affection. Mama was right; she'd grown too cold, to have to remind herself of such things.

She pressed harder against the warm, strong frame of his ribs, and felt his pulse quicken in reply. His dark eyes were opaque by habit; when she pulled away now and he let her see everything, his regret and his hesitance to be honest with her, it was because he willed her to see them. "Yes," he said. "You're right. That's what I thought." His hand cupped her cheek; his thumb stroked the corner of her mouth.

Her relief at this candor made her boneless. She felt almost like kissing him. "Thank you," she whispered. Her free hand groped at his arm, pulling it down so she could feel for the scar at the base of his thumb. "You know that I have scars, too."

"Yes," he said simply.

It did not surprise her at all that he had noticed and decided not to remark on them. He had a talent for waiting, and for subtlety of all kinds; he let her go at her own pace. But sometimes she could startle him. "You were so amazed, when I woke you with the coca."

She reached up to trace the curve of his faint, answering smile. He spoke around her finger. "If I was surprised, it was by your design. You didn't want me to see you."

"Yes." How clever she had felt. She'd thought she was

doing Mama a great favor by saving Ashmore, that her daring would mean their escape from Collins. And for a time, it had meant such. Four years. Only four. She put her face back against his chest, the tears starting again. Had it been worth it? She would not know until she knew the truth about her mother.

But had she acted differently, the body that held hers so fiercely now might be dead, rotted, brittle bones. One could never know which small decisions would spin out like webs, creating new worlds, unimagined possibilities.

The lifting sensation inside her didn't seem right. What if Mama *was* dead? Then these thoughts, this conversation, would be appallingly self-indulgent. That she should sit here talking of herself and him, of moments long forgotten, as if such trivia even mattered when her mother might be gone— "Perhaps you were right," she said, and let go of his wrist. "You saw me clearly. I am still a featherbrained trollop. Look what I did with *you*."

His reply was barely audible, but she felt the vibration of it in his chest where her cheek pressed against it. "Don't," he said. And then, more clearly, "You don't need to do this. The ring should have melted."

That was true. The fire had destroyed the whole building. "I *should* not do this," she corrected, more for herself than him. One could grow accustomed to being held so.

"It doesn't matter."

Though he did not mean this remark in reply to her thoughts, she wondered if he was right. Mama had always let men choose her. Maybe it was the woman who should do the choosing. *She* could choose *him*.

A shiver touched her at the idea, so strange and rare. She tightened her arms around him to steady herself against the unbalancing thought, and his own arms tightened in response. She liked that. As if he needed her as much as she did him. *I don't need him*, she thought. *I want him*. And if she did? Did it require surrender? Ashmore had chosen to hold her, but with her arms wrapped around him now, no passerby would know who had initiated this embrace.

They sat entwined for long minutes as the train rumbled onward. "I always said I would not punish myself," she said. "So I think I will choose to believe him. I will wire Jane. But if I find out later he was lying—"

"Don't think on it right now."

"But—"

"Quiet," he murmured.

How easy it was to take his order and let herself slump against him. She was sick of fear. It was coming to her now that she'd never been as brave as she thought. Why else would lying in this man's arms feel so novel? Fear had been guiding her for years now. She'd felt so afraid of being trapped that she'd never let anyone hold her close. But was that freedom? Or was it simply one long, endless act of fleeing? In those moments when she had believed with her full heart that Mama was dead, she had realized that she had no destination for her flight. New York was not enough for her.

"You're still thinking," he said into her ear.

She let her eyes close. Suddenly, she felt exhausted. "Are you really a cynic, Ashmore?"

His lips against her ear turned up in a smile. "I think," he said, "you should call me Phin."

They stopped for the night at Bristol, visiting the telegraph office before finding an inn. Over dinner, she said little; now that the wire was sent, they must wait, and the task weighed heavily on her. But when they climbed the stairs to their quarters and the innkeeper's idle conversation as he unlocked a door made it clear that Ashmore had secured separate rooms, her fatigue shifted and changed. It gathered in her chest, a full and swelling pressure, and then migrated into her throat, clogging her windpipe. "No," she said to Ashmore. "You're sleeping with me."

The innkeeper was a wizened man in his seventies, but he lifted his lamp spryly enough, inspecting with bristling brows this newly interesting tableau: she staring so adamantly at Ashmore, and Ashmore with his shoulder propped against the wall, giving her an amused survey. "Flattering," Ashmore said. "But I think we both need our sleep."

The innkeeper muttered something and thrust the other key at Ashmore before clomping away, his footsteps heavy with the weight of sins witnessed. She put her hand on the knob of the open door. "Sleep next to me, then."

He ran a hand over his face. "Not tonight," he said. "The day we've had—"

She made an impatient noise. "Oh, yes, no doubt you're about to tell me I don't know my own mind, that the shock has overset my female sensibilities, Bonham and the fire and whatnot. I won't bother to argue, simply to point out that my faculties feel sharp, and if they aren't, then you may take advantage of me with my full permission."

His lips twitched; the speech seemed to have taken his fancy. But he made no move. "Tell me why," he said.

She glanced past him down the darkened hallway, the wooden paneling glowing a rich red in the gaslight. But if someone overheard, who cared? Such things had never concerned her. "For distraction." When he looked unimpressed, she unearthed a little more courage. "For the . . . comfort of your touch." Quickly she added, "Only that, if you insist. You told me you were not a boy—that you were able to master yourself."

His head tipped. "I also told you my interest wasn't idle. I recall you dismissing the idea as naïve."

The statement touched a newly exposed nerve. "I was lying," she said. Tears wanted to come to her eyes, and she swallowed and breathed very deeply to repress them; she did not want to give him fodder to dismiss her desires as ill reasoned. "Even to myself. You see . . . I always understood the view from the window." She had understood it in Hong Kong, as Mama cried in her arms. She had understood it at Ridland's, as she looked for Tarbury and found only empty rooftops. She did not want to be alone. She was sick of loneliness. "I see something better when you look at me. And I understand . . ." She took a great breath. "I understand you have seen things in me worth acquiring. If you want them, you'll come lie with me."

"Oh, I think you are trickier than that," he said softly. "Did Hans acquire anything of you?"

It took her a moment to place the name. She had thrown it at him during their sparring in his drawing room. "I don't know anyone named Hans," she said with an uneasy laugh. "It was meant to irritate you."

He pushed off the wall, coming close enough that she hoped for victory. His knuckles brushed lightly down her cheek. "I gathered that," he said gently. "Someone else, then. It doesn't matter who."

She inhaled the scent of him, this man who could blush, and who let her put his back to the wall. Who did not scruple to admit his faults, even at the cost of his pride. He had held her down without conscience in his study, but once she had been honest with him, he'd grown honest as well. He had held her today as though she was precious, and Henry seemed so completely irrelevant to this conversation. "He didn't linger long," she said. "I will warn you, the whole package rarely pleases. I . . ." She felt herself color. "I am not always so entertaining. I am stubborn to a fault."

One brow lifted. "Oh? How good to hear you admit it."

His open humor encouraged her. "It's true; I'm rather proud of it. And that's not all." She took a breath. "I am reckless. Shameless and intemperate. Especially with champagne," she added, and gave him a flirtatious look. His mouth quirked. "Also, overly demanding of my bodyguard, so deceitful that gentlemen occasionally mistake me for obtuse . . . is that all?" She looked up to the rafters. "Shrill," she remembered, and looked back to him. "Only when I wish to be, but occasionally I do wish to scream. Prideful, yes. Cunning, no doubt. A little bit manipulative. And on top of it all"—she laughed—"I'm disliked by my cat."

His smile grew lopsided. "Do you think I need this warning? Correct me if I'm wrong, but I believe you're only quoting me."

"Maybe." But she felt uncertain, suddenly. "If your interest is . . . not idle, then you should know I value my stubbornness. In fact, that's my main fault: I'm terribly proud of my faults. I don't mean to change."

"It sounds to me as if you're trying to warn yourself."

"Maybe," she whispered, and pushed the door open wider. "Come inside."

He sighed. "I think you should go back to New York."

She wasn't sure, at first, that she'd heard him right. "What? Bonham—"

"I can handle this," he said. "Bonham's actions today—he's at the end of his rope."

"But if I have the records—"

"Someone else can deliver them. I want you as far away as possible. You have resources in New York, and I can also arrange for your protection there."

"So your interest *is* idle."

"What? No." His voice softened. "Give me your trust, Mina. For a few weeks only. After four years, surely that isn't so long."

She felt a wild urge to laugh. If he thought to persuade her with tenderness, he took the wrong approach entirely, and her hopes were thoroughly baseless. "Trust you by hiding myself away? Like some fragile flower, leaving you and my mother to deal with it?"

"*Trusting* me," he said more sharply, "not hiding. You understand, I have some practice with such things—a great deal more than you do. Let me fix this without having to worry about you."

"I don't want your worry. It doesn't flatter me. I want *you.*"

He took her by the arm and pulled her inside. She had no interest in the room—bare floorboards, a sagging mattress, an overstuffed chair that looked dirty in the dim light, its seat shiny with wear; she stood near the bed, watching only him, bracing for a fight she was determined now to win. He stripped off his jacket with brute economy, then unwound the old-fashioned stock cloth at his neck in quick, angry jerks. "Oh," she said, not bothering to keep the jibe from her voice, "have you decided that we're getting undressed after all?"

He tossed away the cravat; it streamed out, and she plucked it from the air, wrapping it around her hands to give an outlet to her nerves. He turned on her in his shirtsleeves, tall and dark and scowling. "If you stay in London," he said, "you go back to those rooms."

"No."

"I won't bother to argue it," he said grimly.

"It won't work. It won't work if you're going to be this way." It seemed her tears had not evaporated but had migrated instead from her eyes to her throat, clogging it. "And before you answer, you should know that my interest in you isn't idle either."

His face changed; the anger melted away, and he

looked as if he would reach for her. She blushed and stepped back, promptly hating herself for it, for the embarrassment she felt at his expression.

She did not want his pity. She did not want to be ashamed of looking blotchy and sounding like a frog; she was sick of feeling she must be pretty all the time. The bed frame hit her calves; she sank onto the mattress and stared at the cloth in her hand. It no doubt smelled of him, and she wanted to press her nose into it. "This is absurd," she muttered.

A brief silence. "What do you mean?"

She managed a little laugh as she cast aside the cravat. But she could not look up at him. "What is my interest but idle? We're strangers, aren't we? Strangers with an interesting history."

The bed sank beneath his weight. His trousers were dusty at the knees. "You're a brilliant woman, but you've been wrong in every way tonight." He laughed huskily. "Your cat doesn't hate you, you know."

She wiped her nose with the back of her wrist. "You know nothing about cats. You said it yourself."

"I was lying. The Sheldrakes had several, and they all adored me."

"They would," she muttered. "Perverse creatures."

His hand settled on her thigh, palm up. After a moment, she put her fingers into it. As his hand closed, the connection of their flesh made something in her relax. "We can't trust this," she whispered.

"If we were strangers, I would not want you to go to New York."

She frowned. "Of course you would. You wouldn't care."

"On the contrary, it would be very convenient to have you here. I want Bonham. Bonham wants you. Voilà: you are bait. It speaks ill of me, Mina, but if I didn't care about you, I would not hesitate to use you in that way. I tell you this because maybe we should discuss my faults as well. I'm not the best of men by any measure. My conscience has decayed over the years. I'm trying to reform myself, but . . ."

She snorted. "You think you need to tell me? I'd already noticed you don't concern yourself overmuch with honoring your obligations. At least, not in any *mannerly* fashion."

His soft laugh was accompanied by a squeeze of her hand. "Then you should believe me, shouldn't you? You have firsthand experience. If I worry about you, it means something."

She scuffed her heel against the floor. "As compliments go, that leaves much to be desired."

He cleared his throat. "Do you want compliments?"

"No."

"I thought not. You don't trust flattery, do you?" When she only shrugged, he said gently, "No, I'm right about that. Because, you see, we're not strangers." He paused, so long that she finally lifted her eyes to his. His expression was grave. "Perhaps it's easier said this way," he murmured. "Can you learn to hate in a day?"

She heard the implication in his question. What a mad idea. Almost, she withdrew her hand. But there was courage in how frankly his dark eyes held hers. She would not prove less brave than he. "I suppose," she said, and shrugged. Still a cowardly response, then, but it was the best she could manage.

"I know it," he replied steadily. "And I promise you, I have learned to hate in a day, and that hate will last my whole life long. Do you want to hear, then, how a mapmaker became a spy?"

She knew what he was asking. Four years ago, her life had also acquired a central narrative. These were not tales to be told lightly; they were keys to the soul. "Yes," she whispered.

His fingers played lightly over hers. "I was an officer with the Survey, mapping the Himalayas. I got to places most men don't go. One of my superiors took a particular interest in my achievements. I thought nothing of it, really; we had an old friend in common, a retired mapmaker and astronomer who had mentored me during my years at Eton. If I did have a moment or two of doubt about this officer, an uneasiness I couldn't explain, then our mutual friend's recommendation silenced it.

"One day, this new mentor summoned me to Simla. He claimed to have lost a confederate who'd strayed over the westernmost border of the North-West Frontier Province, into Afghan territory. It was bad news. Disraeli had been pressuring Northbrook, the viceroy, to take a harder line with Sher Ali against the Russians, and Northbrook was fighting it. There was no reason an Englishman should be wandering into that mess without official instruction; it was like tossing a match onto tinder. But my new mentor was persuasive. He said my skills were the best chance for tracking down this man and getting him out without detection. If I failed, we'd have an international incident on our hands."

"A noble mission," she said.

"Precisely." His lips shifted into a black curve. "Very noble, no doubt dangerous—exactly what I'd hoped for, when I enlisted. A chance to prove, once and for all, that I was not my father's son."

His fingers were slipping away. She caught them, aware of the roughness of his scar. "You are nothing like him." She knew that much. She could recognize such men from a mile distant. Collins had taught her that skill.

"I have tried not to be," he said. "But Ridland made it difficult."

"Ridland was the officer."

"Yes." He was looking through her, now, at the wall. "What he did not tell me was that his man had infiltrated the territory deliberately, in order to unsettle the viceroy's authority. This man was conspiring to make his own retrieval as difficult and public as possible, in the hopes of forcing a war. I was also uninformed that if I was caught, the government, including those sections that had designed this mission, would disavow my official involvement. I would be branded a traitor, my presence in the territory construed as proof of my disloyalty." He sighed. "Even had I known this, I still might have been forced to obey, of course. But at least I could have prepared my team. I took two assistants with me. They died before we realized we'd walked into a trap."

His fingers had tightened on hers. She gripped him now as hard as she was able. Sometimes that was what one needed. She had learned that in the train today. "I'm so sorry."

He shrugged. "The point is, in less than a day, I

learned to loathe Ridland with all my heart. And I had no choice but to relearn the wisdom of that hatred for a decade afterward." His attention focused on her. "Every day, I relearned it. Never more so than when I left you behind in that window."

"You hesitated," she said softly. "You tried to take the knife from me."

"A moment's bravery. And then I put my instincts aside."

"You said you had no choice."

"Yes, I told myself that afterward, too. But it's harder to believe when I know a woman who made choices for herself when none seemed to exist." She felt herself flush, and his lips shifted into a softer curve. "I chose to ignore my instincts that day, just as I had when I decided to trust Ridland. So I hope you will under-stand when I tell you that I don't mean to ignore them again. Indeed, it is a wondrous thing to recognize how right they are."

He reached up, very gently, to brush away her hair. His touch was seductive; she let herself lean into it, and shut her eyes.

"Your instincts are good as well." His fingertips pressed very lightly to her cheek. "If they tell you some-thing, Mina, you should not ignore it."

She did not bother to move. Her instincts were hardly fluent in the language he was asking them to speak, but the eagerness of their attempt suggested a native talent for it. How odd. She had never thought she would fall in love. "And if they disagreed with yours?"

"On small things, I would argue with you," he said

readily. "On the larger questions? If they disagreed, we'd not be having this conversation."

She opened one eye. "But if they do disagree," she said. "On the larger issues."

"Then I won't tell you what to believe. I was told for a very long time to mistrust myself. I would not do the same to you."

She let herself look her fill at him then, his long lips and the soft brush of his hair across his strong jaw. She had never mistrusted herself until she had begun to long for him. That made it easy to take his advice. And if he differed with her on what should count as a larger issue, they could wrestle with it tomorrow. "Lie with me," she said, and drew him by the hand up the bed to her side.

He came willingly. Maybe he'd been foolish enough to believe her when she said she only wished to lie beside him, for when she turned and closed her teeth on his jugular, he made a startled noise and went very still. Thus did a wolf kill its prey. Thus did she choose. She lifted her mouth, just enough to ensure that her words would trace hot moisture across his skin. "You're going to have to trust me, Phin."

He rolled over and put her beneath him in one swift move, catching her wrists and pinning them over her head. "I could say the same," he murmured, and bit her back, very lightly, on the chin.

She lay quiescent for a moment, mastering the reflexive urge to balk at his teeth. She could find it in herself to trust him, but only in her own way.

His hands opened, and hers slipped down to his sides,

gripping him lightly. The shirt annoyed her. It bespoke his hesitance earlier, when she had cast at him every lure in her arsenal. "I like you better undressed." She heard his breath catch, and opened her eyes to find him staring down at her. He smiled, which was not the reaction she wanted. "You're supposed to say—"

"That undressing is not always required." His mouth lowered to hers; she moaned, simply for the fun of it, and then the moan became real as he kissed her more deeply than she'd expected. His tongue was honey, coasting over hers; it famished her. She arched up, wanting to swallow him, to eat him whole. He would make a feast for a woman, his brain and his body and his humor and his sensitivity—this last still a thing of wonder to her. He saw her so clearly.

Her thoughts tangled as his hand slipped into her bodice. His palm found her breast, stroking her nipple, almost lazy as he kissed her. She relaxed beneath him. She liked the weight of him pressing into her, how solid he felt. That she could support his weight made her feel larger in her own right. Her hands skated across the broad expanse of his back, confirming her capabilities; she cupped his buttocks, squeezing, and the muscles there contracted. Slipping lower, pressing into the seam of his trousers, her fingers found the soft weight of his testicles, and when she stroked him, his lips broke from hers on a groan.

It reminded her of her earlier plans, which had involved his acquiescence, not hers. She slid out from under him and pushed him by the shoulder until he fell willingly onto his back. The cravat lay discarded at the foot of the bed; she started to reach for it, but he caught her arm and hauled her back atop him, her neck in line with his mouth. Down her throat his kisses moved, lower, until they circled around her nipple. His teeth came into play again, and then the soft sucking of his lips; she splayed weakly, limp and obedient—temporarily, she told herself—atop him. His hand pulled up her skirts, bit by bit. A fingernail trailed up her calf, moving along the inside of her leg, higher and higher, suggesting the goal but refusing to arrive there. He drew lazy circles on her inner thigh. He was going to overwhelm her in a second, which was not how she'd intended it at all.

She pushed herself off him and leaned backward, her hand blindly groping, finding luck as it closed on the cravat. When he spotted it, his eyebrow cocked. "No," he said.

She smirked. "Afraid?"

He smoothed his hand down her bottom and cupped her between her legs, rubbing, now pressing. "Oh, terribly," he said, as she squirmed for him. "And you?"

"Not at all," she managed. She loosed a shuddering breath, then leaned forward and looped the stock cloth behind his head. His hand found the slit in her drawers, stroking her sensitive flesh, stirring the moisture that rose at his touch. "You will not distract me," she whispered, but her breathiness made him smile too smugly for her liking. She pulled the cravat loosely over his eyes and knotted it at his ear, catching his free hand when it rose and forcing it back to the bed. "Behave," she said.

His finger nudged up through her folds, finding the spot that pleased her most, and she bucked. "I can do this in the dark," he said, his voice low and smoky. "I expect I can do it blindfolded, too."

She paused, not having considered this point. And then an idea came to her. She slid down his body, pushing up his shirt to lick his chest. He liked this; his hands came to her neck, massaging, encouraging her. His trousers were not difficult to open. She licked him up the length of his cock.

He swore; his hands tightened and then fell away from her. "Mina," he said, but she could not tell if it was a warning or praise. So she did it again, taking the tip of him lightly into her mouth, tasting the salt and musk of him, suckling him as he had done to her nipples. The way his body jerked beneath her, and the sounds that growled from his throat, decided her: praise, definitely. She tried to take him deeper, opening her mouth and using the full length of her tongue, simply for the pleasure of making him shake. So easily he writhed for her.

But his patience snapped. He took her beneath the arms and pulled her up, and when he ripped away the cravat, his expression afforded her a premonition. "I've a better use for this," he said, and took hold of her wrists.

"Wait," she said, her heart quickening. "I don't—"

"You do." He put her arms over her head, looping the cloth around them and tying a loose knot. "I saw your face," he murmured into her ear. "I saw your face when I suggested this before."

"But I was thinking I would bite your throat out," she said hoarsely.

He laughed and moved down her body. It became clear, very quickly, where he was going: he took her by the bum and lifted her skirts free, and they came up over her face so that she was blinded as well as bound. "Unfair," she gasped, but her protest broke off as the wet heat of his mouth touched the crease of her inner thigh. His tongue danced over her flesh, licking up the very seam of her, retreating and returning, teasing her delicately; the violent throbbing she felt was all out of proportion to it. For a moment it frightened her again, and in that moment, she recognized that the choice was still hers: no cravat, no blindfold, could make her give him anything of herself. She could still hold herself away from him. But why would she want to?

She let her thighs fall farther apart and gave herself over to his mouth. The pleasure rippled up behind her knees, past her thighs, and down the backs of her arms; she seized beneath him and did not try to stifle her sob.

He kissed his way up her body then, freeing her wrists, nipping at her fingers. Her palm caught his attention; he nuzzled it, his tongue tasting the fleshy mound beneath her thumb. The indolence of his interest puzzled her. She knew he was not yet satisfied; she could feel the stiffness in him, feel his erection against her leg. "I want you inside me," she said.

He pressed a kiss into her hand and took her by the hips, twisting so that she fell atop him. Briefly she hesitated, baffled by this position. Did he not want her, then?

He caught her eyes. "Then have me," he said, and thrust upward with his hips. The brush of his cock suddenly suggested possibilities she'd never contemplated. A little awkwardly, she came up on her knees.

Too late, she realized the matter would require assistance; his long brown fingers closed over his own length, and he positioned himself against her, his eyes on hers hot and unflinching. There was no need to be embarrassed; there was nothing between them of judging. Slowly she seated herself.

The sensation of fullness took her breath, made the aftermath of her climax shiver through her again. The pressure of his hands coaxed her to rise, and then sink back down. She took his tutorship for two long strokes, and then planted her hands on his shoulders and pushed herself up without prompting.

His eyes fluttered shut, and he gave a soft moan. Amazement flooded her, hot and tender and weakening: that he could close his eyes with her and surrender to his pleasure so unabashedly, when with this body of his he might have demanded anything, might have *taken* anything. She rocked back and forth now, rubbing herself along him. Her hunger had announced itself again, pulsing and building between her thighs. A daring thought came to her. She reached down to touch the place of their joining.

He made a guttural, choked sound and caught hold of her hips to stop her. For a moment she thought she had done something wrong, but no—he was only fixing her in place for his own designs. His grip tightening, he pulled her hips down as he thrust upward, into her.

She felt herself tighten—at first a startled response, and then, with a whimper, from pleasure alone. Again and again he thrust, pulling her and pushing her, working her harder and more deeply with each stroke, until she could not hold herself upright any longer. She collapsed forward, pressing her forehead to the hot hollow of his throat, splayed over him, willingly limp as he penetrated her.

He was right, all of this was far from one-sided; he gasped and she gasped back, their bodies communicating toward a mutual goal. He set his face into the crook of her neck and groaned, unafraid of what she might hear in it, and she thought, *Love, yes. I am not afraid anymore.*

Chapter Fourteen

They slept that night with limbs overlapping like puzzle pieces. Phin woke once; she lay peacefully, her lips parted slightly, as though thirsty for the moonlight falling through the window. Her dreams did not appear to trouble her. Perhaps that was partly his doing. He wanted to think so. *Love makes everything that is heavy, light:* trust a theologian to misinterpret the fleshly equation. In fact, he felt curiously heavy as he looked at her, a not unpleasant sensation, but also tired, like a ship anchored in harbor after a long trial of rough seas.

It seemed unwise to feel restful when so much lay ahead. But he remembered her advice, and permitted himself to breathe out the tension that wanted to stiffen him. He stroked her cheek for a minute, then fell back to sleep almost immediately.

The next morning, a new silence sat between them. She put on her mother's diamond ring, and as they boarded the train and the guard called out their destination of London, she gave him an indecipherable look. *Not yet in port*, he thought ruefully. They sat side by side in an empty compartment, but he did not buy a newspaper, and she did not pretend to take an interest in the scenery out the window. London was coming up on them like darkness, clouding their horizon.

He was not going to indulge her at her own expense. As they entered the outlying suburbs of the city, the crouching houses hunched in rows, he touched her hand briefly. "Let me book you passage."

She glanced from his hand to his face. "I'm the one who has what he wants. I can lure him out. Let me help you."

He thought of her face in the window so many years ago, and the cost of stifling memories and guilt. He had stifled himself in the process; he was not willing to abdicate his responsibility to her again. "What will help me is knowing that you're safe."

Her mouth hardened. "I am not one of your pens," she said. "Don't try to order me."

For a long minute he sat there, meditating on the violent force with which the train wheels passed over the ties by watching the small, rhythmic jerk of her shoulders. In retrospect, of course, it made perfect sense that Bonham had been a spy, and a traitor. As the self-made son of impoverished colonists, a man who dreamed of making his name in England, he'd been perfectly positioned to catch Ridland's attention. What had Ridland offered him? A chance for advancement in the motherland? No matter the lure, he had fallen in line; he had courted Collins's favor and trust.

But Ridland rarely delivered on his promises, and Bonham must have quickly realized that Collins offered a better chance for his continued advancement. Somewhere along the line, he'd switched his loyalties. Phin could almost understand the temptation. How sweet it must have felt to take Ridland's orders with a smile, only to skewer him promptly in the back.

Certainly Bonham had seemed a cheerful man that last night in Hong Kong. Standing beside Phin, his idle conversation laced with amusing anecdotes, he'd very casually proposed a drink. And when he'd relayed the order for brandy with a presumption that rightly belonged only to the master of the house, Phin had found it unremarkable. He had assumed—carelessly, in retrospect—that with the gesture, Bonham only wanted to mark his own closer affiliation with Collins's household.

A single drink was all it had taken; belladonna worked quickly. But before moving off to let him die, Bonham had commented on Mina. *The man who catches her will have to cage her.* It seemed irrelevant whether that insight had been based on a clear view of her or on a subscription to her routine. What mattered was that the insight was correct, and that Bonham had reached it before Phin had even begun to perceive her ingenuity.

The man was not to be underestimated.

"I don't want to lock you in," he said. "But I will do it for your sake."

She sighed and looked at her hands. "I don't wish to break your windows. But I will do it for our sake."

He did not miss the adjustment of pronoun, but that small encouragement could not make up for the larger implications of her statement. If she would not cooperate, he was going to be forced to do things that would drive her away more effectively than hatred. "Don't."

"I have no choice," she said softly. "My mother—"

"I have rooms without windows."

When she looked at him now, her face was naked of any pretense, and the fear in it knocked the breath from his lungs. "Not if you love me," she said. "You will never put me into a room without windows."

He held his tongue, wrestling down dangerous whims. If they were going to speak of love, it would not be in service of this debate. "Don't trust a desperate man." It occurred to him that he might as well be speaking of himself. He forced his thoughts to focus. "He may well try to kill you."

"And I won't sit in a room waiting for him to try."

He took her chin and forced her face up to his. "How do you think Bonham found you? Ridland is publicizing your whereabouts to save himself some work. He has made you into bait."

"Then *let him use me*," she said sharply. "Parade me about. I'll play cheese in the mousetrap, willingly."

"How noble of you," he said through his teeth. "But there's no need. If the documents are indeed what he wants, then I can deliver them just as easily."

"It's not a question of ease, Phin. It's—" She drew a long breath. "I *need* to act. I can't be shut up again, to wait helplessly while my mother's life is at stake. Not again." Very softly she added, "I'm only helpless, I'm only chased, so long as I'm not the one chasing."

He realized from her tone that she was making some sort of confession. But, God above, he could not let the intimacy of her offering make any difference to his opinion. This was her *life* they were arguing over.

He dropped his hand, lest his irritation vent itself on her flesh. "An illusion of control is still only an illusion." As her expression tightened, he said more sharply, "One of us is going to have to yield."

She looked away. "Then we are both doomed to disappointment, for I don't think either of us is the yielding sort."

"If you can't trust me to find her—"

"Ask me how I got my scars."

His throat closed. Of all times to decide to tell him, of all the reasons to tell him, this was the least fair. "Mina. *You* are the one at stake here."

"Ask."

He spoke through his teeth. "It makes no difference to this moment."

"Yes, it does." Her blue eyes turned on him, unveiled, challenging him openly. "I saved you in Hong Kong. There's no reason for you to think I don't understand the possible consequences, the dangers of helping you now."

He exhaled. "Can you shoot a man between the eyes from fifty paces?"

"No. But I can think clearly through terrible fear." She paused, and her face went whiter. "I can sit in a windowless room and listen to my mother be tortured for hours on end."

His next protest dried up in his throat. He knew it grew worse. He had seen the scars on her back. He had felt them. They were jagged, not methodical; they spoke of unrestrained rage, with no design to it at all.

She was waiting. She wanted to see his reaction. He drew a hard breath, and for her sake, he let his impassivity fracture. "Go on," he said hoarsely, and took her hand.

Her voice was the barest thread of sound over the clattering of the train. "I can bide my time and keep my sanity when the darkness seems as though it's going to smother me. I don't like darkness. I need light now. I needed you to lie next to me last night."

And he had done that, he thought. That was a small comfort: he had given her that, at least.

"I can listen to her scream," she said more slowly, "knowing it is for *my* sake that she does not apologize. Just this once, she won't apologize, because she knows that if she does, his anger will turn away from her. It will turn on *me*."

He felt a wave of dizziness. Blood draining from his head. "For me," he said. "For helping me."

Her fingers closed hard on his. "No," she said. "It really had nothing to do with you. Believe me, Phin. I was only trying to win our freedom, and you were the way I saw."

And he had left her behind. And refused to let himself think on her. That next day, recuperating in a shack in Aberdeen, he had slept dreamlessly. He had boarded that damned ship without looking back. "Not again," he said. His anger was not for her, but she flinched; he cursed himself and said more evenly, "Bonham and Collins won't touch you this time. I won't let—"

"You won't *let* them," she interrupted. "Yes, that's how I know you're not listening. Let me finish. A day of that. And then, for whatever reason—a visitor, some-one who couldn't be turned away, I never knew—Collins had to move me from that room. And he made the mis-take of moving me into a room with a window." A weird smile quirked her lips. "Did he think I would sit there and entertain myself with the view? I suppose. It was on the second floor, after all. But he thought wrongly. I threw myself through it. *That* is how I got my scars. I went for help, and I met it coming through the gates, a day too late for my mother's comfort. A few minutes too late for my own." She paused, and touched his jaw very lightly. "I would throw myself through glass again for her. She has earned that from me. And I would do it for you, too, even if the window was yours. But I hope you won't make me do it."

He was starting to feel panicked. He had forgotten the sensation in her presence, but the drumming of his pulse made him wonder how he had ever sat quietly be-side her, the whole of this morning. They had to resolve this. She had to bend. "I won't lock you in, then. The run of the house is yours."

Her face shuttered. "Like a dog in a kennel."

"Like a woman being preyed upon by a criminal," he retorted.

"Like a *woman*, yes."

Air and his patience were growing short. "Christ, Mina, it does not come down to that!"

"Don't make me want to run," she said.

This was ridiculous. He fought for a clear breath. "Don't try. It would only embarrass you."

"Oh, I think we would both regret it."

He forced himself to turn away. *Not in front of her. Not now.* But the tattoo of his heart filled his head, sharper and faster than the wheels over the tracks. His fingers dug into the soft upholstery of the armrests. His knuckles were white, but he could barely feel his flesh.

"Phin." Her voice came to him dimly. One second he was trapped in his pounding head, constricted by his clothes, stiflingly hot. The next he was outside himself, so light he felt nauseated. "Are you all right?"

He realized her fingers had covered his only when she squeezed hard enough to drive her mother's diamond into his flesh. The pain focused him. He looked down at her hand, and then forced his eyes up to hers.

She was watching him with a deepening frown. Perhaps, finally, she realized her foolishness. One did not make oneself bait unless one was very confident in the skill of the trap. If his grip on the armrests had loosened, she would have seen that his hands were shaking. She would have thought better of her faith in him.

"Go home," he said hoarsely.

She shook her head.

It was not a truce that commenced between them that day, but a curious and largely silent form of warfare, which Mina waged with every wit in her head. He was as good as his word, and she expected no less of him: her door remained unlocked, and she was free to move about the house as she wished. But while it was a large house, and his presence in it made it more interesting than it ought to be, she could not forget that the exits stood

closed to her. Over the next week, whenever she ven-
tured too near them, her constant shadow, the brawny
footman Gompers, would make it known, at first with
a strongly cleared throat and then with an explicit plea
("It would be awkward for me, miss"), that she must not
attempt to leave. He slept in her anteroom, like a dog
guarding a bone.

For a time, at least, she found patience. Jane spent a
fortune wiring transcriptions of the documents Mina
had stolen. Amongst the gibberish was a list of names,
some of which, Phin determined during a conference
with Ridland, matched those of known associates of the
bombmakers recently arrested at Birkenhead. Ridland
tasked a force to crack the code.

Meanwhile, Phin spent most evenings making public
appearances, hoping to draw Bonham from the wood-
work. When home, he did his best to keep Mina entertained, and his ministrations were inventive and largely
successful. They took their meals in her rooms or in his,
making conversation that rarely touched on the issue between them but that seemed designed to lay him bare to
her with increasing clarity. He talked of his childhood,
and she of hers; she learned that what she'd mistaken for
arrogance was, in fact, a shield that a child had developed
to protect himself from the scorn of his peers. She could
not imagine any schoolboy so stupid as to look at him
and mistake him for an object of pity, but she quite liked
his stories about thrashing Mr. Tilney, and applauded
him for being sent down in style.

He also talked a great deal about maps, about the philosophies of knowledge that had shaped how men fixed

the curves of the earth onto paper. She had never given it much thought, but it made sense to her that premonitions of danger, or convictions of superiority, would yield a different view of the world than would hopes for profit or miracles. She tried, wandering the house, to ignore the closed doors, and when she managed to do so, she found herself enamored of what it told her about him. He was a collector of objects, with an eye for unusual beauty; every nook and niche delighted her.

But when her impatience was heavy upon her—waiting and wondering were so much worse than pursuing a solution—she also saw how every room could have predicted her dilemma. The slew of antique maps pointed to a man determined to hold the world in his palm, to master every knowable order that had been imposed on it. In the morning room, where she went to read, a glass cabinet held a display of striped and curiously colored rocks, all the earth's secrets disgorged, a chronicle of the birth and death of mountains and the violent expulsion of ocean floors into sunlight. Even the bedrooms served as a catalog: decorated by period and place, one was filled with Georgian furniture and scrollwork silken chairs, the next with Turkey carpets and ebony wood inlaid with mother-of-pearl, exotic paintings done in miniature framed along the wall.

In their conversations, he sought to catalog her as well. He was trying to understand her fully, but as the days passed, she grew cautious about whether he would put the knowledge to proper use. The more he understood how much she loathed this situation, the more determined he seemed to make her predicament comfortable.

He wanted to know what sort of frame or case or cage would suit her best, although his own darkening moods suggested he'd already discovered the right answer: none of them would content her.

She slept alone, although she preferred not to—that was the one matter on which she refused to yield. If a man showed an interest in traps, there was no need to offer him the most obvious method. But it was a double-edged mutiny, as unpleasant to her as to him, and her refusal, too, became something of a game to keep her occupied.

Teaching her one night to play skittles, Phin found numerous opportunities to touch her, and she let him do so, curious, in a manner made more piquant by fear, about how strong she would prove in resisting him. When his long body pressed behind hers, bending her over the table to line up a shot, she felt the urge to set her forehead to the felt, to bare her nape to him like a submissive animal. It angered her. "You could touch me anywhere," she said, "if I knew I was free to make my own choices, take my own risks."

The abrupt introduction of this argument did not give him a moment's pause. It sat between them always, speaking even through their silences. "Not if you were dead." His eyes were shadowed by exhaustion; he was leaving the house now in the late hours of the night, trawling back alleys to chase rumors of Bonham. "In a coffin, I couldn't touch you at all."

The second week, she discovered that he'd intercepted a letter to her from Bonham, proposing a place and time for a trade: her information in exchange for the whereabouts of her mother. "Take his offer," she said over dinner. "We'll give him everything."

A muscle ticking in his jaw, he set down his glass and said, "We tried it."

She absorbed this in silence. "When?"

"Two nights ago. He never appeared."

"Because *I* wasn't there," she said fiercely. "He requires *my* presence. You botched it!"

"Listen," he said. "There is something more to this than we know. There's no cipher or key in those documents. Nor could any paper prove his innocence after his actions in Providence. He wants something else from you, and if you cannot come up with a theory, the only option is to wait." When she would have argued, he said more curtly, "He's been spotted in London, and with the number of men looking for him, it's only a matter of time—"

"And meanwhile, my mother remains missing," she said coldly.

"I'm sure she likes you better alive," he retorted.

"At least return Tarbury to me." With Tarbury to hand, she would not feel so helpless.

"You may write to him," he said. "He's quite comfortable in a hotel across town. But as for your care, forgive me if I prefer the men in my employ."

She grew deliberately colder after that. She began to call him Ashmore again; she remarked on Collins regularly. "You call him to mind," she said. "Forgive me." His charm wore thin now; he did not like the comparison. When he touched her, her desire made her furious. Bonham showed no sign of emerging from his lair, and her thoughts dwelt on her mother with a blackening intensity.

They might have continued like this, growing increasingly bitter, had Mina not woken one night to find a stranger in her bedchamber.

It was the sound of her jewelry box spilling that first penetrated her awareness. At first, it did not even occur to her to scream. She had been dreaming of Hong Kong. The cold pressure of the gun, the hot points of pain where fingers dug across her neck and clamped down on her shoulder, wove seamlessly into her nightmare.

Her eyes opened beneath the hot, sour breath of the man standing over her. "Up," he whispered. She stumbled onto her feet, reality separating and solidifying out of the watery remains of sleep. "Walk," he said.

The blunt nudge of the gun pushed her into the anteroom. Beneath her bare feet, the carpet turned hot and wet. Gompers's robust form lay slumped on one side, blood pooling around his head. A shadow detached itself from the corner. Two men, then.

Her head seemed to grow lighter, like a balloon straining at the leash. She had learned four years ago the difference between panic and fear. Panic was the anticipation of catastrophe; fear announced its arrival. It was fear that steadied her footsteps and shoved blood through her veins as the gun guided her into the corridor. Her senses seemed to expand. Old candle smoke clung to her captor's clothes, and stale traces of moldy hay.

She caught Phin's scent a second before he came hurtling through the darkness.

The collision of his body struck her forward into the

opposite wall, and she went down hard on her knees. A gunshot rang out; now came a series of short, sharp thuds. A muffled curse, and a cry. A thick, crunching sound turned her stomach before her brain made sense of it. Hair brushed over her ankle. She recoiled from the fallen body, then scrambled around on all fours.

Two men struggled against the opposite wall. Difficult in the darkness to discern any subtleties, but their forms strained against each other. Now she made out the silhouette of arms outstretched, grappling for control of a gun.

A deafening explosion, a whining shiver past her ear. She threw herself aside as the wall behind her burst, disgorging chunks of plaster onto her head. Her eyes locked on Phin's taller form, her breath, her mind suspended. No question of helping. The other man was pinned beneath him, out of her reach.

Phin made a sudden sharp move, and the other man seemed to lunge away from the wall, only to stagger suddenly back. Phin whipped him around so his back slammed into the wall. The gun clattered to the floor.

She realized how foolish she was. There was no need for her help.

Still, the gun lured her. She inched forward as Phin lifted his elbow and smashed the man across the face. The nauseating crack did not satisfy him; he brought up his knee, and the man curled over it like a rag doll.

Her palm closed over the butt of the pistol. "I have it," she gasped.

Phin gave no sign of hearing her. He snapped the man's body flush against his, into a mockery of a lover's embrace. A wheezing noise filled the air. He was crushing the man's throat.

"I have it!" Why was she speaking? Her voice sounded grotesque, too clumsy and jagged for the delicacy of this operation. Killing a man without a word.

He grabbed hold of the man's hair and, with one sharp move, snapped his neck.

Her fingers around the gun hilt went abruptly slack.

Silence.

Her knees gave way. She sank into the plush silk of the carpet.

He must have looked at her, for she caught the glint of his eyes in the darkness. He still held the body clutched to him. Not even his breath made noise.

Her own rasped heavily in her ears. "I have it," she whispered.

He relinquished the body, his hands subsiding somehow elegantly, like a gesture to accentuate some ongoing conversation. The corpse folded to the floor.

"Are you hurt?"

His voice sounded strange. Colorless.

"Mina." His voice sharpened to a command. "*Speak.* Are you hurt?"

"No." But her joints seemed to have dissolved. Ice was sprouting in her stomach. The cold bloomed outward; it was going to make her shake.

He stepped over the body, toward her. It was not in her to flinch from him, but she would not have blamed some other woman for doing so. The hands that now reached for her shoulders had killed two men with soundless efficiency. The men had cursed and cried out, and he had never made a noise. Their silent, faceless executioner, this man who had touched her so gently.

He pulled her up, guiding her face into his chest. She was indeed trembling, and he gripped her harder and harder yet, as though to hold her together. "It's all right," he murmured.

She wasn't going to lapse into hysterics. It occurred to her to tell him so, but her mind was skipping between other curiosities: that she could feel so safe in his arms, even now. Safer, even. It seemed strange, unhealthy, that he did not shake as well. Every muscle pressed against her was hard, braced for more. *I have some practice with such things.*

A deep unease awakened in her. She put her arms around him, the butt of the gun lodging by his spine. Her intuition was stirring, suggesting the cost that such practice might exact from a man. He did not shake, but that seemed a worse thing to her by far than trembling. "You're all right," she said into his shirt. He was solid, large, whole, and hale. His heart beat steadily beneath her cheek; it actually seemed to be picking up speed now, as though safety were more alarming to him than the threat of death.

The acrid bite of gunpowder scorched the air. Down the corridor, doors were slamming, voices lifting. The servants would be upon them soon.

He pulled away. "Come," he said quietly. He took her wrists in one hand and bent to retrieve the other pistol.

"Your man is hurt," she said, remembering.

He stepped inside and hit the button to call the electricity. Gompers's eyelashes fluttered in the glare. His face looked pale against the dark corona of blood soaking the carpet. She thought Phin would go to him, but he pulled her onward, keeping her directly behind him as he surveyed the corners and alcoves in the room.

"There's no one else," she murmured.

His grip tightened until it was a hair short of painful. The open window had caught his attention. When he turned to face her, his tanned skin looked abnormally pale and his expression was flat and lifeless, clay yet to be animated by the breath of life. "You see the use of windows," he said.

She opened her mouth, but found no reply at the ready.

His glance switched to the doorway. The footman was now awake and groaning, struggling to push himself upright. "I need to deal with this." When he looked back at her, there was nothing in his face that she felt able to speak to. "You will not argue," he said. "Come with me."

He deposited her in his inner sanctum, a dark, sparsely furnished room that indeed had no windows. She might have found it intolerable, had every appointment not spoken so intimately of him. The maps, the opened books on the table, the carefully sketched drawings of mountains and deep valleys, they were his, and she felt enfolded by him.

All the same, she would have preferred his embrace.

Curled up on a sofa, she listened to the dim, distant sounds that managed to penetrate the walls. Doors opening, closing. The comings and goings of men, debating on matters, drawing up plans. The sun must have risen, but she would not have known it save for the ticking of the clock on the mantel.

As the shock wore off, she found herself wondering at her compliance. Waiting never worked. Tonight had proved it. If Bonham wanted her so badly, he would come for her anywhere.

And if Phin needed her, she half thought that he would never come. The shadows in his face tonight were not all owed to rage. Some of them had looked like resignation.

She stepped out through the antechamber, into the hall. Two new guards stood there, men she thought she recognized from her brief time at Ridland's. "Take me to Ashmore," she said.

"He is not to be disturbed." This from a young blonde with a lantern jaw and something of Ridland's cold humor in his eyes.

She still had the purloined pistol. She lifted it and watched him recoil. "Take me to him," she repeated.

On the threshold of the study, she stopped. Phin sat in an armchair, staring into a fire that smoked low in the hearth. The disarranged chairs, the uncapped decanter and emptied glasses testified to a meeting recently adjourned. But it was not the uncharacteristic disorder, or even the darkness of his expression, that gave her pause.

A long pipe sat in front of him.

Of course it did. How had it escaped her? That night when he had caught her in here, the air had been dirtied with it. She had spent too much time in Hong Kong not to recognize the odor. But its apparent mismatch to the circumstances—and to the man himself—had blinded her.

"Opium," she said on a breath. "How intriguing."

His eyes remained on the fire. "Only for a woman raised among wolves."

The air smelled pure. He had not smoked it yet. "True enough." She stepped inside, pulling the door shut. "I wasn't raised in the woods to be scared by an owl."

Now his head turned. His lashes were not thick enough to veil the unnatural flatness of his regard. "Your woods were not dark enough," he said. "You have no idea what I am."

She hesitated, her fingers moving nervously over the pistol in her palm. She weighed her next words carefully. "I saw you earlier. It was not so dark that I couldn't see you, Phin."

His laughter was short and dull. "Yes, that's right. Were you impressed?"

She considered him, her eyes lingering on his languid posture in the chair, the loose drape of his legs stretched out before him. "Yes," she said, and was only a little surprised to realize that she meant it. "I've told you before, if I could master such skills, I would. There's no virtue in becoming a victim."

For a long moment, it seemed he would not respond. Then a bitter smile curved his lips. "How generously you render it. A funny thing, Mina. I have never been glad of my skill at killing. I told myself I had no choice. But tonight . . . perhaps it would disarrange your admiration if you knew that I almost enjoyed it."

"I would not believe that," she said softly.

He shrugged. "Believe as you like. But getting that bastard's throat between my hands—that had nothing to do with clear thinking. It was . . ." He shook his head. His hands lay open on his lap; he spread his fingers to look into his palms, his long fingers flexing once. "I would do it again," he said softly. "Gladly."

She snorted. "Yes, I should hope so. You were saving my life. I should *hope* you took *some* satisfaction in that."

He looked at her, his expression inscrutable. "True. I think I would kill anyone who touched you with violent intent. That shouldn't comfort you, you know." His glance brushed briefly over the pipe. "My judgment stands in question. I cannot afford to lose control."

"I have no fear you will," she said. "Not unless the circumstances require it."

"Oh?" Black humor moved across his face. He reached out to flick a finger against the pipe in one of his curiously elegant, almost feminine gestures. "I used this last night." His self-contempt sounded detached, analytical. "Since I returned, I am a goddamned lunatic whose brain cannot be trusted. My thoughts go awry." He paused. "You've seen it. On the train."

She frowned. Coming into London, he *had* seemed near to losing his composure. But it would not have been the first time she'd overset a man. Evidently, he believed there was more to it.

Well, perhaps there was. She would be the last person to scoff at the complexities of the mind—she, who had unlearned the art of sleeping peacefully alone; she, whose mother had startled from unseen terrors for a year or more after their return to New York. "The trials you've undergone . . ." She could only begin to guess at them all. "They warrant disquiet, Phin." He would share them with her, and thereby halve his burden: she silently made the vow. "If they didn't trouble you, *then* I should worry about your judgment. But as it is— time is what you require. It gets better; slowly, it does. I promise you that."

He sat back. "Comforting," he said dismissively, and she felt her heart fall. "In the meantime, while I wait, I smoke poison to calm myself. As a result, I almost slept through your murder." He paused, his stare challenging. "You see in whose judgment you place your trust."

Impatience burned away her sympathy. "Trust is always a risk," she said flatly. "One you refuse to take, on either yourself or me. Self-pity, though—I see *that* is a choice you'll gladly make."

"That again?" He sprang from the chair with violent force. "I grow sick of this goddamned debate. I will not take it on my head to risk you simply so you can say you had a *part* in it!"

She scoffed. "A part in it? You think I want the right to brag?"

"What the hell else can it be? Unless you think me utterly incompetent?"

"That's the last thing I think you," she said bitterly. "Alas, you don't feel the same for me. You would have me wait with my hands tucked beneath my skirts so you can *fix* the matter for me, because God forbid I should have any say in it whatsoever! Yes, you can fix my messes—but can't I do the same? Certainly I did *not* require your guidance when I saved your life four years ago!"

"And what a trouble it would be to you," he said scathingly, "to be given an option for safety—"

She gave a wild laugh. "To be *kept* like a stuffed bird of paradise. Do you think that's how I want to live? In a very pretty cage? Do you think I *want* to live, if that's the cost? My mother made that trade, and you see how it worked out for her. Thank you very much, but *I* will not do it, even for you!"

After a long moment, he exhaled. "So. You would play bait in a trap of our making. What difference? It would still come down to depending on *me* for your safety."

She slammed the gun onto the table and spread her empty hands. Defenseless. "Yes," she said. "And here we get to the heart of the matter. I am very willing to depend on you. Of all people, it is *you* I would depend on. But you refuse to understand that. It's not enough for you. You say you care for me, but—"

"Mina." His eyes met hers, dark and unblinking. "*Care* is not the right word."

She caught her breath. "Don't tell me you love me," she whispered. "Not like this."

He ran a hand over his mouth. When it fell, a sneer curved his lips. "By some sick and twisted joke of the universe—"

"We've found each other like this," she snapped. "Yes, and love isn't always a blessing. You want to make this love *convenient*. And so you will make decisions for me at my expense, knowing that you tread on my nightmares. How *comfortable* for you."

"God*damn* it! Can you not be bloody reasonable for once?"

"Reason? What would a *madman* know of it? My God, I must be mad, too, to think that I love such a mule-headed fool! You think your *thoughts* are disordered? For God's sake, Phin, you're a man who orders his dratted pens! And that's your problem! If you'd cast off your goat-hair shirt, you would realize there's no need to be orderly all of the time! But if you insist on it—of course you will drive yourself mad. And me too, if you have your way!"

Turning on her heel, she stalked out, past the guard. She would not go back to his rooms. The hallway passed in a blur; no matter how fast she walked, the blonde was always at her heels. She threw the door to her apartment shut on his nose.

"Miss!" Sally, caught scrubbing blood from the carpet, clamped a hand onto her mobcap. "Oh, miss, it's glad I am to see you! Are you sure you're all right?"

"I'm brilliant." She fell into the chair by the window, glowering out at the blasted garden. The morning sunlight was spilling over the boxed-in flowers. Someone should set fire to it. Someone should turn the soil up and plant nothing but weeds.

"Miss?" Sally spoke hesitantly. "I thought you should know, a piece is missing from the jewelry box."

She spoke absently, unable to pull her eyes from the garden. "The jewelry box?"

"Yes, miss, they upended it, but all the pieces are accounted for save your locket."

"I have that," she said. She had fallen asleep wearing it, but it had scratched her in the night, and she had taken it off and cast it under the bed.

Her thoughts sharpened. Surely they hadn't been looking for it?

A warm weight landed in her lap. By instinct, she gasped and threw her hands up to shield her face. But it was only the cat. It took a moment to comprehend this. The *cat* had jumped into her *lap*.

"Perverse," she muttered. He butted his head into her torso. Of course, after hiding like a coward last night, he would want attention now, when she had all but given up on him. He hit his head harder against her and then rubbed himself along her rib cage. She sighed and scratched him behind the ears. Such stubbornness had to be rewarded, she supposed.

The door smacked open, frightening Washington to the floor. She came to her feet. Phin paused on the threshold, his face black with fury. "Not even bothering to knock," she said sarcastically. "Yes, you're getting the way of it now, aren't you?"

He strode toward her, his hand reaching into his jacket. "Here," he said, and pulled out the pistol she'd abandoned.

Sally gave a strangled squeak. Mina did not take her eyes from his face. "Go," she said to the maid.

His nostrils were flaring with the force of his breath. Even had he sprinted across the house, it should not have winded him so. The latch clicked shut behind Sally. He extended the pistol, the muzzle pointed toward the floor. "Take it," he said harshly. "You want to kill yourself to make a point about the tragedies of womanhood? Do it here. Now. Make me watch."

Her pulse was thudding in her throat. "Don't be stupid."

He snatched her hand and forced it to the butt of the gun, lifting it so the barrel settled against his chest. "Or maybe you want to shoot me? I'm the villain here, after all. I'm the one who's driving you mad. The trigger is yours, Mina."

She forced herself not to recoil. She had never seen him in such state. His eyes were bloodshot, wild, and his fingers trembled over hers, for all that they gripped her more unbreakably than iron. If she yanked back, he would not let her go. She knew, had learned last night, not to trust guns in such a tussle. "Stop it," she whispered.

He spoke slowly, each word distinct and cutting. "What do you want, then?"

"Your trust," she said.

"Christ. Take it," he said curtly, and she caught the gun as he pulled his hand free. Shoving a hand through his hair, he turned a tight circle. When his eyes met hers again, he looked no calmer, but his exhaustion seemed more marked, the lines around his eyes deeper. "This is not a matter of trust," he said. "I did not think you so goddamned *stupid*."

Her hand tightened around the revolver's grip. What a terrible weight it exerted on her hand, as cold as the feeling in her chest, pulling her down. "I want to know that you believe me capable. That now and—and in the future, you will let me take risks, not simply try to . . . protect me."

He shook his head slightly, whether in disbelief or denial, she could not tell. "All I want to do is protect you," he said, but there was something resigned in his voice, as if he loathed himself for it or thought she would mock him for the sentiment. "It's not weakness that makes me worry about you, Mina. It's love, and you bloody well know it. I love you."

She drew a hard breath through her nose. "Yes," she said. "I know. And—I love you as well." As his frown faded and he stepped toward her, she retreated a pace.

"But . . ." *Love does fizzle, with time.* Her mother had said that once. And if it did, what would remain but this? Obligation, worry, concern, *if* she was lucky. Otherwise—only his power over her, to keep her in this house when she might want to leave.

"You are testing me," he said flatly. "You don't even realize it. You want to prove something. How do you not see that it will come at your own expense?"

"I'm not trying to prove anything." Was she? It was true that she wondered how hot a flame his feelings might manage to withstand. But she did not want to hold his hand to the stove. She had no desire to hear him cry uncle. "It's only—if this is what your love means—if we are not to be equals, if you can't believe in me . . ." *Then I can't accept it.*

Did she mean that? If she did, surely she would be able to bring herself to speak the words. But they lodged in her throat, a solid pressure difficult to breathe around. "I expect nothing from so many people," she said haltingly. "But from you, I find myself expecting . . . so much."

His face shuttered. "And I fail to deliver it, you mean."

"No, I—"

"Yes, let's be honest here." His voice had sharpened into a jibe. "Of course you can't leave it to me. I've failed you. You've never forgiven me for Hong Kong. Those scars you wear—*they're* what stands between us."

"No." His idiocy astonished her. "Why won't you *listen* to me?"

"Oh, I've been listening. And it all seems very clear to me, suddenly. I ran out on you, yellow as a dog. You have no cause to depend on me." His laughter hurt her ears. "And you are wise for it, no doubt. *I'm* the fool here. If my father—"

She raised the gun to his heart, and he fell silent. Her hand was shaking with the force of her revelation. "Coward," she said. "At least I own up to my fears. I vowed never to make my mother's mistakes. But you? You're rationalizing your actions on the assumption that you *will* make his mistakes. You think I'm testing you? What is the opium but a test for yourself?"

His mouth thinned. "Mina. If something were to happen to you—"

"What? Do you think you would turn into him? That the demon inside you would take hold? That you would turn to the drug every night?" Her laughter sounded ragged. "I take it back. It's not me you need to trust, Phin. It's *yourself*. You're right. I would make myself bait only because I trust you. And damn you," she added fiercely. "I am *not wrong* to do so."

Slowly, very slowly, he raised his hand. His fingers closed over her wrist, steering the gun away, toward the wall.

She loosened her grip, letting him pull away the weapon, watching as he crouched to set it on the floor. As he straightened, long-limbed, loose, and rangy, she whispered, "I know you. You know I'm right."

He stared at her, expressionless. And then all at once he moved. His fingers plunged through her hair, painfully hard, hairpins springing free. He dragged her head to his. He was trying to prove his own blackness, perhaps; the kiss was hot, punishing almost. She kissed him back just as hard; she was not afraid.

He stepped into her, making her stumble over her skirts. Her palms came up to his hands where they gripped her, her nails cutting into his flesh, digging in for balance as he walked her backward out of the sitting room. Her calves hit the bed. Down she fell, and he came down atop her, his lips fierce, brooking no objection.

If he thought to ravish her, he was in for a disappointment. She closed her eyes to block out the sight of this room like a jewelry box; she closed her mind to the objections she'd entertained so successfully for two weeks now in denying herself this pleasure. She would take it again; she would ravish him.

The sunlight felt warm on her face, but his lips were hotter; beneath her roaming hands the muscles of his arms bulged stubbornly, immovable. Their mouths made soft sucking noises of communion, belying the rough scrape of his teeth. Her skirts rustled as he yanked them up, and the starched sheets protested as he came down fully atop her; the rub of cloth sounded like shocked whispers from a distantly observing crowd.

But the moment held no scope for subtleties or demurral. She reached down to help him, to yank her skirts all the way to her waist, spreading her legs for him without hesitation. She felt his surprise in the brief pause of his body, but then his hand was delving between her legs, stroking without hesitance, drawing a crude design between her lips. She thrust against his hand and he pushed a finger inside her, and then another, widening them to stretch her, as if he was the one who wanted to test limits. Which, of course, he was.

"Open your eyes," he growled into her ear.

His lips looked unexpectedly soft in the light, glossed by their kisses, but his exhausted eyes demanded things of her. She craned up to press her mouth to the cleft in his chin, running her tongue along it as his hand set a steady, hard rhythm below. Slipping under the hem of his shirt, up the hard, ridged plain of his belly to the slight rise of his nipples, her fingers traveled him. She set her nails into his flesh and raked them down to his navel, and he shuddered and cursed beneath his breath and bit her on the shoulder through the thin silk of her gown.

None of this was civilized. She scratched him again, even harder, and bit him on the neck. If he had a demon, so did she. He removed his hand to lick his thumb before laying it back atop her slit, and she arched beneath him, her back coming off the bed. She had learned from the cat that moving away from a touch could be as provocative as moving into it, but perhaps Ashmore had known this all along; he had walked away from her in Hong Kong, and she had chased after him because of it.

She moaned beneath his insistent strokes, and he laughed, his hot breath moving like a flame down her décolletage. A wild sound; it made her nape prickle, and from a stranger it would have made her run scrambling for safety. But the danger he presented came all from within. She gasped as his teeth closed around the fabric over her nipple. She opened her mouth on his shoulder and laid her hand against his cock, holding the length of him through his trousers.

And suddenly, a strange pause overtook them. Their bodies fell still by some silent accord, his hand inside her, his mouth pressed to her breast and hers to his shoulder, their ragged breathing warming each other's skin, her fingers cupped around him, the birdsong outside. Stray motes of dust floated in the sunlight, and his hair rippled in waves from his scalp, shining dark.

Peace came over her in a long, loosening wave. She did not want to leave him. She wanted to wake up beside him in the mornings.

When he lifted his head, the unguarded look on his face made her breath catch. It triggered grief, always near the surface these days. Tears pricked her eyes, and he leaned up to kiss her, very softly, on the mouth. He drew back, then returned once more, his tongue slipping across hers, sipping from her lightly but deeply, as his hand between her legs adopted a gentler and more specific focus. Her muscles tightened, but everything else in her melted; her fingers moved to the fly of his trousers, and then, as his flesh made hot contact with her fingers, she rubbed him gently, his tongue and his cock both.

A small noise broke from his throat, curiously soft, almost lost; she did not want him to feel lost. She was with him. She lifted her arms and wrapped them around his back very tightly, pulling him up against her, squeezing his hips with her thighs, enveloping him as fully and tightly as she was able. His hardness brushed against her, and she tilted her pelvis to bring herself into fuller contact. "Come," she whispered.

He pushed inside her little by little, easing her open to him. As he hilted himself, they both sighed. The coincidence made her smile a little. If only it were all so easy as this. The slow rocking movement he set up made her feel dreamy, at once everything fleshly and also free of flesh, unbounded and limitless, adrift like a dust mote, illuminated as fully.

Behind her eyes even the darkness looked soft, soft as his hair against her cheek; she stroked the stubble on his jaw as they moved together. The rhythm itself was dependent on repetition, but it moved one forward anyway; she sensed her oncoming crisis as her senses expanded in every direction. The sheets smelled of lemon and a faint trace of vinegar; the salt on her lips was from him. Dim distant noises from the street: the rumble of a carriage, the happy cry of a child, the scrape of a broom over dusty bricks. She felt capable of knowing and absorbing everything. He moved within her and she was the world.

"Mina," he whispered.

"Yes," she murmured back, and broke apart, so simply and comfortably in his arms, trembling with it.

He went still over her, the veins on his arms corded, as though the force of his pleasure strained his ability to contain it. And then, with a short, gusting breath, he leaned down to kiss her again, and she felt the slight ache and twinge of his withdrawal, the stickiness between her thighs.

Risk. Objectively unnecessary. Her instincts had demanded it.

When he rolled off her, she followed, coming up on her elbow to look at him. His lashes were long, curved sweetly as a child's; his lips pouted, full as a boy's. She ran a finger over his bottom lip, then down his chin. He stared at the ceiling, and his chest lifted and fell on a long breath. The light falling through the lace curtains laid a gold filigree over his face, and the delicate pattern touched off a stray thought. It made so much sense, now: what the men last night must have been looking for, and why Collins had kidnapped Mama.

She leaned forward to kiss his ear, intending it to be a brief project. But the softness of his lobe intrigued her startled lips; she ran her tongue along the edge, and now he exhaled a longer breath, as though finally his lungs could rest. "I will trust you," she whispered. "I'll do as you ask. But only if you trust yourself."

Chapter Fifteen

Trust yourself. Her edict stayed with him after he left her rooms, the locket safe in his pocket. It echoed in his head as he wrote the note to Ridland, whose men would circulate word of his proposed trade: the locket for Harriet Collins. With a hairpin, he and Mina had bared the secret of the necklace that Collins had given his wife, so many years ago. Beneath the miniature painting of roses in bloom lay a cipher disk, a set of tiny circular scales that, when spun, would help to unlock a code. No doubt, for a man with so many enemies, a woman's neck had seemed the safest place to store it.

Trust yourself. The words continued to puzzle him as he dressed for the evening. He wanted to keep Mina safe from a goddamned criminal; surely that was not an unusual urge for a man in love. He could not understand, then, why she insisted on connecting that desire to the question of his own trust in himself.

But as he contemplated the matter, his rising anger gave him pause. It suggested that his confusion concealed some deeper knowledge that he did not wish to face.

He was not accustomed to thinking of himself as willfully ignorant. As Fretgoose arranged his necktie, he stared into the mirror, watching his own eyes. Even he could not read them. He had no idea how she managed to do it so well. Alas, his own insight into her seemed equally clear. She was speaking the truth to him. If Bonham didn't take the bait tonight, he would need to enlist her aid. Otherwise, he had no hope of keeping her.

He dismissed Fretgoose and went to fetch his pipe. In the small, railed area outside the kitchen, he smashed it to pieces. Afterward, he dusted the fragrant ash off his hands and watched the flakes flutter away, dissolving in the breeze like stray regrets.

His plan was to spend the evening with Sanburne's circle. He had told Ridland to advertise his plan to visit the Empire; the music hall would be crowded and raucous, an excellent place for Ridland's men to position themselves unnoticed. Sanburne had responded to the proposition of an outing quite enthusiastically; apparently, one of his friends had just come into money and required a celebration.

Sanburne came for him at nine o'clock, Dalton and Tilney in tow. The carriage already smelled like a gin palace on payday, Tilney flushed as red from booze as Dalton's hair. Sanburne's mood seemed strangely muted, but when Tilney held out a bottle, he took it rapidly enough and downed half of it in one go before handing it back. Tilney then turned toward Phin, extending the bottle just as the coach thudded into motion. Wine splashed over Phin's knees.

"Brilliant," said Sanburne. He snatched the bottle and upended it on Tilney's trousers. As the man shrieked, he raised his voice. "No need to cry like a girl, there's another around here somewhere."

Tilney rummaged around by Sanburne's feet. He came up with a new bottle, which he tried to present to Phin.

"Doesn't drink," said Sanburne.

"What!" Tilney gawked at him. Dalton leaned forward, squinting, as though to inspect a sea creature brought up from the deep.

"Occasionally," Phin said. "But only to anesthetize my boredom with the company."

The Empire was bustling, its cream-and-gilt facade brightly lit, the curb packed with carriages. Swells in tall hats, ladies in gaudy satins and feathered headdresses, porters in their red-banded caps, match women and urchins pleading for coins, helmeted policemen attempting futilely to disperse the throng—the hubbub of the crowd trailed them inside, up the red-carpeted stairs, until it faded to a muted roar not unlike the sweep of wind on a winter's night.

Their box sat high above the stage, at one end of the U-shaped balcony next to the fall of the blue velvet curtains. It gave Phin a good panorama.

Drinks were ordered. Phin, with a pointed glance at Tilney, called for a whiskey. Sanburne looked approving. Phin took a sip, then waited for the act to start before pouring the liquid onto the carpet. At the next round, he demanded another. Now Sanburne looked puzzled. The viscount was a very curious alcoholic, wasn't he? By the third drink, Sanburne was watching him narrowly. *You're right*, Phin thought, *I can't do it so well as you can.* Tilney disappeared and returned with a ballet dancer, who batted her lashes at Phin and complimented his cuff links. Dalton said something loud and eager, and the men laughed, an ugly, sharp sound that made the dancer flinch. She looked very young. Did they not notice that their boisterousness scared her? She was clearly new to this routine. He would not wish it on her; he would wish it on no woman, but all too often they had no choice in the matter.

He closed his eyes, breathing deeply. Bonham was not going to show. He felt this in his gut. He was going to have to let her play a role. He was not a praying man; he had no idea how the hell he was going to get through it.

Dalton leaned over to harass him, complaining that he was not being properly celebratory. And then Sanburne, pursuing a new line of investigation, leaned forward and gave Phin a sniff. "Opium?" He sat back. "Even gin would be sweeter to you. Arsenic would be softer on your brain."

Lectured by Sanburne on matters of health and clean living—here was rich irony, indeed. A man could mine it for months and not tap out the vein. "No doubt," he said evenly. "Thank you for your concern."

"I'm worried for you," the viscount said.

Apparently, Phin was not the only one who required a look in the mirror. "You needn't worry," he said.

"The hell I don't."

"Have you a mirror, James?"

Sanburne recoiled. He looked as if he wanted to say something else, but all at once his mouth twisted, and he stood. "More drinks, then," he said to the box. "Anyone?"

He disappeared for a good deal of time. Phin was growing restless now. Bonham's absence made the night a pointless exercise, and he did not like to leave Mina alone. Tilney and Dalton addressed him; he had no interest in responding. She was right, he thought. There was no use pretending to be one of these people, or attempting a life like theirs. He had no use for this mask.

When Sanburne returned, nudging his shoulder and asking him to step outside, he was glad to oblige. They stepped into the snug little hallway that curved behind the boxes, all dark red velvet and the faint smell of smoke. "I need your help," the viscount said. He looked surprisingly grim in the smothered light. "Are you sober?"

Phin propped his shoulder against the wall. "Sufficiently. What is it?"

"I need you to put out an ear for underground rumors." Sanburne paused. "To be brief, some boy has been writing me about curses and tears and whatnot, and just now he popped up on the stairs and tried to gut me."

"I beg your pardon?" Phin said, thrown off by the delivery of such tidings in this casual manner.

The viscount shifted impatiently. "You heard me right. And I want him found. He's delivering the notes somehow; perhaps a watch on my house would work." His brow arched; the pregnant pause lent his next words a deeper significance. "Can you do that?"

"I could arrange for it," Phin said carefully. What fresh mess had James gotten himself into now? "Tears, you say. And a curse."

"Yes." Sanburne's gray eyes narrowed in study of him. "Perhaps some information as well. I expect you must have friends who play in that part of the world."

By habit, an evasive reply sprang to Phin's lips. But he hesitated. He had no pride in his dark connections, or in the fact that he was still privy, through them, to strange and dangerous knowledge. His past did not do him proud; he had stumbled into his occupation out of idiocy, and survived through sheer will and native talent, the sort that might allow a mule to pull a cart up a mountain. For almost six months now, he had tried to forget it, to be someone different.

But the silences required by his routine had led to this. He looked at Sanburne now and saw a stranger, and a stranger looked back at him warily, asking for help with no confidence at all that he'd receive it. "I'd appreciate it," Sanburne added. It was as close as he would ever come to saying please.

And why should he have to say please? They had known each other since boyhood. Phin ran a hand over his eyes. Did his skills so diminish him? He would always regret the applications to which they'd been put, the pain he had inflicted and the death he had dealt. He would carry that regret to his grave. But he had also aided people in his time. And last night, he had saved a life more precious to him than his own. When she had called that a talent worth having, nothing in him had been able to disagree.

Surely regret could exist side by side with hope. An unsheathed knife was not dangerous so long as it was wielded justly, and put to a deserving target. There was no shame in being able to help, and he excelled at what he did. He was a *natural*. Didn't she realize that? Why didn't she trust him?

I will trust you if you trust yourself.

He looked at Sanburne. He'd thought the man childish in his concerns. But wasn't it the height of childishness to disavow one's own abilities and sulk in a corner over a past that couldn't be changed?

"Yes," he said, testing it out. "No question that I can help."

Sanburne exhaled, nodding once, and gave him a grateful grin. "Just like old times," he said.

No, Phin thought. Far better, from now on. Let her dance as close to cliffs as she demanded. He had it in him to catch her if she fell.

Mina sat on a park bench, watching geese graze the bank of the Serpentine. It was noon, and the sun had yet to emerge from behind the clouds; fashionable society was still abed, and she sat waiting for the arrival of a criminal. Bonham had chosen the location very cleverly. Elms flanked the opposite shore of the lake, but a bullet could not travel so far with any accuracy, and on this side, nary a tree grew for cover. The flowerbeds and carefully tended lawns and shrubberies of Rotten Row lay ten minutes distant; the grass here cropped up in sparse patches, too discouraged by foot traffic to grow more ambitiously.

She was nervous. She was armed, a gun hidden beneath her skirts where they spilled across the bench. She was taking action. That was what she had required, and it was the opportunity that Phin had finally offered her.

He was watching. She would not look for him, but the knowledge that his eyes were on her from a distance somewhere made her feel as warm as though she were standing in his embrace. He had left her at the edge of the park and, with a press of her hand, had told her not to glance back. She had gone on tiptoes to kiss him, because the look he gave her brought home what a great leap he was taking; he looked at her as if trying to memorize her face, and the deep breath he'd drawn had made her heart turn over for him.

She would make it through safely. She felt it. A dozen pedestrians strolled past, couples and lone gentlemen, some of them charged to protect her. The manpower and discretion required for this operation had forced Phin to work closely again with Ridland, who'd seemed positively jovial during their morning conference. "I confess," he'd said over coffee, "I was uncertain at first of the traitor's identity. But I felt quite relieved when Bonham incriminated himself. Much trickier to pin treason on a peer of the realm."

A gentleman walking past spared her a sharp look. She avoided his eyes and focused on the geese. But he halted and turned back, approaching her hesitantly. Her heart quickened. It made sense that Bonham would send an emissary, but she had not thought of it. How sloppy of her.

"Forgive me," the man said. His hair was silvered at his temples, and the skin beneath his chin hung loosely. But he was well dressed, his black chesterfield of a fine cut and quality, and his blue eyes looked more bewildered than conspiratorial. "I do not mean to be forward, but you look so . . . I must ask you: is it possible that you're a relation of Mrs. Harriet Collins?"

Her hand slid under her skirts, her sweaty fingers slipping across the butt of the gun. She had not confessed it to Phin, but she half feared she would shoot herself in the leg. She much preferred to hold her weapons than to sit on them. "Yes," she said. "I'm her daughter. Who are you?"

Her rude address made him blink and clear his throat. "I did not mean to give offense." His voice was shaking a little, which made her frown. "I know this is most untoward. My name is Robert Thompson. I had the pleasure of her acquaintance once."

A little shock prickled through her. "Robbie," she said.

He pressed his lips together for a moment, as though struggling to contain some strong emotion, then cleared his throat. "She spoke of me, then?"

"Yes." He did not look like anyone's idea of a hero; his hand, clutching so desperately the gold knob of his cane, was freckled with age, the veins prominent.

But he was still handsome in a slim, unassuming way, and there was a terrible dignity in the way he squared his shoulders and nodded. Mama had not done right by him. She had fallen in love with him at a country house party and accepted his suit in private, only to jilt him a week later, without a word of warning. A richer prospect had appeared on her horizon, and ever since, she had regretted reaching for it. "She spoke of you often," Mina said softly.

"Spoke?" Now alarm made him pale. "Is she—"

"No," she said. *Pray God not.* The thought drew her back to the moment. He must leave, and quickly. If Bonham spotted her in company, he might not approach. "A pleasure to have made your acquaintance," she said, and forced her eyes back to the geese.

But in the periphery of her vision, he lingered, staring at her with a sort of helpless wonder. "She spoke of me," he said. "I have—I have never forgotten her. Please tell her that, won't you? If you can take pity on a stranger, who will regret his forwardness in an hour and rue it ever after."

His hushed words spoke far more than that. *Some love does not fizzle, Mama.* She blinked rapidly against a misplaced surge of emotion. "Yes," she managed. "Yes, I will tell her."

"Thank you," he said, and turned away.

From the corner of her eye she watched him go, marveling. His hand had been bare of rings. What did that signal? Had he never married? Some Englishmen did not wear wedding rings, but surely, if he had a wife, a man so concerned with manners would not have shared such a message?

All at once, she became aware that she was no longer alone on the bench. Her hand closed on the pistol butt. A soft breath touched her neck, lifting the hairs at her nape. She turned, and something hard came into her ribs.

"Unclasp it very slowly," said Bonham. He smelled strongly of sweat, and his beard was well on the way to a tangle.

She lifted her hand and shoved her own gun against his belly. "A standoff," she said hoarsely.

His eyes were no less green than she'd remembered; the eyes of a poet, a visionary. They locked on hers. "All right," he said slowly. "I throw mine away, and you do the same."

She hoped Phin was watching closely. "Very far away."

He nodded. "On the count of three. One . . . two . . . *three.*"

His pistol went flying, a splash announcing its arrival in the Serpentine. Her own aim was not so good; her weapon landed on the bank.

She rose, and he did as well, in one sudden move that left her no time to spot how he managed to produce the knife. But its touch against her throat was unmistakable; she went very still.

"I would remove the necklace myself," he said quietly, "but I fear, with one hand, I would botch the job. Your neck would not like that, and I need you in one piece to escape. So, very slowly, I want you to unclasp the locket."

She reached for her nape. Her fingers were shaking; they fumbled on the clasp. "Where is Mama?"

"With Ridland, I expect." At her indrawn breath, he laughed sourly. "You're surprised? He found them in Providence before I could get there."

"You're lying," she said.

The blade twitched. "*Hurry.* Carefully. Don't damage it."

The moment the necklace came loose, he snatched it from her hand and gave her a push forward, one arm around her waist, the other still holding the knife to her neck. "Better to let me go," she said, forcing herself to keep her eyes on the ground, lest he see her scanning the green for Phin. "Easier for you."

"I would prefer it," he said. "Money is a problem. Once I've decoded the account numbers, we'll revisit the question." His arm abruptly stiffened. "Tell him to get back."

Phin was walking toward them, straight and calm, his arms outstretched, his gun leveled at Bonham's head. "She'll be dead before you fire!" Bonham yelled.

She met Phin's eyes and shook her head almost imperceptibly. To her astonishment, he smiled at her, nothing grim or dark in it: thus might he have smiled at her at their wedding altar, or over their newborn lying in the cradle.

The tenderness of it, the absolute certainty, seemed so weirdly miraculous that her heart filled with an answering joy. She smiled back at him.

He pulled the trigger.

The explosion deafened her. It took a moment to realize that Bonham's arms had fallen away, and the knife was caught harmlessly in her skirts. She kicked it to the ground, then caught sight of the locket glimmering in the dirt. She picked it up and walked forward, her ears ringing. Phin had lowered his gun. Men were racing down the green now, their guns drawn, but his eyes remained fixed on hers as he strode forward. He looked at her as though she were the world and the world was his.

She had never seen the point to patience. She broke into a run.

They collided hard. The breath went from her as he dragged her up against his chest.

For a long moment she was content to be gripped by him, and to dig her fingers into his back, so solid, her shield. When she located her voice again, there was no creativity in her. "I love you."

"Never again," he said hoarsely into her hair. "Don't ask it of me, Mina."

"Oh, I won't," she said, and laughed, giddy in the sunlight. "I'll make sure I don't have to. From now on, I borrow no jewelry."

A commotion caused them to turn and look down the

field. By some miracle, it seemed that Bonham was not dead, despite the bullet in his brain. Ridland's men were making frantic preparations to transport him. One man broke off to run toward a coach that had drawn up at the edge of the grass. After a brief conference through the window, the pane slammed shut and the door opened, disgorging Ridland.

Mina pulled away from Phin. "Bonham said *he* has her. Since Providence!"

Phin gave a soft curse. "Of course he does." He took her arm, leading her forward.

"Of course?" she asked in bewilderment.

"How else would he have ensured that you stay in England?" His laughter was dark and harsh. "Pawns on a chessboard."

Mina's glower did not appear to faze Ridland; he paused a few feet away from them to sketch a congratulatory bow. "Excellent work," he said. "I was just asking after the locket. Do you have it?"

Mina stepped forward and slapped him.

Her palm stung, but the old man barely blinked. "Ah," he said. "Figured it out, did you?"

"Yes," spat Mina. "I have the locket. What say we make a trade?"

He rubbed a hand over his cheek. "Surely thanks are in order. I know your mother was quite grateful when I fetched her from Providence. I rather doubt she'll complain."

Phin sighed. He dropped her arm and took Ridland by the throat, shoving him back against the glossy side of the coach and pinning him there. "Enough," he said flatly. "Where is she?"

"Be sensible," Ridland wheezed. "We needed Bonham. He'd taken an interest in your lady. And if she'd known her mother was safe, what would have persuaded her to stay and draw him out? *You?*"

"I am going to destroy you," Phin said. "Delicately, gradually. It will be greatly amusing."

"Phin," Mina whispered. Someone else was in the coach, hands struggling with the window latch. And she thought—despite the shadowy interior, it seemed possible—

"If she is hurt," Phin began grimly, but Ridland cut him off, sounding anxious now.

"I took her from Collins, didn't I? That bastard is six feet below ground now. She was thanking me for it. I have never done you wrong."

The window slammed down. A blessedly familiar face filled the frame, a frown of disapproval on her pale brow as she eyed Phin head to toe. "I am well," Harriet Collins announced. "Although why it concerns you, I can't guess."

"Mama!" Mina clapped her hands over her mouth. "Mama—oh, step aside!" She grabbed the handle, trying to yank the door open, but it was obstinate and slipped from her sweaty palms.

"Do calm down, Mina." Mama peered over the window. "No one wants a public scene. Mr. Ridland, if you would be so kind?"

Phin stepped forward and gave the door a yank. Mina tried to clamber up inside, but the height was too great. She found herself being lifted by Phin into the compartment, and then her arms were around her mother. Mama went tumbling back onto the bench, crying a protest which Mina roundly ignored as she squeezed harder.

For a minute Mama bore her attentions, patting her awkwardly and making soothing murmurs. Then she grew impatient. "All right," she said, "enough. Calm yourself, Mina. What is this—tears?"

Mina pulled away, stung. "Yes, tears! I thought you were dead!"

"But Mr. Ridland found us very promptly. Didn't he tell you?" When Mina shook her head, her mother made a brief sound of annoyance that won a muttered apology from Ridland, eavesdropping from just out of sight. "How very bad of him," she said more loudly. "But"— her voice lowered—"he did do away with Collins, dearest, so you will grant him pardon."

"Pardon!" Mina gaped. What a talent her mother had for forgiving rascals! "You've been missing for weeks— and I was being hounded at knifepoint for your stupid locket!"

"I know. That was a surprise to me. And here I'd thought it was simply a very lovely piece."

A noise escaped her—anger, disbelief, amazement, she didn't know. "It was a *cipher disk*! To Collins's documents!"

"Shh!" Mama laid a cool hand against her cheek. "Darling, calm down. What need to worry? I knew you were clever. I knew you would figure out my letter. And so you did. And I knew"—her glance flicked to the doorway; turning, Mina found Phin watching them impassively— "you'd handle it brilliantly. You always land on your feet. Remind me, who is this gentleman? I feel sure we've met before, although I'm afraid I can't quite recall . . ."

Phin cleared his throat to speak, but Mina was feeling the beginning of a very ill temper and did not see the need to reassure Mama of anything. "He's my lover," she said. "It's utterly scandalous. I seduced him."

"Her fiancé," Phin said, with a dark look for Mina. Mina scoffed, but he lifted his voice to override her. "Phineas Granville, Earl of Ashmore. How do you do, Mrs. Collins."

Mama looked briefly puzzled. "Ashmore," she murmured. Then, with a shrug, she gave him a smile that, as it shifted toward Mina, became smug and unduly vexing. "Yes," she said, "you always do land on your feet, darling."

"He hasn't asked me to marry him," Mina said. "He's lying."

"Not for long," Phin said.

"Always lovely to meet a man who will give you a push when you hesitate," Mama said serenely. Her eyes strayed past Phin, and to Mina's horror, her smile landed on Ridland, who had inched into the doorway. Worse yet, he was smiling back.

"That reminds me," Mina said sharply. "I ran into Robbie Thompson. I believe he's a widower. He sends his most tender regards."

A blush colored Mama's face. "How very . . . interesting."

With an urgent, apologetic glance to Phin, Mina pulled the door shut on Ridland's dawning scowl.

"It's perfectly nauseating," Mina said to Phin.

They were lying in his bed. Now that the danger was past, Mama had remembered propriety and had insisted on removing herself and Mina to a hotel. Mina had waited until she was asleep to slip away.

Privately, though, she hoped Mama woke before she returned. A bit of scandal might restore her good sense. Currently she languished in the most vexing and giddy of contentments, delighted as a schoolgirl at the prospect of two men vying for her hand.

"Nauseating," Phin agreed, too mildly for Mina's satisfaction.

"Really, though! For her to have sat there flirting, in the house where I was held prisoner! Where I made myself sick with worry over her. And did you see her thank Mr. Ridland for the clothes he supplied her? As if a hundred Worth gowns would make up for her daughter being used as bait to expose a traitor! She has *no* head when it comes to men."

He laughed and sat up. The sight of his well-muscled chest briefly distracted her from her pique; she ran a finger along the edge of his pectoral, which had pressed against her own so splendidly only twenty minutes before. "Perhaps the difference here is that she was never worried about you," he said.

She dropped her hand. "Well, yes, that's my point exactly!"

"Because she knew she didn't need to be," he said. "You heard her. She knows better than anyone what her daughter is capable of." When she began to protest, he added with a grin, "I don't mean to argue, Mina. I have no intention of making Ridland part of the family. Mr. Thompson, on the other hand, can set up a camp in the lobby to wage his campaign."

She exhaled. "Yes," she said. "We'll give him every aid." The thought encouraged her; what could she and Phin not do, when they set their minds to it? They had bested each other, after all. In comparison, her mother was no large challenge.

The thought made her warm. She leaned forward to kiss him, and he pressed her back against the bed. For a long moment their tongues tangled, and when he pulled away, she sighed. "I don't want to leave you," she whispered.

"Excellent, since I intend to marry you. Beware—in a moment, I'm going to ask."

She felt her pulse trip and a blush spread across her face. "But I love New York as well. Not as much as you, but nearly, I'll confess it."

His lips took on a teasing quirk. "I suppose New York is bigger."

She laughed. "Oh, did I hurt your pride?"

He came up on one elbow, looking more serious. "We have choices, you know. I don't need to be in England year-round."

She paused. "I could acquire a taste for London in the spring."

"And a motive," he said. "The title comes with a great deal of land in the south. I hear lavender grows very well there."

Here was news. She lifted her brow. "High-quality lavender?"

"Nothing but," he said.

"Would that be your dowry, then?"

"Dowry?" He fell back onto the pillow. "*Dowry?* Miss Masters, I will have you know that I'm a man."

She put her hand between his legs, and felt his interest stir. "So I've noticed," she murmured. His head turned toward hers, his eyes dancing. "But reminders are always welcome. One might mistake you for a girl, with these." She reached out with her free hand, very delicately, to touch his lashes. They fluttered beneath her fingers, and she laughed again. "Especially if you bat them."

He rolled on top of her, pinning her arm very neatly. "Then you should know your place," he said. "It's your role to bring the dowry."

"Oh, yes?" He had not tried to knock her away from her main objective, she noted with amusement, and her effort was yielding a very firm result. The harder he grew, the weaker her limbs seemed, and the stronger she felt inside, where it counted. Together they were more brilliant than anyone she knew. She felt very proud of them, and rather gleeful. "And what would you request of me, your oh-so-fearsome lordship?"

"You," he said gently, and kissed her mouth. "Forever. Will you marry me, Miss Masters?"

She deliberately withheld her reply, waiting until he frowned and laid his lips against hers again. "On one condition," she said into his mouth.

"Name it," he breathed.

She smiled. *Excellent.* "I keep all the keys."

True love
is timeless with historical romances from Pocket Books!

Delve *into a* passion *from the* past *with a* romance

from Pocket Books!

LIZ CARLYLE
Never Romance a Rake
Love is always a gamble....But never romance a rake!

JULIA LONDON
The Book of Scandal
Will royal gossip reignite her husband's passion for her?

KARIN TABKE
Master of Surrender
The Blood Sword Legacy
A mercenary knight is bound by a blood oath to reclaim his legacy—and the body of the one woman he desires.

KATHLEEN GIVENS
Rivals for the Crown
The fierce struggle for Scotland's throne leads
two women to courageous new destinies...

**Available wherever books are sold
or at www.simonandschuster.com.**